THE FLAMINGO RISING

THE FLAMINGO RISING

Larry Baker

ALFRED A. KNOPF
New York 1997

THIS IS A BORZOI BOOK
PUBLISHED BY ALFRED A. KNOPF, INC.

http://www.randomhouse.com/

ISBN 0-375-40050-8
LC 97-73822

Manufactured in the United States of America

First Edition

For Ginger, Jenny, and Ben.

My family.

ACKNOWLEDGMENTS

First, an apology. To those I have hurt or disappointed in the past, I am sorry. Especially to Tim, who deserves better than he got.

The true history of this book will probably never be known. Still, certain people merit special attention. To my first readers in Iowa City—Karin Franklin, Julie Tallman, and Mike Lankford—many thanks for their enthusiasm. Special thanks also to Cathy Denny in St. Augustine, a friend and reader.

At Sobel-Weber, Laura Nolan and Sarah Jackson handled my questions and insecurities with both skill and humor. I even forgive Sarah for not letting me through the door the first time I went to Nat's office. And, contrary to what Sarah and Laura think, there is no way they will ever get the truth from me about some of the characters.

My profound gratitude to Nat Sobel for taking this orphan book and selling it in three weeks. Nat's faith in this story helped restore mine, and every writer should be so lucky. His Sunday night calls will always be memorable. I hope we will be friends and partners for a long time.

At Knopf, proper recognition of all the people who worked on the book would take more than a page, and those thanks would still be inadequate. But I will be grateful to them forever. That Wednesday afternoon meeting in Sonny's office is indelible.

Very special thanks must go to Jenny Minton at Knopf. Not only for her patience with me over the phone and her acrobatic juggling of all the little details as we edited the book, but especially for her insight into the role of Abraham's father at the end. A small change, but necessary for his redemption.

ACKNOWLEDGMENTS

How to thank Sonny Mehta? I thought I had written a good book. He made it better. He constantly reminded me of the basic rule of writing: Individual words matter. Hours with me in his office, in his apartment, over the phone, line by line, word by word. I hope we get to do it again.

Finally, singular thanks to Katie Arnold, wherever she is when she reads this. I might have written a book anyway if I had never met her, but it would not have been this book.

THE FLAMINGO RISING

Abraham's Voice

My name is Abraham Isaac Lee, and I am my father's son. This is a story about Land and Love and a Great Fire that consumed all my father's dreams. If my voice sounds too . . . too artificial, then I am happy. I sound like my father, my wife tells me. Even my sister, who has escaped her parents, who lives in the West, even she tells me that I am her father's son. At this moment I am wearing his clothes: a sweater seldom worn by him when it was new, a pale blue tie given to him by my mother, his brown penny loafers. I am in his image. My southern accent is subtle. My hair is parted as his was, but black, not red. Combed as close as possible to being like his on his wedding day. My speech is usually dramatic; my gestures are precise. Grace, my wife, tells me that I have been this way since even before my mother died. Grace, my precious and essential wife, whose name my father loves because he believes all names have power. My father, who believes every material object is a symbol that requires interpretation. My father named me; my mother named my sister. I am Abraham, and I am Isaac. Because of my father, I have never liked irony.

My father, my mother, Grace and her father, my sister, a short black man named Pete, a dog named Frank, a pilot named Harry, a girl named Polly, and a few others. All of them have a role to play.

And Alice, whose voice I hear even now, twenty-five years later, whose sad and smirky voice tells me that I must forgive myself. I always remember Alice when I go to Mass with Grace and my children. I was raised Catholic, as was Alice, but she lost her faith long before I accepted mine. When I sit in my photo gallery, looking out toward the ocean, I can hear her laugh and tell me that I need to get on with my life. That history did not stop in 1968.

3

Land and Love

Turner West saw the land first, but my father was rich and bought most of it. Unlike other stories about land, this is not about farming or crops or man taming the wilderness. The land of this story was one square mile of Florida real estate halfway between Jacksonville and St. Augustine. A mile of beachfront and a mile deep into the scrubby interior, cut along the eastern edge by Highway A1A as it went south toward the Keys.

West saw the land in 1950 and knew it was where he wanted to build his funeral home. His father had been a mortician before him, and his brothers had gone into the same business in Georgia. In 1950, West had been driving down A1A and saw the sun rise over the Atlantic. He told his father, but the elder West was skeptical that a funeral home so far from a major city would ever be successful.

"The future," West had said to his father, "you have to think about the future, even in the funeral business."

West borrowed from his father and brothers and was able to buy two acres on the west side of A1A. The land sloped up and there was a clear view of the ocean, so the West Funeral Home opened its doors in 1951 on Easter morning. My father thought that was a nice touch, especially after he found out that Turner West was an atheist.

West may have been an atheist, but he was also an American Puritan. His work ethic was impeccable, and his funeral business prospered. He had no paid employees. His wife and six children worked with him. He personally trained his three oldest sons in mortuary science—a fact my father particularly admired about Turner West. In his own case, until he was ordered by the Duval County courts to obey the law, my father had educated me and my sister at home. I was twelve years old before I saw the inside of a classroom.

As an atheist, Turner West belonged to five churches and a synagogue. On Sunday morning he was up at dawn and attended services first at the downtown Jacksonville Baptist Church, then at the First Church of Christ at 9:30, followed by the Methodists at 11:00, the Episcopalians at 1:00, a late lunch at home, and finally 5:30 Mass at the Cathedral in St. Augustine. He was in temple on Saturday. He absorbed hours of religion every week, but he never volunteered for any committee work at any of the churches and always insisted that his name not appear in any printed material, except for the regular ad in each church's bulletin. His priest, pastor, and rabbi friends appreciated his humility. I know this because Grace West later explained to me why her father went to church.

"Contacts," she had said. "Everyone wants a friend in a time of need. Daddy is there for them because he has always been there. When the moment comes, Daddy says, they are lost. The living, that is, and they want someone who can understand their grief. Daddy has always been part of their congregation. Who else would they choose?"

My father understood perfectly how West's mind operated. My father, the agnostic.

"Abraham, he is a worthy opponent," my father would say. "He understands the power of symbols, even though he does not realize that he is the ultimate symbol himself."

On his two acres, West built his business and his home. The funeral home was styled after a southern plantation house, white columns and Jeffersonian arches. The West family lived in the back: Turner and his wife in a large bedroom over the garage full of hearses and limousines, their six sons sharing three small rooms on the ground floor next to the embalming room.

For my father, Turner West was an adversary. He was Death personified. My father was Life. If you think my father was crazy, you would find many people who agree with you.

My father saw the sun rise over the Atlantic a year after Turner West did, and my father also saw the West Funeral Home and Chapel.

"This is the spot for my Great White Wall," he had told my mother, pointing to a large half-moon-shaped indentation that pushed A1A in a long arcing curve away from the ocean. Another visionary might have seen a perfect spot for a tourist hotel fronting a hard beach that could accommodate pale and flabby easterners and their two-ton cars. My father saw a drive-in theatre.

It is a story my mother loved to tell. My father looked at the rising sun, turned 180 degrees, and faced the West Funeral Home. With both arms spread wide, he had said, "I will blot your sun out with a Wall of Life. I will put you in the dark."

"I told your father that he was crazy"—my mother would laugh—"but that I loved him anyway."

It was not really a personal vendetta against Turner West. That came later. But on that first day, my father had simply had a vision about what to do with his money, the ample and undeserved money handed down to him as the last of the Lee family from Winston-Salem.

I give you these details to make sure you do not fall into the easy interpretation that others have. Too many people have told me that the war made my father crazy. But that's not true. My father was disjointed even before going to Korea a week after seeing his land in Florida. My mother told me all the stories about his family, the death of his parents in a murder-suicide, how he found them the summer before his senior year in high school.

"He was different after that, the rest of his family told me," she would say. "Not as quiet, not the shy child they had known before then, just not the same. And he went to Korea knowing that he would not die, that he had to come back here to build his dream. He sent me drawings every month, gave me specific instructions for the contractors, and even made me go to California to buy those giant redwoods. He also told me that you and Louise were going to be our children, described you exactly as you were, even before I saw you." She told me all this, and then she would smile that smile my father must have loved the first time he saw her.

Turner West married his high school sweetheart. They were virgins in both body and heart. I have seen their wedding pictures. Imagine a handsome version of Abraham Lincoln, literally, and you have Turner West. Tall, angular, sad eyes, coal-black hair, long arms, but with a movie-star quality. His wife was short and a bit plump. They had kissed at seventeen, pledged their love at eighteen, married at twenty-two, and deflowered themselves on their Atlanta honeymoon. He had told her that he was going to be a mortician like his father and grandfather, and she had still agreed to be his wife.

Her name was Grace, and she was a natural consoler. It was she who had early contact with the next of kin in those brutal first moments on the phone when the living start the dead on their last journey. West could never believe his luck in finding her. She was his wife, lover, mother, friend, and partner. In the first ten years of marriage, they had their six sons. By the time the West Funeral Home was opened, the three oldest were trained to be their father's assistants, and the younger three were destined for the same career. The youngest was old enough to drive one of the limousines in the daily processions that began under Turner West's bedroom.

On the day two barges landed on the beach—two barges each supporting one end of the first of those hundred-foot redwoods that had been shipped from California down the Pacific coast, through the Panama Canal, up past Cuba to float offshore of the land my father had bought—on that day, Turner West's wife died.

They had been foolish, they told themselves. She was too old to have another child. It had not been planned. It could have been terminated. Even in those unenlightened days, there were ways. But then they had looked at each other and knew that things would be all right.

In the waiting room, however, Turner West had been told there was something wrong, and his long legs had outraced the doctor back to the delivery room. His wife was dead, but his daughter was alive.

When the nurse asked what her name was, West had thought she meant his wife. "Grace. Her name is Grace," he had said, and that was the name they put on the birth certificate.

If you had asked Turner West what he remembered about the next three months he could not tell you, because he remembered nothing. Then, sitting in his bedroom one dark morning, he heard a

baby cry. Grace was in a crib in the room in which she had been conceived, in the room where she was to sleep in a bed next to her
father's bed for the next five years. Turner West had rocked his
daughter back to sleep, and then he walked to the front of his funeral
home to look out the window. At that particular moment he saw the
Flamingo Drive-In Theatre blocking his view of the morning sun.

Hubert Thomas Lee met my mother in a graduate class on Dante at
the University of North Carolina in Chapel Hill. When the professor had said, without a trace of irony, that the punishment in the
Inferno for adultery was to suffer eternal orgasm, pleasure so prolonged and intense that it became pain, my father had whispered
loud enough for everyone to hear, "I'll take my chances."

Only one person laughed. My father looked at her and decided
to ask her for a date. When she stood up to leave, he had second
thoughts. Edna Marie Scott was six feet tall, a beautiful but sturdy
six feet tall. My father was five nine.

Neither was a virgin, but nobody knew that about Edna Marie.
Everybody knew that Hubert T. Lee was a rogue. Loud, not as
charming as he thought he was, too quick to spend the famous Lee
tobacco money, a drinker, and a lover of women. He had always
bragged about his goal of marrying a movie star, of himself being a
movie star. A month after meeting Edna Marie Scott, Hubert Lee
was engaged to her. The wedding was a Roman carnival. The Scott
family of Greensboro was richer than the Lee family of Winston-
Salem. And everyone agreed: My father did not deserve my mother.

When I was sixteen, Alice Kite pointed out to me an obvious
truth about my parents.

"Everybody says your daddy is crazy, Abraham, but have you
ever asked yourself what kind of person marries a crazy person?
Your mother must be as crazy as him, but in her own way. Don't you
think so?"

My father was five feet nine inches tall. My mother was six feet. He
weighed 140 pounds; she weighed 160. He had red hair and green

eyes; she had blond hair and blue eyes. Can you imagine how my sister and I look? You are wrong.

For the last time: My name is Abraham Isaac Lee, and I am my father's son.

My father handed me over to my mother when I was three months old, placed me in her arms as she met him on a dock in Seattle. He was home from Korea with me and Louise.

I was born in an orphanage hospital in Seoul. Louise was born the same day. The woman whose body carried me was eighteen years old, and the man who impregnated her was probably in his early twenties. He was a soldier in the Korean army, but little else is known about him. The young girl was a high school graduate and in excellent health. They were not married, and they were not my parents.

I am a full-blooded Korean. Black hair, black eyes, a broad nose, skin a blend of yellow and brown. For my eighteenth birthday my father took me back to Korea "to see your roots," as he put it. Even then, I was wearing his clothes, because we were the same size. We went to the orphanage and looked for more records about my biological past, but there was no paper trail. I was introduced to Bertha Holt. She and her husband, Harry, had founded the Holt Adoption Agency. My father sends her a thousand dollars every year, and every year, my father says, "They send a thousand babies to their parents." He likes the number connection, but Bertha Holt told me that my father tends to exaggerate. She was amused when I said, "Oh, really?"

The Holts were my father's friends during the war, and they helped him adopt me and Louise even though, as she said, "Your father did not fit all our guidelines."

My blood is Korean. We all have some doubt about Louise. I have always been self-conscious about my appearance, especially since it doesn't match how I see myself. I have been told that I am handsome. Even if I discount the opinion of my parents and wife, others have often remarked on how "distinguished" I seem. I look "wise," my teachers would tell me. The only person I have ever seen who I thought looked like a wise man was Turner West. I said that to my father once. He looked down at me, peering over the top of his glasses, and said, "Turner West looks like the Devil. Dressing all in black, Isaac, does not make you look wise. It just makes you look like a preacher or an undertaker. And both of them are doing the Devil's work."

So, I look handsome, distinguished, or wise. And I always look Korean. Louise simply looks like no one else in this world. The woman who gave birth to her was thirty-five; the man who impregnated that woman was a mystery. At least, the woman who gave birth said she had no idea who the father was. Looking at Louise, you can come to only one conclusion: The man was not Korean. She has the best of Asian and Caucasian features. Beautiful skin, dark eyes but not narrow, a perfectly shaped American nose. Even today, men and women stare at her when she passes them.

When we were tiny, my mother used to tell us, "They would stop me in the grocery store and ask about both of you. They would pat you on the head, Isaac, but with Louise they would reach out with the tip of one finger and touch her cheek as if they were seeing if she was real."

Before you overinterpret, forget about trying to tie my father to the mysterious white lover of a Korean woman. Louise has no feature in any way remotely similar to our father's. He would often joke about the possibility, telling her that she was a "half-baked Lee pie." But we all knew it was not true. If anything, Louise looked more like my mother, especially the way they both would stare at my father when he was trying to be funny but failing, a look of infinite patience and pity. "Lee pie" jokes were never funny.

My father found us in Korea.

"I was in a room of crying babies, and you two were the only quiet ones," he would say. I believed that story for years until my mother told me the truth.

"Your father had found a baby in a ditch, abandoned and crying, and he was taking it to Harry Holt. The baby died before he got to the orphanage, but he did not know. He made one of his grand entrances, telling the night nurse to make way for Jehovah and baby Moses. And he handed over a dead child. After the nurse told him, your father sat in a corner waiting for Harry. He sat there for hours, he told me, thinking about me and the land that was waiting for him in America. Surrounded by sleeping babies, your father found you. Your Korean name was written on the card attached to your crib. You were Lee Sung Kyung. You know your father, Isaac. The moment he saw that Lee name he knew it was a sign of something. You were his."

After she told me about how my father found me, I asked my mother about Louise.

"Oh, her." She laughed. "Your sister was supposed to be your twin. At least in your father's mind. A boy for him, a girl for me. She was in the crib next to yours, and when he picked you up *she* started to cry. In fact, I think she cried for the first three years of her life. Ear infections, allergies, pneumonia, every plague available to torture a parent. Your sister was an unattractive chore for all of us. Not like you, so calm, so happy. Louise was never happy, not even when she turned out to be so beautiful."

My sister is indeed beautiful, with only one physical flaw. She limps when she gets too emotional—mad or happy, anything. By sheer force of will and self-control, she can walk straight. Doctors could have fixed it with leg braces when she was still growing up, but my mother did not let them.

Even today, as famous as my sister is because of her acting career, few people know. No studio, no producer or director, no critic, no paparazzi . . . nobody has ever seen her limp.

If you go to the library you can find a copy of the June 4, 1953, issue of *Life* magazine. All of us are there: my father, mother, sister, me, Turner West, Grace, and the Flamingo Drive-In Theatre. A two-page article with six pictures. My father has had a lifetime subscription to *Life,* and I have all the copies in my garage. Grace tells me that they are a fire hazard. My father thinks she is being ironic.

The story is titled "A Southern Wonder of the World." The editors had wanted to emphasize the geographic and architectural oddity of the Flamingo. In their minds, its being in the South and my father's being a remote descendant of Robert E. Lee combined to make an obvious statement about southern culture. When my father saw the article, after weeks of waiting, he exploded. "I am no southern cracker, and I represent nothing but myself!" For my father, southern culture was an abomination. My father cursed the South; my mother was a Southern Belle.

"Hubert Thomas Lee," she would say to him as they sat at opposite ends of our fifteen-foot dining-room table, "you may deny your own southern heritage, you may desecrate the temple of your southern elders, you may ignore your own southern accent, but never forget that your children were born in *South* Korea."

I would look at Louise and read her minced lips—"They're *both* crazy."

Life had come to record the construction of the world's largest drive-in theatre, but the writer would not quote my father as he wanted. "Not in size, young man, not in size is this wall large, but in meaning. This is my challenge to God. My fist in his unseen face, the chip on my shoulder, the line in the sand."

Years later, I would come to understand that my father had lost his faith in God as he, seventeen years old, listened to a preacher try to explain his parents' death to a church full of mourners. For the rest of his life, my father wanted God's attention, to force God to answer to him, Hubert Thomas Lee. The Flamingo was an invitation.

The *Life* writer left confused, and the story became a simple tale of a "colorful southerner" and his "charmingly attractive" wife, descriptions that earned the writer the lifelong wrath of Hubert Lee and Edna Scott.

The words of the story were a complete distortion of reality, but the pictures did not lie. The Flamingo was a wonder of the world in 1953. If anyone tried to do the same thing today, he would be flailed by every environmental group and harassed by every government agency charged with protecting the public interest. My father's vision was a white monster that violated the natural world and turned night into day.

"Isaac, you must remember, with enough money you can build anything. You can even turn back the ocean." That was my father's explanation for the Flamingo.

On the first day, my father was overseer to the construction of a half-mile-long seawall that divided the beach along a north–south line that marked the highest water point of the year. Thus, at high tide the Atlantic threw itself against this six-foot stone wall and then retreated. At low tide, we had a hundred feet of hard white sand on the east side of the wall. The actual work took a month, but my father divided his paid labor into biblical units. The wall was day one.

My father called that wall his Maginot Line. "No illusions, Isaac, about the wall. When the time comes, God will jump this bump and head for Paris."

Paris was the screen tower. And it was the Tower that *Life* had come to photograph.

The Tower was a hundred and fifty feet high, two hundred feet across, and fifty feet wide at the base. Facing the ocean was the blank white screen. Facing A1A was the world's largest neon marquee, a glaring pink flamingo whose head continually dipped and whose body rested on one leg while the other extended and retracted. Florida nights along A1A were more pink than black, a glowing pink that softened everything, a pink that Turner West called "worthy of a New Orleans whorehouse."

In May 1968, Alice Kite took me out on the ocean in a leaky boat to see my father's Tower. A mile offshore at three in the morning, just as the closing credits had finished on the last movie of a triple bill, the screen went white and then dark, and, for the few minutes left before Pete Maws turned off the marquee, she and I gazed at the pink glow that seemed to pulsate out from the sides and top of the Tower, a rectangular void surrounded by halos of pink light.

"Izzy, you live in Wonderland. You know that, don't you?" she said, a month before my sixteenth birthday.

So, my family lived in the world's largest screen tower. That was the "hook" of the *Life* story. Southern aristocrats, Asian children, and Hollywood—believe it or not.

One of the pictures that *Life* published showed the inside of the Tower. My father had insisted that the world see how it was held together. "Not just size, but strength," he had told the writer. My mother would tell me these stories about my father when I was sick and had to stay in my Tower bedroom while the movies were showing on the other side of my shuttered window.

"He would tell that young man exactly why we had used certain materials and certain designs, and I could see him taking notes. But he never used the exact words. I suppose he thought your father was just teasing him. But, Isaac, you know your father. When he told the young man that he had built this Tower to be his home, to be indestructible, to withstand the mightiest hurricane, to protect his family from the wrath and pettiness of almighty God—well, your father was not teasing at all. Your father was serious. Of course, sometimes even I can't tell, but that time with the young man I knew he was serious."

Six ancient redwoods, one at each corner and two facing each other in the middle, were the strongest part of the Tower's skeleton. Severed and stripped in California, they were replanted twenty feet deep in the Florida sand and dirt. The crossbeams were Texas oak trees, squared at twenty-four inches, shortened to fifty-foot lengths. Connecting the redwoods and the oaks were hundreds of short steel rods and thousands of oak planks. Within the white skin of the Tower was a maze of lumber held together by a ton of nails, bolts, and screws. My father's engineers told him that he was "overbuilding," but he told them that when God came knocking he wanted to be ready.

On top of the Tower was a custom-made RCA speaker horn. Some of you reading this might not have ever been to a drive-in theatre. If you have, chances are that you never went to one that did not have car speakers. In the beginning, all drive-ins had a large horn on top of the screen tower. That was the reason most drive-ins were built away from populated areas. As cities spread farther out, drive-ins developed the car speaker. My father hated them, but even he had to acquiesce to the change in 1960. For those first seven years, our parking surface was unblemished by speaker poles. But the voices on-screen, the crack of gunfights, the violins of love, the drone of airplanes, the weeping of infants—all could be heard for miles offshore. Until John Kennedy was elected President, anyone with a boat could see a free movie at the Flamingo.

So *Life* had six pictures. A mile offshore looking back to show how that white screen dominated the view. From across the highway to show the Flamingo marquee. My mother and father holding

Louise and me, still in diapers, in the concession stand. The playground at the foot of the Tower, a playground that impressed parents because of how many slides and rides there were. A fifth picture showing how we lived inside the Tower, including our dining room that could seat twenty people.

It was the last picture, the two-page full spread, that my father liked the most. Taken from the top of the Tower, it showed the Florida landscape stretching out for miles. That was also the picture that showed Turner West. A quarter mile down A1A, the West Funeral Home was reduced to the size of a toy. A magnifying glass would show you Turner West himself, standing at his front door and holding Grace in his arms, staring at my father, who was standing on top of the Tower looking down at him.

The Great Fire occurred the summer of my sixteenth birthday. The year was 1968. My father always appreciated the overlap of social and personal symbolism.

Pete Maws

I remember everything about the day Pete Maws came into our lives. It was my eighth birthday. Of course, I remember earlier times in my life. Some fuzzy, some stark, some that may not have even happened. But I remember everything about my birthday on June 4, 1960.

"There's a caboose at the box office."

We were coming down A1A back from Jacksonville, Louise and my mother in the backseat, my father and I up front driving. It was also Louise's birthday, but she had insisted that she did not want a party. My father had teased me about neither of us having a party if the other did not want one. I had tried to negotiate with Louise the night before, but she was adamant. I went crying to my mother. She told me to go see my father. He looked at my pitiful face and then announced that we were all going to Jacksonville the next day to buy me a present. I asked him not to buy anything for Louise.

"There's a caboose at the box office," I had said as soon as we made the last curve toward the Flamingo. My father slammed on the brakes and pulled off the road.

"Hubert, you've stopped the car," my mother said in a tone that was more a question than an observation. "Would you prefer we walked home from here?"

My father simply stared, and I sat there beside him experiencing the first epiphany of my life. It was the same one he was having at that moment. The present he had bought me in Jacksonville was a Lionel train set. There was a caboose at our box office. There had to be a connection.

We slowly drove past the caboose into the sanctuary of the Flamingo. Even my mother and Louise seemed curious. The caboose itself was actually on a flatbed trailer hooked up to a large, but very old, truck. The railroad wheels were off the caboose, and the truck had two flat tires.

The four of us soon stood at the end of the caboose, eight feet planted firmly on the earth, looking up at the back door.

"Anybody in there?" my father called out.

Do you remember that movie *The Day the Earth Stood Still*? Michael Rennie lands a flying saucer in some baseball stadium, and some robot has some sort of laser-death-vapor-ray power?

"This means something," my father whispered to us.

"Why are you whispering, Hubert?" my mother asked. When she took a step toward the caboose, the door opened and out stepped a tiny black man.

It was a tableau. The four of us looking up at this short dark figure who was standing with both hands on the back rail of his caboose looking down at us.

"You folks got anything to do with this movie place?" were his first words.

My father became himself again. "Hubert T. Lee and family," he beamed, pointing back at us. "Owners and operators of the Flamingo Drive-In Theatre, largest theatre screen in the world, brightest lighthouse in the world as well." He was very proud.

"Those *your* children?" Pete Maws said, staring right into my soul and even causing Louise to blink.

My father hesitated, as if he did not understand the question. My mother answered immediately, "Abraham Isaac and Louise Janine. Today is their birthday."

"Beautiful children, Mrs. Lee," Pete Maws said, "and proof that the Lord makes no mistakes."

With that declaration, Pete Maws had won my mother. My father took a few more minutes.

"Your name, sir?" my father asked.

"Peter Maws. Just been—"

"*Pete Moss!*" my father exploded. "Come to help us grow."

Pete Maws looked directly at me but he spoke very slowly to my father. "Peter Maws," he said, enunciating and lengthening his last name. I could read his mind as his eyes held mine, and his face had the expression of a man who had heard the same joke every day of his life. At that moment I desperately wanted to tell him not to take it personally. My father had always wanted to hire a crew of Pete Moss, Harley Davidson, Peter Bilt, and especially Sara Lee.

"Are you a Negro?" Louise had finally spoken.

Pete Maws nodded.

"We don't get a lot of Negro customers," she said.

"You show many colored movies here?" he asked.

My father changed the subject. "You need some help with those tires?"

But then my mother changed our lives. "Mr. Maws, would you like a job? Do you have any skills that might be useful? Carpentry, painting, electrical?"

My father tried to interrupt her. "Edna, we have a full crew, and I don't think . . ."

"Not really, Hubert," she said. "That Taylor girl will be quitting tomorrow, and besides, you have the speaker posts to put in this fall. I think Mr. Maws here might be very helpful."

It was the first time I had ever seen my father not in control of a conversation, and, for reasons I did not understand myself, I wanted Pete Maws to stay with us too. Years later, my father admitted that he had been wrong to hesitate.

"But, Edna, surely Pete here has a job to get back to, so if we just help him get back on track, so to speak, he can get along down the road to where . . ." he said, and then shifted his attention to Pete Maws, ". . . to wherever it was you were going."

Pete stepped down to the ground, and we all got a better look at each other. He was at least four inches shorter than my father and probably did not weigh much more than a hundred pounds. His skin was a deep brown, and his hair was not much more than stubble. In fact, he was going bald and as he grew older he began to look more and more like a miniature version of Uncle Remus in that Disney movie *Song of the South*. Louise pointed that out to all of us after she had left home.

"I've been working on the railroad . . ." he began, and I was immediately scared that my father would start singing that old song, ". . . for twenty-five years. Retired this week. Started as a linen boy on the sleepers, then waiter in the dining car, spent the last ten years on the caboose. Doing maintenance"—glancing toward my mother—"just odd jobs to keep the cars in shape. Whatever it took, I could usually do it."

He shook hands with my father and me. I was enthralled. He was the shortest adult I had ever known. By the time I was twelve I could look down at him when we talked.

"I got my pension, bought this old caboose. Looking for a place to put it in the ground."

"You worked for the Palm Coast Line?" my father asked.

Pete nodded. "Twenty-five years."

My father persisted. "*You* got a pension?"

I did not understand what my father was getting at, so I looked at my mother. She put her hand on my shoulder.

"I'm just a little surprised that the Palm Coast would put a Negro on the pension plan. No offense, but you know what I mean?" my father said.

"I was hired with a bunch of my friends while we were boys in Palatka. I could read and write, so I filled out the forms for all of us. Form had these two lines—colored or white. I checked the white box for me, colored for the rest of them. Turned in all the forms in a bunch at one time. Boss put them in a stack with a hundred others. Years later I start getting mail telling me how much I was getting on the pension plan. Palm Coast is a big company. Lots of forms in the Miami office. Peter Maws seemed like a white name. My handwriting looks white."

"Wasn't that a lie?" I said, surprising everyone.

I regretted saying it as soon as it came out. I wanted him to like me.

"Young Abraham, you're right. It was a lie. But, you see, when I was fifteen I wanted to be white. I didn't want any pension. I just saw those two choices and I decided to be white. Some clerk in some office somewhere who will never see me—to him Peter Maws was just another white man."

Just then Pete Maws said something to me that he knew I must have been thinking about.

"I was a boy then. I didn't like my color. Young boys sometimes don't know that they can't change the truth about themselves. Know what I mean? I wanted to be white back then."

"And now?" I asked.

"You learn some things as you get older. Such as there are some things you can't change." He gently pinched my cheek. "You can't change *this*. You are what you are."

He turned to my father. "I'd like that job if you think you need me."

Negotiations began between the two men while my mother and Louise went back inside. I remained there and saw how Pete Maws finally won over my father.

To work for the Flamingo, you had to live with the Lee family. Not metaphorically, literally. In addition to equipment and supply storage on the ground level of the Tower, my father had built one-room apartments. We lived on the second level, and that is where our giant dining room was filled every Sunday as my father held court. To work for us, you had to live below us and eat one meal a week with us. Of the dozens of people over the years who sweated in the field with us during the day, only Pete Maws stayed forever. And he stayed only because my father allowed him to live in his caboose at the far edge of the field.

When my father told him that all the employees had to live with us, Pete said that was fine. When my father made it clear that he meant living *in* the Tower, Pete simply said that he had been living in a caboose for a decade and he intended to live in the one he had been dragging up from south Florida. My father hesitated. He did not like exceptions to his rules, but he agreed to let Pete put the caboose in the northeast corner of the lot if he painted it sea-green. Pete would take over the projection duties from my father, and he would be expected to watch all the property when our family went on any trips. He would not have to eat Sunday dinner with us unless he wanted to. In fact, I probably heard Pete Maws talk more that first day than I did on any one day since then.

Business concluded, my father went into his P. T. Barnum routine about the Flamingo, a routine heard by all new employees.

"You're a lucky man, Pete Moss, lucky to be part of the Great Wall of Life. Off the iron line of necessity, the tracks that go nowhere, you are now part of this Grand Design, a small agent in the universe of Free Will."

I stood off to one side and watched Pete listen. He never looked directly at my father, as he never looked directly at anyone except me or Louise over the years.

"This is *the* Wall, Pete Moss, the symbol of human power and aspiration, the stairway to heaven, the Tower of Babel, the symbol of my life."

Sometimes my father just liked to hear himself talk.

Pete Maws squinted his eyes and looked up at the sky and then at the Tower.

"It's a big wall, Mr. Lee, and you've got a giant bird out front here. But I'm not sure about that other stuff."

My father was silent. "Pete, I mean to say . . ." But he stopped.

"Like I told your boy," Pete said, touching my shoulder, "some things you can't change. Some things are what they are."

I was eight years old that day. It was the first time I began to understand my father better. Perhaps understand is the wrong word. I began to see that he was more than one person. For the next half hour, Pete Maws and my father had an adult conversation about gravel and lumber and all the maintenance problems involved in running the world's largest drive-in. My father did not exaggerate; he was not ironic. He and Pete often laughed, but it seemed to come out of some common experience they had had with faulty pipe connections or hammers hitting their thumbs. My father laughed hardest when Pete told him that in addition to lying about his color to the Palm Coast Line he had also lied about his age.

"Told them I was thirty. Afraid I wouldn't get the job if I said I was fifteen."

"But *fifteen* years' difference?" my father asked.

"Wasn't taking no chances. Tall then as I am now, had a mustache, and the man at the desk wasn't looking at us singly anyway. So I turn forty and Miami thinks I'm fifty-five and white. I get the letter saying I'm eligible for early retirement. Twenty-five years of loyal service."

My father was hysterical by then.

"You telling me the truth about all this?" he said, winking at me as he stood next to Pete.

"Yessir. I wouldn't lie to you," Pete said, his face turned toward the Flamingo. "I'll never lie to you."

Pete and my father were happy with each other. They might have been friends anyway, but Pete sealed my father's affections by insisting on one non-negotiable term of his employment.

"One thing, Mr. Lee, before I set this car"—motioning back to the caboose—"in the ground."

My father tilted his head and arched his eyebrow.

"This is my home. Nobody comes inside unless I ask them. Never. Is that fair?"

"Fair is fair, Pete." My father nodded. "Fair is fair."

More than thirty years later, Pete Maws still lives in his caboose by the ocean. He sees the sun rise every morning, and almost every day he sees my father and me and my youngest son. More than thirty years after my eighth birthday, the only person to have ever seen the inside of Pete's caboose was Turner West.

Frank Sinatra
and Turner West

My father will tell you that the feud between him and Turner West began when West had the audacity to complain about Frank Sinatra. My father loved to listen to Frank Sinatra sing. During the day, when we were all working in the field, he would pipe Sinatra music through the giant speaker horn on top of the Tower. This was usually not a problem, because the sound drifted on summer winds out to sea. But in 1960, a week after Pete arrived, a strong wind coming in from the Atlantic carried "The Lady Is a Tramp" back to the West Funeral Home just as services were beginning for the daughter of the Mayor of Jacksonville. She was seven and had died of leukemia. The Mayor's wife had wanted a downtown funeral home, but the Mayor and Turner West had become friends. This funeral was to have been a breakthrough event for West, and my father, if left to his own judgment, would have ruined the moment.

West had sent his eldest son to ask my father to turn off the music. The son failed to mention anything about the funeral being for a little girl. He just asked for an hour of silence from the Flamingo. I was there, and I saw my father puff up and begin to launch into his routine about white walls and symbols of life.

"Your father's domain stops where mine begins," he began, "and if I wish to fill the air with . . ."

The music stopped in his mid-sentence, and the son of West thanked my perplexed father for his kind understanding. My mother had turned off the music. She told me later, "Abraham, sometimes your father is not very mature. A kind man, but not a mature man."

My mother gave specific instructions that the Flamingo was to remain silent from an hour before to an hour after any funeral at the West home. Each day she posted a schedule of services in our kitchen. On weekdays, when she was teaching in St. Augustine, she would call periodically, listening for music in the background. But my father never went against her wishes. He grumbled, he shook his fist in the air in the direction of West, but he obeyed my mother.

Pete Maws told me something else about my mother a year after she died. We were sitting on the back of his caboose, our feet propped up on the railing, looking at the Atlantic.

"Your mama told me that the reason we put in those speaker posts was more than just to keep up with the times. She had made a promise to Mr. West that the big horn would be replaced. You know your mama, Abraham, she always thought your daddy was unfair to Mr. West."

My first memory of Turner West himself is when I saw him and my father on the Flamingo lot, arguing about the titles on the marquee. It was two weeks after the Frank Sinatra incident, and we were all busy installing the four hundred speaker posts to replace the giant horn on the Tower. My job was to help carry the thick metal tubing that was used to insulate the underground wiring. Hanging from my belt were rolls of tape and tubes of special glue to seal the joints of each six-foot section of pipe. Pete and my father were digging the long rows. Pete was then doing the welding of pipe and splicing of wire. Louise's job was to fetch any miscellaneous material or refreshments we might need. My mother was teaching in St. Augustine. I was eight. I did not know that Grace existed.

"Mr. Lee, could I speak to you for a moment?"

Turner West had appeared out of nowhere to stand beside us. From my point of view, he was a giant dressed in black, looming over all of us. My father had talked about Turner West for as long as I could remember, and there he was.

"Is this about my marquee?" my father said without turning around to face him. "I thought we had that settled."

"I wish you would reconsider. There is no reason some accommodation can't be reached. All I ask is that you give me some consideration during the day," West said. "The night is yours."

Still holding his shovel, my father had turned to face West. He was six inches shorter than West, and at that moment I thought he was the bravest man in the world. But, you must remember, I was only eight years old. My understanding of courage had come from the movies. David and Goliath was one of my favorite Bible stories.

"Consider this, West," my father said, shaking his shovel. "A thousand cars a day go past my marquee. It's the cheapest advertising a theatre can have. People see it coming; people see it going. A blank marquee in the daytime is simply a wasted opportunity."

Pete would not look at either man, but he had stopped working and was holding the end of a pipe in his left hand. Louise and I were staring at the demon my father had described to us dozens of times. As a demon, Turner West was oddly disappointing.

"A compromise then," West said firmly. "You remove the titles whenever I have a service scheduled. If you wish, I'll have one of my sons do all the work. Take down the letters and put them back up. You won't have to bother with anything."

My father's voice got louder.

"*You* will not touch anything of mine!" he said, gripping the shovel handle with white knuckles. "Not God himself will touch my property."

All this anger occurred eight years before the Great Fire, but it began even before then. I had always assumed that Turner West was the Jack Palance of my father's movie, the villain who threatened our way of life. Indeed, *Shane* was the first movie I could ever imagine actually being in. I had always assumed that my father was justified in his feelings toward West. I did not know why West was evil, but I trusted my father completely.

I always assumed that West's grievance against the Flamingo had something to do with the movies we showed. That was partially true. But it was not just the movies, at first, it was the titles. The Flamingo marquee could be seen up and down A1A for a mile in each direction, well before anyone saw the West Funeral Home. From that distance a driver could see in stark type the shows for the week.

That week when I first met Turner West, my father had booked a triple feature: *Body Grinders, Invasion of the Body Snatchers,* and *Flesh Feast*. My father often booked a horror combination to draw in the teenage crowds that could get out in their parents' cars. Horror movies were excellent date movies. He also advertised concession specials: hot dogs became finger sandwiches, meatball sandwiches became cat-brain gumbo, chili became gut creole.

Turner West stood there that day a victim of my father's showmanship, or so my father told me later.

Perhaps two other men could have reached a sensible and fair compromise. If my mother had been there, perhaps she could have dealt with West more diplomatically. When she was home later, she and my father left Louise and me inside the Book Room, our family library, while they argued on the lot below us. I could see my father waving his arms and pointing; my mother was motionless. But my mother did not sway my father this time, even when she suggested that the marquee be blank when West had a specific service scheduled in the afternoon.

Pete Maws thought my father was inflexible on this particular issue because Turner West had actually appeared on my father's property. By not using a phone call or a family emissary, West had stepped over some territorial border, albeit more mental than geographic, and my father had formally declared war after years of simmering disputes.

West had stood there that day long after my father had declared the Flamingo off limits to God himself, stood there silent for a long moment, looking at my father as if he were some drunk who had driven a truck through the plate-glass entrance of a flower shop, some drunk who could not be reasoned with or made to take responsibility for his actions, some drunk whose delirium and self-absorption had destroyed a thousand roses.

I know what you are thinking now. No eight-year-old child could see that in an adult's face at that moment. You are right. I did not see it then. Years later, Turner West told me how he had felt at that moment. I was an adult, in my thirties, and we had gone to bring my father home from the hospital. I was driving because West was blind. Grace was in the backseat with our first son.

I do clearly remember West's final words from that first meeting in 1960. He had turned to walk away, but then turned back and said the words that must have meant something to him, something that was his own justification.

"I was here first," he had said quietly, as much to me and Pete Maws as to my father.

It was the wrong thing to say at that moment.

"No! No!" my father screamed at him, slamming the shovel down and leaping forward.

The two men were ten feet apart, West as solid and upright as a new tombstone, my father gaining momentum as he seemed about to hurl himself at the granite man whose mere existence had become a provocation.

In a split second, Pete was out of the ditch and between the two white men. His back was toward West, and he had his arms around my screaming father.

"You shall be last! You shall not take what is mine! You are not the first! You will never . . ."

Turner West was gone. I had been frozen to the spot, staring wide-eyed at my father, and I had not seen West disappear. West was gone, but my father was still screaming at the empty space where he had been.

"I will destroy you and your family! I will burn you down! Turn your home into ashes!"

That was the day my father bought the five-gallon gas can and put it in the projection booth. I had no doubt that he was serious, but Pete convinced me that he would save my father from himself.

From that day, my father seemed to delight in tormenting Turner West. He booked more horror movies than usual, played the Tower horn until my mother would catch him, and started putting a line in every Friday's *Jacksonville Sun-Times* ad about the Flamingo being located "right next to the West Funeral Home on A1A." It was a gratuitous insult, but the depth of my father's hate toward Turner West was too deep even for my mother to mitigate.

Frank the Dog

I want you to know my family and the others in my life as well as I do. But I do not understand my sister. How can I expect you to understand her any better? I have seen Louise afraid only once in her life. But in that moment of fear I caught a glimpse of the adult she would eventually become. That moment was the first time that Pete Maws saved her life, a week after my father and Turner West had their confrontation.

Louise and I are the same exact age, almost to the minute. Pete first saved her when she was eight; she was a child. He saved her again when she was sixteen; I was still a child.

To understand the first rescue, to understand Pete and Louise, you must know about Frank.

On our seventh birthday, our parents gave Louise and me a dog. Louise named him Frank.

Frank was rescued from the Jacksonville dog pound a day before he was to be put to sleep. Louise and I had walked up and down the rows of cages, a canine death row. I wanted a puppy, but Louise saw this pathetic dachshund-terrier mongrel shivering by itself.

"That's Frank," she had said. My father was impressed. His daughter had evidently had a vision of the dog she wanted long before she actually saw him. Indeed, Frank the Dog was something Louise had always talked about.

Frank was a tragic dog. We were told that he had distemper and would probably die within a few weeks anyway. The Animal Shelter saw itself as a mercy killer in Frank's case. But Louise pointed at him, and Frank was saved.

The first few weeks back at the Flamingo, Frank was fun to watch. He would run in circles and make himself so dizzy that he would fall over. He would howl every time he heard a siren. He would sit when told and fetch sticks with joy. Louise loved Frank.

Within a month, however, it was obvious that something was wrong with him. The distemper crisis had passed. He had lived, but he went insane. Frank became vicious. In August of 1959, he got loose and bit an off-duty policeman who was there with his family. The bite was only a scratch, and the policeman was a dog lover. But my mother banished Frank to the Tower kitchen as long as the Flamingo was open for business. Only during the day was he allowed to roam freely over the grounds, and he seemed harmless as long as we and the other employees were the only people around.

Then he started snapping at the employees. Two quit without notice. One made the mistake of saying to my father that he must choose between keeping the dog or keeping a good employee. I was there when he issued the ultimatum. My father's anger was not feigned; his response was not a performance.

"*You* do not offer me a choice. *You* do not set the terms of your employment. That dog is part of my family. That dog is my daughter's pet. That dog might be the Devil's disciple, but that dog stays," my father had said.

I was there. I repeated every word to Louise. At dinner that night she walked over to my father as he sat at the head of the table, and she hugged him from behind his chair, whispering something in his ear. He simply nodded and said, "I know."

By the time Pete Maws was hired, Frank was loved only by Louise. He had bitten my father, me, my mother, two other employees, and had gotten loose from his pen so often that he was chained *and* penned when the Flamingo was open. During the day, he was kept on a chain even when he was playing with Louise. With her, he was as gentle as a lamb; with anyone else, he was potential stitches.

Five weeks after Pete arrived, Frank finally turned on Louise.

My parents had gone to St. Augustine for the afternoon. Pete was painting his caboose. I was sweeping the patio in front of the concession stand. Louise was in the pen with Frank. The other employees were out on A1A doing patch work on the asphalt entrance to the box office.

I heard her screaming, and I froze. Frank's pen was next to the Tower door to our living quarters, about fifty yards away from the concession stand, a hundred yards away from Pete's caboose, but he was already at the pen before I started to run. When I got there, Pete was inside the pen, his jacket wrapped around his left arm.

Louise was stiff in the corner, her face a crucifixion, betrayal and despair manifested in a look I would see years later. Her white blouse was ripped, her fingers bloody. Frank was five feet in front of her, his hair bristled up on his back, his head trembling, his teeth clenched. He was a small dog possessed by a demon. In a blur, it all happened.

"Dog!!!!" Pete shouted, and Frank lifted off the ground and spun around in one motion, flying toward Pete's face, his jaws open wide enough to consume the universe and howling like a siren announcing the apocalypse. Teeth and arm met in a union of flesh and bone. With his right hand Pete grabbed Frank's throat, pulling him close to his chest as he yelled at me.

"Abraham, get your sister!"

I was paralyzed.

"Abraham, get her! Can't hold him like . . ."

I ran into the pen and grabbed Louise's red hand. We were out in a second with the pen gate slammed behind us. Louise collapsed on the ground, and I turned back to see an allegory. Frank was writhing and moaning, as if in pain as well as wanting to inflict pain. Pete, I realized, could not let go of him. If he did, he would be attacked over and over. Frank was an exploding star of malevolence. Pete was trying to embrace and hold the energy.

My strangest memory of that moment is that I distinctly recall thinking that I wished my father were there to see it. I was only eight years old, but I knew my father would see more than a man and a dog. He would see what I was seeing. It was the moment I first realized that I was turning into my father.

I ran to call the police, pulling Louise into the Tower and to the kitchen, where I made her start washing her hand. Frank was not rabid, I intuitively knew that, but I also knew that Louise had to start some sort of cleansing process. Then I ran back to the pen.

Pete was lying on the ground, facedown, his back arching up with sporadic jerks. I thought he was dead, but he was just lying on top of Frank, letting his weight drain the force out of the dog.

"Things okay now," he said to me, not looking back. "I got him down. Almost choked him to death, but your daddy wants him alive." Taking a deep breath. "Just going to hold him down, make him eat some grass, wait for your daddy."

My parents arrived an hour later. In a few minutes, my father had slipped a rope around Frank's neck and freed Pete. You can still see the scars on his face and arms.

Pete ate dinner with us that night for the first time. In the trial that night to decide Frank's fate, Pete was a witness for the defense. For saving her life and the life of her dog, Louise accepted Pete into our family.

My mother was for death, my father for life. Pete offered life imprisonment.

"Just put him away," he said.

"Can't do that, Pete. You know that," my mother said. "He has gotten out of every pen, chewed every rope, snapped the chains out of their pegs, and I think I saw him climbing the fence at one time. He has to die."

"Put him in the Tower," Pete said, looking at me. "In the space above young Abraham's room. By himself. I'll take care of the cleaning and the feeding."

Supply rooms and employee apartments were on the ground level of the Tower. The dining room, kitchen, Book Room, Louise's bedroom, and my parents' bedroom were on the second level. My bedroom was on the third level. Above my ceiling all the way to the inside top of the Tower was open space broken only by hundreds of cross beams.

Pete prepared Frank's new home. He put in wood flooring and then hauled up, bag by bag, two thousand pounds of dirt to cover half the floor area. Every day for as long as Frank lived, Pete would take a bag of fresh dirt up to Frank's space, sniff out the wet spots or solid piles, shovel the waste into an empty bag, and put fresh dirt down. Thirty minutes a day, every day for years. Pete never took a vacation.

Pete also protected Louise when she made her visits to Frank, even though she insisted that Frank would never attack her again. Pete always kept within a few feet of her, and he never let her reach out to pet Frank. But she was right. Frank never growled at her, never bared his teeth. Seeing them together was like seeing one of those prison movies where the prisoner and his visitor are separated by some glass wall, always watched, never alone, close but never touching.

When I was fifteen, and my parents were gone one night when the Flamingo was not open, I managed to sneak Grace into my room. She had never heard the story of Frank, and she did not believe me when I told her. We were lying side by side on my bed, and the lights were off.

"Do you hear that?" I whispered to her. She shook her head. "Listen closely," I told her.

Minutes passed, and I was happy just being that close to her, so happy that I almost wished Frank were asleep. But he was not.

The clicking began soon enough. The space right above my ceiling was the wooden floor of Frank's room. His nails had walked across above me for seven years. That night with Grace, Frank was in a good mood. He ran in circles above us, and we could hear him slide when he got to going too fast.

I called his name and he barked. Before I could stop her, Grace also called his name. There was abrupt silence, and then a low growl.

Church vs. State

For the next four years, Pete and my father took care of me and Louise during the day while my mother taught at Flagler College in St. Augustine. I did not know that Grace existed, nor did I think it strange that Louise and I had never been to school. And to this day, we have never learned how the county found out about us. Whatever the reason, my father suspected that West was the cause, a suspicion that my mother would laugh about. But the county *did* find out, and my parents were forced to open up an old wound. Making the decision to send us to parochial school was the first time I had ever seen them argue in front of us. Argue for real, that is. I now understand that it was not just about going to school. It was an argument about God.

Both my parents were raised Southern Baptist. My mother had lost faith in the Baptist church, but not in God. She took instruction in Catholicism and never looked over her shoulder back at the incensed Scott family. She also never had a day of doubt in her life. My father walked out of the Coverdale Baptist Church when he was seventeen, right in the middle of his parents' funeral service. He had rejected the preacher's call to accept the "mystery" of God's plan. As my mother explained to me, "Isaac, your father was a very angry young man."

Up until we were twelve, my parents had compromised about how to raise Louise and me. My mother would take us to Mass every Sunday, but we were not formally christened. We did not take communion, but we did pray. I believed; Louise did not.

The St. Augustine Cathedral was built in 1787 and has been meticulously maintained over the centuries. Every Christmas we

34

went to hear the Hallelujah Chorus. My father was silent when we got home, but even he could not resist joining in when my mother and Louise did their version of "Unto Us A Son Is Given." After 1960, Pete went with us to hear the Chorus, but he never went to church any other time. I knew, however, that Pete believed in God, believed as much as my mother did. That tied him to her; not going to church tied him to my father. I have seen Pete's Bible, a big leather King James Version with the ink rubbed dim on many pages after years of tracing his favorite passages with his finger.

Pete helped me understand my father's relationship to God.

"Your father wants to believe. You understand that? He just wants proof. Seems to him to be more proof that God doesn't exist than that God does."

Even I knew there was no proof that God existed. I was twelve, and I was beginning to have answers to all the big questions.

"Pete, everybody wants proof. I believe in God, and I still wish I could see the ocean part or the sun stop or something that really defies the laws of physics."

"Difference is, young Abraham, you already believe. Something happened to your father, something somewhere, and he didn't believe anymore. Something killed his faith. Something bad happen to you, your faith might not be enough. You'll want real proof. Earth, not air."

"Class, these are the Lee children. Please make them feel at home."

Thus, Louise and I were introduced to our first schoolmates. My father had lost his battle with the State of Florida, and his children were to be thrown into a world that he had told us did not exist. Given the choice between the secular and the temporal, he had acquiesced in my mother's wishes.

"Hubert, you can send them to the public schools, with all the trash that goes there, or you can send them to St. Agnes. At least at St. Agnes, they will already know some of the children from church."

If it had been solely my father's choice, he would have sent us to the public schools. But even I knew that the decision was made by my mother, and my father was merely given the opportunity to act as if he were the judge. By the time I was sixteen, I knew, like my father, when my mother was not to be crossed.

Louise and I stood in front of the class. Every boy in the room was staring at her. I was staring at Grace West.

You must remember that up until the age of twelve my sister and I had had no friends outside of the Flamingo. My mother, my father, Pete from the time we were eight, a few employees who never seemed distinct until those that worked for us in 1968—that was my environment. If my Lockean slate was blank at birth, it was initially filled with a limited range of experiences. My world was shaped by my family, the movies we showed at the Flamingo, and a weekly issue of *Life* magazine. Thus, all current events were experienced at least a week after they happened. There was no news in my life, only history.

My parents did not allow us to have a television at home, nor did we listen to the radio. Big events like the death of John Kennedy I knew about when they happened because somehow my parents always seemed to know and let Louise and me know. But even those events never affected Louise and me like they did my parents. There was never a context out of which we could react. My science teacher at St. Agnes once compared me to a child raised in the woods by a pack of wolves. A bit hyperbolic, but not completely unfair. Louise and I were not savages, but we had certainly been isolated. If I had started school at eight, or even at sixteen, perhaps my reaction would have been different. But I was twelve, and I was just beginning the ritual of puberty. My body was outracing my ability to understand it, and it was beginning to embarrass me in private. I was awkward, and I ached with a surge of hormones that shifted blood away from my brain and into the nether regions of my loins. Sometimes I was dizzy at night at work, watching the screen as two adults touched and then fell into an embrace as the picture faded to black or time jumped to the next morning. Not really watching—staring. Louise always seemed to catch me and know what was in my mind. I could never imagine her having the same thoughts as me.

You must understand all of this—all the prior isolation and the physiological tides—to understand how I felt that morning at St.

Agnes. I had no real concept of beauty before that moment. I had seen the most gorgeous actresses in the world on the Flamingo screen. But they were larger than life. If you have seen my sister in the movies today, you would say she is one of the most beautiful women in the world. So, you would tell me, surely I must have known my sister was beautiful even back then. I did not. She was simply my sister. Not so immune were the other boys at St. Agnes.

Before Louise stepped into that classroom, Grace West had been the most beautiful, the most popular girl in school. She had been going to St. Agnes since the first grade, but she had never been at Mass in the Cathedral when I had gone with my mother. Turner West wanted his daughter protected, and St. Agnes, nestled a few blocks from downtown St. Augustine, was as close to the Middle Ages as Turner West's atheist money could buy. Grace had been going to school with the same boys and girls since they were all six years old. She had ascended the pecking order of adoration steadily from the first grade. When St. Agnes had its annual chocolate sale, most of the boys competed with one another to see who would be allowed to sell Grace's allotment. So, Louise's arrival was like a star that blazed into a solar system, shifting the laws of gravity to realign the orbits of planets. For the next six years Louise and Grace were the twin suns of their parochial cosmos, exuding heat and light as we revolved around them. Even though they are sisters-in-law today, they are not friends.

When introductions were finished that first morning, Louise and I started to walk to our seats. It was the only time Grace had a momentary advantage. Louise began to limp, not like a cripple, but noticeably enough to cause a pock-faced boy named Mike Welch to snicker.

I understood why Louise limped. We were both nervous. More than nervous, we were terrified. For those first few seconds, Louise had lost control of her emotions, and her legs betrayed her. It was the only time they ever saw it happen, but it was a streak of imperfection that Grace needed to keep her from completely resenting my sister.

When it happened I held Louise's arm to support her, and

we stopped in mid-aisle. I then understood my father's morning admonition.

"Abraham, you must always protect your sister," he had said as we got in the car with my mother to go to St. Augustine. "It is a wicked world."

I felt Louise's arm stiffen, and then she walked, she floated, flawlessly to her seat. I stood watching her, seeing my sister leave me behind and become the actress you know today. I saw her as my parents must have always seen her—as a wonder of creation. I became my father at that moment: Pride and Rage possessed my soul.

Mike Welch had quickly stifled his laugh, and he was looking down at his desktop. But he knew I was looking directly at him. I wanted him to look at me and see that I was never going to let him laugh at my sister again. He was the first person I ever wanted to hurt. More than that, he was the first person whom I ever made *plans* to hurt. Louise was standing by her desk about to sit down, but then she looked around and took back control of her life.

"Is this where I sit?" she asked the nun. It was an odd question because the nun had been very clear a few seconds earlier about that specific seat. It took me years to appreciate what Louise was doing at that moment, but I see it clearly now. Speaking her first words, she had pulled all those embarrassed adolescent eyes back to focus on her. Even Mike Welch looked up. Then my sister took a slow and deep breath, a very deep breath. Even I blinked when it became obvious.

Louise had breasts.

It was a challenge and a provocation. Those other twelve-year-old children were divided and conquered. My sister had breasts. Even through the white uniform blouse, the shape of a woman was cleaving the class into camps of masculine desire and feminine jealousy. Above the blackboard in front of the room was a crucifix. On the wall at the back of the room was a picture of the Virgin Mary. Louise Janine Lee stood in the middle and smiled, and then she sat down. Grace West was in the seat behind her.

I did not realize it then, but that morning marked the division of my life into two worlds. The Flamingo, with my father and Pete, was now sharing time with St. Agnes. For the next six years those two worlds would seldom overlap. The thirty-two children in Sister Claudia's sixth grade would follow me up through high school. A few dropped out or moved, to be replaced by others, but the central cast never changed. With time, Grace came into the world of the Flamingo, and then Gary Green, the pudgy boy who sat in front of me. And with time I came to be accepted into the world of St. Agnes. I had friends at St. Agnes that never came to the Flamingo; my father never came to St. Agnes. My first day at St. Agnes also marked the time when I first became aware that my skin separated me from most other people around me.

"Are you Chinese?" were the first words Grace ever spoke to me.

We were on the concrete playground, sitting on a bench under a hundred-year-old oak tree. I had been watching Louise on the swing across the yard, her plaid skirt billowing out with each downward arc. "I was born in Korea," I said, stating a fact that had never seemed significant to me before. "I was adopted when I was a baby."

"Do you know who your mother and father are?" she asked.

I looked at Grace as if she were retarded, and then I laughed, but she had handed me the apple of knowledge, an apple unbitten before then.

"They own the Flamingo Drive-In," I said, "where we live. Hubert Lee and Edna. My mother teaches at Flagler."

"No, no," she persisted, "your real mother and father."

Grace was lucky that my father was not there to answer her question. It was that word—*real*—that provoked him as no other word in the language. Louise and I had always seemed to know we were adopted; even before we could speak we had heard *that* word over and over. And other people had sometimes asked the same question that Grace was asking. Louise and I even understood the mechanics of pregnancy and childbirth. From our earliest consciousness, we knew that we were conveyed into this world through the body of some woman who had had sex with some man. My father and mother had insisted that we understand that basic biological syllogism: sperm and egg equals baby. My father had always warned us about the "real" question.

"Some fool will ask you about your *real* parents, some half-wit human slug with a rock-level IQ," was one variation of the same message that Louise and I had grown up with, "and you just tell them that your parents are Hubert T. Lee and Edna Marie Scott, the most real parents in the world."

But that was bombast, and even my father knew it. My parents had established their claim on Louise and me not by those pronouncements. I know that it is politically correct today to differentiate between biological parents and adoptive parents. Even to this day, however, my father rejects that distinction.

More than once a day, every day from my earliest memory, my father asked me, "Who is your favorite father?" It was a game. I would say, "You are." And then he would ask, "Who is your only father?" I would say, "You are." We might be in the car together, or working in the Flamingo field, and he would simply ask the questions. He might fake an accent or feign a lisp. But the questions were asked every day, of both Louise and me. Never by my mother, who often rolled her eyes when she was present or in hearing range of the questions. "Hubert," she would say, "enough is enough. These children know who their parents are."

Call it indoctrination, or anything else you will, but it was part of the air we breathed and the food we ate. And it was part of the ritual that even my mother participated in every night.

I was twelve years old, and I had never gone to sleep without one of my parents sitting beside my bed, talking to me as I faded out. More often, it was my mother. She would sing softly and slowly to me. I don't remember the lyrics, only that her voice was always there. After Louise and I got our separate bedrooms, my parents usually alternated putting us to bed.

In the daytime, my father would rant that "biology's got nothing to do with parenthood," and at night he would make up bedtime stories for Louise and me. Sometimes I would act like I was asleep and listen to my parents talk to me even though they thought I could not hear them. I do this with my own children now, talking to them when they are asleep, assuming that the words will somehow go deeper into their subconscious.

I was kissed every night and told that I was loved. I do not mean metaphorically. I would sometimes wake up in the night and discover my mother or father asleep in the chair beside me. My mother would sometimes lie down on top of the bedcovers, with her arm across my chest, and whisper songs in my ear, telling me how much she loved me, and sometimes she would go to sleep that way before I did. My father did the same. Pete Maws explained it all to me, explained a truth that I had come to know intuitively. "Young Abraham, your mama and daddy need you more than you need them."

My father had told me that fools would ask about my real parents. Sitting in the shade of a tree at St. Agnes, Grace had asked me about those mythical real parents. Grace was no fool; even my father would admit that. I was twelve. I was in a new world. I did not understand the real significance of the question, but I had my first doubts about my father's explanations.

If these parents were not real, who really were my parents? I sat there with Grace and thought about the bodies of the man and woman who had created me. In that oak shade, for the first time, I clearly visualized, at least I deliberately tried to visualize, how they must have looked. I thought of my own image. I looked nothing like my parents. I looked at Grace, her smooth and pale skin, her short brown hair, her long fingers, her dark eyebrows.

"Who are your parents?" I asked, trying to shift attention away from my parents.

"My father is Turner West," she said, looking over at a group of older boys who were pointing at Louise.

"Your father is Turner West!" I blurted out. Then I was speechless. I did not want him to be the father of Grace.

"Who is your mother?" I asked, trying not to think about her father. Grace did not answer, so I asked again. With only a slight tremble in her voice, she finally spoke.

"My mother died when I was born."

A Desire for Television

"Did you make any friends at school today?"

It was an innocent question, probably asked by every parent of every child who had just come home from their first day of school. But how could I answer my mother?

"Can we get a TV?" I said, surprising even myself.

We were sitting down for dinner, my father silent because that was his way of showing displeasure about the mere fact that we had been taken away from him by the State and then given to the Church.

"Abraham, did you hear me?" my mother said, a carving knife in her left hand.

I was flustered, so I looked to Louise for help. She looked straight up at the ceiling. I then looked to my father, who was staring at his plate.

"Abraham?" my mother persisted.

How could I tell her that I wanted a television because Grace had asked me if I watched "American Bandstand"? I had told Grace that I did not, but I had not admitted that we did not even have a TV. When she asked me what I *did* watch, I had mumbled something about not watching much television, and she had seemed disappointed.

"Some of the kids from Mass are there," I finally said. "You know, Gary Green and some others."

"Oh, yes, I remember Gary. He seems very nice," she said. "I have met his parents."

She made that last remark with a tone in her voice that told me that Gary was nice despite being raised by the two people who had spawned him. My mother's first appreciation of other children was always tempered by what she called their "background." Three years after my first day of school, Gary Green was eating Sunday dinner with us every week. He was to be my best friend for the rest of my life, my co-worker, and partner with Pete Maws in the future rescue of my sister. That night at dinner in 1964, Gary Green was simply a diversion to keep me from answering my mother about the other friend I had made in school.

"Did you learn anything today?" my father suddenly said, still looking at his plate. "Did they teach you anything you didn't already know?"

Louise and I looked at each other, reading each other's mind, knowing that my father was really talking to my mother, not to me.

"Hubert, that is an unfair question, and you know it," she said calmly. My parents' arguments were always calm.

My father relented, but he did not change the subject.

"I want to see your books," he said.

As long as I was in school, even all the way through graduate school at Notre Dame, my father never abdicated his role in my education. From that first night, he asked to see all my homework. He scanned my textbooks, looking for papal fallacies even though most of the books were the same ones used in the public schools. The Catholic religious texts he held in silent contempt, a compromise with my mother and, eventually, out of respect for me. I believed in my mother's God. He knew that. I still do.

My sister's and my education had begun long before we went to St. Agnes. Between the dining room and my parents' bedroom on the second floor of the Tower was the Book Room: their library and study. Books from their own childhoods, their parents' books, their own college books, books bought since they went to school—my parents never threw away a book. The Room itself smelled of leather and paper and ink. It was the largest room in the Tower, and I still have pictures of Louise and me sitting on the floor reading together when we were not yet six. Behind us were some empty shelves that were filled up in another picture taken the next year.

In the shelf space not occupied by books, my mother would arrange all the framed pictures from her and my father's past. As part of every new employee's orientation, they had to endure a tour of the Book Room given by my father. Hubert Lee would explain the history behind every picture: who this was, who that was. He had bought every roll of film taken by the *Life* photographer back in 1953, had all the pictures developed, and had dozens of them enlarged to fill up empty wall space in the Book Room.

Besides books and pictures, the Book Room also had every knickknack from all my parents' trips, many of the "projects" that Louise and I had done when we were tiny children, and, finally, any significant artifact that had some meaning to my family. The objects, as my father would say, explained us.

The Book Room Tour usually took three hours, and then the employee was never allowed back in that part of the Tower. Grace West was the only person who ever saw the Book Room without my father as a guide, but I knew the Tour by heart by then.

"Why won't you let anybody back in here after they see it?" she had asked me that time when my parents were in North Carolina. I gave her the answer my father would have given, even though I had never actually heard him explain it to anyone else.

"Grace, this is where we live," I said. "Not just in the Tower. In this particular room. This is our home."

She did not understand, but I did, and Louise now does, grudgingly, whenever I force her to remember the past. Louise will admit that she was the happiest in the Book Room of all the times of our childhood. She and I learned to play quietly in one corner of the Room while our parents sat at the other end, reading or talking. Persian rugs on the floor, leather chairs, two overstuffed couches, two writing tables, a card table where we all played pinochle and where my father taught Louise and me to play checkers and chess, two ceiling fans. The Book Room was also the first place in the Tower that had an air-conditioning unit.

When my father was designing the Tower, he had imagined this room first. The others were functional and developed organically, as they were actually used. But the Book Room was completed exactly as my father had planned, even down to the furniture selection and arrangement. The chairs were from his home in North Carolina, the rugs from my mother's home. Even the books on the shelves were arranged according to a list he had written down long before the Room was finished. New books were placed according to his own Lee filing system. My mother was in charge of the non-book arrangements. Even with them, there was an order, an order that became clearer to me the more I heard my father's Tour.

If you began in the southeast corner of the room and went clockwise, you saw the chronological pageantry of my family's life. A complete circuit around the Room gave you two and a half centuries of history. Lees and Scotts from the time of the First Great Awakening eventually evolved into the last picture of the Tour: a black-and-white group picture of the white Lee and Scott, their Asian children, and Frank the Dog—a picture taken by Pete Maws.

My father's favorite part of the Room was the window that went from one end to the other, an eight-paned window that began only two feet from the floor and went all the way to the ceiling. When the outside shutters were open, we could see forever. The outside white shutters, which folded down from above the window, were shut when the winds were strong and when the movie was showing. The only problem with the window was that the salt air left a film on the glass so that my father had to wash the window every other day, a job he bequeathed to me when I was twelve.

"*This* is your home?" Grace had laughed that day when I gave her the Tour. "Your home is a room in a movie screen?"

"And *your* home is a funeral parlor?" I countered, savoring the pleasure of my own quick insight.

We stood there silent for a few seconds, and then we both laughed at each other and at ourselves. Our children love hearing that story over and over again.

"Why does your father hate my father?" Grace had asked after we stopped laughing.

"Why does your father hate my father?" I asked her.

"But he doesn't, Isaac. I've told you that," she answered.

We had had that debate many times before Grace was in the Book Room, and we had never come up with an answer. But I still would not admit to her that she was right about her father. I did not really believe that Turner West hated my father. West simply dismissed my father as a lunatic, a major annoyance, an example of too much money and too much genetic inbreeding. Turner West had never responded to my father out of malice; more often, he acted out of self-defense. West did not see my father as a symbol; he was simply a bad neighbor.

After dinner that first night after our first day at school, we were all in the Book Room, Louise and I trying to act like we were not hearing our parents argue.

"Hubert, did you really expect to keep them at home forever?" my mother asked, a book in her hand.

"No, but I did expect you to help me fight this a little harder. You could have at least done that."

"Hubert, whether you admit it or not, Abraham and Louise are not . . ." She spoke in a voice so low that I could not hear clearly, so I went over to a shelf to get a book and did not retreat as far back as I had been. Louise stayed in the farthest corner.

". . . and St. Agnes is the perfect choice for them. You must admit that."

My father protested. "No, I do not admit that, but I will agree to it. You want them to have religion. So be it. But, Edna, the uniforms? The nuns? The dogma? The . . . the . . ."

" 'The mind-forged manacles'?" my mother said, silencing my father. Her words made no sense to me then. It was years before I understood the reference points of my parents' universe, that my mother had her Ph.D. in eighteenth-century literature, that my father never finished his dissertation on the American Romantics.

"I will not let them become mindless," he began again. "I will not let them be hurt. I will not let them be like everyone else."

"But, eventually, Hubert, you must let them be themselves. They cannot be *you*."

They were sitting on the blue couch, turned toward each other, their feet almost touching. My mother put a cushion behind her head and stretched her legs across my father's lap. She was as long as the couch.

"Do my feet," she told him, beginning the ritual massage that ended all their arguments. I could hear the bones in her ankles pop as he squeezed and slowly turned her feet.

"Abraham, would you please put on some music," she said to me, her eyes closed.

I looked at my father, who smiled and nodded. It was all part of the ritual of my childhood. Music in the Book Room as my parents sat on the couch, background music of Mantovani or Ferrante and Teicher or Andy Williams or Johnny Mathis or Frank Sinatra or, later, Herb Alpert.

I was standing at the window looking down on the Flamingo lot. It was the first day of November, the first day I went to school, the first time I saw Grace West. The sun was not completely down yet, but the Tower was casting a shadow over the lot that separated it from the beach to the north and south of it. The first day of November was when we closed the Flamingo for that season, not to reopen until the first Wednesday in March. Four months of hibernation.

I could see Pete Maws below me, walking the lot, going speaker post to speaker post removing the two-watt bulbs that illuminated each post, and then tightly wrapping each speaker in a plastic bag to keep them dry until spring. It was his own ritual. He did not need to take the bulbs out. If the speakers were kept dry, the bulbs would have been still good four months later. But Pete took the bulbs anyway, and then he would put them in an electric string that he wrapped around his caboose, so that the outline of his private domain was stitched with four hundred tiny lights. When the Flamingo was dark in the winter, Pete's caboose could still be seen by the midnight shrimpers.

Pete looked up and saw me in the window. He waved, and I waved back. I then found a record for my parents. Andy Williams started to sing about a river wider than a mile.

"Pete's taking out the bulbs," I said, sitting down to do my first night of homework.

"Time to rest," my mother whispered to herself.

Down below me were Pete and his caboose, and the concession stand with the projection booth above it. In a dry corner of the booth was a five-gallon can of gasoline. My father had put it there four years earlier, changing the gasoline every few months so that, as he told us all, "It will be fresh enough to burn that place down when the time comes." That place was the home of Grace West.

My father had put Pete in charge of the projection booth. Therefore, the gas can was under Pete's supervision. He told me not to worry.

"Your daddy gets a bit excited," he told me that first year when my father bought the can. "But I won't let him do it. Time comes, I won't let him have the gas. He'll come to his senses."

That evening when I was twelve, I looked at Pete and was happy that things seemed to be under control. I was safe in the Book Room of my home, thinking about the future. I thought Pete would keep my father safe from himself. When the time came in 1968, my father started the Great Fire.

Pete Maws gave him the match.

Education

"Did you make any friends at school today?" I asked Louise that first night before we went to bed.

We were in my room. Our parents were still in the Book Room listening to classical music, the sound of Mahler's First, my father's favorite, seeping up through the floor.

"Not as many as you did," she said, smirking at me.

"I don't know what you mean," I said defensively.

Louise still had on her St. Agnes uniform, which surprised me because the night before, as we had anticipated the new world we were about to enter, she had been adamant about her distaste for plaid skirts and white blouses. Getting home, I had immediately changed clothes, but not her. For the next six years she would wear that uniform almost everywhere, much to the increasing annoyance of my father. He told her more than once that he expected such behavior from me, but he had never thought she would give up her identity so easily. My mother told him that he was missing the real point of a uniform, but she did agree that Louise should not wear it while working at the Flamingo. Too much of a contrast, she admitted, with the pirate costumes that we usually wore.

"I thought you were going to offer to say *grace* at dinner tonight," Louise said, sitting on the floor next to my giant globe but not looking at me.

"Louise, you know we don't . . ." But then I understood her real point.

"You know, I think Grace West is the prettiest girl in the class," she said.

I was pleased, because I thought so, too, and I wanted to talk about her to someone. It only took a few minutes, however, to realize that if I wanted to talk about Grace with anyone, it was not going to be my sister.

"And the boys say she is the smartest person in the whole class," she said, looking up at the ceiling.

At that moment I was secretly proud of myself. My intuitions about Grace were being justified. Even my sister seemed to be saying that I had chosen to fall in love with my other half.

"And she certainly likes you. That's obvious," she said.

I must have been blushing, but I wanted her to say more.

"Too bad, though, about her father," she said in a matter-of-fact voice. "Too bad."

It was the cruelest thing she could have said to me. She knew I was trying to ignore the obvious.

"Maybe we'll have a double wedding. You and Grace, me and one of her brothers. Our fathers weeping and letting bygones be bygones and all that. Whatja think, Abe, peace on earth?"

Louise and I were born on the same day. Why was she so much older than me?

That night I struck back the only way I knew how.

"You know, I haven't heard Frank walking around for the past few days. Do you think Pete and I ought to check on him?"

Louise knew I was lying, and she must have known how weak an attempt at a jab it was, but for as long as Frank lived I knew where Louise's armor was the thinnest. After Frank died, she was impenetrable. She limped out of my room without speaking. Thus ended our first day of school.

Grace was not to remain the smartest person in our class. Within a few weeks it became obvious that Louise and I had had the benefit of a better education than our classmates. My mother had taught us to read; my father had taught us to write.

My father would laugh at the books we brought home from St. Agnes, and our writing assignments were, according to him, an insult. The Catholic teachers were quickly impressed with our knowledge and skills, however, which led to my first educational crisis. Sister Mary Francis, the Director of St. Agnes, suggested to my mother that Louise and I be shifted into the seventh grade immediately. My father loved the idea, saying, "The sooner they get out, the better." My mother initially approved, but I convinced her to let me stay in the sixth grade.

"I have already made friends," I told her as we walked along the beach on the first of December. "And I never had any friends before this."

It was the truth, but not the real truth. Gary Green and I were, indeed, friends. I had seen him knock down Mike Welch that first day of school in the playground. I never asked him why, but I knew. Gary was also a smart boy, and he had been the first person to offer me help in math. I did not really need the help, but I was developing a routine that would continue all the way through high school: Let others think they were helping me so that they would like me. Basic math skills I had gotten at the Flamingo: counting money at the box office, keeping ticket records, doing concession inventories, even helping my mother do the payroll. When I got to high school and really did have problems with algebra and geometry, Gary just assumed that I would need his help again. I was glad he was my friend, and I once told Louise that I thought she ought to date him, but she informed me that she was not interested in boys her own age.

"Why would you assume that these are the only friends you'll ever have?" my mother asked me that day on the beach. Louise was in her room sulking, and my father and Pete were in Jacksonville to buy white paint for the Tower screen.

"But we just started," I pleaded. "And there are some really nice kids I know and . . ."

"Is Gary your only friend?" she asked.

We were carrying two beach lounge chairs and had walked about a half mile south of the Flamingo lot. My mother took a walk on the beach every day, usually by herself. That day, she had suggested I come with her. Chairs planted in the sand, we sat side by side looking at the ocean and talking. The temperature was in the sixties, too cool to swim, but there was not much of a breeze coming in from the east, so we did not need our coats.

My love of the ocean comes from my mother; my love of the water comes from my father. Even before we could walk, my father had Louise and me in the water learning how to swim. When the water was warm, we went swimming almost every day. Until the sixth grade, we even went swimming at night without our clothes. Sometimes even in the day. I can remember the three of us running up out of the water naked and lying down on towels around my mother, who had been watching us while she sat in her lounge chair. We would threaten to throw her in the water, but she was stronger than all of us put together. Or so it seemed. She could carry my father on her back, me and Louise under her arms, and then take us down to the edge of the ocean and throw us in. It was a wonderful game.

My father said he was not ashamed of the human body; my mother said he was shameless. Any guilt I had about my own body came from my mother. Not that she was repressed or repressive. But my mother always said that a body was not for public display. I saw my father naked hundreds of times, as did Louise. I have no memory of my mother's naked body. Indeed, my father always joked that my mother disappointed him. She could not swim, and she did not like carnival rides.

That first day of December, I was coming to understand why she loved the ocean so much. We sat there under a noonday sun watching the tide come softly in, the surf almost apologetic as it crawled toward our feet.

"I do not want you bored at school, Abraham," she said. "I want you excited about learning every day. Perhaps you need more of a challenge."

My mother would often say the same things my father would say, but her voice was never as strident or emphatic. Her voice was a wish, not a command.

"Please, let me stay where I am." I could not articulate, perhaps not even to myself, the real reason I wanted to stay in the sixth grade.

We sat there without speaking for a few minutes. My mother's eyes were closed, and I thought for a second that she had fallen asleep. I closed my eyes, and then I found myself praying sincerely for the first time. In a purely theological sense, I was trivializing the existence of God. I know that now, and I try to tell my own children that God shapes the important things in their life, not the mundane. But I do not begrudge my son's prayer that he be given some divine intervention in the outcome of a soccer game or that his mother and I take him to Orlando next week. My own life that first of December hinged on my staying with Grace West. I wanted God to reason with my mother.

"Abraham, what do you see when you look at the horizon?" my mother asked, her eyes still closed.

I stared hard, assuming this had something to do with my future. My mother was often indirect.

"A straight line," I said, hoping this was not a trick question.

"Look harder," she said.

I stared harder, and then I saw that what I had always assumed was a straight line was actually very wavy and uneven. It *had* been a trick question.

"A wavy line," I said.

My mother nodded.

"And what do you hear?" she asked.

That *was* a trick question. There was nothing on the beach to hear except her and me. There was not even a bird in the sky.

"Just us," I said.

I was wrong, I know that now, but it was the answer that kept me in the sixth grade. God, as you may know, moves in mysterious ways.

"Perhaps you're right," my mother said, "perhaps you should stay where you are for now. No need to hurry."

Grace and I were to be classmates for the next six years. I was to become class valedictorian; Grace was salutatorian. Gary Green had the third highest average. Mike Welch did not graduate. In a class of thirty-two, Louise was ranked twenty-third, a distinction that required her to work harder than I had done to be number one. I always thought my sister knew more than me, certainly she was a better reader and writer, and the first few months of the sixth grade had revealed the width of the gap between us and the rest of the class. Even today, my father still wonders why she had such a mediocre record. By the time we were in high school, when grades seemed such a clear indicator of merit, my father would become so exasperated with Louise and her indifference to her studies that he and she would often yell at each other across the dining-room table while he was trying to "help" her.

From that first day of class until her graduation, Louise slowly, but inexorably, separated herself from my father's vision of our future. My success in school made him proud, but I also knew that I was merely fulfilling his expectations. He assumed I was to be the smartest child in school; I was not strong enough to ever question his assumptions. Louise, I think now, was stronger than both of us.

I enjoyed going to school, and not just because Grace was there. After the first few weeks, everyone seemed to accept me. I did not feel as foreign as I had that first day, and I quickly got a reputation as a brain who was willing to help someone else. I played games at recess with enough skill to be included very quickly when teams were being chosen. My teachers liked me, except for Father Tucker, who had been a missionary in China and who always went out of his way to find fault with me. I was going to tell my father about him, but I quickly realized that if I told him about anyone bothering me at St. Agnes there would probably be a melodramatic scene, either at home or at school. Louise was right about our father. As much as I loved him, I did not want him to come to St. Agnes.

So I told my mother. Father Tucker was made a fifth-grade teacher that year, and then reinstated to the sixth grade as soon as Louise and I were in the seventh. I was not surprised. If my father could not stand up to my mother, I assumed that no one else could, either. Louise found out the truth years later. My mother had gone to Sister Mary Francis, described the problem, and then pointed out that the Lee family pledged three thousand dollars a year to the St. Agnes building and scholarship fund, as well as another two thousand for the Bishop's Annual Appeal. Five thousand 1964 dollars. My father would have tried to confront Father Tucker and challenge him to some "angels on the head of a pin" debate at high noon on St. George Street downtown. My mother quietly asked if there was anything we could do to make everyone happy. Sister Mary Francis was a reasonable woman.

By the end of that first year, the spring of 1965, I had made a place for myself at St. Agnes. Although I worshipped Grace West, I managed not to be too obvious. Except, of course, to Louise. I sought out Grace's company almost every day, managed to ask her questions about assignments, accepted her help on certain projects, and purposefully missed a few spelling words every Friday to make sure she had the top score. I had to stop doing that when my father saw one of my tests.

Living in a drive-in theatre did not hurt my popularity. Two or three times a season, when we were showing a western, my mother arranged for all the boys in my class to come as a group to the Flamingo. I was not even embarrassed by my father, even though he performed his usual routines. For those nights, I was exempt from work and became the leader of a parochial pack. John Wayne was free, popcorn and chocolate Toddies were free, tours of the projection booth were conducted by Pete Maws, and we got to sit in the patio seats in front of the concession stand. Movies over, my mother drove a St. Agnes bus full of sugar-saturated boys back to St. Augustine and delivered them individually to their front doors. The first time we did all this, Gary Green asked my mother if she would adopt him. My mother also had the same arrangement for the girls in class, but Louise was not the natural leader I appeared to be. The girl movie was usually a comedy or perhaps a Doris Day romance, and my mother would take personal charge of the activities. The tour was much the same, but the girls were not allowed in the projection booth. That was my father's only restriction, and my mother agreed.

Of all the times my class was brought to the Flamingo, Grace West was never among them, and I never had to ask why.

Grace eventually pointed out another reason I seemed to be accepted so soon into St. Agnes.

"All of us girls saw how you helped your sister that first day, how you held her arm and seemed so protective. It was nice, Isaac, and you seemed so much older than the other boys. Of course, all the boys saw your sister. For them, you are the brother of Louise."

Two years ago, at a movie premiere in New York, a TriStar pub-licist introduced me as "the brother of Janine Lee." Grace was with me, and she poked me in the side, whispering, "Told you."

I have seen all of Louise's movies, even the ones she would like to forget. In fact, I have seen most of them more than once. Unlike some women in the movies, Louise is not a star, but she *is* an ex-traordinary actress. And she is still beautiful, but only when she wants to be. I am very proud to be her brother.

The Loved One

When I first discovered that Grace was the daughter of Turner West, I knew that I must never tell my father that we were friends. Considering everything that had happened between the two men up until that point, I could only imagine an Armageddon of cosmic proportions, some final resolution that left a scorched earth and Grace forever out of my life.

Until we were in the eighth grade, Grace and I assumed that we were a secret from our parents. We did not see each other anywhere except at St. Agnes. Louise knew, despite my constant denials, that I loved Grace, but she was not going to tell our parents. After we graduated from high school, she made a confession about what she had planned to do.

"I figured you would want to keep it a secret forever, so I knew I had some leverage to get things from you," she told me.

"Louise, what could I ever have that you would want?" I had asked her.

"Oh, Abe, when the time came, I knew you would lie for me when I needed an alibi. But then they found out about you and Grace before I could really threaten to expose you. So all my best-laid plans for blackmail were ruined by her showing up that day. She always did make my life more difficult."

When we were almost fourteen, Grace came to the Flamingo as an unannounced agent of her father. She had not even told me she was coming, which was probably a good decision. I would have aged prematurely if I had known she was about to meet my father.

It was the Saturday before the opening of the 1966 season. We were all in the concession stand, stocking shelves and making sure the fryers and poppers were clean and working. Pete was painting the patio chairs in front. My parents were doing an inventory of boxes and cups. Louise was holding a bottle of Windex and a roll of paper towels for me while I stood on a ladder cleaning the overhead menu boards.

"Mr. Lee, could I talk to you?"

Without turning around, I knew that voice. My vision blurred and I felt myself falling off the ladder, but Louise had grabbed my legs. I looked down at her, my eyes clearing. She was grinning like an idiot.

My mother and father were down on their hands and knees behind the counter. I could see my father's puzzled expression as he looked at my mother. She stood up first. Then my father stood, his clipboard still in hand, his pencil between his teeth. I held my breath, assuming that my father would instantly know who Grace was and instantly see that she and I had been secretly betrothed. But his face showed no sign of recognition.

Grace was standing next to the cash register. Next to her was Pete, an inch shorter than she.

"Young lady has a message for you," Pete said. I could have sworn that he had figured out that Grace and I were in love, just by the look on our faces when we made eye contact. But I was wrong. Pete did not know until my mother told him later.

"My father . . ." Grace began to speak, and I knew it was the end of my life as I had known it, probably the end of life on earth. I sat on top of the ladder, looking down at my family, afraid of my father for the first time in my life, afraid he was about to hurt *me* and someone I cared about, wanting him not to be himself.

"My father wants me to ask a favor of you," Grace said. She was wearing a solid black dress and her hair was pinned tightly back. The resemblance was unmistakable.

"And your father is?" my father asked slowly, as if knowing but wanting her to admit it first.

"Her father is Turner West," my mother said. "Am I right?"

Grace's composure faltered for a second, and she blushed, a blush made more deep because of her pale skin. At that moment, if my father had said the wrong thing, I would have ceased to be his son. But my father redeemed himself.

"Why has he sent *you?*" my father asked, but his voice was soft as he walked around the counter and sat on a bench next to the window. Sitting, he was shorter than Grace. I looked at my mother. She had one of those expressions on her face that I knew she only got when she was absolutely, truly, deeply in love with my father. I had seen it often, but less and less during the past two years.

"I don't know," Grace confessed, and I could see that she was as confused as I was at that moment.

"Doesn't matter," my father said, smiling. "The important thing is that you are here, and you have a purpose."

"I told him that I knew Isaac," she blurted out.

I felt as if I were in a thunderstorm. I could see the lightning coming but I was unable to move. I knew the bolt was about to incinerate me, and I would be ashes. Louise swallowed hard. I could hear her throat clear itself, and then she pinched my leg. My mother was looking at Grace; my father was looking at me, with a look that said "We will talk later."

"You know my son?" he said.

"From school. We are in the same class."

My father did not look at me. He was staring at my mother, as if some conspiracy were being revealed to him. My mother's look said "We will talk later."

For a moment my father was speechless, but he soon refocused on Grace.

"You have a message from your father," he said, still surprisingly calm. Certainly he was more calm than I was.

Grace took a deep breath and began to speak in a measured tone that indicated that she had practiced her delivery more than once.

"He would like for you to reconsider showing that movie you are going to show in April. The movie about the funeral business."

I was outraged. Why had Turner West sent his daughter to do this? He knew of my father's capacity for wrath. He had seen my father's reaction to any request to alter his behavior. He knew my father's potential for violence. I hated Turner West at that moment.

He was a coward. He had sent his youngest child into a pit of snakes, a den of lions, from which he had barely escaped years earlier. My father had been right about West. He *was* an evil man.

"My father would like for you not to show that movie," Grace continued, her voice shaking only slightly.

"Tell your father I will think about it," my father said, standing up and turning Grace back toward her home. "Pete, would you walk this young woman back to her father's house?"

Pete took Grace's hand. I had told her all about Pete, so she accepted his hand without hesitation. Everyone felt safe with Pete.

As she was about to leave, Grace turned and said, "I was supposed to tell you why my father thought you should reconsider."

My father laughed happily, almost hysterically. "Oh, young lady, I know exactly why your father wants me not to show it. I know exactly. You just tell him that I will let him know tomorrow. I just have to talk to Abraham's mother."

I was totally confused. Nothing in my father's past behavior had prepared me for his apparent conciliatory mood.

My father was about to speak to me when I noticed his brow furrow and his eyes blink. He turned quickly back to Grace as she was leaving.

"Young lady, I'm sorry, but I did not get your name," he said.

Her hand in Pete Maws', the future mother of my children looked at my father and spoke in a woman's voice.

"My name is Grace. I was named after my mother."

My father's mouth opened, but he did not speak. Grace had done to him what she did to me.

The movie was *The Loved One*. I saw it for the first time when I was in college at the student theatre. It never came to the Flamingo. I was proud of my father as I sat there in the cramped smelly room with a hundred other sophomores. It was a brutally funny movie, a parody of the funeral business. If I had not been me, I would have laughed as much as anyone else.

You probably have not seen *The Loved One*. After it came out in 1966, there were rumors that funeral directors all across America colluded to keep the film out of their communities. See it. You will understand why.

Jonathan Winters played a double role: the sinister funeral director of a giant Forest Lawn–type mortuary and cemetery, and his incompetent twin, who operated a nearby pet cemetery. Rod Steiger was the effeminate chief cosmetologist who lived with his obscenely obese mother. Milton Berle played a Hollywood star whose dog had to be buried with an elaborate service because the star's wife was inconsolable. Gap-toothed Robert Morse played a young man on the make, trying to succeed in any business, dancing amid the nude statuary in the memory gardens, and falling in love with the assistant cosmetologist, a beautiful young woman who eventually commits suicide by embalming herself.

My father must have planned on showing *The Loved One* as his ultimate insult. He must have anticipated Turner West's objections with relish. He must have known that Turner West would have done something to retaliate, something that would in turn justify a darker outrage from him. My father might have been mad, but he could be very methodical.

The day after Grace made her father's request, my father sent me to her home with a note informing Turner West that *The Loved One* would never be shown in the state of Florida.

The Wall
of Turner West

When my father wanted to teach me something, he would make me sit with him in one of those green wooden chairs on the patio in front of the concession stand. Whenever he said, "Abraham, would you meet me on the patio?" I knew that I was supposed to learn a valuable lesson. Supposed to. Sometimes, however, my father began in one direction and arrived somewhere else. My mother always seemed to begin with no direction in mind, but she always got to where she wanted to go.

"Abraham, would you meet me on the patio?" he said that afternoon after Grace had left the Flamingo.

Louise whispered just loud enough for me to hear, "Forgive me, Father, for I have sinned." My sister's sense of humor is probably proof that nature has as much power as nurture.

Louise and my mother stayed in the concession stand, but I knew that they could see me and my father through the big windows. My mother said to me, a week before she died, that she had always wished that she had had a movie camera to record those conversations between my father and me. Not the words, just the picture. My father usually standing and pacing, his arms waving around, fingers pointing, him pushing his hands through his thinning hair, and then the finale—him and me shaking hands, as if some verbal contract had just been negotiated.

"So, Abraham, how well do you know this girl?" he asked that afternoon, a question I had expected.

"Since the first day of class when Louise and I went to school," I said, trying to anticipate his next question.

"A nice girl?" he asked, his arms crossed across his chest.

He had turned around to face the screen, so I was talking to his back.

"I'm not sure I know what you mean—nice," I said.

"Is she smart? Is she well-mannered? Is she a real Catholic? Is she someone that you *like?*"

His emphasis on that last word brought back all my insecurities. How transparent were my feelings?

"She is the nicest girl in the class," I said, deciding that I might as well tell the truth. But as soon as I said it I realized that Louise was also in the same class, so how was my father going to react to me saying that Grace was nicer than my sister? But my guilt and apprehension were unnecessary. I should have realized that my parents never assumed that Louise and I were comparable to other children. If I said Grace was the nicest girl in class, or the prettiest, that was a reflection on the other girls, not Louise.

With his back still toward me, and with his hands clutching the patio guardrail, my father held a knife over my heart.

"How long have you known that this nicest girl in the class was the daughter of Turner West?"

Saying the name of his adversary, my father whirled around and seemed to leap at me.

But that was my imagination. He had simply turned and stepped toward me. Still, the last vestiges of puberty betrayed me. My voice cracked and quivered between octaves.

"Since the first day," I sputtered out, trying to clear my throat while not looking at him.

Then my father did the unexpected. He did not raise his voice; he did not shake his fist at the universe and curse his neighbor. For the first time in one of these conversations, he sat down beside me. He put his legs over the chair in front of him and slouched back in his seat. I did the same. Both of us were looking at the largest blank screen in the continental United States.

"You could have told me," he said, but I did not believe him. My father was lying either to me or to himself.

"You hate Turner West," I said, my voice harder than I thought I was capable of. "You said you wanted to burn his house down.

Destroy him and his family. You said that. I'll always remember that. You said you wanted to burn down his home, where he and Grace live. You said it. You said you were going to kill them!"

My father was silent, so I turned to face him. He kept looking at the screen, but his brow seemed furrowed. As if he were sorting out the past, or trying to find words for the present.

"I said all that?"

At that moment, I hated my father *and* Grace's father.

"And he probably hates you! Probably wants to . . . wants to . . . wants to blow up all this." I had stood up and started pointing in every direction, toward the tower and screen, the concession stand, even Pete's caboose. "He probably wants to see you dead as much as you want him dead. To see us all dead."

My father was looking up at me, and my mother was watching me through the window.

"Abraham . . . ," my father began to say, but I turned and walked away, hitting my fist against the railing as I headed for any place other than where I was.

"Abraham!" my father shouted.

I kept walking, but then I saw Pete out of the corner of my eye. He was shaking his head. I stopped and looked at him and then stared at the screen, the screen my father was always painting and pointing at, the white surface that, from my earliest memories, had reflected a world that did not exist except in the imaginations of a thousand writers and directors. I turned to look back at my father, but I saw the ocean first. Focusing closer, I saw my father still sitting on the patio, my mother standing behind him but separated from him by the window. I walked back to them.

I did not sit down. My father had stretched his arms across the seats on both sides of him, and his feet were still draped over the seat in front of him.

"I want you to do me a favor," he said.

At that moment, I desperately wanted him to say that it was okay for me to like Grace and that it was okay that she like me, but I knew that was not possible. I expected the "favor" to be that I was not to have anything to do with her, ever again. But I was wrong. We were not to be the Capulets and Montagues. My father would not have me reject Grace, nor would Turner West banish his daughter to a nunnery. In a few years, I would learn that the conflict between my father and Turner West was older than Shakespeare.

"Tomorrow, I want you to take a message to Turner West," my father said. "I'll write it down and put it in an envelope. Just remember, it's between him and me. You are not to read it."

Then he put out his hand.

"A deal?"

"A deal," I said, putting my hand in his, seeing him smile.

In my room that night, I listened to Frank pace back and forth over my head. A police car went speeding down A1A, its siren wailing, and Frank began to howl. Even through the thick walls of the Tower, the sound of sirens always seemed to hurt Frank's ears. My parents were in the Book Room. I had thought about eavesdropping on them, but the music they were playing made that impossible. You must remember, the really serious conversations between my parents were always almost whispered.

Sitting there in the dark, I had opened my shutters to look out at the ocean. There was a half-moon in the sky. My chin resting on the windowsill, I looked for the shrimp boats.

In the morning, my mother prepared me for my visit to the West Funeral Home. She picked out my clothes, made me take an especially long bath, and supervised my dressing. I was to wear my St. Agnes uniform: blue shirt, gray slacks, black dress shoes, dark blue tie, but with a special blazer that had hung in the closet so long that it was almost too short. My father had protested when she suggested that we go to the store and buy a new coat before I make my visit.

"I will sacrifice some of my pride in this matter"—he had laughed—"but that man will not change my budget."

My mother and I both laughed with him because we both knew that my father had spent lots of money making life miserable for West. Ten dollars for a new jacket was the smallest of small change.

I was surprised and puzzled by my parents' good mood, especially my father's seemingly casual approach.

Before I was allowed to put on my uniform, my father trimmed my hair. He wrapped a sheet around me and clipped the hair over my ears and evened out my bangs. Then my mother brought in my father's Vaseline hair tonic, combed my hair straight back, and poured on the oil. I once told my oldest son about this scene. He was in his Hemingway phase, having read almost everything written by him. My son said it was like I was a matador being dressed by handlers. I think he might have been right. I remember that my parents did not even let me button my own buttons. When the dressing was completed, they made me stand in front of their full-length mirror. I was between them, and we all looked older than we were.

Did you ever wish that you had a picture of some particular moment from your past? Most of the pictures anyone has from their past are usually posed self-consciously for *a* picture. Cameras are seldom there for the really important moments. Events, yes; moments, no. I still have a picture in my mind of the three of us at that moment, my mother and father each with a hand on my shoulder, each looking at my reflection in the mirror, me looking at my own image. In my memory, I see all of us. In the mirror that morning, I saw only myself.

Envelope in pocket, I was walked to the edge of A1A and released. My father told me to wait for an answer; my mother told me to say hello to Grace for her. Then I was walking by myself down the highway to the funeral home that I had always been told was the embodiment of every evil in the world. I thought about what my mother had just told me as I began the trip. Was it only my mother who knew that I was more than my father's messenger that morning? Or did he know, but not admit that he knew, that I was actually doing what I had always wanted to do? I did not look back, but I knew they were both watching me walk away.

For some reason, I had expected Turner West to open the front door when I rang the bell, so I blinked that first second at the way that West had seemed to change his appearance. Perhaps my father had been right, perhaps West had the Devil's power to shift shapes and forms. In front of me was a much younger Turner West. In fact, it was his youngest son, with darker hair and an unlined face, but a replica nonetheless.

"My father sent me with a message for Mr. West," I said, my self-confidence in a puddle at my feet.

The young West was soon replaced by an older West, who was then replaced by the elder West. I was motioned into the hallway. The first part of my body to respond was my nose. Grace, I realized, must live in a flower shop. Then I was led through a parlor, following Turner West like a soldier follows his leader through a mine-field, trying to put my feet in the same spots as West did, afraid that a misstep would atomize me. I was afraid to look to my left or right, sure that I would see a corpse in every corner. Neither Louise nor I had ever been to a funeral. My only image of death had come from the movies, and, thanks to my father, I had seen too many horror movies.

"You have a message from your father?"

I was sitting in Turner West's office, not quite remembering how I got there. Without speaking, I handed him the envelope. Before he opened it, West asked me if my father expected an immediate answer. I just nodded, afraid my voice would crack if I spoke out loud. I sat there while he read the note, wondering if my father had written something inflammatory, some message that might cause Turner West to harm the messenger. West's face had no expression that gave me a hint as to how he felt. He looked up and then straight at me. I could only look at him for a second until I looked away. I told my mother later, when we were alone, that I thought I had seen his face in some movie we had played at the Flamingo. Or perhaps it was in a dream I had. It was a handsome face, I said, like somebody in a movie. She seemed interested in my description, but I did not tell her that it was also a cold face, a face not like my father's, which concealed no emotion. Even at fourteen, I wondered if the face of Turner West was the inevitable face of a man who had looked at death too much. How many dead faces had Turner West touched in his life?

On the wall behind West were certificates and pictures. Shots of West and his wife, in which he looked like the son who had answered the door. Pictures of his six sons. A group picture of all the sons and their father together, seven men dressed in black. There was a picture of the West Funeral Home taken a few weeks before it was opened for business, with West talking to some carpenter about something. A picture of West with a group of men in business suits at some sort of luncheon. In a large frame over his right shoulder, under tinted glass, was an entire page from the *Jacksonville Sun-Times* full of stories about a bus crash that had killed the Jacksonville University basketball team. At the top of the page were small individual pictures of each of the young men. Eight of the eleven pictures were carefully circled. In small frames next to the newspaper were eight letters, some typed, some with pristine penmanship, some barely legible. Each letter, I would read later, thanked Turner West for his consideration. I told my father later about those letters. He said he remembered the procession down A1A, and he did not make a joke about it.

Another wall was also filled with pictures, dozens of them, all of Grace. Of all of West's children, Grace was the only one who had pictures as a baby and child on the wall. Her own special wall. The smallest frame held a picture of her taken the day she was born. School pictures from every year at St. Agnes were there, as well as the group class picture from each year. Grace on a tricycle and Grace on a Shetland pony at the parish fair in St. Augustine. Grace reading a book. Grace with her brothers, all of whom looked like Turner West. Grace on the beach when she was seven years old, looking away from the camera and toward the ocean. Next to that picture was its almost exact duplicate, but Grace was thirteen, still looking away from the camera and toward the ocean, wearing a bathing suit that might have been simply a larger version of the one she had worn six years earlier. I had never seen her legs above the knee before I saw that picture.

Of all the pictures of Grace, none of them showed her and her father together.

"Would you excuse me for a moment," West spoke, breaking my reverie about his daughter. I was instantly afraid that he could read my mind. "I will have an answer for you to take to your father, but I would like for you to remain here until I get back."

And then he was gone and I was alone. I sat rigid in that revolving office chair, stopping myself when I felt tempted to rock back and forth. I kept looking at the wall of Grace, sometimes glancing back at the other wall to look at her mother's pictures, seeing very clearly the resemblance, and then at pictures with West in them, seeing her resemblance to him as well. I tried to imagine some part of my father's face in mine, some trace of my mother. I envied Grace.

A minute passed, then another, and I was getting more nervous. Had he gone to do something about the message from my father? Or had he gone to do something connected to his business? Had I interrupted a secret ritual in another room of his home? Were he and his sons in the middle of an embalming process? I tried to remember what his hands had looked like, especially the right hand that had shaken mine at his front door. Whose flesh had he pressed before he pressed mine? I tried to remember any smell that might have given me a clue, but, at fourteen, I had no sense of what formaldehyde smelled like, so how would I have interpreted any scent that I could have detected? Then a more important question came into my mind: Where, after all, did they keep the dead bodies?

I stood up and began to pace the office, casually touching his desk, stepping closer to the wall with the certificates, reading them and then the eight letters. Then I turned around and faced the wall that had been behind me, a wall of small print.

At first glance, I did not understand what I was looking at, but then the significance began to suck the marrow out of my adolescent posture. I exhaled deeply and sat my bottom on the edge of Turner West's desk. Facing me was the largest bulletin board in the world, a board covered, very neatly, with what must have been almost a thousand newspaper clippings. Some were only a few inches long, others were two columns wide and five inches deep. Each had a single name in dark print at the top, then, in small print, the history of a human life. I was face-to-face with the Wall of Turner West, the obituaries of every person whose last vision, had they been able to see after they were dead, would have been Turner West looking down at them as he closed the lid of their coffin.

"My father said you were here."

Grace stood in the doorway, dressed in black, smiling at me. In all the time I had known her, we had never been alone before.

I was speechless.

"Don't you get enough of that uniform at school?" she asked, walking around to sit in her father's chair.

"Do you *really* live here?" was my suave and sophisticated opening line. From my brain down to my mouth, those words were a regret even as they escaped me. But she did not seem bothered by my lack of tact.

"*You* think I live in a strange place?" She laughed.

Thus was born our own private joke. We had had a similar exchange the first time we ever met, and we will do variations on that theme for the rest of our lives.

"Oh, Isaac, this is not so bad. I told you that."

I sat back down in the chair, the West Wall behind me, his daughter in front of me, trying not to say anything silly.

"I've never been in a funeral home," I said.

"Would you like a tour?"

"You'll show me around?" I said, somehow excited by the idea of her and me walking around looking at her world together.

"Oh, I can't do it by myself, but my father will. He's very proud of this place."

I was disappointed, and then hesitant. I was not yet comfortable being around the man who was to become my father-in-law. I think about that now, about how Turner West intimidated me for as long as I lived at the Flamingo, and how he and I never had a long conversation until that early morning when Grace was in labor with our first son. Her pregnancy had been very difficult, and we had been in the waiting room for almost twelve hours. It was 3:00 a.m. when a nurse came to tell us that mother and child were both healthy. I had been listening to West tell me the story of his life before he met my mother and father. Grace, I had realized that morning, had known only part of the story, as I must have known only part of my own parents' story. Hearing that his daughter and grandson were safe, Turner West had cried. I know he wouldn't have done that if my father had been there.

"Do we have to have him be with us?" I asked Grace there in her father's office.

"Isaac, he won't bite you."

"No, no," I protested, "I just wanted, wondered if . . ."

But I stopped because I did not want to admit that it was not really her father I did not want with us. I just did not want anybody to be with us. Grace looked at me, and I knew she was quickly figuring me out.

"Sometime later. Or maybe on a Sunday when he is at church, I can do it then. My brothers will keep a secret for me," she said, adding as if almost talking to herself, "My brothers will do anything for me."

"And I can give you a tour of the Flamingo," I said, grasping at any excuse to put us together.

"Would you really?" she said with noticeable pleasure in her voice. "I've always wanted to see a movie there, but my father says no. Even when all the other kids in class get to go, he says I have to stay away."

"I've noticed," I said, letting an unnatural sarcasm slip out.

"But I told you all the time, Isaac, it's not my fault. If it were left up to me, well, you know, I would have gone to see you, I mean, to see the movie."

It was the first time I had ever seen her get flustered, so I changed the subject.

"I like your pictures. I can see how you look like your mother. Probably more than your father."

Grace shrugged, but she did not speak. I was now seeing that she was as nervous as I was. So we sat there for a minute, working ourselves up to a conversation, but her father reappeared. Grace looked up at him and then quietly got out of his chair and slipped out of the room, turning at the last second to give me a waist-high wave of her hand.

"Give your father this," he said, handing me a brown envelope. "Tell him"—clearing his throat—"tell him thank you."

Around the dinner table that night at the Flamingo, I told my family about my adventure, about the pictures, the West Wall, the smell of the flowers. My father listened closest when I described the wall with Grace's pictures.

"She obviously means a great deal to him," he said. "Much more than his sons do. That happens. Out of many children, one becomes, for some reason, most important."

My father was speaking to himself, as if to a co-conspirator.

When Grace and I take our three sons to Mass we always sit in the same pew in the same order. She on one end, me on the other, the oldest boy next to her, Dexter, the youngest, next to me. The arrangement never varies.

Dexter is different from the other two boys. Even at five, he is wiser than they are now. The other boys are distracted at Mass, but not him. Grace tells me that when she was pregnant with him, that late and unexpected miracle, she felt something different inside her. I would lay my head on her stomach and listen to his heartbeat. Grace was afraid. I knew she always thought about her own mother's late pregnancy.

After he was born, I remembered all those stories my mother would tell me about Louise's sickly baby years. Dexter was like that. Always sick. But strong. He would squeeze my thumb with his fist as he coughed. At nine months, when he almost died from pneumonia, he would grip the bars of his crib and wail until his mother or father came to pick him up. His breath would be raspy, his lungs rattling, but as soon as one of us picked him up he would wrap his arms around our neck and go to sleep. We paced the floor of his room for hours, letting him rest. It was when I realized that his brothers did not resent the attention Dexter got that I knew that they would be happy adults.

I look at my own children now and wonder if they will ever understand me and their mother. How much of the simple routine of our adult life is a mystery to them? Do we even exist in their lives except as to how we feed them, clothe them, or constantly harass them into grudging obedience?

Compared to my childhood, my children lead remarkably normal, upper-middle-class existences. A home in the suburbs of Jacksonville, an A-frame beach house, parochial school, private music lessons, money in the bank for college, braces on their teeth, and parents who dote on their every awkward movement.

Grace shows them pictures of the Flamingo, of their grandparents, of me and her when we were their age. My oldest son rolls his eyes and whispers to his little brothers, "No wonder Daddy is so silly." I glare at him, and he smiles. He is fifteen, very tall, and I see Turner West more and more in him every day. My father also sees the resemblance.

When our sons are asleep, Grace and I always sit and talk as we listen to music. Nothing soul-searching, nothing profound. Just about the day. We both have a glass of wine. She has usually been busier than I have been that day, so she has more to tell me. I will sometimes stand behind her and rub her shoulders, and she will talk without seeing my face. Rolling her neck around and around, sometimes resting her cheek against my hand. I kiss the top of her head, kidding her about a bald spot that does not exist. I say it, and she always reaches behind her to slap my leg. Except for a few lines around her eyes, and skin that is softer than when I met her, Grace seems not to have aged. Then we go to bed. Except for the time with my sons, it is the best part of the day.

A Truce

According to *Life*, 1966 was a turbulent year in America. Civil rights confrontations, race riots, bombings, the escalating war in Vietnam, a country primed to self-destruct.

In my memory, 1966 was one of the best years of my life. North Florida was a peaceable kingdom, and I went from fourteen to fifteen looking forward to each new day, my voice maturing, my body shooting up to look my father in the eye and down at Pete Maws, my mind daily absorbing another small fraction of the collective knowledge of the human race, my heart held on a string by Grace West.

For one entire season, the Flamingo did not play a single horror movie. By the end of spring 1967, my father had managed not to curse Turner West in front of me for more than a year. I knew he had not changed his mind about West, but he held his temper in check. Or so it seemed.

When school was in session I saw Grace every day. Her father had even relented enough to let her visit the Flamingo, but not to see a movie on those nights when our entire class was treated. She could never come at night. Her father, she told me, never thought it was safe at the Flamingo after dark. But she could come on a weekend day, and we could sit on the patio and talk, or walk on the beach, or help Pete with some maintenance problem. Best of all, we could go to the playground at the base of the Tower and spend hours on a carousel or sliding down one of the five slides. We were too old to be playing on a playground; we both knew that. And we never told anyone at St. Agnes about it. Even Louise kept our secret.

My father had built the largest playground between Jacksonville and Miami. Not just two of everything, usually four or more. All sizes, painted with the gaudiest of colors. Even a trampoline. Sand pits, concrete tunnels made out of massive sewer pipes, and off to one side an eight-car Ferris wheel. When I describe the playground to my own children, they all agree that it was a lawsuit waiting to happen. Even Dexter seems jaded.

"Your father loves children," my mother always said. "But sometimes I wish he weren't so earnest about it."

My father's playground was, indeed, excessive. Most nights there was more equipment than children. Seldom did we play the kinds of movies that drew lots of families, so much of my father's time was spent chasing teenagers out of the playground after the movie had started. Teenagers no longer excited by backseat sex, teenagers seeking a thrill level one plateau higher.

My father might have loved children, but he hated teenagers.

In 1966, I think my father did not see me and Grace as we were. He would, from a distance, look at us on the playground and sometimes wave. But he never came close to us, seldom close enough to Grace to even say hello. I was very thankful for his distance.

Louise also ignored us. When Grace would come over, Louise would find something else to do. Only once did she intrude, and we did not speak to each other for a week afterward.

"Have you ever been skinny-dipping?" she casually asked Grace one afternoon as we all sat on the patio.

Grace did not answer at first. I was blushing, and I hated my sister.

We were all fifteen, but Louise was going on thirty. She had breasts, and hips, and lips, and eyes that were windows into a world of eternal damnation. I knew all that because I had been listening to three years of St. Agnes boys who were willing to sacrifice their souls for a touch of my sister's flesh. And I understood their temptation because I would have done the same for a moment's union with Grace. I was fifteen, and I wanted more than the heart of Grace West. Louise knew I was dying to be Grace's knight; she also knew I would never lay siege to the castle of my desires. My sister; my scourge.

"Have you?" Grace finally mustered up a weak reply.

I saw my sister's answer coming, but I was helpless.

"Oh, sure, me and Izzy have done it since we were kids," she said, fluttering her eyelashes at me. She also knew I hated to be called Izzy.

"The both of you?" Grace said, not looking at me.

"Sure, sure, lots of times. Ever since we could swim. Our father—"

"Louise! Do you have to be so—" I tried to interrupt.

"Oh, Iz, why is it that you won't admit what you do? You may be a virgin, but don't be a hypocrite," Louise said, cutting me off. She was at the phase in her life when everybody was a hypocrite.

In thirty seconds, she had managed to expose my deepest insecurities. I was a virgin and did not want to be. I desired Grace but did not think I was worthy of her. I had the most vile thoughts in my adolescent mind but wished I could consummate every one of them. In all the time I had known Grace, we had managed to skate around the thin ice that was . . . that was sex. Louise was now chasing us with a pickax.

"I don't swim," Grace said, stopping me from defending myself.

She had shifted the terms of the conversation. I was immensely relieved. She could not swim, so she did not have to really face my sister's question. Not a swimmer, she, of course, had never been in the ocean naked nor would she have to face that decision in the future. I was relieved, and I was immensely disappointed. For the briefest of moments, I had envisioned my sister accomplishing a design that would have lured Grace into the ocean to swim naked next to me. I hated myself, and I loathed my sister.

"Too bad," Louise had said. "You should try it, swim or not. You should go into that water and feel the ocean next to your skin and feel the current lift you up and away. You really should, Grace, you should really try it. Some night, you and me. I could hold your hand and let you float out there."

"But why do you have to be . . . naked?" Grace asked, looking directly at my sister. "I mean, I have a swimsuit."

"Mary Grace"—Louise laughed softly, giving Grace a name that she was to use every time they talked after that day—"you and my brother are meant for each other. Name your first daughter after me." And then she walked off, leaving Grace and me alone.

After our first son was born, Grace and I hoped we would have a daughter. Grace and Louise would never be friends, but it was not Grace's fault. A daughter named Louise might have softened up my sister, but Grace and I only had sons.

"Is it true what your sister said?" Grace asked that day after Louise had left. "About you being a virgin?"

I was thankful I could tell her the truth.

"Yes," I said.

"Good. I think that's important. A person should only do that with someone they love and plan to marry."

I briefly noted the "*plan to* marry" and then asked her if she wanted to go for a walk on the beach. Ten years later, almost twenty years ago, she was a virgin on our honeymoon. I would have been if 1968 had never happened, if I had never met Alice Kite and Polly Jackson.

Judge Lester

Dexter loves science fiction. Of all the types of science fiction he likes, we both agree that time travel is the most interesting. He dreams about traveling to the future. I dream about the past.

He always likes to hear me describe a game I sometimes play with my friends at dinner or at parties. The rules are simple. If you could travel back to the past and change only one small specific thing, what would it be? You are not allowed a major revision. You cannot erase wars or plagues. You cannot stop a bullet after it has left the barrel. In fact, you cannot reverse an action, only a decision. Then you must predict the future.

I once played this game with Louise. It was a test to see if she was really my sister. On our thirtieth birthday, with Grace visiting her relatives in Georgia, Louise and I were helping Pete Maws with his annual caboose painting. I had explained the rules of the game to her, and she had answered almost as soon as I finished, as if there were only one possible response.

"I would tell Daddy not to hire Judge Lester," she had said, proving that she was, indeed, connected to me.

Pete had been standing there with a brush in his hand and a white towel wrapped around his head. He nodded, but did not speak.

Louise and I had heard of Harry Lester long before we ever saw him. And we saw his work long before we saw his face. Harry was a sky-writer and air advertiser. My father had hired him first in 1960 to advertise the movie *Psycho*. It was a short title, so the banner was cheap, and my father gave him a hundred free passes to drop over downtown Jacksonville. My father was especially impressed by how low he was willing to fly, low enough to go between buildings as well as over them.

Harry Lester helped make *Psycho* a sellout because he put himself and the title on the front page of the Jacksonville papers. My father was a great believer in the Barnum school of salesmanship: Any advertising was good advertising, and the best advertising was free advertising. The day before we opened, the boldface headlines of all the papers were some version of "Psycho Pilot Grounded" or "Psycho Flyer Shot Down."

Harry Lester had strafed the busiest street in downtown Jacksonville at high noon. You would have thought he was dropping hundred-dollar bank notes instead of two-dollar passes. Thousands of people were running around trying to catch the fluttering paper, dodging traffic and each other, but not being too successful at either. There were a dozen minor car crashes, and three people went to the hospital. My mother insisted that the whole episode proved the existence of God. How else, she asked, were those idiots saved from themselves and not killed?

Harry Lester was endeared to my father all the more because he had been willing to risk life and limb to promote the Flamingo. He had been flying about fifty feet above the street when his banner got caught in a power line, snapping it off the plane. Unfortunately, the tail of the plane was still attached to the banner, sending Lester into a nose dive and rendering eight city blocks powerless. His Piper Cherokee planted prop down in a city park, Harry Lester walked away from the wreckage into the waiting handcuffs of the police.

Although not legally responsible for the actions of his advertising agent, my father gladly paid for everything: car bodywork, street repairs, broken bones, power lines, and new shrubs for the park. He even hired a lawyer to help Lester keep his pilot's license. When he offered to buy a new plane for him, my father guaranteed himself a vassal for life. Harry Lester worshiped my father.

In his own way, the Judge was a legend long before he came to live with us. Louise and I saw his plane a dozen times every season, a banner trailing his new, bright-red Piper. Or, on those days with almost no wind, his white smoky skywriting floating over the ocean. After a day's work, he always buzzed our field. Louise and I came to hate Judge Lester only after 1968. Before then, he was a romantic figure, a flyer, a daredevil, the man who dipped his wings just as he thundered over the Flamingo field. He seemed heroic to us, especially after the time he flew so close to the top of the screen tower that his wheels actually touched the tar roof.

My sister and I were thrilled when our father told us that Harry Lester was coming to work full-time at the Flamingo, to live and work with us. That was the summer of 1967. We did not understand our mother's hesitation, nor Pete's silent hostility. We did not know what they knew, that our father was the only person who would hire Harry Lester for *anything*.

I had expected him to land on the road in front of the marquee, but he had parked his plane at the airfield in St. Augustine and my father had given him a ride to the Flamingo. He did not own a car.

He was not what I had expected. He did, indeed, look like a pilot. He stepped out of the car wearing a leather jacket and aviator sunglasses, and he was tall, and he was glamorous in his own way, but he was also an old man. His wavy hair was totally gray, and he had liver spots on his hands. I had expected Charles Lindbergh, as had Louise. In front of us was Lindbergh's father, or so it seemed. In fact, Lester was the same age as my father, but he looked older. Then he spoke, spoke like he was paid by the word and every conversation had a time limit. And as he spoke his face twitched and contorted, his eyes swelled and blinked, his large lips puffed and seemed to almost flap, his jaw jutted and swung from side to side.

"You kids look just like I expected. Just like your old man said. Just like your pictures, which I have seen about a thousand times. And you, missy, look even better than your pictures. You look like a model. You ever think about modeling as a career? Lots of money in modeling. You there, honest Abe, you look like a doctor. Look like a man who people can trust with their lives. Know what I mean? How about some candy for you two?"

He had reached into his jacket and pulled out two Hershey bars, but kept talking without missing a beat.

"Nothing like chocolate to get you going, know what I mean? Got an almond and a plain here. Take your pick. Might be a bit soft, but that makes them taste better . . ."

Louise and I were struck dumb. Harry Lester was a cartoon.

"So you kids take your pick. Always more where that came from. I got connections with the candy kings of North America. Always a chocolate bar with Judge Lester. But more than that. I got gifts from the East for your mama. Myrrh and frankincense and singing birds on a wire. Mrs. Lee, may I?"

"Harry, we've known each other too long for gifts," she said.

"Probably so, yes, that's surely true, but the lady of the house always deserves a gift when guests arrive for a long visit. And I do hope to settle in and be a part of the most famous family in the southeast United States, a family known for its charm and its—"

"Harry, enough." My mother had raised her hand and motioned him to stop. In mid-sentence, Harry Lester was silent. But he kept nodding his head a bit too emphatically, so my mother tilted her head slightly, and he froze. Harry Lester, I would discover, was the most nervous man in Florida.

Louise stepped behind me and whispered, "Ask him about giving us a ride."

She and I had talked for days about how when Harry Lester arrived we were going to ask him to take us up in his plane and let us see the Flamingo from a mile high. But I had undergone a complete change of heart once I met him. I was afraid to be in the same plane with a man who acted so strangely.

I turned around and whispered back to her, "You ask. But not now. Wait until we're alone."

Actually, I had lost my interest in flying with him, and I thought that if we put off asking about it, then Louise might change her mind, too. But I was wrong about Louise, as usual.

"Mr. Lester, Abraham and I would like to ask you a favor," she promptly said.

"Little Miss, Little Miss, I am your eternal servant, your knight of the air, your . . . ," Harry began.

"Harry," my mother said quietly.

"Yes, ma'am." Harry stopped, but you could see his whole body suffer from the effort. You could almost see the vibrations in his head slowly travel down his body until they seemed to stir the dust at his feet. "Yes, ma'am," he repeated, his hands in his pockets.

"Louise, I think we should let Harry get settled in before we ask him for favors," my mother said.

I was thankful that my mother had saved me. But Louise was not to be denied.

"All we wanted . . . ," she began, and I found myself slowly shaking my head so that my parents could see that I had disavowed any alliance with my sister, "all we wanted was a ride in his plane."

You could have heard the proverbial pin drop. I looked at my mother, who was looking at Louise. I could hear Pete clear his throat. Harry Lester's eyes were as big as tennis balls. Then my father spoke.

"Louise, you and Abraham are probably a little young to go flying this year. Maybe next year."

It was an evasion, I knew that even then. I knew my father, as volatile as he seemed to be, was not about to put me or Louise in harm's way.

"Daddy!" Louise exploded. "We just want to fly for a little bit. And you promised."

My father had indeed promised many times that one of these days we would go for a plane ride. Harry Lester, however, had never been part of the same promise.

Louise was adamant. "You promised."

Then Louise turned to my mother, and I had another of those revelations that are understood only in hindsight. My mother was stronger than my father, but she was not safer.

"Louise, why do *you* want to fly?"

My mother had excluded me from the drama. My father, Harry, me, and Pete were relegated to the audience. I had seen this happen all my life. In the Manichaean world of the Flamingo, my father and I were one half; my mother and sister were the other. I first noticed it when Louise was going through puberty. She and my mother had become part of the same secret world that all women have in common, a world alien and mysterious to men, a cyclical world of blood and rhythms and fluids and flight.

Louise and my mother shared the world of all women, and they shared a world of their own: mother and daughter, Edna and Louise. It was this second world, not of physiology but of psychology, that I had seen even before Louise's body turned into that of a woman. The patio talks between my father and me had always been public theatre, but Louise and my mother, too, had been sparring in short dialogues all their life together. At this moment in front of the Flamingo, I knew, they were saying more to each other than the rest of us could hear.

"Why do *I* want to fly?" Louise asked, stepping away from me.

"You," my mother said.

"I want to fly that way," she said, pointing east toward the Atlantic. "So far out that when I look down all I can see in any direction is the ocean. Don't you remember?"

"Edna, you and I should talk about this tonight after dinner," my father interrupted.

"Hubert, we'll talk, but I tell you now that I think Louise should get her plane trip, as often as she wants it," my mother said, and I could see Harry Lester blush.

"Harry, my daughter wants to fly with you," my mother said, snapping him back to attention. "Can I trust you with her?"

His huge lips clenched tight together, Harry Lester nodded slowly.

"Yes, ma'am," he said, forcing a pause between each word. "I will take care of her."

"I know you will. I know. You will."

My father was in a panic, but the expression on his face at that moment was comic compared to the reaction he showed when my mother finished her next sentence.

"Because you are going to take me up first and show me that my child will be safe in your hands."

My mother, who never went in the water, was going to fly. To fly with Harry Lester. A man whose whole body was an exclamation point.

"Louise, if Harry is as safe as I think he will be, you can fly with him. If he is not safe," she said, turning to him, "he will not live with us."

I called Grace that night, after asking my mother if she could come with us the next day.

"Your mother is going to do what?" She laughed.

"Grace, this is serious. She's going to get in a plane with a man who can't drive a car! Don't laugh."

Grace could not help herself.

"Isaac, your mother will be fine. It's Harry Lester I wouldn't want to be."

"That's my point, Grace. You haven't seen this guy. He's . . . he's not . . ."

"He's not going to disappoint your mother, Isaac. Relax."

The next day in St. Augustine was clear but windy, not a comforting environment for any would-be flyer or passenger, but my mother showed no emotion. Harry Lester was sweating through his pants.

My father, Louise, Grace, and I watched the two of them climb into the shiny red Piper. I should have known things would be okay because there was no dramatic farewell. My mother offered no profound exit lines, no grand gestures. Seated in the cockpit, she waved through the window to us. Harry did an exaggerated salute. And they were off.

Do you remember the takeoff scene in *The Spirit of St. Louis*? The silver *Spirit* lumbering down the runway, trying to bounce itself into the sky before it hit some trees at the end? Jimmy Stewart pulling the throttle back and coaxing the gas-gorged plane up at the last second, clipping branches and sputtering into a cloudy sky?

Harry Lester's no-name Piper went from zero to a hundred in five seconds and lifted off the concrete with a half mile to spare, nosed up at a forty-five-degree angle, leveled off, then banked right and headed for the Atlantic's horizon.

For the next hour, my father and I were silent. Grace tried to start a conversation with Louise, but that was always a mistake. It was one of the few times I would ever see Grace angry.

"You people *are* weird," she muttered under her breath, walking into the small airport control tower looking for a bathroom.

My sister and I and my father waited for our mother and wife to return.

They had left at noon, and Harry had promised to have them back by one o'clock. At 12:59 a red dot appeared in the east, and then at one o'clock a silent Piper seemed to float effortlessly down to earth. The plane was on the ground before any of us had time to digest the fact that it had landed with the engine shut off. The prop spun into life only when it was necessary to taxi back to where we waited.

My mother was out first, as calm as when she had gotten in an hour earlier. Louise was holding her breath, waiting for a pronouncement.

"Everything's fine, honey. Harry is a fine pilot. I told him you and he could go up anytime you wanted," my mother said, with the same tone that she might have used to say that the salt she had just added to a certain recipe was just right. Satisfactory, but not significant.

Louise clapped her hands and ran to hug my mother, who folded those long arms around her and kissed her on top of the head, whispering something that made both of them laugh out loud.

As they walked past my father, arm in arm, my mother turned to him and said, "Hubert, you really should learn to fly."

Back in time. Time travel. Change a decision. Hindsight that always prints the clues in bold, black ink. A lifetime of a million words and gestures. You need a fine-screen sifter, blocking the boulders that mean nothing, shaking until the single grain drops into the oyster's mouth, and the irritation begins, the calcification that does not always end in a pearl.

My father should never have hired Harry Lester. But that day in St. Augustine, how were any of us to know? The day was a triumph. Even I felt happy for him as he jumped out of his plane, bouncing toward us, a white scarf around his neck, stopping under the end of his wing, spreading his arms and proclaiming, "*Here come da Judge!*"

Grace was the only one of us who laughed. My family stood there knowing that we were supposed to have *some* reaction, but not knowing what. Harry seemed disappointed. Evidently, the line had some significance for him.

"They don't watch television," Grace said to Harry, explaining us to him.

Eventually, Grace explained it to me, and I went to her place one night to watch a certain comedy show. Harry Lester watched a lot of television, and sometimes he and I would sit in his apartment in the Tower and watch TV together. But not much. My parents hated television.

"You folks never watch 'Laugh-In'?" he asked increduously.

Our collective blank expression must have been an answer.

In the Book Room that night, my father and I played chess at one end while Louise and my mother talked softly at the other. I asked him what he planned to do with Harry Lester when he was not flying his plane. My father kept his eyes on the board while he spoke.

"Probably put him at the box office. Your mother thought he would be good at security with all the money there. And he can do traffic control when the line gets too long."

"You trust him?" I said, moving my bishop to put him in check, thinking two moves ahead.

"With money?" he said, moving his king a space.

"No, no, directing traffic," I said, watching the board and wondering what Louise and my mother were talking about.

My father laughed softly and moved his queen to put me in check. "Abraham, you're too young to worry so much."

I took his queen with a knight. My father was a very bad chess player.

A week later, after Harry had moved into an apartment in the Tower, he took Louise up for her first plane ride. It was another family affair, with Pete as an added spectator.

My mother had suggested that I go along for the ride, but I declined. My father and Pete nodded in agreement, and Louise whispered, "Your loss," as she walked off. My mother put her arm around me, and we both waved. Then she asked me a frightening question.

"I wonder if Grace would like to fly?"

I was quick to respond.

"Mother, Grace won't get in the water. I'm sure she—"

My mother stopped me with the obvious rebuttal.

"Neither will I, Abraham. But that is water. Flying is different."

I grabbed at straws, at any argument that would discourage my mother from luring Grace into the air.

"But her father. He won't let her do anything. He's more protective than even you and Daddy."

My mother leaned down and said quietly, so very low that only I could hear, as if we were sharing a secret, "I'll talk to him."

Within another week Grace had taken her first flight with Judge Lester. At the airport that afternoon, the audience was smaller. Just me and my mother and Turner West himself. That morning before we left for St. Augustine, I had seen my parents in one of the few arguments in their life that did not conceal the anger they must have felt.

Louise and I were sent to the Book Room while they stood on the patio far below. We could see them from above, and we could hear fragments of their conversation. My mother had stood there with her arms folded; my father had swayed back and forth, kicking stray rocks at his feet, clenching his fists tightly to his side. Then my mother did something out of character. She sat down.

My father was suddenly taller than she was, and he became speechless. Neither one of them spoke for a minute, and then my father walked off, shaking his head.

At the airport that day, I began to see Turner West in a new light. He did not speak to me, except for the perfunctory hello and goodbye, but he and my mother acted like old friends. With Grace in the air, they leaned against the hood of West's new black Cadillac. I sat in the front seat of our 1952 Buick, my vision alternating between the sky and the ground, worrying about Grace and my mother at the same time. I did not like seeing her talk to Turner West. I did not like seeing him laugh at something she said. I wondered if they were talking about my father. I did not like seeing him smile and nod slowly as he listened to my mother. I was my father's son, and I hated Turner West. I wanted Grace to return to earth and her father to return to his side of the highway.

The hour passed, and Grace returned to me excited and happy.

"Isaac, Isaac, you should have gone with us!" she said, running up to hug me as soon as she touched down. As she held on to me, I could see over her shoulder to where my mother and West stood. They were both smiling the smile of proud parents.

Grace turned fifteen the day of her first flight. It was a present from her father.

After that flight, Grace explained to me how it was possible for my mother to fly with Judge Lester even though she avoided the water.

"Isaac, you have to see him in the air. I was scared to death when your mother talked me into flying with him. But she told me to trust her, that I would see the difference."

"The difference?" I had said.

"The man is absolutely calm when he is in that airplane."

"Sure," I said sarcastically, "cool as a cucumber."

"No, listen, this is true," she insisted. "Harry, or Judge, or whatever you call him, is a happy man in the air. You're right about him down here"—pointing to the sand as we walked on the beach—"but up there he . . . he . . . well, you have to see it to understand. You really do. Isaac, you should see the waves. Like I did. Like your mother and Louise did. Not just up high, but almost on top of them."

Grace was describing her own first flight with the same excited voice that Louise had used when she got back.

"We flew right along the tops, as if we were landing on the water, and Harry was completely in control. And straight ahead was this wavy horizon."

Harry Lester had become the thread that held the three women in my life together. When my mother and Louise began calling him "Judge" we all did. All of us except Pete, who had almost taken a shovel to Lester's head when the Judge called him "shortcakes."

Pete insisted on calling him Harry, even after the Judge apologized profusely to him.

Two weeks after that first flight, the truce between Turner West and my father was broken. In between was the season's first hurricane, but it had nothing to do with my father and West resuming their feud. Judge Lester was the cause of the breakdown, but it was the hurricane that ensured that my father would forgive the Judge for anything, even the Small Fire.

"God is coming," my father announced at dinner the night after Grace's birthday. Judge Lester was the only employee invited.

"Hubert, why do you persist in this mockery?" my mother said, her voice without the usual patience it had when my father spoke of God. "If I thought you really believed it was God, I could excuse you. But it is just a joke to you. An old joke. A tiresome joke."

Louise and I were not used to such disgust in our mother's voice. It was if she did not like our father, but we knew that could not be true. My father ignored the obvious irritation my mother was showing.

"Come to blow us down," he said, much slower, but more directly to my mother, as if she were his only audience. "Come to test us, to test our faithfulness."

My mother and Louise left the table at the same time. Judge Lester, his fork still trembling, broke the silence.

"Mr. Lee, is there anything I can do?"

"Do you believe that God is coming?" my father asked, resuming his performance.

Judge Lester was totally confused.

"Someday," he said, but without conviction, almost like he was afraid a wrong answer might get him fired.

"Not someday, Judge . . . in a week," my father said. "The feminine side of the Lord, the watery wrath of a God scorned. Wind and water spinning around a heavenly center of peace and calm."

I listened to my father and knew that he was merely going through the rhetorical motions of a sermon. With the first hurricane of every season, he had delivered much the same speech. Judge Lester, however, was spellbound.

"The hurricane?" the Judge said, like a student in front of his favorite teacher.

My father looked at the Judge and me, lingering for a few seconds in his gaze at me.

"Do you think this will be the one you keep expecting?" I asked my father, without irony, without contempt or derision, asked with the realization that I had become an actor on a stage with my father, each of us depending on the other for the lines that justified our own lines. I was on stage; I was in the audience. My role was small, but, as you know, I was only fifteen. Not even old enough to be my father's understudy.

"Could be," my father said, taking a deep breath.

The best acting I did at that moment was not in my father's drama. No, my best dissembling was to hide my sorrow. In front of him were two people: me and Judge Lester. My father deserved a better audience. The vast auditorium of his life, scene of all the grand gestures and metaphysical monologues I had witnessed for years, that auditorium was reduced to five chairs, two of them empty.

"I heard it was a big one. Biggest thing ever this early in the year," Judge Lester said with growing enthusiasm. "Big enough to blow that commie out of Cuba. That's what I hear."

Pearl *was* the monster storm we were promised, but like every other hurricane since 1952 she never got as far as Jacksonville. Daytona was flooded, but Pearl had already begun her eastward swerve by that time and she eventually spun herself into oblivion somewhere out over the Atlantic. The Flamingo did suffer extensive damage, and Pete's caboose was flooded. The seawall had been breached, as my father predicted, but at the last moment Pearl and God seemed to lose interest in my father's Tower.

But it got close enough to throw ninety-mile-an-hour winds at the Flamingo, and Judge Lester was the only person who would stay in the Tower with my father. My mother took the rest of us to North Carolina, and Pete stayed in his caboose.

When the Judge accidentally set the West Funeral Home on fire the week after the hurricane, breaking the truce, my father, who had been depressed and moody, not only forgave him, he bought him a new color television.

"Loyalty"—he beamed—"should always be rewarded."

The Fourth of 1967

From the spring of 1966 until July 5, 1967, Grace and I saw each other almost every day. On the weekends, she could come to the Flamingo during the day, or my mother would take us to Jacksonville for a matinee, leaving my father and Louise behind. I could go to her home, but there was not much to do there. And, unlike at the Flamingo, we were never left alone at the West Funeral Home. One of her brothers was always nearby, not always seen, but always in a position to hear us. Unobtrusive, silent, their faces blurring together in my mind, they ignored us most of the time, but as soon as she and I came anywhere close to certain rooms one of them would appear, as if casually arriving at that same point in the universe just as their sister and her "friend" also arrived.

To this day, her brothers have never accepted me as a brother-in-law. And to this day I cannot keep their names straight. At reunions, with their own wives and children, or on holidays, when we have those giant dinners or picnics, they look at me and my children as if we were illegal aliens. My sons and their cousins are great friends, and Grace is adored by her brothers' wives. Much like their father, however, the West sons have never forgiven my father.

At my wedding, Turner West told me about the first time he was able to separate his feelings for me from his feelings toward my father.

"It was when you brought those clippings," he said after dancing the first dance with Grace. His eyes were still wet from crying, and his breathing was ragged. Although we did not know it then, his heart was beginning the irreversible disintegration that would take ten more years and make him an invalid for the last year of his life.

"I thought to myself then, it was something your mother would have done."

On my second trip to the West Funeral Home, having first been my father's emissary, I went bearing gifts for Grace from myself. I had spent the previous week collecting every newspaper in Duval and St. Johns Counties. In newspapers that Turner West had never seen, I had found eight obituaries of people whose funerals he had arranged. I clipped them out, put them in a wooden cigar box that Pete gave me, walked down A1A without telling my parents, and presented them to Grace. You would have thought I had given her a box of diamonds.

During the weekdays at St. Agnes, Grace and I were inseparable. We studied together, we did projects together, we ate lunch together.

After Gary Green became my best friend, the three of us would plan our schedules around each other. Grace told me that Gary's real parents were dead, and the people who I thought were his parents were actually his aunt and uncle. It was a secret that he had kept from everyone but her. I promised her that I would not let Gary know that I knew, but I made the mistake of telling my father.

"He must come live with us," my father said at dinner, announcing a decision as if it were an inevitability.

My father had gotten to know Gary because of all the times that he came out to the Flamingo. Two or three times a week during school, almost every night during the summer, Gary would show up and work for free, helping me patrol the ramps or carrying film cans for Pete, then staying to help me clean the concession stand after we closed.

When I told Gary about my father's pronouncement, he was embarrassed at first, then seemed interested, but was also quick to say that my father couldn't be serious.

"Why would he do that, Abe?" he asked me one night as we were spying on a double date of lovestruck teenagers in a station wagon in the back row. "Does he really think my parents would let me do that?"

"But your parents . . . ," I began to say, but then I realized I couldn't explain my father's plan to him unless I revealed that Grace had not kept his secret. "Well, if it is okay with them, I mean, you're right, it's up to them."

There were no heads visible in the station wagon.

"I'll ask them," Gary said, as if it were a question about going to sleep over at a friend's house for the night. No big deal.

Eventually, I found out that Gary's parents were not dead, and he did not live with his aunt and uncle. He lived with his parents, had always lived with his parents. They might not have been the best parents in the world, but they were certainly not like my parents. In fact, they loved Gary in their own way, as all good parents do. But his parents were able to separate their own lives from the lives of their children.

Gary had lied to Grace about his parents when he and she were in the sixth grade. He had wanted Grace to feel sorry for him, because he had wanted her to fall in love with him. Until I arrived, he told me at our graduation, he thought that he and Grace would be a couple.

Chinese Dragons were actually made in Tulsa. So were Bangkok Boomers, M-40 A-Bombs, Starburst Comets, Screaming Streamers, Kamikazes, Buzz Bombs, and a hundred other fireworks that you cannot buy today.

You cannot buy them for two reasons. They are illegal, and the Sooner Fireworks Company, which alone knew the secret process, blew itself up in 1974, leaving a sixty-foot crater in the red Oklahoma clay and vaporizing the seventeen pyrotechnists who worked double shifts from April through June. Sooner fireworks were apocalyptically explosive and inexpensive, and they came with a double-your-money-back guarantee.

My father was Sooner's biggest single customer. Once a year, north Florida held its collective breath and turned its collective eyes toward the Flamingo and celebrated America's birthday with a psychedelic eruption of sound and color that lasted as long as Handel's "Music for the Royal Fireworks."

You have to go back to your own childhood and recall the first big fireworks display you saw. The colors and sounds in the sky, the crowd below all voicing that group *aaah* as the skyrockets exploded overhead, the night sky lit up with a giant flash, and then the tiny sparkling streamers floating to earth, blues and golds and reds and greens. You have to recapture that moment and then magnify the effect by ten. You then have to imagine how it must have been to have that effect intensified by Handel's music blaring out from a giant speaker horn on top of the Flamingo Tower. You have to imagine a field full of cars, their horns honking. You have to see thousands of other cars lining both sides of A1A, blocking traffic from the Flamingo box office north to Jacksonville and south to St. Augustine. Even more, you have to imagine hundreds of boats bobbing in the Atlantic just offshore of the Flamingo. Yachts, tour cruisers, small powerboats, a few full-size freighters, dozens of shrimpers, and once even a destroyer from the Mayport naval base, which closed the display with a twenty-one-gun barrage of cannon blanks. (Only once—the captain was reprimanded.) Tens of thousands of faces lifted up to see America's largest fireworks display, or so I was told.

If you can imagine all this, then you can imagine my father's Fourth of July.

From the summer of 1953 until the Great Fire in 1968, my father treated us to fireworks. Until Judge Lester came in 1967, there had never been an accident.

"Mr. Lee, you got to get them things up higher," the Judge had said to my father when we were unpacking the Sooner shipment. "You got to get some elevation. Get them"—he paused as if he knew how ludicrous the idea was—"get them up on top the Tower, and you'll have a show that those crackers in Georgia can see."

"Too dangerous," Pete Maws said quickly. "Too dangerous."

"No, no, no," the Judge protested. "Not all of them. Just for the finale. Eight or ten big ones. Me and young Gary can set them off quicker than Dixie."

In the past, my father had hired a barge to float offshore and serve as the launching pad for the fireworks. The duds fell into the ocean, and the mortar shells were pointed east, away from shore. Only once had a strong wind brought some fragments back to the coast. But the Judge had found my father's weak point.

"I bet you *could* see them a lot farther off," he meditated. "But we would have to be careful. No doubt about that. What do you think, Abraham?"

I was caught off guard. I knew that my father was not really asking for my opinion, at least not in a way that would affect the decision that he had probably already made.

"I'm not sure," I hesitated. "Pete might be right. It might be dangerous."

My father looked at me and then at Pete, who was not looking at any of us. The Judge's head was bouncing on his neck, and his eyes were blinking. He looked like he actually believed it was a good idea, an idea that might be fun to do.

"We'll do eight," my father announced. "Just as a test for this year. Four Dragons, two Boomer Sooners, and two"—he mentally reviewed the inventory—"two Earthquakes. Or maybe just eight Dragons."

Pete snorted, but he did not openly disagree. He did, however, try to save my father from himself.

"You want me to handle it?" he said. "I can set them off and get back to the booth to start the show. Wouldn't be any problem."

I knew what Pete was trying to do: keep the Judge away from the fireworks. It was the right move. Pete had worked on the barge in previous years. He was a man who was never careless. But he had not reckoned on my father's sense of loyalty. Judge Lester had stayed with my father in the Tower during Hurricane Pearl the previous week.

I have come to see all of us that summer in terms of our roles in chess. My father was the King. Pete was the Rook. Judge Lester was a Knight. Gary was to become a young Knight. I was to become a Bishop.

"No, thank you, Pete. You stay on the barge. I'll put Gary and the Judge on the Tower," he said, turning to me. "You, Abraham, you want to work on the Tower or the barge?"

I knew the answer my father wanted.

"The Tower," I said, seeing his pleasure.

"Just one more thing, men," my father said, rubbing his hands together. "Let's keep this a surprise. Just among us guys. Deal?"

We all nodded, even Pete, all knowing from whom we were keeping our secret.

All this took place on July 1, 1967. I had four days left in the first phase of my relationship with Grace. For over a year, we had been melting into each other. The future seemed clear. We would graduate together, probably go to college together, get married, have children, grow old together, bury our parents, and then die in each other's arms. Looking back at that "future" now, I can see that it will all happen. Some of it already has, other parts will happen soon enough, and other parts will be amended. If you ask me now, I will tell you that, overall, my life has been happy. After the Fourth in 1967, I would not have predicted that would be possible.

The night before the Fourth, I asked Grace if she would like to see the view from the top of the Tower. She quickly accepted, not appreciating how difficult that ascension was to be. It required that we deceive her father and my parents. Turner West had been very lenient for the previous year in letting his daughter spend as much time as she had at the Flamingo, but he had been very clear in not allowing her to visit after dark. After dark, however, was exactly when I wanted to get Grace to the top of the Tower.

"How will you get out?" I had asked her that afternoon.

"Some way, I'll do it," she had said. "But I hate to lie to him."

I was becoming very good at rationalizing behavior.

"Don't lie to him," I said. "Just don't tell him anything. Figure out a way to meet me after the box office closes. Can you do that?"

"How will you explain it to your parents?" she asked, almost whispering into the phone.

"I won't," I said casually. "They will not know. It'll be our secret."

Moral evasions aside, getting to the top of the Tower was more difficult than I let Grace anticipate. Inside the Tower was a seventy-foot, absolutely vertical wooden ladder beginning a foot away from the trapdoor that was in the corner of my bedroom ceiling. Even Gary, who was to go up the next night, had no idea how dangerous the climb was.

There was another reason the climb was taken by few people. Getting to the ladder after climbing through my ceiling usually required only one motion and a few seconds. If done very quietly and quickly, you could get up the first few rungs of the ladder before Frank the Dog could react. The first time he went, Judge Lester had not been quick enough. Pete had somehow failed to mention anything to him about Frank, and the Judge had been saved only because of his thick boots.

Pete had told me how the Judge had cursed him and Frank all the way up the ladder. "Course, when we were halfway up I reminded him that we still had to come down the same way." He had laughed to himself. "And weren't no surprise to Frank on the trip down. He would be waiting for us."

If I had told my parents about asking Grace to go with me, they would have objected, but for different reasons. My mother, no friend of Frank's, would have said it was too dangerous. My father would have simply said that the top of the Tower was no place for a girl. He had forbidden Louise to go up a long time ago, and even though she often went with Pete to visit Frank she had never gone higher. I had been surprised that neither she nor my mother had simply gone ahead and done it anyway. But neither seemed that interested in going up through the belly of the Tower to its roof.

I had been up there dozens of times, sometimes by myself after I thought everyone else had gone to bed. More than a few times, I was surprised to find my father already up there. He had somehow managed to get to the top without going through my room, and he would never explain how. "My secret," he would say, and to this day he still refuses to tell me. But in those times in the past, he and I would sit near the edge of the roof and look at the dark Atlantic. I was looking for the lights of boats. My father was just looking.

At 3:00 a.m. on July 4, 1967, I quietly pushed open the trapdoor in my ceiling and poked my head up to look for Frank. Not a sound, nothing.

"Isaac, is he there?" Grace asked.

"Oh, he's always here. Sometimes you just can't see him," I said, trying to be nonchalant.

My plan was simple. I would get through first, stand there as a shield in case Frank suddenly charged, pull Grace up after me and get her on the ladder immediately, and then follow her up, under her in case she slipped. Within a few seconds she was up with me and then on the ladder. We had gone up about twenty feet when I heard something scratching at the foot of the ladder.

"Just keep going," I said to Grace.

The scratching turned to whimpering.

"Frank," Grace said before I had a chance to stop her.

She had spoken as if she were speaking *to,* not about Frank. But I was afraid that any strange voice would set him barking. The whimpering stopped, and the two of us froze to the ladder. I soon realized that I had reached up to grab Grace's leg when she spoke, as if my touch would stop her. Both of us motionless, I kept my hand on the back of her calf, just above the ankle. I was sweating, and her skin was moist. I was dizzy.

Don't try to overinterpret this part of my story. Grace had said Frank's name, and he had become silent. Then I could hear him drop his body to the floor, curling around the base of the ladder, as if waiting calmly for our descent. I knew he would not hurt Grace. I can tell you all this now, but I knew even then that I could never tell Louise about the effect Grace had on Frank. Louise was very possessive about Frank, and, except for Pete, she resented anyone else even seeing him.

Two minutes later, Grace and I were on top of the Tower. She was breathless. I walked over to the side facing the ocean, but she went the opposite direction, standing on the highway side and looking down at the West Funeral Home.

"That's where I live" was all she said. Then she turned and walked over to me. We stood there holding hands and looking at the ocean.

If I told you there was a full moon, you would say I was hopelessly romantic. I have been accused of worse things, I suppose. But you can go back and check some farmer's almanac and see that on July 4, 1967, there was a full moon shining at three-fifteen that morning, and the tide was at its highest point. The crests of the waves were like a thousand silver threads rolling toward Grace and me, but we were absolutely safe there on top of the Tower my father had built. I could not imagine that after that morning I would not see her again for two months, not until we were back in St. Agnes.

The Small Fire

Every year my father gave the Florida Highway Patrol, the Duval County Sheriff's Department, and the St. Johns County Sheriff's Department each a five-thousand-dollar gift to their pension or Christmas fund. He also gave all the local officers a season pass to the Flamingo, good Sunday through Thursday except on holidays. He knew most of the men in each patrol car by name. A few, who often stopped by the box office to linger and talk with my mother, those few got gifts for their birthdays. My father's first law of commerce was "Advertise. Advertise. Advertise." His second law was equally important: "Keep the law happy."

My father could measure the law's happiness in very specific ways. How often they would drive by the box office, for example. How often they would cruise silently through the field on the weekends, an unpaid security force. How often they would carry an early deposit to the bank when we were sold out. How often they would handle traffic control on especially busy nights. Most important, by how much slack he was given on the Fourth of July.

Traffic on A1A usually became blocked by five in the afternoon on the Fourth, and the box office did not open until seven. A1A is still today only a narrow, two-lane, winding highway. Back in 1967 it was even narrower, more winding, and with less space along the shoulders. If you were not coming to the Flamingo for the movie or to sit outside and see the fireworks, you always cursed whoever was responsible for the largest traffic jam of the year. For you, the police were not much help.

Turner West had given up complaining after the first year my father had his fireworks display. Like a fort under siege, he closed his doors and endured the assault. If you were dead that day and not in the ground by noon, well, then, you waited.

Traffic was more congested in 1967 than it had ever been. My father had advertised the biggest fireworks display in the history of Florida. It might have been. Who can really measure things like that? It was not the longest, but it was probably the most intense.

The Fourth was also one of the few times when my father hired extra employees. In 1967, most of the kids in my class worked that one night. Extra help in the concession stand, an extra box office open, two people to sit at the exits and turn away gate crashers, five St. Agnes seniors specially trained to help Pete Maws on the barge along with three pyros from Sooner Fireworks, a girl and a boy hired just to keep the restrooms clean and stocked, ten sophomores on bicycles with giant baskets full of popcorn and Cokes who went up and down the line of cars on A1A selling-selling-selling until sold out and who then restocked to go back to sell-sell-sell.

My father had an army of temporary help, young Christian soldiers from St. Agnes, each and all part of the patriotic orgy that was my father's Fourth.

The Fourth of 1967 was amended by Judge Lester in two ways. First, the rooftop finale; second, he convinced my father to push the fireworks back to the intermission instead of having them as soon as the sun had gone down.

"Build up the expectation, Mr. Lee. And you can keep those folks out front buying those treats. Lots of corn and pop you can sell with a captive audience in an hour and a half. Lots of Hershey bars," he had said, his hands twirling like he was skipping rope.

Of all the contradictions that were fighting each other in my father's mind, Judge Lester had managed to find the one that my mother found least attractive.

My father was a rich man. Making a profit was the least of his concerns. Spending money meant nothing to him. But my father loved to see people spend their money at the Flamingo. He loved to see the cash and coins piled on the table in the Book Room at the end of the night. Of all my memories, the image of my father counting money, the sweaty and crumpled fives, tens, and twenties neatly pressed and stacked corner to corner, bills all faceup and going in the same direction, the absorbed look of bliss on his face: that memory is the one my father himself remembers best. He can recite dates and deposits and then beg you to pull out the ledgers and see if he is right. But those ledgers don't exist anymore.

When the Judge suggested the delay, I could see my father's mind totaling up the potential extra concession sales. An hour and a half could mean almost a thousand dollars.

He turned to me.

"Abraham, how many more kids can you get me from the Vatican?"

I had learned to frown like my mother.

"Daddy . . . ," I began.

"Okay, okay, *mea culpa,* forget that stuff about the Vatican. But I will need some more help. Can you get it for me? Five dollars flat plus ten percent of their gross sales. Fair enough?"

It was more than fair; it was superfluous bribery. In fact, I had a list of boys from St. Agnes who had been begging me to get them a spot at the Flamingo that night. My father did not need to offer so much, but I did not tell him.

The Fourth of 1967 is etched clearly in my mind, but neither I nor my father can remember the titles of the movies we were playing that night. He usually booked a western and a comedy for the Fourth, so that was probably the double-feature combination in 1967. He and I should be able to remember them precisely, as we do most of the other dates and titles that were shown, but those particular films have been erased. The real show was to be at intermission.

As soon as the sun went down, I knew we had made a mistake. Most of the people in cars along A1A had been there every Fourth. They had no intention of seeing a movie; they just wanted to see the fireworks. They had come to expect the show as soon as the sun was down, then they could go home. Usually by intermission A1A was clear, but not in 1967.

Fifteen minutes into the first feature, horns started blasting out in front of the Flamingo. So many, so loud, that you couldn't hear the movie through your car speaker. The concession brigade out front had been instructed to go car to car and let everyone know about the change of schedule. Told that it would be after eleven o'clock before the fireworks began, north Florida became less of an audience and more of a crowd, and then it became a mob. Hundreds of cars decided not to wait, and so a game of musical parking spots began. With one car close to the Flamingo pulling out, two others farther down would race to the new empty spot. The result was always one more unhappy driver, usually a husband with his family. North Florida then became more like south Georgia, with some genetic honor code being tested. A gentleman could not be insulted in front of his family.

A1A became a drag strip, and my father's law enforcement influence was soon being tested. Police reinforcements were called. Soon, a dozen police cars were cruising in front of the Flamingo. I saw my father out in front of the box office conferring with men in three different uniforms.

Turner West had called for help. The chain he had stretched across the entrance to his parking lot had been rammed by a Volkswagen van full of Florida hippies who then had the bad sense to back into a Ford pickup full of Florida veterans from WWII. As those two groups were debating their choice of weapons, dozens of other cars edged around them to fill up the West parking lot. West and his six sons were no match for the children who were soon chasing each other around and over the unfortunate West hearses parked in back, nor could they convince the hundreds of women and children who were planted on blankets or in lawn chairs on the West front lawn, the immaculate West front lawn, that they were on private property. There was to be no help for Turner West.

Those carloads inside the Flamingo who had actually paid to see a movie as well as a fireworks display soon began to honk their own horns because they could not hear the movie. Pete turned up the volume, but it did not help. Headlights began flashing in sync with the horns. Southern males began blustering into the concession stand demanding to see the manager.

If all this had happened in 1968, when Alice Kite was in charge of the concession stand, she would have known how to handle all that testosterone. But in 1967 the concession stand was left to me and Louise, a few St. Agnes temps, and a woman named Betty

Burnett, who, confronted by a phalanx of shouting men, began to cry and pointed to me.

"Talk to him," she wept.

There I was, a fifteen-year-old Korean wearing a pirate hat, a black eyepatch, and an excessively flowered Hawaiian shirt. I stood there with my hand on the cash register, trying to muster up an older voice. Then Louise began to scream.

"They're shooting at us!"

Betty Burnett fainted.

"Izzy, look at them! Have you ever seen anything so gorgeous!"

Louise was at the concession entrance, pointing toward the Atlantic. Everyone in the concession stand, angry men and all, had rushed to the door.

The shrimpers were attacking us.

Like the cars on shore, the shrimp boats and other ships at sea had expected an early display. But, unlike their landlocked kin, the shrimpers had their own fireworks. Compared to my father's arsenal, they were underarmed. But they had the advantage of surprise. Deciding not to wait for the Flamingo, they launched a broadside at the Tower. Instead of shooting straight up, they had aimed their mortars toward the coast.

I did not know then that it had all been part of a surprise my father had planned for this Fourth. He had given them most of the ordnance, but he had not given them much direction except that they were to be part of the finale. My father, however, had never appreciated how independent shrimpers could be, especially when they had been celebrating the Fourth since four in the afternoon with a buffet of Schlitz and Pabst. Hearing the horns, the shrimpers had taken that as their signal to open fire.

Fortunately, they were far enough offshore so that the rockets never reached land. But the effect was spectacular. As soon as the customers on the lot realized that they were being assaulted from the rear, they turned their collective vision to the east and saw the incoming streamers. Some of the shells hit the water before they exploded, ending in a whimpering hiss. But most arced gracefully away from the shrimp boat that had launched them, flew in a gold or silver line toward thousands of patriotic souls, and then, at the last moment, seemed to slowly drift toward the ocean to explode with a blinding flash and deafening roar only a few feet above the water, which then reflected the burst of colors on its liquid and wavy face.

My father's hand was on my shoulder.

"Get to the Tower with Gary and the Judge. I'm telling Pete to stop the film and get to the barge. We should be ready to start in five minutes. Do you remember the signal for the finale?"

Three Buzz Bombs launched simultaneously, I remembered.

"Daddy, is everything going to be okay?" I turned to ask him. Only later would I understand how really dangerously close we were to losing control of the world around us.

"A piece of cake." He laughed, as if it were all part of a plan that was running like clockwork.

"Louise, five minutes till showtime!" he then shouted to my sister, holding up five fingers.

I could see Louise muttering something about God, something profane, but then she walked back to the cash register, knelt down to pat Betty's face—she was slowly coming to—and then shouted to my father as he ran out of the concession stand, "I want a raise!"

Then she looked up at me as I was taking off my eyepatch.

"I want a frigging raise, Abraham, and I want out of here."

Actually, frigging was not the exact adjective, but you get the picture.

I weaved my way across the field, going in the direction opposite to where everyone was looking, sorry that I could not stop to enjoy the psychedelic display they were seeing. In less than a minute, I was with Gary and the Judge in my bedroom.

Pushing open the door in my ceiling, I suddenly felt obligated to tell Gary about Frank the Dog.

"Gary, I forgot to tell you something about getting up to the roof. We first . . ."

Judge Lester vaporized.

"For chrissakes, you didn't tell him about the hound from hell!"

Gary froze.

I was suddenly an adult.

"Just follow me. I'll explain later. Whatever happens, just keep climbing. Whatever. And Judge, please shut up. I'll take care of Frank, and you follow Gary up."

My mother was very proud of me when I told her this part of the story. Even my children are impressed.

I was through the door in a second, and Frank's nails were clicking across the floor in the dark as soon as Gary shot up through the trapdoor and began climbing the ladder. He was very quick.

Like a soccer goalie, I tried to anticipate which way Frank would fly toward the ladder, hoping to block his trajectory long enough for the Judge to escape.

I guessed wrong.

Frank flew past me and clamped his jaw around the Judge's thick boot.

"Holy Mother Almighty Christ the King!" the Judge howled.

Gary stopped to look down.

"Gary! Keep going!" I shouted up to him.

The Judge was hanging on to the ladder with only his hands. His left foot was trying to kick Frank off his right foot, and he was cursing every dog that had ever been born. His two legs swinging wildly, the Judge was probably going to fall off the ladder, and if there was one place he did not want to be it was on the floor with Frank.

"Judge, just be still. I will get him off of you," I said as forcefully but also as calmly as I could. I was remembering how Pete Maws had held Frank in his arms seven years earlier.

With both my feet solidly on the floor, I reached up and put my hands around Frank's ribcage. As I told Louise later, I was fascinated by how fast his heart was beating. It seemed that nothing should be able to live at that tempo for very long.

I knew what I had to do.

With one motion, I yanked Frank off the Judge's boot and spun around to throw him as far as I could, shouting, "Go!" while Frank was still in my hands. By the time Frank hit the floor, the Judge and I were halfway up the ladder. Gary was already on top.

The next few minutes were like the eye of a hurricane. Absolute peace that would not last, but valued all the more because it was temporary.

From the top of the Tower, the view of the shrimpers' fireworks was even more beautiful. The lines were longer, the explosions bigger, the colors and their reflections even brighter. I looked down at them and remembered that Grace and I had been up on the Tower alone only a few hours earlier. I wished she could have been with me to see the sight at this moment. Then I walked to the other side of the roof and looked toward her home.

Cars were everywhere. The flashing red lights of the police cars were bouncing off hundreds of other car windows and bodies. Small crowds of people were wandering up and down the highway. Horns were still honking. I could see the sons of Turner West racing around their brightly lit parking lot in futile pursuit of a covey of children. I could see Turner West in his front yard shaking his fist at a highway patrolman. Grace was not to be seen anywhere.

I turned to see Gary and the Judge walking in front of the giant speaker horn.

"Better stay away from there," I said.

Gary walked toward me as soon as I spoke, but the Judge hesitated. He had been pointing toward one of the shrimp boats.

"Judge . . . ," I started to say, but Handel interrupted me.

The blast out of the giant horn was loud enough to blow the Judge off his feet and almost off the Tower.

With that first note, Pete Maws set off the first of my father's Oklahoma fireworks. These were the big ones. With that first arrow into the sky, the crowd out front forgot its earthly quarrels and turned its vision toward heaven. One last, long blast from the disgruntled car horns, and then the masses in front and behind the Tower were united in a series of communal and orgasmic oohs and aahs, amplified by applause for the really, really big explosions. My father had to be right: This must have been the biggest display in the world.

On top of the Tower, the three of us had about nine minutes until the finale. Gary and I helped the Judge up.

"You okay?" we asked, each shaking one of his arms. I felt sorry for him. My mother's observation was obviously true: Judge Lester was safe, and happy, only in a plane.

The Judge was dazed, but he shook his head and seemed to get his bearings.

"You boys do me a favor, okay? You don't tell that colored fellow about this, okay?"

"Put this in your ears," I said, handing Gary and the Judge some wads of cotton.

"Eh?" said the Judge.

"In your ears," I shouted over the music and explosions. "Just remember the hand signals."

Gary gave me a thumbs-up sign, and the Judge just kept nodding. I had about five more minutes to think about Grace, so I walked over to the front edge of the Tower and looked toward the West Funeral Home. I promised myself that I would convince my father never to do this again. I wanted Grace to be with me on the next Fourth, and I wanted us to just sit there on the patio and be spectators. My thoughts about the future were interrupted by Gary. He was pointing to his wrist. I nodded, and then I motioned for him to light his railroad flare.

The Judge had already loaded the first four mortars, and an eighteen-inch fuse was hanging over the lip of each shell. I waited for the three Buzz Bombs. Gary had his flare, I had mine, and the Judge was holding four Chinese Dragons.

If everything went as planned, I would light two of the mortars, Gary the other two. The Judge would count a slow ten and then re-fill the mortars, allowing the shell to cool down just enough. Gary and I had agreed to make the Judge the reloader because we were afraid that he might light the middle of a fuse, throwing all our timing off.

If everything went as planned, it would be a perfect universe.

To be on the safe side, Gary and I were to start at opposite ends and opposite sides of the mortar trail. We would carefully light the two on our end and then run like crazy past the other two. Our entire role in the finale should not have taken more than twenty seconds.

If everything went as planned.

Out on the barge, Pete and his crew had just gone through a flawless program. The Sooner pyros, three of whom would die a few years later in the big Tulsa explosion, had even managed to snuff out a dud that had popped up only a few feet out of a shell before falling back on the barge, a pyro's worst nightmare.

The inventor of the Buzz Bomb must have lived in London during the Blitz. The sound of those falling bombs had to be the only inspiration for an Oklahoma Buzz Bomb. As soon as it was lit, the BB started its ascent with a loud vibration that got louder the higher it went until it exploded with a kaboom that rattled windows and unborn children for miles. "Opening guns of the Apocalypse," my father called them. Our instructions on the Tower were to light our rounds as soon as we heard the first of the almost simultaneous BBs being launched. If everything went right, three quick BOOMs would be followed almost immediately by four Chinese Dragons, whose individual epileptic paths would crisscross, making the night sky look like a Jackson Pollock silent movie. Silent because the triplet Buzz bombs would probably render most of north Florida temporarily deaf.

I took one last long look toward the Atlantic, seeing beyond the barge and shrimp boats. Storm clouds were rushing in from the east. The ocean was waiting for something.

zzzzzzzZZZZZZZ went the first Buzz Bomb. Gary and the Judge and I looked at one another. Handel was smiling in his grave.

Gary and I began the race past each other. Four Dragons were soon chasing across the sky, trailing glory behind them.

BOOM went the Buzz Bomb, then CHANG went the first Dragon. In quick succession: BOOM-CHANG-BOOM-CHANG-BOOM-CHANG-CHANG!!!!!!!!!!

Gary and I had ten seconds to watch the show, the most beautiful ten seconds of our lives. My father had been right. The effect was a metaphysical union of art and religion. I sometimes meet people today who, when they realize who I am, their eyes light up and they tell me that they were in the crowd that night and that they can still remember those ten seconds, remember them as well as any other moment of their lives. Of course, they then usually laugh and want to talk about what happened next.

Gary and I should have been watching Judge Lester. When we looked down we both realized that the Judge had been watching the show, too. He was standing there with his arms full of Dragons, the mortar shells empty. My father's plan was to have the first broadside of the finale followed by a string of Texas Twisters blending into another round of Tower Dragons.

"Judge! Load the shells!" I yelled, but the Judge just stood there. He was deaf. He was in clinical shock. The Twisters had already exploded, and the sky was empty. I could imagine my father and Pete Maws wondering what was wrong. I hoped they thought we had been blown up in the first round.

Gary reacted as soon as I did. We grabbed the Dragons out of the Judge's arms and loaded the four shells, pushing him out of the way. It was as if we were dancing two steps out of sync with some music, and we could not catch up. Cars began honking again.

Four Dragons were lit. In slow motion, Gary and I watched the fuses burn up the sides of the shells and then down into the shells themselves. Then we both saw the end of 1967.

Judge Lester was standing over the outside shell, peering intently into the dark circle where a Dragon was about to leap out of its cave. The Judge was frozen in place, and I knew what was about to happen. But Gary changed history. In one motion he had leaped to knock the Judge away from a premature death.

SWOOSH, SWOOSH, SWOOSH, away went three Dragons.

"A dud! A dud!" Gary began to laugh hysterically, still holding on to the Judge as they both lay on the tar-paper roof. The fourth shell had been kicked sideways and was tilted at a forty-five-degree angle toward the home of the girl I loved. The three of us did not move. Somewhere out beyond the Atlantic I could hear a tiny pair of dice being shaken and then rolled.

The fuse had been jarred loose. The Dragon was either dead or it was hibernating. Snake-eyes or seven, the dice were tumbling to a stop.

"Gary, I'm sorry I didn't tell you about Frank" was all I could say, my eyes fixed on the mortar shell. I knew he was looking at the same thing. Neither one of us was breathing.

"It's okay," he began to pant. "Grace told me. I just didn't expect him to be—"

SWOOSH went the fourth Dragon, screaming a path up and then whispering itself down to the roof of the Turner West Funeral Home. I did not see it descend, but I have imagined it over and over. Grace described it to me. She was standing with her father on the front lawn. Turner West was not a religious man. In his world, God and Fate were responsible for nothing.

Gary and I had run to the edge of the Tower roof just in time to see the Dragon explode. The crowd around the West building thought it was all part of the show. Even though sparks and burning paper were flying everywhere, they cheered and clapped. In less than a minute, a dozen small fires were starting all over the West roof. More entertainment.

From the top of my father's Tower, I could see the sons of Turner West try to save their home and business. You had to admire them. They did not hesitate. They did not panic. The youngest son quickly had a garden hose attached and was standing on top of a hearse shooting water up on the roof. Turner West himself was up on the roof with three other sons, all with blankets, smothering the fiery circles only to have new circles erupt somewhere else. It was dangerous, but they must have known they had no alternative. The nearest fire station was miles away, and with A1A as blocked as it was, there was no way a fire truck could get to the fire. When the spectators realized that they were watching a real fire, they opted for self-preservation. Pickups were plowing into other pickups, cars were racing in reverse over the curbs and out of the West parking lot, knocking down the shrubs along the driveway.

Other spectators turned into allies of the West family. Two more garden hoses appeared out of trunks and were soon engineered onto faucets in the house. Extensions of hoses materialized out of other cars. Later, I wondered why someone would have a garden hose in their trunk.

On his roof, looking at a corner fire that would not die, Turner West made a decision that he had not wanted to make. With the possibility that the entire building would be consumed, he told his sons to evacuate the premises.

I could see Grace making all the arrangements in the parking lot. The first coffin out was solid white, a child's size. Blankets and sheets were spread in each car parking space, and each soon held a coffin. Mahogany, maple, cherrywood, steel, pine—I counted twenty-three when they were finished. Some were wheeled out on gurneys, others were carried on the shoulders of West sons and helpers. I knew most of the caskets were empty, but which ones? Last out, because they were inside in a room farthest away from the burning corner, were two unembalmed bodies in black bags. They were put in a hearse, safe from touching the asphalt lot. Turner West watched from his roof. I wondered if he could see me.

Pete Maws had been right. Sometimes faith was not enough to make you believe in God. You wanted proof. In my world, I had never had a doubt until that moment. No part of the scene below me made sense.

I wanted rain. I prayed for rain. I tested God. It rained.

I should have never doubted my mother.

Purgatory

The morning after the Fourth of 1967, I called the West Funeral Home but was told that Grace could not speak to me. Nor could I come to see her. Her oldest brother had told me in a voice whose delight was not disguised, "She is not to see you ever again."

I found out later that her father had planned to take her out of St. Agnes, but she and my mother had convinced him to keep her enrolled. Still, I was not able to see her or speak to her until the fall session began, almost two months later.

My sentence in Purgatory began with Sunday lunch after the Fourth. My parents, Louise, the Judge, Pete, and Gary did not seem to appreciate how the world had come to an end. They ate as if eating made sense, as if there was a purpose in nourishment. My plate stayed empty.

"I want some changes made," my mother suddenly said.

"So do I," said my father, staring straight at her, but they were not talking about the same changes.

"Hubert, you have to start being more considerate of other people. You are not the center of the universe," my mother said with the tone of a parent.

"Yes, yes, I have certainly come to know that." My father glared.

"I have told Mr. West that we will pay for any damages," she said. "And I apologized to him."

I did not understand my father's anger. The disaster of the Fourth *had* been his fault. I had been cut off from Grace. That was his fault, too.

"Mr. West, indeed."

There was no mistaking the acid in my father's voice. Louise laughs at me today, remembering how I had never seen the obvious.

"Mrs. Lee, I think I should apologize to the man himself," Judge Lester had tried to interject, a gesture toward conciliation that I would have appreciated, if I had been paying attention. It was Gary who eventually came to defend Judge Lester's memory. His recollection of that luncheon conversation has become my best record of that hour of my life.

"It was more my fault than anybody else's," the Judge said, trying to sacrifice himself in the fire of my mother's wrath. "I will go see him today if—"

"No!!" both my parents said at the same time.

Then Gary tried to speak.

"I was up there, too. I should try to . . ."

But he stopped in mid-sentence, knowing that the best of actors cannot save a wretched script. I was silent. Louise was frowning at me. Pete took a deep breath, but he did not speak.

Looking at only my father, my mother said, "Gary, you and the Judge are not responsible. Accidents happen, but they do not happen without all the elements being brought together so that the chance for disaster meets the possibility. Chance and Possibility are not the same thing."

Gary still shakes his head every time he tells me about how Judge Lester heard my mother's discourse on Chance and Possibility and did not have a clue as to what she was saying.

"Louise and I almost laughed out loud," he tells me now, "when the Judge spoke."

"Yes, ma'am, that's certainly true," the Judge had said slowly, nodding his head as if in deep thought but his eyes twitching like a bulb burning out.

Louise snickered, and my mother leaped on her.

"And you, sister, you and I are going to talk later about your social life in St. Augustine."

Louise immediately looked down at her plate while Gary and I blushed for her. I *do* remember our collective guilt at that moment.

Gary, who loved my sister, and I, whom she tormented, had both thought that Louise's flirtations were still our secret. Louise had been breaking Gary's heart for a year, but he forgave her.

My father jerked his head around to face Louise when my mother shifted the conversation to her.

"Your social life?" he asked.

Louise glared at my mother, and then she opened the door that could never be closed.

"I don't think you are in any position to judge me, if you know what I mean," she said to my mother. "You of all people."

The two women looked at each other, but my sister blinked first. Then she threw her fork down on her plate, scattering food all over the table, and walked quickly out of the room, slamming the door behind her.

A few years ago I asked Louise why she had to say what she had said. I had come to know all the details about my mother's own "social" life in St. Augustine, and I suppose that all those details would have become obvious to me eventually, as obvious as they had already become to my father and sister.

"Oh, Iz, I was fifteen," she told me. "I was fifteen. Doesn't that excuse something? I'd take it back, but just because you didn't know anything about Turner West and Mama doesn't change the fact that Daddy already knew. We all knew, but none of us was going to admit it out loud. And then Mama came down on me, and I had to get back at her somehow. Oh, Iz, I was fifteen."

A long time ago I was fifteen, and I thought my world had come to an end. I had been grievously wronged by all the adults around me, and I had withdrawn into a shell occupied by a tiny throne on which I sat to pass judgment on those around me. I was fifteen. In my heart and mind, my life was a drama, and I was the only character that mattered. If I had been older, perhaps I would have seen and heard more clearly. The Sunday after the Fourth of 1967 was one of those pivotal days in my life, and I was not paying attention. I should have seen the distant look on my father's face, seen the tightness around my mother's eyes, heard the rip in the fabric they had wrapped around themselves.

Pete Maws had brought the conversation back to the subject of restitution and contrition.

"I have offered to help with some of the repair work," he said, speaking as if there had been no break in the discussion about the Flamingo's obligation to the West Funeral Home. "Mr. West thinks he can be fixed up in about a week. I'll help his boys reshingle the roof."

It was a reprieve, and my father seized it and tried to be himself again.

"Pete, I can pay for a dozen roofers. You don't have to do anything."

"No, sir, that's right, I don't have to do anything," Pete said, his voice absolutely neutral. "Nothing at all."

My father was about to repeat himself, but he stopped and looked around the table. Only Pete was looking at him.

"But you're probably right," my father relented. "Why spend money when you don't have to."

"I can help, too," Judge Lester offered. "Bound to be some odd jobs I can do."

"Probably not a good idea, Harry, might still be some hard feelings. Mr. West is a forgiving man, but his boys are a hard lot. Best you stay away. Work on your rope climbing," Pete said, winking at me and Gary.

Judge Lester went from penitent to sulker. Pete had found the soft underbelly of his ego. The Judge had refused to come back down off the Tower roof through my bedroom after the fireworks fiasco a few days earlier. He was not going to confront Frank ever again, he insisted. So he stayed on the roof throughout the rain that had put out the fires on the West roof, had stayed until sunrise, and then my father had had to go up to the Tower roof and arrange a rope ladder so that the Judge could climb down the face of the screen instead of through its dark insides. Until the Judge died, Pete managed to always slip in some reference to Frank or ropes just when the Judge was feeling good about himself.

If I had been alert, and wiser, I would have stopped all the misdirected talk about roof repairs and hemp descents, about how much damage was done, about fireworks that had misfired. I would have slammed my fist on the table, forcing all of them to face the real issue. *We have to talk,* I would have said. *Why can't we talk about two fathers who are ruining the lives of their children!* But I was fifteen.

My mother closed forever the possibility of such a discussion when she threw Judge Lester a lifeline.

"Judge, you stay away from the Wests," she said, raising her right hand and spreading her fingers. "But I would like for you to take me up for another ride whenever it is convenient for you. You choose."

The Judge beamed.

And so we began our lives all over again, as if nothing had changed. The Fourth had merely been an awkward, but temporary, glitch in the routine of the Flamingo. My mother would go flying with Judge Lester every Sunday afternoon, and even Louise began to fly with them, mother and daughter reconciled. Years later, Louise would tell me how she and my mother would look forward to those flights after Mass. They would go straight from the Cathedral to the St. Augustine airport, where the Judge had been dropped off earlier. I would wait in the car while the three of them were gone for an hour. It was during those single hours that my mother would talk to Louise about how Turner West had fallen in love with her.

Everyone I have ever cared about came to know a piece of that puzzle. Pete knew more than he ever told me. Judge Lester died before I could ask him, and before I could hate him. Turner West himself would spend hours, as he lay dying, going over and over the same details, trying to understand why it had to happen the way it did. Grace and I had to hear the story from all of them. To this day, my father has his own version, and I have heard it a hundred times as we have sat on the back steps of Pete's caboose. Of all the people who knew, my father knew the least.

My Mother

I rely too much on my memory, and I assume that all memories are somewhat flawed. It must be impossible to hold on to any moment *exactly* as it happened. My mother is a memory, as is most of this story. Before I began telling you all this, I sat down with letters, those *Life* photos, certain mementos, all the material artifacts of my life. I talked to Grace, to my father, to Pete Maws, to my sister, to Gary Green, to anyone who remembered 1968. I wrote notes, tried to organize my life into a narrative pattern that would explain everyone I have loved. Out of that past, one precise moment with my mother kept coming back to me, but my father tells me it never happened.

I am very young, perhaps only five or six. My mother and I are alone in a boat watching a Jerry Lewis movie. Our being in that boat is the major reason I can understand why my father said all this never happened. First, my mother would not have been away from the theatre when a movie was showing. Even though she had a full-time teaching job during the day, she always helped my father run the show, seven nights a week, during the eight months of the year that we were open. She was always in the concession stand or the box office. She never rested. More important, she was scared of the ocean. She could not swim. Except for this one memory, I know she never got in a boat, no matter how big. She loved the ocean, and she could not live out of sight of it, but she was never in it.

That night, however, she and I are in a motorless boat on the Atlantic. I cannot remember the title of the movie, but I do remember that she and I are laughing hysterically. I am sitting between her legs, my back to her chest, her arms around me, and we are happy.

Sometimes she will lean forward and kiss me on the top of the head, singing softly and slowly "You Are My Sunshine."

Suddenly there is a tremendous roar, a blast that almost causes me to capsize the boat as I jump up out of her arms. I am young, remember, and it is dark, and we are a mile away from shore, about to be eaten by a monster.

The monster is a shrimp boat. I must have been asleep in the dream, or I would have heard the muffled engine. I am young, and I am terrified. I bury my head in my mother's large chest, but I am soon coaxed out to see that we are surrounded by a dozen shrimp boats, all of which are coming in from a full day on the ocean. Their nets are up, and each has a flickering white light on the tip of a forward spar. One of the shrimpers has seen our boat and sounded his foghorn. As Pete Maws always reminds my father, all mysteries have a rational explanation.

For an hour my mother and I float with the shrimpers. They tell her that they come to that spot every night on their way home. Drop anchor, drink beer, relax. They tell my mother that we should play more John Wayne movies. Some days they would take their wives and children out on the shrimping trek just so they could all stop on the way back. In my memory, my mother and I go aboard one of the shrimp boats, and I explore the smelly bowels while she drinks with them.

My father says it never happened, and he may be right. But I do know that as long as movie sound tracks blared from the speaker horn on top of the Tower I could look out toward the black horizon, see a dozen bobbing lights, and smell fish and shrimp and beer.

Of all the people who knew about my mother and Turner West, Alice Kite finally explained it best to me. Alice, who entered my life in 1968, who was there for the Great Fire, who was my mother's best friend, who was the oldest woman I was ever to meet. Alice Kite made it simple.

"You, of all people, you, if you really love Grace like you say you do, you should understand Turner West. Iz, you say you loved Grace from the moment you saw her," she told me on my sixteenth birthday. "No explanation, no rational reason. So why can't someone else fall in love at first sight?"

She hit me hard on the shoulder, a habit of hers I was never to get used to. "Why couldn't Turner fall for your mother? You got a monopoly on love, Iz?"

And then Alice, who was as tall as my mother, put her arm around me and whispered, "Do you really know everything there is to know about love?"

If I ever see Alice again, I will tell her that I do not know everything, but I know enough. I love Grace. I love my sons. I love God, as my mother did.

In the Beginning

In 1954, Turner West met a tall, attractive woman in church. For no good reason, he had decided to go to an early Mass instead of the late-afternoon service. It was pure chance. The woman was Edna Marie Scott. He watched her for weeks, his mind focused on her every move. Being an atheist, and in the St. Augustine Cathedral as part of his commercial endeavors, West would sit through every Mass with his mind clear of all the religious clutter that seemed to preoccupy the true believers around him. His ritual participation was flawless, and he performed all the outward motions as if possessed of a faith that gave him all the strength that he needed to brace himself against a world that had gone terribly wrong sometime in the distant past. Unlike my father, however, who desperately wanted to believe in something, Turner West was comfortable in his disbelief.

As he was dying years later, I tried to offer him one last chance to accept God. I was worried about his soul. He was too good a man, I told him, not to believe in God.

"It doesn't matter, Abraham," he told me. "You keep your god. It doesn't really matter."

I had then tried the cruelest of arguments to pull him toward my faith. "Turner, do you know how much I believe in God?" I asked him.

"More than you should, Abraham. But if you and Grace are happy believing as you do, then it's okay."

"No, listen to me," I insisted. "You must believe me when I tell you this. I know that someday, in some form, somehow, I will see my mother again. In a way I cannot imagine, I will see her again."

He shook his head.

"Abraham, your mother is gone" were the last words Turner West ever said to me.

In 1954, Turner West had convinced himself that he would live out his life as a man whose value was determined by how much help he could be to the survivors of death. He would train his sons to follow him, and he would shelter his daughter as best he could from an indifferent world. Then one day after Mass he saw a woman almost as tall as himself kneel down to light a candle in front of a statue of the Virgin Mary. Not since his wife died had he noticed another woman. But as this tall woman knelt in front of an icon that Turner West did not believe in, his heart moved. He stayed to watch her. Then she stood up, turned in his direction, smiled, and walked past him.

"I just sat there," he told me as we waited for the birth of my own first son, "for no good reason. I had thought that she might come back and speak to me, but she did not. I told her that later, and she told me that she had not noticed me. That should have been my first clue."

West looked for the tall woman the next week, and he asked Father Denning who she was. Told that her name was Edna Scott, West had imagined a life story for her, and he always watched her after Mass. The candle was always lit, a prayer said.

Decades before it was politically correct, my mother had not adopted my father's name when they got married. To her students, she was Dr. Scott. To Father Denning, she was Edna Scott. Only at the Flamingo was she Mrs. Lee.

"I found out soon enough," West had told me. "In our first conversation. She never misled me. But I had watched her for weeks, had even stood close enough to listen to her talk to other people. She told me soon enough, and she even told me that she had always known I was the Turner West from down the road. I suppose I didn't hide my disappointment when I found out who she was married to. No offense, Abraham, but I disliked your father long before I met your mother. After that, I hated him."

I was surprised to hear Turner West use the word "hate." Unlike my father, he was seldom extreme in his emotions or actions. But he was right. He did hate my father, and my father hated him. Long before I met Grace, my parents and Turner West had a life more complex than I would ever know.

Turner West loved my mother. Hubert Lee loved my mother. My mother loved only my father, but he came to question that. My mother knew that Turner West loved her. He told her in 1960. She told him that she cared for him as a friend, cared deeply for him, cared especially that her husband had for some irrational reason chosen him to suffer for all that was wrong with the world.

"I was not even a temptation for her," West told me. "But your father . . . your father turned me into something I wish was true. In his eye, I was your mother's lover. He had nothing to justify that vision, but, I suppose, in his mind, it made sense."

The triangle of my parents and Turner West turned into a five-pointed star when I met Grace. My mother was happy for Grace and me. In his own way, so was Turner West, or so he eventually told me. My father was harder to understand. When I'm in my blackest moods, I think my father must have seen me as his revenge on Turner West. If Turner West wanted my mother, my father might have thought, then he must lose his daughter. My father, of course, does not see the past the same way I do.

The summer of 1967 would end with me going back to St. Agnes and to Grace. I would ask her about her father and my mother. She asked me why I had never asked before.

Everything that happened after that summer was shaded by my newfound knowledge about my parents and West. Still to come were Alice Kite and Polly Jackson and the Great Fire. It is an old story, and not always original, but it is all I have.

The Cowboy

The year 1968 began with the Tet Offensive. I read about it in *Life*. By the end of January, Lyndon Johnson was a doomed President. Bobby Kennedy and Martin Luther King were still alive. Eugene McCarthy was tilting at New Hampshire windmills. Nolan Ryan was about to begin his first year in the major leagues. Arthur Ashe was profiled in the same issue as Bill Cosby, each man an example of the racial progress that America was making. George Wallace was foaming about welfare mothers breeding children as a cash crop. The pictures of him in *Life* were never flattering, but the pictures of Johnson always seemed to show a thoughtful and kind elder.

Life was full of pictures. Lots of pictures of the war. My father would sit in the Book Room and mutter to himself with every page. Then he would hand me the magazine and say, "Look at this," and I would see the dying faces of boys only two years older than me. My father never editorialized; he assumed the pictures would be self-explanatory. "Look at this" was the refrain.

Some of the pictures I will never forget. A one-legged Vietnamese girl being outfitted with a new wooden leg to replace the one blown off when her village was "accidentally" strafed by American jets. The copy of the story betrayed no irony. She had been hiding in a ditch with her mother. The jets came and went. She had been carried to an American base, and her life had been saved. The last picture in the story was of her smiling, a big and happy smile, as she stood on crutches and held on to a smiling American medic, another young man. You could look at that picture and see the genuine joy for each of them in that moment. She was going to walk again, and he had helped save a child who had come to him at the brink of death.

Pictures from Tet were in the same issue as a profile of Ho Chi Minh. Rubble and refugees. Ho as a young man in France, a tiny man next to a tall European in a top hat. Ho was a communist, but *Life* also said he was a nationalist who distrusted China.

"Look at this," my father said.

A black American soldier was on a stretcher, his eyes glazed as other soldiers looked up at the sky, watching for a helicopter.

Munitions and other supplies were piled next to the runway at Da Nang. One picture had a soldier standing next to a pile to show how high it was, as tall as three of him, so much that they had no building to put it in, and more was unloaded every day. In the background you could see a giant C-135 cargo plane about to land, bringing more supplies. The next picture showed the plane only a hundred feet off the runway, then a picture of white smoke coming from one of the engines, then a picture of the plane's wings tilted so that one was touching the ground, then a picture of the nose hitting concrete, then a fireball, then a blackened and broken giant eggshell with silver-hooded aliens spraying white foam over it, a black ash of a body being swallowed by the foam, only the stiff arm rising up as if to protest. In the last picture of the sequence, a bare-chested GI is waving to someone behind the camera, waving to someone fifteen thousand miles away, someone whom he loved and had left behind. The soldier is thin and wears those plastic-framed military glasses. The picture's caption identifies him as Pfc. Larry Mohn from Fort Worth. In the upper-right-hand corner of that picture is a dot, another C-135 coming in for a landing.

Pictures of a golf course in Saigon, officers resting around a pool on the nineteenth hole. Pictures of nightclubs in Saigon, Asian girls onstage. Pictures of soldiers with puppies. Pictures of Westmoreland and McNamara and Richard Nixon.

In February of 1968, a substitute teacher at St. Agnes asked me if I was Vietnamese. Always before, the question would have been was I Chinese or Japanese. I shook my head vigorously. No, no, I was an American. I tell my son Dexter about those questions I was asked when I was young. Of all my sons, Dexter is the one who looks most Korean. He will be asked soon enough about who he is. The answer for him will be more complicated than it was for me. But he will find an answer sooner than I did.

On the first day of February, my father handed me the latest issue of *Life*. We were alone in the Book Room. My mother and Louise were in St. Augustine.

"Look at this." There was a picture of a thin Elvis Presley. I looked back at my father.

"No, no—*this!*" he said, tapping his finger on the opposite page. Then I saw it—the future.

There was a full-page picture of a giant Cowboy marquee. The world's second largest drive-in, the Cinema-70 in Oklahoma City, was going out of business. The Cowboy was a freestanding neon marvel. Both of his thirty-foot arms moved, one to throw out a lasso and pull it back, the other to pull out his revolver and shoot it, yellow fire coming out of the barrel. The article explained how the Cowboy's fifty-foot legs, through the magic of sequential neon, would flex at the hips and seem to flare out and then snap back at the knees to click the spurred heels of the boots together. It gave new meaning to the concept of bowleggedness. As a work of popular art, the Cowboy had potential if it had been simply a neon statue. But the Cowboy was built to serve Mammon. Across its midsection was a giant white screen, illuminated from inside to backlight five lines of advertising copy, each line long enough to accommodate twenty red plastic letters, each letter two feet high.

"Look at *this*," my father was whispering to himself.

I looked at the Cowboy but could not see how it would fit in with the Flamingo. There was no place to put it, I thought. The front of the Tower had to be kept clear for car traffic, and the neon Flamingo itself needed lots of unobstructed visual space so that it could be seen from a distance. The Cowboy was just too big to have it stand anywhere near the box office. I could not understand my father's interest.

"Daddy, what's the big deal?" I asked him.

"Oh, I was just thinking, son, just thinking," he said. "Thinking about bumping up the ante."

I Meet Alice

On the first day of March, Louise was sick and stayed home from school. When I got home that afternoon she had made a miraculous recovery.

"You've got to meet her," Louise said when I walked into the kitchen.

"Her?" I asked, trying to be indifferent.

"Oh, Abe, are you going to go through your whole life being so blessed calm?" She was almost giddy. "Just put those useless books down and go to the concession stand."

My first look inside the concession stand turned me into a pillar of salt.

Polly Jackson was bent over the edge of the popcorn popper tray, cleaning out the salt and grease left over from a pre-opening test pop. I had to lean on the crowd control railing that led to the cash register.

She was wearing short jean cutoffs and a white sleeveless cotton blouse. The blouse was soaked with sweat, and I could see her bra strap clearly. Better yet, the bottom of the blouse was tied up high around the edge of her ribcage, leaving a field of unprotected flesh between ribs and hips, a field of tanned and perfect flesh. As she scrubbed the inside of the tray, the lower half of her body swayed in the opposite direction, proving for me that the basic laws of physics that I had been learning at St. Agnes were indeed true. I was fifteen. I was trying to remember Grace's name.

Polly Jackson then stood up straight and began the process of sucking the air out of my body. Her back must have been aching from leaning over so much, so she stretched her arms out and rolled her shoulders, arching her back. I stared at her bottom.

Her shorts were too short. Pushing out at the bottom edges were two firm mounds, two swelling white ribbons of flesh that screamed in contrast to the tanned upper thighs.

All this part of my story I have never told Grace or my sons. But I remember these details, remember them as you remember the same moment in your life. Doesn't matter if you're male or female. You remember. The first time you fully understood how the war between your Body and your Soul would never be a fair fight.

Her bottom pulled tight and then spread apart by a Levi's seam, Polly Jackson did the most sensuous thing I have ever seen. Not knowing I was behind her, she simply began to wipe some of the grease off her hands. An innocent act. She started to rub her hands on the back of her shorts, her fingers seeming to massage the exact surface that I longed to touch. I wanted to be her fingers. I wanted my face to be her hands.

I had kissed Grace West less than a dozen times in my life up until then. Short kisses, soft, tender kisses that left me dizzy and breathless. If the phrase "making love" had ever meant anything before it became a hackneyed euphemism, it was what I felt about Grace West. I wanted to make love with her, to achieve that Platonic union of homesick halves at last reunited. I desired her with the totality of my being.

I did not want to make love to Polly Jackson. Nor did I desire her with the totality of my being. I had simply surrendered to that part of my being that had drained the blood out of my brain, blood rushing to another extremity of my body.

This is embarrassing, this admission. I am older now, a parent, a husband. But the recollection, the effort to put it into words, the memory—these are not unpleasant.

"A penny for your thoughts."

The haze of the previous eight months had finally lifted. From those first words from Alice Kite as I stared at Polly Jackson, 1968 began.

"Did I underbid?"

I had heard her voice, but I could not turn away from looking at Polly.

At the sound of Alice's voice, Polly had turned to look over her shoulder. How to describe that face? A pornographer's dream? A trashy beauty queen? Too much makeup, but just enough? Lips that seemed like puffy scarlet . . . puffy scarlet . . . puffy, glistening scarlet . . . I can't describe those lips. Polly Jackson was nineteen years old, but all I could see was that girl in *Lolita*, a movie we had played in 1962 and which my parents had kept Louise and me from seeing, or so they thought. Polly turned completely around, and the vision was complete. Breasts, of course, but those were not what I first saw. It was her stomach, the perfect flesh that curved ever so gently from under her ribs down to those shorts with the top two buttons unbuttoned so that another tan line was just visible, a stomach with a mystical center, a stomach sculpted by Satan like a work of art, a stomach that took your eyes and forced them to follow invisible lines inexorably to that magnetic center. A stomach like a roller coaster ride. Start at the hipbone and rush down and then up again as you reach the soft swelling crest at the center, to poise yourself at the brink of that navel and then plunge down into the darkness, to become weightless as you fall, pulled to earth and your death.

I know, I know. All this is excessively self-indulgent. But you must understand that as long as Polly was around I was willing to set aside Grace. In all my life, there was no greater sin.

Alice then taught me another basic lesson about pleasure, a lesson not so fashionable today. She hit me in the shoulder with all her might, her fist knocking me sideways. She had gotten my attention and given me the first of a season of bruises.

"I was talking to you, Romeo. You can't look and hear at the same time?"

Who was this woman?

"Is your name really Romeo?" Polly had spoken.

"No, Polly, his name is Abraham Isaac Lee, and he is the heir apparent to the Ponderosa here," Alice said, smiling at me with that smile of hers that had a hard time not being a smirk.

Polly looked at us, and her face said that she had no idea what Alice was talking about. In my memory, Polly will always be a blond, even though when I first saw her naked I knew she was not really blond. I apologize for the simplistic stereotype. Polly deserved better from me, but that realization was to come later.

"Forget it, Pol, go back to work. We still have to paint the store-room," Alice said, turning back to me.

Who was this woman? And why was she bossing Polly around as if she owned the Flamingo?

Alice Kite was almost six feet tall. Even today I could not de-scribe her shape to you. Other than tall, she hid everything else. Unlike Polly's spray-on clothes, Alice always wore the baggiest of shirts and jeans. She never wore shorts. But when she looked at you, not just in your direction, but really looked at you, you never forgot. Natalie Wood, I tell people, she looked like a Natalie Wood who had aged as gracefully as a human would ever age. An unlined face with old eyes.

Alice Kite was twenty.

"Stare much?" she asked me.

I did not know if she meant my looking at Polly or at her.

"I'm sorry. . . ." My voice cracked, the last lapse of what had been an excruciatingly extended puberty. I must have blushed.

Polly laughed without turning around, and Alice threw her long arm over my shoulder and steered me out of the concession stand onto the patio. I tried to sneak one last look at Polly as we left, but Alice caught me.

"You'll burn in hell, you know that," she said.

"Am I that obvious?" I asked, surrendering to her.

"All boys are obvious. Even the good ones," she said softly, and then her voice became a whisper as she leaned her face down to mine and put her lips next to my ear. "Don't worry. And don't ever tell anyone this, but I want her body more than you do. Of course, not for the same reason."

Alice had the same effect on everyone who ever knew her. That is, everyone that she ever let know her. It was one of the three unique traits that separated her from anyone else I ever knew. She could form an instantaneous bond of intimacy with you. I would see her do it with other people, the same way she did it with me. Even in a crowd, she would lean over to someone and whisper something to them, and they would smile or nod or whisper back. In a textbook social setting, it might have been considered rude, but you forgave her when she did it to you. It was as if she was letting you in on a secret that no one else knew, and she seemed to reveal the most private parts of her own heart and mind. You always wondered what she was saying to the other person, as they must have wondered about her secrets with you. I pointed this out to Alice once, and she shrugged, saying, "Yeah, but none of you ever hear the same thing." I would see her put her arm around my father, my mother, my sister, Gary, Polly, Pete, and even Judge Lester. I always wondered who they thought they were talking to. Especially my mother, the only other woman I knew then who was as tall as Alice.

Her other two traits?

Alice Kite was a puncher. Out of nowhere, she would pound her fist into your shoulder or slap you on the top of your head. But she only did it when she was happy, and she only did it to people that she liked. I'll never forget the look on Pete Maws' face the first time she did it to him. Alice was the only person I ever saw who could get away with violating Pete's sense of personal space.

The last trait?

Alice was the most vulgar and profane person I have ever known. It was almost gratuitous obscenity, a constant and casual stream of *S* and *F* and *C* and *MF* words that always shocked a stranger. Sometimes I even thought she overdid it just for effect. It was a part of her that I will not show you in this story. Everything I tell you that she said—every line has been cleaned up. But you'll know what I mean. Take every line from Alice in this story and add your own favorite dirty words. Most of you won't even come close.

For as long as I knew her, Alice censored herself only in the presence of my mother. In fact, the harshest words Alice ever spoke to me came after I had made the mistake of letting slip a *d*—— in front of my mother.

"You do not speak to your mother that way, you hear me"—pointing her finger in my face—"or to me," she said one day when she was responsible for bringing me and Louise back home from school while my mother stayed in St. Augustine.

That first day in March, Alice had pulled me out of the concession stand and pushed me toward the Tower.

"See you later, Romeo," she said. "And go tell your sister I have a job for her."

Back in the Tower kitchen, Louise grabbed my hands and pulled me over to sit at the small breakfast table.

"Isn't she something!" she asked breathlessly.

"She's gorgeous," I admitted, reluctant to gush too much about my first sight of Polly Jackson. "But she doesn't seem too—"

"*Gorgeous??!!*" Louise interrupted. "Izzy, I don't mean that little tramp from St. Augustine High. I'm talking about Alice. Don't you think she's great! That Polly, she's just this year's first huggathemonth. She'll be gone in a week."

Louise would be wrong about Polly. At that moment we both assumed that our mother would get rid of her soon enough. I was just thinking that I hoped it was not too soon. But Polly was to be the first hug that stayed until we closed.

"Alice! Alice! Don't you know who Alice Kite is?" Louise asked me as she squirmed in her chair.

The name was beginning to become familiar, but I could not get it placed clearly until Louise reminded me.

"She is *the* Alice Kite that went to St. Agnes years before us. Didn't anyone ever tell you about her? Not even your precious Grace? *The* Alice who had to drop out of school for some reason that nobody knows exactly. The Alice who seduced a priest! A *priest,* Izzy, a priest who taught at our school. For God's sake, Izzy, she slept with Father Thomas. His picture is still on the wall in the main office. He's gone, but that picture is still there."

I was confused.

"She's a legend, Iz, a frigging legend. And she is going to work for us. Heck, she's going to live with us."

"Alice Kite slept with a priest?" I wondered out loud, thinking that I could imagine Polly Jackson doing that, but not Alice.

"Well, that's what everybody says," Louise said, calming down.

"Everybody?" I asked, knowing that I would have to ask Grace.

"Well, some people say that. Maybe the truth is probably less interesting. But I do know that she once told Sister Elaine that the Pope *was* fallible and Mary wasn't a virgin. And, Iz, she *did* have to leave school. Oh, wow, I think this is going to be a great year."

I had seldom seen her so happy.

The Perfect Crew

The Flamingo always opened a new season on the first Wednesday in March. A crew was usually in place by the middle of February, and we spent a hectic two weeks cleaning and polishing, testing all the equipment—sort of like coming out of hibernation. In all the years I could remember, we never had a crew that seemed to fit all together. My father always insisted on having seven people to balance the seven of Turner West. When he anticipated busier nights than usual, he would hire part-timers, usually from St. Agnes. Louise and I were the core, then Pete came along, then Judge Lester and Gary Green. It wasn't until Alice and Polly were hired that my father found his ideal combination.

In the past, there had always been complications. Someone turned out to be lazy or incompetent, sometimes a thief, or someone who, for whatever reason, simply quit without notice, muttering about my father's moods. My father's "hug" seldom lasted a complete season. Sometimes we went through two or three over a summer. And then there was always the problem of finding someone who was compatible enough with the rest of us to actually live with us in the Tower. Betty Burnett in 1967 presented that problem.

As sure as Louise and I were that Polly would be gone within a week, we were wrong. Of all the young girls who had ever worked at the Flamingo, she was the most attractive, the most decadent, the most tempting. Always before, Louise and I could count on the hug's dismissal, sometimes with an argument from my father, but most often we would simply wake up and the hug would be gone. My father might grumble, but his usual response was to hire another one just like the one who had disappeared. But Polly was allowed to stay. Despite those shorts, her bottom, that stomach, those lips, and even after my mother caught Louise and Polly naked in the ocean with two boys from Flagler College—Polly stayed.

Louise had a theory about Polly's survival.

"It's a compromise, Abe," she explained to me and Alice. "Daddy gets Polly. Mama gets Turner West. She can't complain."

Alice and I were down on our hands and knees scraping the concrete floor of the patio in front of the concession stand. Louise was sitting on the railing.

Alice spoke without looking up.

"So you think your mother is sleeping with Turner West?"

"I didn't say that," Louise said, getting defensive.

"Sounds like it to me."

"Oh, Alice, you know what I mean," Louise protested. "I just think it's a convenient arrangement. Daddy gets a cheap feel and Mama gets a cheap thrill."

She was pleased with her weak rhyme.

"Cheap?" Alice asked, still looking down.

"Oh, Alice, why do you have to pick on a single word? I'm just joking. You know that. Mama and Mr. West see each other on Sundays. They're probably studying to be saints," Louise said, squirming on the rail.

"Words count," Alice said. "That's all. Just that words count."

"Thank you, *Mother*," Louise said, and then pouted off the rail and into the concession stand.

"Why do you think Polly is still here?" I asked Alice.

"Does she work hard?" Alice quizzed me.

I nodded. We all had to admit that Polly worked as hard as anyone else around here, and she never complained. She and Alice were in charge of the concession stand. The grills and menu boards had never been cleaner. The food even tasted better. She could pop corn, box it, bake pizzas, grill burgers, and keep the steamer cabinets full—all at the same time. I'll never forget how one night she had both hands full of french fry baskets when she walked by a pizza oven and opened it with her elbow, all in one fluid motion, without stopping or dropping a fry. And she had a talent that I did not appreciate at that time. Polly never overcooked or overstocked. There was never a wasted crumb, and that was important because my father never sold reheated or leftover concessions. Even my mother was impressed by how small our concession write-off was.

"Is she dumb or dishonest?"

"Alice, I never said those things."

"No, you haven't, and it's not even the right question to ask. I suppose the real question is why you are surprised she's still here. I know all about those other girls. I just wonder how much that matters."

"But, my father, he always—"

"Izzy, your father probably flirts when he's asleep. He can't help it. He wants every beautiful girl to think he's cute, or something, and if I was married to him like your mother I'd probably get as perturbed as she does. It's probably genetic, which explains why you're different. But, of all the bad habits for a man to have, your father could do a lot worse."

I was thinking about that phrase "you're different" when Alice spoke up again.

"Of course, your father *is* as crazy as the Mad Hatter." She laughed, not looking at me but knowing that it would make me angry. "Remind me to tell you about my job interview, when me and Polly were in the projection booth with him."

I was about to dive into that opening, but I heard Polly behind me.

"Y'all need some help?"

Before I could answer, she was down on her hands and knees in front of me using a knife to scrape up some dried gum from last year. It was all too quick. The transition from Alice to Polly. On all fours, she turned her blond head and looked back over her shoulder at me. I just stared.

There we were, all three of us down on our knees. Polly smiled and then turned her head back to concentrate on the ground. I had not moved. Alice crawled over next to me, spatula in hand, and whispered in my ear.

"You know, she does that on purpose. She knows exactly how you are feeling. Dumb, she's not."

Alice then stood up and looked down at me. Always before, whenever she caught me staring at Polly, she would have that repressed smirk on her face, as if I were simply another confirmation of some human failure. But that day on the patio she had another look, a look that Grace called her "professor" look. A look that turned the object of its vision into a problem to be solved, a look that sought the answer to some Gordian knot of a question. The look never lasted more than a moment, to be quickly veiled by the ironic detachment that most people saw.

"Like father, like son," she said, blowing me a kiss.

Everything came together those first few months of 1968. By opening day, I understood my father's intuition. All of us *were* meant for each other.

The day after Polly and Alice were hired, I had asked Grace if she knew anything about Alice Kite. I did not mention anything about Polly. Grace had listened to me as I told her all the gossip about Alice that I had heard from Louise.

"I don't believe any of it. Somebody started saying mean things, and then everybody else repeated it. But I never believed it. Alice was just different from everyone else, that's all."

"So why did she leave? And where has she been for the past five years? And why does she look so old?"

I was talking to Grace, but I was also thinking about Polly. I did not want to mix those two worlds, but the effort was beyond me. The next thing I knew, Grace was walking away from me.

"I said I didn't know," she huffed over her shoulder as she moved away. "Nobody knows."

I watched her glide toward the gymnasium, and I focused on her plaid skirt as it bounced in time with her walk. I tried very hard to imagine how her bottom must have looked at that moment. I had thought about her body a thousand times before, but this was the first time I did not feel guilty about my most base desires. Something was happening to me.

The next day, Grace and I had our first argument. Louise had told her about Polly Jackson. Grace did not tell me anything was wrong at first. She simply refused to sit with me at lunch. In fact, it was the first time I had ever seen her and Louise act like they were friends. My sister, the Judas. Gary Green, however, followed me around all day asking about these "new girls." He had been hired as a full-timer, but he wasn't going to move into the Tower until May, when school was out. Unlike Grace, Gary told me that he believed all the stories about Alice.

"Abe, she was not your average Catholic girl. Know what I mean?"

I did not. When pressed about it, neither did Gary.

"Heck, she was just different from the other girls. That's all. And most of the sisters did not like her."

Alice Kite, however, was not Gary's real interest.

"So when do I get to meet this other girl? The one your sister says you are going to have sex with. When do I get to meet her? How about tonight?"

I had looked at Gary and seen myself. He was reacting to Polly without ever having seen her, but reacting as I must have. Of course, every boy at St. Agnes who was hired for busy nights at the Flamingo was to have the same reaction. Alice was right, we are all the same.

Triplets
and Polly Jackson

The Cowboy arrived a week before we opened. The legs came first, each one on a flatbed semi-trailer truck. Then the arms. The body and head came together. The giant parts were stacked in front of the Tower, waiting for the stomach, the marquee, to arrive. It was late, and my father fretted that he would not have the Cowboy in place for opening night.

Turner West, the mildest of men, bought a pistol the day after the Cowboy's first leg was planted.

My father put the Cowboy right next to the line that divided his property from that of Turner West, so close you could almost hear the neon hum if you were in the West driveway, so close to the West Funeral Home that some people thought that it was actually part of that business rather than the drive-in down the road.

West had been the first funeral business in Florida to offer pre-death contracts. You know, make all the arrangements early and spare your loved ones the grief of handling the details of your funeral. A week after the Cowboy began glowing, four of those contracts had been cancelled.

As I approached my sixteenth birthday, I was beginning to understand how petty my father could be.

"I had many reasons to hate your father," West told me a long time after my mother died. I had gone with him and Grace to his own father's funeral in Georgia. "Your mother, of course, and the years of harassment. But most of all because he made me lose control of myself. I had finally come down to his level, and he knew it. He had wanted me to act like he did, and he succeeded."

We had been driving in one of his limousines. Grace and I were his passengers, and he kept his eyes straight ahead as he spoke.

"Your mother had shown me the pictures of that monstrosity. She and your father had argued, but it was one of the rare times she had lost. She apologized to me, but I had the feeling then that your father had won. I had known all along that his goal was to make me leave, to destroy my business. I knew that. When I saw those pictures I knew he would make it impossible for me to stay there. I was even looking at a new site in Jacksonville. By the time everything burned, I was already planning to leave."

Grace and I were in the back, holding hands and dressed in black. I felt like one of his sons. I was remembering opening day in 1968. Except for the Cowboy's shadow, everyone at the Flamingo had been excited.

My father's first film of 1968 was *The Birth of Triplets*. You have probably never heard of it, but *Birth* was the highest grossing drive-in picture in America in 1968. It never played indoors. Indoor audiences were different. A man named Saul Mixon had put together three separate short documentaries about childbirth. The first was a 1950s version of sex education, complete with diagrams of crusading sperm and fortress eggs. The second was about pregnancy. The third was the wonder of birth.

Mixon's contribution was to dub in a new sound track linking all three together, and he created the most effective advertising campaign in theatre history. *Birth* was not a documentary; it was to be sold as an exposé. He was the P. T. Barnum of the Sexual Revolution, and my father has always been sorry that he never met Mixon in person.

When Mixon called my father, he told him to have the largest staff he had ever had for a movie. My father liked Mixon's optimism. A deal was made. The Flamingo would have the southern premiere. Mixon would pay one hundred percent of a saturation ad blitz and get seventy percent of the box office gross. The theatre would get thirty percent of the gross and one hundred percent of the concession revenue. Mixon even agreed to pay for two weeks of Judge Lester's aerial advertising.

"Get your pizzas and meatball sandwiches stocked up, Mr. Lee," Mixon said over the phone. "There is nobody, I say nobody, who eats more than mama-to-be. You'll set records."

Part of the advertising for *Birth* promised that customers could buy certain sex education books that had been banned in most parts of the country. "Only at this theatre—the book they don't want you to read!" I was put in charge of the bookselling. Mixon made a separate deal with me: ten cents on every dollar book sold was my commission. My father even let me talk to Mixon on the phone.

The gimmick on the books was that there were actually two of them: a blue book for men, a pink book for women, to be sold car-to-car on the lot. I was assured that every car would want one of each. Never mind that the only difference between the books was the color of their covers. Mixon promised me that the two sexes would never let the other see their own books, books that were actually not much more than a thick pamphlet of bold print and dry prose.

Judge Lester started whetting the public appetite in mid-February. Sometimes my mother flew with him as he pulled banners over north Florida promising *"Birth Shown at Last," "The Mystery of Birth," "The Birth of Triplets, See It All," "Banned in Boston, Sex and Birth, One Week Only"*—a new phrase every day for two weeks. Hundreds of thirty-second radio spots on all the major stations. Quarter-page newspaper ads. Even television, which my father despised. A black screen with white lettering, a pulsating bass drum in the background, Saul Mixon's voice warning anyone with a weak heart or prudish sensitivities to stay away from the Flamingo, to not even drive by. Mixon even had me and Gary Green put leaflets on every windshield of every car in every parking lot of every obstetrician in Jacksonville and St. Augustine.

The day before we opened, my father was dancing.

"Do you feel it, Isaac, do you feel those people making up their minds? This'll be the biggest opening ever. Bigger than any Fourth! Like we are Mecca!"

The truth is, I *could* feel it, that mass of humanity that was beginning to slouch toward the Flamingo.

On Wednesday afternoon, by five o'clock, A1A was packed with cars. The box office wasn't scheduled to open until seven. My father called his crew together and gave us a pep talk. His seven knights, as he called those who lived in the Tower, and a dozen pawns from St. Agnes. His enthusiasm was contagious.

I tell my sons this story and they laugh, as they do at most of my stories. Grace tells them how she was sent to Georgia for the week, and she tells them to be careful about the details.

"I was not there," she says, "and you know how your father exaggerates."

My sons don't care. They are very tolerant of me and their mother. I tell the story, and Dexter always, when I tell him about the end of the movie, always says, "Gross, Daddy!" But they all want to hear it again.

The part of the story that I can never convey to them is how I felt the next day, when I understood my father's pride in his seven knights, the crew he had always wanted. After that first night, I knew that we would never hire another person to work and live with us. Alice and Polly were the last of my father's family.

My mother was always in charge of the box office, selling the tickets and making change in a blur. Judge Lester was stationed with her: ticket-taker, crowd control, and security. After the box office closed, usually two hours after the beginning of the first feature, he was to stay out front and watch for gate crashers while my mother went to help in the concession stand. When he was not taking tickets, he was also supposed to write down the license number and description of any car with only one ticket-buyer in it. Later, Gary and I were to check to see how many people might have mysteriously materialized after getting on the lot. Sagging car trunks were always a clue.

Alice was cashier in the concession stand. Louise and Polly were each in charge of one half of the self-serve lanes. The concession stand had a T-shaped arrangement. Customers came in from the sides and walked through a maze of railing that kept them organized and all going in the same direction. The top corners of the T eventually met at the bottom where Alice had customers coming at her from two sides. But she would use both hands—ringing up sales, taking money, making change, pointing out condiments, and giving directions to the restrooms, all at once. With *Birth,* Louise and Polly were cooks, and each had three St. Agnes part-timers popping and stocking like crazy. Alice, however, had no backup, except for me whenever she had to go to the toilet.

Gary and I were the rampboys. With *Birth,* we had six part-timers whom we sent up and down the ramps checking for faulty speakers and looking for any possible trouble. Two of the part-timers were girls who were also supposed to keep the ladies' restroom clean and stocked. I had asked my father to hire extra rampboys so that Gary and I would be free to handle the book sales, and so we would not have to split the commission with anyone else. Four hundred cars buying eight hundred books, with two separate showings a night, meant sixteen hundred dollars gross and eighty dollars apiece for Gary and me. It would be a gold mine.

Pete Maws was always the projectionist. The booth was beside the concession stand, and he would help at the stand until showtime. Once the movie started, however, Pete was not seen again until the last reel had been rewound and put back in the cabinet. On slow nights, Pete would train Gary and me to be projectionists. There would be no slow nights with *Birth.*

My father? My father's only job, on any night, was to wander around and watch everyone else work. He might step in to help in a rush, or he might not. At intermission he would get on the speaker system and make his spiel about going to the concession stand. It was a routine that made people tell their friends the next day, "You'll never believe the pitch I heard last night at the drive-in. This guy ought to have his own nightclub." They were right; my father could be a funny man, more so if you never met him.

On especially busy nights, with a full lot, my father had another routine before the show started. He would stand on top of the concession stand, just outside the projection booth, with a microphone in hand and with Pete keeping a spotlight on him, and he would act as the Flamingo's master of ceremonies. On those nights, like the *Birth* showing, he would be in full Flamingo uniform: pirate hat, eyepatch, Hawaiian shirt, Bermuda shorts.

My first clue that my father was right about finally finding his ideal crew came when Alice and Polly actually got excited about wearing the Flamingo uniform. Louise, the future actress, had always liked the costume. Gary and I had resigned ourselves to it. Judge Lester used it as a disguise; in it he could become someone else and overcome some of his nervousness. The eyepatch was optional for all of us, but only my father was allowed to carry a giant wooden saber painted silver. Even Pete participated in this Gilbert and Sullivan operetta, but he negotiated a provision with my father that allowed him to change clothes as soon as the movie started.

Only my mother was exempt from the uniform. She would laugh at my father and accuse him of "mixing metaphors." My father would always laugh back and tell all of us that my mother's education had ruined her sense of humor, to which she would simply say that her marrying him was proof of her sense of humor. They had always joked like that as Louise and I grew up, but less and less after the Fourth of 1967.

Birth was going to be a big night. My father was ready.

"Open the gates!" he shouted at six o'clock, a full two hours before showtime. Judge Lester took down the chains in front of the box office, and the Flamingo quickly began swallowing life.

Gary and I had been down at the box office to help with initial traffic control, but the Judge was a master of hand signals, so we headed back to the field. As we walked, cars sped by us racing for the best spots.

"Do you see what I see?" Gary asked as we got to the concession stand. I thought I knew what he meant, but shook my head anyway.

"Every car is full of kids," he said. "Whole boatloads of kids. I thought this was supposed to be a sex movie."

"Where do you think kids come from?" I tried to joke, but humor was not my strong point. "Anyway, wait until you see who else is in the cars. Mr. Mixon said I would never see as many pregnant women in one spot in my entire life."

Saul Mixon had been conservative. Not only were the cars full of pregnant women, they had piled their entire families in with them. Each car was bulging with children and a reluctant father. I thought, if anyone should know about childbirth it would be these people. But Mixon was right, we were going to need a lot of extra help that night. As soon as the cars pulled up to a speaker post they belched out hordes of children who immediately streamed to the playground, oblivious to any other incoming cars that were cruising around looking for empty spaces.

Beginning to think like my father, I made a quick decision.

"Gary, get Jack and Nancy down to the playground and tell them to stay there all night. Even after the movie starts, I have a feeling these kids will not be sitting still in their cars."

Jack and Nancy were two of the St. Agnes temps for that night. I was soon wishing we had hired more than a dozen. I was also thinking that we might not have bought enough concession supplies. The cars had children, fathers, and at least one pregnant woman. Dozens of station wagons had more than one mother-to-be. Within fifteen minutes after the box office opened, both concession lines were already stretched outside the building. And it was not just the size of the crowd, it was the size of their appetites.

"Should we go help the girls?" Gary asked. I detected an ulterior motive, something to do with Gary being able to get close to Polly and Louise at the same time.

"Gary, if we start helping in there, we'll never get out, and we only have about an hour to sell books," I explained, almost wishing that I wasn't so perceptive.

The field was full in thirty minutes, the playground packed, and the restrooms had waiting lines. Gary and I split up, him taking the half of the field closest to the playground and me supervising the half closest to the concession stand. He had objected to the assignment, but I had my father's proxy.

Pete Maws found me as I was looking through the windows into the concession stand. All I could see of Polly was her head and shoulders as they moved back and forth behind the serving lines.

"We're out of pickles," Pete said, with a look that told me that I was being tested.

"I'll send somebody to the Tower storage room. We've got ten cases."

"Meatballs, too?" he asked.

"Five cases," I said, proud of myself.

"Gonna be some sick people tonight," he said.

I laughed. "Pete, there's nothing wrong with our food. You know that."

"Yes, Mr. Abraham, I know that. Just think that some of these men aren't ready for this show. We'll see. Course, we might also have to deliver a few babies tonight."

That did suddenly scare me. Pete was right. How could some of those women, so big, *not* be about to deliver.

"You ever deliver a baby?" I turned to ask him.

Pete cackled, "Nozzir, don't know nothin' about birthing no babies," in a Negro voice that he seldom had. He was immensely pleased with himself, speaking as he turned to go help inside, "Been waiting a long time to use that line."

All of us doubled our pace the next hour. I was checking on all the temps in my half of the field; Gary was roving over the other half. I stopped in every few minutes at the concession stand, seeing if they needed any supplies. The smells of popcorn and pizza were fighting for supremacy. Onions and boiled eggs were staging a minor conflict. Polly was beginning to sweat. I could see Louise cursing under her breath. The temps were like frenetic Disney dwarfs, hustling around with arms full of food and drinks. I saw Polly take an ice cube and rub her neck and then reach inside her shirt to rub her chest. Louise dropped a hamburger patty on the floor, looked around to see if anyone had seen her, and then put it on the grill. Alice yelled from the cash register, "Louise Janine!" and Louise took it off the grill.

I looked at Alice. She was mouthing something to me, but I could not understand her, so I went around front. "See me after the stand closes. I've got some news you might be interested in," she said, all the while ringing up sales and sifting through the cardboard food baskets to make sure nothing was hidden.

"LADIES AND GENTLEMEN!!" My father was on the roof.

I stepped outside and looked up. My father saw me and pointed the tip of his cutlass at me. It was a signal. Gary and I were to get our books ready.

"LADIES AND GENTLEMEN! YOU HAVE EXACTLY FORTY-FIVE MINUTES UNTIL SHOWTIME. THREE-QUARTERS OF AN HOUR

UNTIL THE MYSTERY OF LIFE IS REVEALED TO YOU. LESS THAN
AN HOUR UNTIL YOU SEE YOUR OWN ORIGINS. LESS THAN . . ."

A thousand people had turned to look up at my father. Men,
women, and children, some with their arms loaded down with food,
others in line for the restroom, others at the playground. His voice,
crackling through a speaker, flooded those cars facing the screen,
and I could see heads turn toward the concession stand. The sun was
not down yet, but Pete had the spotlight on my father, microphone
in hand, the Pirate.

"AND YOU WILL NOT BE DISAPPOINTED. NOR CAN YOU
CLAIM IGNORANCE. YOU WILL SEE IT ALL. EVERYTHING. AS
WRITTEN IN THE SKY AND HEARD IN YOUR SLEEP." Even I did
not understand that. "BUT FIRST YOU MUST . . ."

That was the cue for me and Gary. We each had a St. Agnes temp
to carry a box of books behind us as we began the car-door-to-car-
door mission. When the box was low, the temp was to race back and
get another.

". . . SEEK THE KNOWLEDGE IN PRINT. THE WORD MUST BE
YOUR GUIDE BEFORE YOU SEE THE LIGHT." I knew my father was
losing them at that point, but he liked to hear himself. "MY ASSIS-
TANTS WILL SOON BE AT YOUR DOOR, OFFERING FOR A VERY
LIMITED TIME, ONLY AS LONG AS SUPPLIES LAST AND THE AU-
THORITIES DO NOT INTERVENE, THAT KNOWLEDGE WHICH HAS
BEEN KEPT FROM YOU BY YOUR SCHOOLS, YOUR CHURCHES,
AND, DO I DARE SAY IT, KEPT FROM YOU BY YOUR OWN PAR-
ENTS. ONE DOLLAR BRINGS KNOWLEDGE. BUT, LADIES AND
GENTLEMEN, THOSE BOOKS FOR WOMEN WILL BE SOLD ONLY
TO WOMEN, THOSE FOR MEN ONLY TO MEN. YOU MUST UNDER-
STAND YOURSELF BEFORE YOU EMBRACE YOUR OPPOSITE.
YOU MUST LIFT YOUR OWN VEIL. ONLY THEN CAN YOU SEEK
THE TRUTH FROM THAT OTHER SIDE OF HUMANITY"—horns
were honking by then—"BUT, PLEASE, DO NOT SEEK MY MEN
OUT IF YOU ARE NOT READY FOR THE TRUTH ABOUT YOUR-
SELF. DO NOT FORCE US TO TAKE YOUR MONEY UNLESS YOU
ARE PREPARED TO BREAK THROUGH THAT WALL OF META-
PHYSICAL AMBIGUITY WHICH KEEPS YOU IN THE CAVE OF

YOUR IGNORANCE." More horns, all seeming to ask "What?" "YOU MUST BE A SEEKER, A QUESTER, AND, AS A BONUS, ONE OF THESE BOOKS CONTAINS A SEASON PASS TO THIS THEATRE"—which was a surprise to me. "OTHERS CONTAIN COUPONS FOR FREE REFRESHMENTS"—also a surprise, but also, as I thought about it, not true. "REMEMBER: YOU HAVE LESS THAN AN HOUR. AND, FOR YOUR CONVENIENCE, WE WILL CERTAINLY KEEP THE CONCESSION STAND OPEN. BUY KNOWLEDGE. SATISFY YOUR SPIRITUAL AND PHYSIOLOGI-CAL THIRST. AND THEN SATISFY THAT OTHER THIRST—SHOW YOUR BOOK AND LARGE COKES ARE HALF-PRICE"—a surprise to Alice, but she adjusted quickly. "I SPEAK NO MORE"—horns and whistling. "LET THERE BE KNOWLEDGE."

For a full two seconds, nobody moved, and then the frenzy began. Gary and I did not get to all the cars. The crowd came to us. We were the bloody body in a sea of sharks. I could not keep track, nor could Gary. We immediately dropped the restriction on who could buy the books. I simply saw a hand with money and I shoved a book in that direction. Sometimes people did not even wait for their change. Billy Mottern, my temp, was smart enough to bring back another temp when he returned with more books. I lost my eyepatch and three-cornered hat in the crush. Gary had his hands and wrists scratched. In forty-five minutes, we sold fifteen hundred books, almost four to a car. The pregnant women, especially, bought more than one, as if stocking up for their friends. I was not surprised to learn later that we were setting records in the concession stand. Food and sex, Alice told me, people could never get enough.

"FIVE MINUTES!" was all my father's voice said after a while, and with one last surge the starving patrons bought the word of Saul Mixon.

It was completely dark by then, and my father was fully illumi-nated on top of the concession stand. He was waving his sword, turning in a circle, speaking low and then up to a crescendo, in a routine that he and Pete had perfected by constant practice since 1960.

"With the setting of the sun . . . ," he said as he slowly turned, seen by all those people. Then he began raising his sword toward the screen. ". . . the show MUST BEGIN." At the exact moment his body stopped and his sword was pointed directly at the screen and his voice said its last word, my father disappeared. Pete had switched off the spotlight and lifted the projection shutter to light up the world's largest theatre screen. Poof! My father was gone and the show began simultaneously. It was a great trick, and the crowds always loved it. Even people who had never been to the Flamingo had heard about the man who ran it. That first night of *Birth,* my father had never been better. You should have been there.

I had expected the concession lines to go down as soon as the movie started, but those women kept coming back for more. I had always been told that a pregnant woman could never keep her food down, so why were these women gorging themselves? And their children! They were everywhere.

"Look at those roaches scramble." My father had suddenly appeared beside me. "The future of America." He seemed to be swaying in time with some music that only he could hear. Then he did something he hadn't done for months. He put his arms around me and hugged me, holding on to me until I was afraid that someone would notice. He was happy. I had the feeling that tonight was the night when Polly was to get her first official hug.

My father and I were motionless, joined at the belly like interracial Siamese twins, and the crowd flowed by as if we were not there.

"Abraham, I love you, and I never want you to grow up," he whispered to me as the rest of the world looked at the screen. At that moment I remembered how my father and mother used to grab either Louise or me and put us between them as they hugged each other. I wanted my mother to be there at that second, to be pressed against my back as she reached her long arms around to encircle me and my father.

"Never grow up," my father said out loud. "Promise me."

I was fifteen; I did not understand my father until I found myself telling Dexter the same thing my father had told me.

"Yeah, okay" was my profound response, but it was enough for my father. He released me and went into the concession stand waving his sword.

"Daddy, we're going to need more of those books," I shouted at him as he went through the door.

"No problem," he shouted back. "You call Saul tomorrow."

Even then, I could see that my father was beginning the long process of turning the Flamingo over to me, tiny bit by tiny bit. It was a paradox: Do not grow up, I was told, but also become your father. I would tell Alice all about my insight later that night, as we watched the ocean.

"No contradiction, Iz," she would say, rubbing my shoulders. "Your father never grew up, why should you?" I can still feel her hands, those incredibly long fingers.

Thirty minutes into *Birth,* we had our first small crisis. One of the toilets in the ladies' room was backed up. I told Louise about it, but she refused to go clean it up.

"*You* do it!" she said to me as we stood in the storeroom behind the concession grills. I knew that Polly was somewhere listening to us.

"But, Louise, it's the *ladies'* restroom," I said crisply.

"Tell Renee and Lisa to do it," she said. "I thought that's what we hired them for anyway. Aren't they supposed to be right there all the time!"

"I'll do it." Polly Jackson had appeared and volunteered. "Probably just a wad of Kotexes. Gimme a plunger or a coat hanger."

I blushed at the *K* word, and Polly noticed.

In five minutes, she was back. I did not ask her any questions.

"I told one of those girls back there to have the women start using the men's room as well. Right now, all four johns are flushing, and the two in the men's will help speed up the line," she told me as she headed back to a grill.

"But the . . . but the men . . . ," I stammered.

"Don't ask me," she said. "It was Alice's idea."

I turned around and there she was at the cash register, smiling that smirky smile, crossing her eyes and then winking at me. Gary would always tell me that he thought that Alice Kite could read lips.

Polly brought me back to the moment. "You know, Alice is right. You are kinda cute, especially when you get that dumb look on your face."

Louise thought this was the funniest thing she had heard in her life.

You could tell me that I was being insulted, but I didn't think so then. It was the way she looked at me when she said the word "cute," the way she arched her eyebrows.

Just then Gary came rushing in the back door of the concession stand, breathless and sweating.

"Abe, get out front! Turner West has a gun and he's shooting at your father!"

For the first time that night, I was moving faster than the crowd around me. Gary and I were out of the concession stand, across the lot, and through the exit gate. On the screen as we raced by was a doctor pointing to a diagram of a woman's uterus.

Running toward the West Funeral Home, I could see three police cruisers, their red lights flashing, blocking A1A. I could see my father standing in front of Turner West, who was being held by a sheriff's deputy. Judge Lester was beside my father; two of West's sons were next to their father. Cars full of fertile women were lined up for half a mile.

Turner West had not been shooting at my father, but he had put a bullet between the eyes of the Cowboy. The neon in the Cowboy's head had been shattered, and its dark brow was sparking and fizzing.

Why was I not surprised by all this? In fact, why was I only surprised by the fact that Turner West had *not* been shooting at my father, but only at his surrogate?

The two men were glaring at each other, but my father was the calmer of the two. Turner West could have been sent to jail, but my father negotiated his probation, calling in some of the favors that he had cultivated with the sheriff over the years. The deputy asked Turner West if there was going to be any more trouble. West was silent. The deputy asked again.

My father answered for him. "No more trouble, sir, I can promise that. Mr. West and I will establish a peaceable kingdom right here in the Sunshine State. No more trouble, I promise."

Of course, it was a lie, but a necessary lie. I knew, we all knew, anyone who knew the two men knew that there would never be peace. I looked for my mother, but she was not there. The Flamingo had been left in the hands of my mother, Alice, Louise, and Polly. My father, me, Gary, and the Judge were under the Cowboy, urinating on rocks to mark our territory.

A week later, I would tell Grace about how I was beginning to see my life as "a series of surreal juxtapositions."

One minute selling books, the next cleaning out toilets, then seeing her father in handcuffs, a giant sightless Cowboy looming over everything, then back to the Flamingo to see four hundred adult males undergo a collective convulsion as the first of three babies sprang from the loins of a leviathan.

Turner West was a free man. The deputies were gone, warning him and my father to settle things. The first night of *Birth* had been a battle that my father had won. He had forced Turner West into a higher level of ritual. West bought another gun the next day, as my father expected him to do. Until the Great Fire, West or one of his sons fired one shot into the Cowboy every day. Just one. My father simply budgeted a daily service call from a Jacksonville sign company. The supplies of glass, plastic, metal, and neon tubing were limitless, as was money. Bullets, too, were cheap, and plentiful.

"I shot him every day," Turner West told me on his seventieth birthday, his last birthday. I understood the pronoun reference.

My father led me and Gary and the Judge back to the Flamingo. He stopped at the box office, and the three of us were told that he wanted a private conversation with my mother. Cars were kept back by a chain across the entrance, waiting for the second show.

Birth was an hour and a half, but it was not until the last fifteen minutes that you actually got your money's worth. Gary and I were standing near the concession stand, waiting to help in what would surely be one last mad rush for refreshments at intermission. Neither of us was prepared for what we actually saw. Triplets conceived in a cartoon, gestated in a sequence of black-and-white diagrams, were born in the flesh. And the camera did not blink.

A real pregnant woman, a really large pregnant woman, was wheeled into the delivery room, and then, on the largest theatre screen in the world, the audience was put where the doctor was—right between her legs looking directly at *Birth*.

When my sons were born, I stayed in the waiting room with Turner West. Grace did not even ask me to stay with her. She knew.

Water broke and poured toward the Flamingo playground. And then from the cradle of civilization came a head, a round bulge that pushed against a reluctant opening, almost out and then momentarily slipping back in, and then, as if on a coiled spring, the whole body popped out, splotchy and still attached to a cord of life that was trailing back to Mesopotamia.

Alice was standing beside me. "Too bad this ain't in 3-D," she said, leaning over to punch Gary in the arm. Then she was back inside. Gary's eyes did not leave the screen.

A newborn baby boy was seen being held upside down. Then another. I could hear the women clapping in their cars, and I prepared for the worst. Surely, I thought, some chain reaction was about to occur. Surely, labor had to have been induced by some mysterious feminine empathy, especially with this crowd. I had even forgotten about my father and Turner West.

Back to the doctor's point of view—we all saw the last of the triplets arrive. It was a girl. I looked around. The concession stand was empty, and all the concession girls, led by Alice and Polly, were staring through the big plate-glass windows. Louise was nowhere to be seen. I looked at Gary. He was turning green.

That should have been enough to see, but Saul Mixon had more. You must remember, all these films had been documentaries, probably intended for some closed-door session of medical students at school in 1955 or earlier. Education and science were to be served. Why shouldn't future obstetricians see the afterbirth?

Gary and I were saved by Alice, who shouted from the concession stand, "Close your eyes, boys!" just before it happened. But we heard that groan pouring out of the four hundred parked cars that had their hoods pointing upward at the screen. It was a masculine groan, but the worst was not over for any of the males on the lot that night.

I opened my eyes to see a happy mother back in her room, a beaming father, three gurgling babies wrapped in white and laid in their mother's arms. Gary and I had almost recovered when Saul Mixon's voice announced that one last procedure was necessary before the newborn boys could go home. Surely not, I thought, surely not. This was not advertised. It was Saul Mixon's bonus.

Between a rubber-gloved thumb and forefinger, a tiny wad of baby flesh was stretched, and then what looked like a medieval corkscrew was placed on the tip, and with a decisive twist the baby flesh became circumcised boy flesh.

It was the most painful and violent ten seconds in American film history. Even the women were quiet. But for all the men, after an hour and half of pizza and Cokes and hot dogs and hamburgers and popcorn and meatball sandwiches and french fries and pickles and chocolate Toddies and ice-cream bars and licorice—it was too much. My own groin had reflexed in self-defense, but I had not eaten anything, so I only felt pain, not nausea. Dozens of male heads leaned out of windows. Some were able to get to a toilet, usually with their wife following for moral support, sometimes having to lean on their wife's arm. Unlike an hour earlier, the men now had to use any available space in the ladies' restroom.

Birth had ended with male flesh being peeled like an apple, and casualties were all over the field. I turned around to find Gary Green sitting on the ground with his head in his hands.

"Abe, I want to thank you for ruining my life," he said, head still down. "Especially my sex life."

"Gary, you don't have a sex life." I began to laugh, and then Gary began to laugh. He and I still laugh about that moment even today.

With that first showing over, cars began forming a caravan toward the exit gates. My father had been worried about this part of the night because we had never tried to clear a field of cars and then reopen. Usually, two or three pictures played once and people had no reason to remain. He had thought that a lot of cars might stay over, but one showing of *Birth* had been enough for this crowd. I could imagine how some of those people must have rolled down their windows as they drove by the hundreds of cars waiting on A1A, shouting warnings and telling them to turn back before it was too late. But I was wrong. Word-of-mouth advertising, which can kill any picture, was almost universally positive. All those women, even all those men after they had recovered, would tell their friends that they had gotten more than their money's worth that night at the Flamingo. My book sales did drop, however, on each successive night. At the end of the week I had to send a dozen cases back to Saul Mixon. He did not seem surprised.

Before the box office opened for a second showing on opening night, my father, like Colonel Travis at the Alamo, called us all together and offered the temps a full night's salary in cash right then and there without an obligation to stay for the second show. It was his line in the Florida sand. Who would stand with him? Louise raised her hand and asked for the cash, but my father ignored her.

Looking back now, I know that I must have been using all the adrenaline that my body would ever produce. It was more than a drug. As soon as the box office had first opened I had felt like I could handle any situation, and as my father spoke I was still on an upward curve in my energy level. I wanted to see the field fill up again, to keep moving, to keep selling books, to see my father on the concession stand again. Having already seen *Birth*, having survived *Birth*, I knew I would not be as affected as I had been the first time. I could pay more attention to the audience and the concession stand.

The second show was just as hectic as the first. Gary and I sold as many books, the crowds cheered my father as he disappeared, and the toilets did not back up. At the end of the second show, Gary and I could look right at the screen without closing our eyes. I even laughed when I looked through the concession windows and saw Alice waving a pair of scissors at me.

And then, as the last car left the lot after midnight, I was tired. I was actually more than tired. I was exhausted. I wanted to go to bed. There was nothing that I wanted more than to go to sleep.

"You going skinny-dipping with your sister and Polly?" Alice asked nonchalantly as she handed me the last of four bags that had been stuffed with concession money. We were at the cash register. Polly and Louise and the temps were cleaning the kitchen. At first, I thought Alice might have been tricking me.

"Are you serious?" I asked her, trying to appear unfazed.

"As serious as soap. That's why I told you to see me after the show. I knew you would want to know."

Alice was serious, I could see clearly. And she had that *old* look on her face that I had seen the first day I saw her. I looked at her and asked a question that was suddenly embarrassing.

"Are you going, too?"

She shook her head.

"Nope, I'm just the lifeguard."

I was being drawn to the ocean, but I resisted.

"I suppose they're going by themselves."

Alice nodded at first, but then she shrugged.

"Not really. Gary and Billy were invited, and there will probably be a few other kids from school."

I knew what she was really telling me. I was uninvited. I could wait around another half hour and nobody would mention anything to me. I was very tired again.

"You want to be the assistant lifeguard? It's up to you. Meet me in an hour, at the south end of the wall. I'll be there. You and me can look for sharks."

I thanked her for the offer, but I said I was going to bed. I thought I was telling the truth, but an hour later I went looking for Alice. It was unseasonably warm for March, even in Florida. You could start to sweat even if you were standing still.

I walked quickly and quietly by Pete's caboose and then climbed over the seawall. The tide was out as far as it would go that night, and there was a half-moon.

If you have never done this, you should try it: Go to the beach late at night when nobody else is around. That night as I looked for Alice, I became acutely aware of how noisy my world was during the day and when the Flamingo was showing movies. There was always something in the background. Music or voices or the whine of cars away on A1A. As I looked for Alice I only heard the ocean creeping away from the shore.

"Over here," Alice said in a low voice.

She was sitting on a blanket, a bag next to her. In the weak moonlight I could not see her face clearly.

"Isaac, sit down. You'll spook the fish."

It was the first time she had ever used my full middle name.

"Where is everybody?" I asked, settling myself down on the blanket next to her.

"They're out there. Don't worry. Louise made a bet that she could swim out farther than anybody else."

"Is Gary out there?" I asked. I wanted her to say that it was only the girls who were swimming.

"Sure, him and Billy and two older guys from St. Augustine. And those two senior girls from St. Agnes. Louise, of course, and Polly."

"You mean the older guys are not from St. Agnes?"

"Nope, they're from Flagler. I met them. Nice enough. And who can blame them for accepting your sister's invitation?"

"Were they at the show tonight?" I asked, trying to figure out where these boys came from and if they were students of my mother's.

"Isaac, your sister had this planned all week. She told me she had invited some of her friends from St. Augustine, and she told me not to tell you."

"But you did," I said.

"But I did," Alice said.

"So she'll be mad if she sees me. Mad at you and me both."

"Iz, your sister is always mad."

Alice and I talked for half an hour. Small talk, bits and pieces of my life. Frank the Dog, where Pete came from, Judge Lester, Turner West and Grace, and Polly. She smoked two cigarettes in that half hour. She must have lied about that when my father asked her if she smoked. He did not hire smokers.

We could hear voices coming in from the ocean. Louise and her friends were getting closer. I recognized Gary first, and then Polly. Then I could see some dark bobbing shapes, but they did not come all the way to shore.

"Isaac, do you ever think about your real mother?" Alice asked quietly, shoving a cigarette stub into the sand. "You know, the woman who gave birth to you."

It was an old question. I was glad that my mother did not hear Alice ask it.

"Sometimes," I said, and I was being truthful. Even today I sometimes think about that woman. When I was in Korea after graduation, I thought I might simply have one of those chance re-unions that happen in the movies. But Seoul has more people than the entire state of Florida. "But, Alice, I can't imagine someone else being my mother."

Alice did not speak for a minute. I heard Louise yelling at somebody named Dan and then a Paul, and then she squealed.

"Sure, you're right," Alice finally said. "I can't imagine you belonging to anybody else except those two people up there."

Polly was yelling at Becky Lennon and Amy Smith, "Gary's got a hard-on! Gary's got a hard-on!"

I was glad I was not out there.

"Iz, I'm going to make you a happy man tonight," Alice said.

"Can you make my parents happy again?" I asked without thinking about it. I surprised myself.

"I'll work on that. But tonight is your treat," she said, spreading her legs wide apart. "Sit over here between my legs, with your back to me. And be absolutely quiet."

Sitting between her legs, I could feel my back up against her chest. She kissed me on the top of the head. Not a real kiss, just a peck, and then she said, "Get ready to see the glory of God."

From the bag beside her, Alice pulled out a four-battery flashlight. Suddenly, a white beam shot out across the water until it began to pick out heads and shoulders. Becky and Amy screamed, but Louise yelled back at the shore.

"Alice, don't be a jerk! Turn off that light! Alice!"

Alice yelled over my shoulder, "Polly, I dare you to come out and show us your butt."

I knew immediately what was about to happen, and I began to shake. Alice tapped me gently on the side of the head.

"Be absolutely still," she said. "With the light in her face she'll barely make out my outline. You, she won't see."

"I will if you will," Polly yelled back.

"Don't hold your breath, girl," said Alice, her right hand holding a steady beam of light on Polly's head in the water, her left hand around my waist. Nobody spoke for a few seconds, and then I heard Louise yelling at Polly.

"Do it! I dare you to do it!"

"Double-dare! Triple-dare!" Gary and Billy Mottern chimed in, and then two male voices I had never heard before began their own chorus, "Gluck gluck gluck! Polly is a chicken! Polly wanna cracker." I knew she hated that. We probably all have a certain phrase that is especially galling. Polly hated *wanna cracker.* "Polly wanna cracker!"

Sitting between Alice's legs, hidden in her shadow, I kept staring at Polly floating in the ocean. I knew she was going to take their dare. I was quickly shedding all those images of flesh that I had seen on the screen earlier that night. Those images of birth that were their own best form of birth control.

"Not a word, Iz, not a word. And I'll never tell her you were here. Not a word," Alice whispered as Polly's shoulders came into view. A word? I was already struck dumb and rigid with anticipation. I could feel Alice's breath on the back of my neck, and then Polly walked slowly out of the water.

She stepped into a circle of light that stopped where the sand and sea met. Feet apart and hands on her hips, she shook her wet hair. Not seeing me, she looked directly at me. Then she turned to walk slowly back into the Atlantic. Glistening, numbing perfection.

"You owe me, Isaac," Alice said as Polly swam away.

At that moment, I would have given her my soul.

Alice Plans My Future

A month after I saw Polly naked, Martin Luther King Jr. was murdered. I had heard about him for years, heard him discussed at St. Agnes and in the newspapers. Most of all, I knew about him because of Pete Maws, who kept a scrapbook with all sorts of stories about King and other black people. Pete took every *Life* magazine and searched it for any news about black people. He did the same with newspapers. It was a big scrapbook.

Pete told me when King was shot. It was early evening, before we opened. He and my father were huddled outside the concession stand. Gary and I were told about it, and my father asked if I was ready to run the projection booth. Pete wanted a night off, the only time since 1960 that he had missed a show. I only missed one changeover that night, and Pete was very proud of me when I saw him the next day.

I own two indoor movie theatres in Jacksonville today, and none of my projectionists has ever had to make a changeover, nor have they ever had to change a carbon arc. With xenon lamps and single giant reels that never skip a frame, the technology is cleaner and simpler. Just flip two switches.

That night in April of 1968, I had Gary right beside me in the booth. You would have thought that those two old Simplex E-7 projectors had been made out of crystal, so precise and careful were our movements. I had seen Pete throw reels on with one hand and slam down the door of the E-7 after changing a carbon. Gary and I were afraid that a heavy breath would split the film, and film splicing was not yet one of our skills. It was a strange perspective that night, watching the big screen through that small window in the booth.

Near the end of the night, after the concession stand had closed, Alice and Polly came to the booth. Luckily, the last reel had already started, so all we had to do was close the shutter and turn off the sound switch. Anything more complicated at that point would have required our full attention, and Polly made that impossible.

Alice lit a cigarette, but I made her put it out. She refused at first, but when I told her Pete would smell even a little bit of smoke, she relented.

"Okay, Iz, this is Pete's place. You're right. He deserves some respect," she said.

Polly surprised me.

"Oh, Alice, give it up," she said, like she was exasperated.

Alice was putting the snuffed Winston back into its crushproof box.

"You got a problem, Pollywolly?" Alice said. Gary and I knew to step back.

"Not as many as you do," Polly snapped. Gary and I stepped farther back. Neither one of us was as brave as Polly, but neither were we as foolish.

"I'll ignore that, cracker girl. Just chalk it up to monthly bloat," Alice said with an edge.

"Sure, but my bloat only comes once a month."

Gary finally interrupted.

"Hey, can someone tell me and Abe what's going on?"

"Parrot girl here is still upset because I made her get a fresh burger for a customer. No big deal, just a fudging fresh burger to replace one his kid had dropped. No fudging big deal," Alice said, looking at me.

"Not once, Alice. Not once. At least three times tonight. Every time some pickaninny whined, we're handing over more free food. You'd think we were the welfare office," Polly said.

"Did it cost you a godblessed dime?" Alice asked.

"That's not the point," Polly shot back.

"And the point is?"

"The point is that I'm tired of niggers thinking I owe them more than anybody else! And I'm tired . . ."

How often have you discovered something about someone that you could not have imagined, something so ugly that at first you cannot believe that it is actually true, even if they show you face-to-face?

". . . tired of having you lecture me. I was there when they integrated my high school. You weren't. All of them came in so high and mighty, and they ruined it all. Both of you"—pointing singly to Gary and me—"went to that lily-white Catholic school. You never had to see it like I did. You'd know. You'd be different."

She was right. I knew that Gary and I had been insulated. In my life up to then, Pete had been the only black person I had spoken more than a few sentences to. Still, I wish Polly had stopped telling us how she felt. Especially there, in Pete's booth.

"But, Polly, why tonight?" Alice asked, her voice suddenly very conciliatory. "Why tonight of all nights? You never said anything before."

"I don't know! How should I know? I just wish things were like they were before. I mean, I'm sorry, I'm really sorry that he got killed, but he brought it on himself. He really did. I really believe that. I really am sorry. I really am . . . but . . ."

And then Polly started to cry. First a shudder, a sniffle, and then she broke down and sobbed, sitting on the stool that Pete used to see out the projection window. Gary and Alice and I did not say a word for a long time. After a while Alice walked over and knelt in front of her. Then she did something odd, something Gary and I never had the nerve to mention again. She kissed each of Polly's knees, and then she reached up to take Polly's hands away from her face, kissed each palm, and then whispered something in her ear, a long whisper that excluded Gary and me. Polly just kept nodding her head, and her crying slowly stopped.

Alice stood up and walked back to Gary and me. There were ten minutes left in the movie.

"Gary, Polly wants you to show her how to run the projector

after we close. You know, show her how you keep the picture on the screen even on windy nights. Will you do that?"

"But Abe knows more than I do," Gary said. "We'll both show her." I have always thanked Gary for the effort to include me.

"Nope, I've got plans for the young Lee," Alice said, turning to me. "And I need a cigarette. Iz and I will be on the patio if you want him. Think you can handle it?"

"You have plans for me?" I asked, disappointed that I was not going to be allowed to stay.

"Oh, big plans, Iz." Alice laughed.

An hour later, with the concession stand cleaned and the field almost empty, with Louise off for her nightly swim, this time by herself, Alice and I sat on the patio and watched the first three reels of The Graduate. Gary was flawless.

Alice was throwing kernels of popcorn up in the air and catching them with her tongue. Sometimes I would knock one away just before it landed, and she would kick me. As Benjamin Braddock was on the screen in front of us, resting on the bottom of his parents' swimming pool in his new scuba gear, Alice told me how my life was about to change.

"I want you and Polly to have sex," Alice said, but those weren't her exact words. "You both need each other."

"Alice! Polly won't come near me, you know that," I said, but then I thought she might be teasing me. "Are you serious? I mean, how can you be serious? She's three years older than me, and she . . . she . . ."

"She doesn't like dark skin? Is that what you want to say?"

I knew how Polly felt about me. Gary had told me some of the things she had said to him. Not mean things, but just casual remarks about how I was "too brown." I was ashamed to admit to Alice that what was really bothering me was how I was beginning to feel about myself. Polly made me want to be white. That scene in the booth, in particular, had made me all the more insecure.

"That's one reason she needs you," Alice continued.

"And why do I need her?" I said. "I don't love her. I'm not even sure I like her. I love . . . I love someone else."

"You *want* Polly. That's enough for now. Worry about love later. Worry about that for the rest of your life."

"Alice, you making a decision about me and Polly doesn't make it happen," I said, hoping I was wrong.

"Nope, and bears don't dump in the woods."

Photographs, Memories, and My Future

In a few years, I will be fifty. Dexter, my late and last child, named after Martin Luther King Jr.'s son, will not even be a teenager. My other sons will be in college. Grace will also be fifty, but she still looks like a much younger woman. She has not aged. I often wonder about the others. Alice will be fifty-five when I am fifty. When she was twenty, she looked much older. I wonder about now. How does she look? Did she ever get to be happy?

I have a picture of me and Alice taken on my sixteenth birthday. My mother was taking pictures of me and Louise, but Louise had refused to stand beside me that day. Alice replaced her. We are very close. I have my hands down at my sides, but she has her right arm over my shoulder. We are standing on the concession patio. Alice is wearing those sort of granny sunglasses that were popular in 1968, her dark hair tied up on her head to keep her shoulders cooler. I am wearing shorts, a sleeveless T-shirt, and holding a shovel. Alice called it "Florida Gothic."

There are other pictures from that day. Me and my mother, both my parents and me together, even one of my parents and Louise and me all together, a rare shot, since Louise was beginning her Greta Garbo leave-me-alone routine. A picture of Polly and Alice together, with Alice making rabbit ears behind Polly's head. A picture of my father and Polly side by side, probably closer than they should have been, my father's hand resting low on Polly's hip. Me and Pete, one of my favorite shots, us looking like a 1968 version of a multicultural poster. Pete and Judge Lester together, Pete with a severely distressed look on his face, the Judge looking bug-eyed. A picture of all the Flamingo men lined up by height. The Judge was at one end, then Gary Green, my father and me level with each other, and then the dropoff with Pete at the other end.

There is also a picture of the Flamingo women, with my mother in the middle, Alice behind her and off to one side, Polly and Louise in front. I often look at that picture. Louise has a copy, and she once told me that when she sees it she is always amazed by how different each one of them looked and yet how so very beautiful they each were in their own way. Louise has never been intimidated by her own beauty, and she is not afraid to be unattractive in some of the character roles she plays in the movies, but she seldom acknowledges beauty in other women. But she is right about that picture. Even in black and white, the four of them are stunning.

I also have a picture of me and Grace on my birthday. It was done in secret, back in St. Augustine. Alice had arranged it, telling my parents that she was taking me to town to help her look for a present for Louise. But we stopped and picked up Grace on the way and went to the plaza across from the downtown Cathedral. Alice took a whole roll of just me and Grace, twelve shots, just to make sure we would find one to keep forever. Of those twelve, the one we both chose was a shot that had not been posed. Alice had taken it while we were looking at each other and waiting for her to tell us to get ready for the next shot. We are sitting on a bench, Grace with her hands in her lap, me with an arm resting on the back of the bench but seeming to be reaching for her. We are close, but not touching. Our whole lives are ahead of us.

I have boxes with hundreds of pictures that my parents took, as if they had tried to freeze every moment in the lives of Louise and me. Grace and I take lots of pictures of our boys, and we have hours of videotape. Beginning with their first birthdays, we took film of every party. But the opening and closing shot is always the same, a close-up of their face with them talking directly into the camera. That tape is set aside until the next year, so that the final image of their face on that birthday is juxtaposed with an opening image of their face on the next birthday. We began with an 8mm camera, and when we got our videocamera we had all the old film transferred to videotape. Each year, Grace and I will watch the birthday tape, seeing that son age. For the older boys, we can see them become men in less than half an hour. Dexter is still evolving.

My parents never used a movie camera, even after my mother had suggested that we buy one. My father resisted for reasons none of us understood. I wish he had changed his mind. I would like to see films of us back then.

I can imagine what I would have wanted to keep in motion.

The time Judge Lester flew his Piper *under* the Bridge of Lions in St. Augustine after Alice had dared him. The Judge had agreed only if Alice was his passenger. She did not hesitate.

The time Louise acted out the role of the Virgin Mary at a St. Agnes Christmas program. She ad-libbed lines and stole the show from Jesus, making all of us weep as she wept at her son's crucifixion.

The time when Grace and I went to our senior prom, me in a tuxedo and her in a formal gown that showed me some of her chest for the first time. How we danced, and how Louise and Gary were in a dark corner kissing. That film would probably show Turner West in his chaperon's role, and my father sulking at the door of the gymnasium, there because he had promised my mother that he would be a part of that moment in his children's life.

Most of all, I wish we had filmed my parents at the Flamingo. I would like to see my mother move again, to hold on to her motion and her voice. There were moments unique to her. I would like to see her on the beach again, sitting there under that oversized umbrella to keep the sun off her skin, turning to look back over her shoulder as she heard me walking up to her, that smile, her hand motioning me to sit beside her. I would like to have recorded those times when my mother and father taught me how to love someone else by showing me how much they loved each other. How they would walk together on the beach, or look at each other in the Book Room as they listened to Frank Sinatra. How my mother would laugh at my father's excesses, causing him to stop and laugh at himself. I would have liked to be invisible and have an invisible camera and follow them around and record their lives without Louise and me, to hear the secrets that only they knew.

Dexter's favorite picture of me as a child is the one where Louise and I are sitting in my father's lap as he sits on the ground in a veterans' cemetery in St. Augustine on Memorial Day. We were both three, but Louise looks too tiny to be the same age as me. It is 1955, the summer my father tried to grow a beard. He is wearing sunglasses, and I am holding a daisy in my hand. His arms are around us, and the three of us are surrounded by hundreds of those uniform white headstones. In front of each headstone is a small American flag. Me, Louise, my father—the three of us are looking directly at the camera. My mother took the picture.

I promised Dexter that he and I could have our picture taken in the same spot in the same pose. It was his idea. Unfortunately, he does not have a sister to take Louise's place.

Grace has been asking me lately if I am going through some sort of midlife crisis. But then she always laughs because she says I have been going through the same crisis since she first met me. A crisis? Certainly not a professional re-evaluation. I have never *had* to work; my parents' money took care of that.

I went to college with Gary. He was an English major, and he took my father's dissertation and completely rewrote it until it became his own, and my father became a series of end notes. It was not plagiarism. His committee knew all about it, but Gary and my father had come to see American literature from the same perspective. Gary, however, worked harder at going deeper. With his Ph.D., Gary now teaches in Ohio. He proposed to my sister once. I had tried to tell him that she might not have the same feelings for him as he did for her. I reminded him that she was probably going to be an actress, but Gary thought he was in love. Luckily for him, she did not accept his proposal. Gary is still a bachelor, my sons' favorite "uncle." He lives in Florida every summer in one of the houses that I own on the beach. If anyone is having a midlife crisis, it's Gary. He is actually beginning to dye his hair, and he once brought a twenty-two-year-old undergraduate to spend the summer with him, a former student of his who worked hard at being her version of an intellectual. Gary has tenure, and he has been working on a book for ten years, fiction about his childhood. I have read parts of it. He is not Fitzgerald or Wolfe, but he is still my best friend. In fact, he often asks me why I am *not* having a crisis.

I have no career with which to be disappointed. I own much property. Empty lots, movie theatres, rental houses, twelve apartment buildings, convenience stores, one large office building in downtown Jacksonville, thousands of acres all over north Florida. But I pay other people to manage all that property and invest my other money. I give twenty percent of my annual income to charity or the church or to my sons' school. But twenty percent is probably too little.

I do not have a career. I have hobbies. I tell stories at the public library during children's hour. I coach the chess team at my sons' school. Most of all, I take pictures. I have my own darkroom, and I have sold my pictures to newspapers and news wire services. I take dozens of pictures every day, and my darkroom is full of rolls of film that have never been developed. I have even had shows of my pictures on display at museums and art galleries. It is a talent I am genuinely proud of, a talent that occupies that time when I am not with Grace and my sons. I take pictures of everything.

I own three houses in Florida. Two for my family and one for myself. There is the big house in Jacksonville for all of us. Grace and I designed it so that our children will grow up in one house and have that one place as their home forever. Even after the boys are grown and gone away, Grace and I will be living in this house, and they will know that we are always there in the same spot where they grew up and that they will always have a place to come back to. We also have a beach house south of Jacksonville. Much of our summers are spent there. It is close enough to Pete's caboose that Dexter and I can walk to see him whenever we wish, close enough that Dexter can even walk by himself whenever he gets in one of his moods. Pete is always home.

Grace does not know about the third house, nor does anyone else, not even Pete or my father. I have owned this third house since before I married Grace, over twenty years now. Her not knowing about it does not mean that I am trying to keep secrets from her. Grace knows everything about me, even about me and Alice. But she does not know about my private gallery.

It is in St. Augustine Beach, miles away from Pete's caboose and Jacksonville. It is one of a long line of undistinguished beach houses, certainly not like the house of a rich man. The coquina siding is dotted with large patches, the metal roof is rusted and painted over, and the large deck facing the ocean sags.

None of my neighbors, as far as I know, has ever seen the inside of my house. There are no bedrooms and almost no furniture. There is a kitchen with a small table. There is a photographic darkroom with a tiny bathroom: toilet, sink, and shower only. From the outside, the house looks like it has the usual amount of windows, each always with the curtains closed. But inside you would see that there are no windows. Solid windowless walls have been built over all the old inside walls. The kitchen and darkroom are at the west corners of the house. The rest of the inside has been gutted and turned into open space. The floor is polished oak. Four large skylight windows in the ceiling supply most of the interior light. The east wall, the one facing the Atlantic, is a series of glass sliding doors. From almost anywhere in the house, you can see the ocean.

The house is my private gallery. Hanging from the reinforced ceiling are three floating walls. The walls are movable because they are on thick wires that can be hooked to any number of the dozens of rings that are embedded in the beams. If I were to let you into this house, you could stand in front of one of these walls and the top of your head would be level with the top edge of the wall, your knees would be level with the bottom edge. Each wall is thirty feet long. Depending on my mood, they float perpendicular to the ocean, sometimes parallel, sometimes at an angle. These three walls are white, as are all the walls in my house. On these white walls are hundreds of photos, none of them framed; some have been there for many years, some went up yesterday and will be gone tomorrow.

Most of these photos were taken by me, but I have reserved the south wall for my parents: pictures taken by them or of them by their own parents. Old, old pictures of people I never met: my American ancestors. On this south wall are three important pictures. Like all my important pictures, they have been enlarged to almost life-size proportions.

The first is of my parents on their wedding day. They are standing in the center of a line of Carolina Lees and Scotts. My mother's gown is starkly white at the center of this picture, my father's tuxedo shirt equally bright. From a photographer's point of view, it is not a good picture. The light is uneven, the people not balanced (I said that to my father once, that the people in the picture were not "balanced"—you should have heard him laugh), and the all-Negro band in the background has too many blurry faces, as if they had intentionally been trembling to hide themselves from the camera's eye. I also have the original print of this picture, the eight-by-ten black-and-white that was framed long ago. On the back of that original are the signatures of every white person in the line. Not merely their names, their actual signatures. It was one of my father's projects as soon as he got it back from the official photographer. He personally went to see everyone in the picture and made them sign it.

The second important picture has my grandfather in it. Just him and my grandmother on their wedding day. Richard Henry Lee was his name, and in the picture he is the same age my father was when he got married. The two men look very much the same, more like brothers than father and son: short in height, light hair, a touch of arrogance in their smile. My grandmother, of course, looks nothing like my mother, but she does look happy on that day, as my mother did on her wedding day. This second important picture is more brown than black-and-white, and you can see where it must have been folded at some time in its past, leaving a ragged white crease across the middle.

This second picture was taken thirty years before the first picture. In this second picture, if you look very hard, you will see the future. Perhaps not. I see it now because I know what happened in the past. My mother told me the story about her in-laws, all about how my grandfather murdered my grandmother and then killed himself. It was inexplicable, my mother would say, gently shaking her head. They were not young and impetuous. There were no rumors about infidelity. Married for so long, they were seemingly still very much in love with each other. Of course, it was not a peaceful marriage, ever. Richard Lee, my mother would say, was not an easy man to live with. My father found his dead parents in their bedroom in their big house.

My mother told me all this in 1968. We were watching Alice and

Louise do cartwheels on the grass in front of the fort in St. Augustine. "Death explains nothing, Abraham," she said to me as she massaged my bare foot. "Only life."

The third important picture on the south wall is one of my favorites. My mother, me, and Louise on the beach by the Flamingo. Louise and I are probably four or five years old. The camera is behind us, and you can see me and my mother's back as we sit and look toward the Atlantic. I am sitting very close to her, my head resting on her shoulder. If you look closely, you can see Louise about thirty feet away, standing waist-deep in the ocean, looking at whoever is taking the picture.

The pictures on the south wall have not changed in twenty years. The other walls are not as permanent.

All those other walls are hung with my pictures. There is no particular order. Shots from a decade ago are next to yesterday's picture. That could change tomorrow. I once read a review of one of my exhibits and learned that I have three recurring themes in my photos: pictures of graves, of trains, and of the ocean. I suppose those are my public pictures, but my private house has few of those particular shots.

I have taken lots of pictures of trains, but most of them are not in my private gallery. I can't really explain why so many. I suppose I got interested when Pete and I took a train trip to Miami for his brother's funeral. In fact, the first train picture I ever took was not really of a train. It was of Pete sitting on the back steps of his caboose, a long shot, but close enough to exclude any signs that the caboose was on a drive-in theatre lot. Since then, I have taken thousands of pictures of trains, tracks, boxcars, cabooses, flatcars, old engines, passenger cars old and new, restored Pullmans, crossing signals, and flattened pennies.

Only one train picture in my gallery has remained constant. It shows the old Palm Coast Railway station in Palatka, where Pete signed up for his first job. Just the station, closed and boarded up, but with dozens of unemployed Palatka Negroes sitting on benches or standing around smoking.

Lots of pictures of Gary and Pete, Grace and Louise, my mother and father, all of us and more. All over the walls. Pictures of people that my family never met, people that Grace never knew about. Pictures of some of my college teachers, especially Dr. Male, who could never keep his pipe lit. Enlarged pictures of my wedding, pictures of my sons as babies, of buildings that I own, of my sons as toddlers, of Dexter on his first birthday, of my trip to Korea, of Dexter in the hospital when he had pneumonia and we thought he might die—pictures of everyone but me.

On the north wall is my favorite picture of Alice. She and Louise were singing that Bobby Goldsboro song about a girl named Honey and I had stopped them in mid-lyric. They had been laughing, and when I told them to freeze they instantly stiffened. But just as I pressed the button on my new camera, Louise stuck her tongue out and Alice pointed her middle finger at me. It was the last picture I ever took of her, and she was unaffectedly, genuinely happy.

Of the third kind of public picture that I seem to take, of the ocean, I have many of those on these private walls. Pictures of the Atlantic, especially, dozens of these are on the floating walls of my gallery. A series of pictures I took of the Atlantic were the first pictures I ever had published, in *Life*. My father was very pleased.

Of all the pictures I enter in contests, my ocean pictures win more often than my train or grave pictures. Each of those winning pictures is on my wall. A writer for *American Photo* once asked me why that kind of picture seems to be more successful than my others. I told him, but he did not believe me.

If you look closely, I said, you will see what I saw when I took the picture. Follow the lines, I tell you, and you will see how the water curves around upon itself, how the lines seem to meet an invisible stone and swirl around it to meet on the other side, how the colors of the water have a depth that no other substance has, how just under the surface there is another layer of line and color. And, if you look long enough at my pictures, at the lines and color and depth, you will see the face in the water that I saw.

Who Loves Whom?

When I looked at Grace I did not see Dexter in our future. I could not imagine myself a father someday, not when I was fifteen. I realize now that I was not even able to imagine being married to Grace. When we finally did get married, I told her how worried I was about the future. After all, I said, my only role models had been my parents. I was not trying to be funny.

"Oh, Isaac," she had said, laughing, as we danced at our wedding reception. "You worry too much. And, at least, *you* had a mother."

Only a few minutes earlier I had watched Grace dance with her father. Everyone was applauding, and I could see the two of them talk privately as they turned in circles. The band was playing "Moon River." I would have let them dance for the entire song, but Gary Green reminded me that I was supposed to cut in and take my wife away from her father.

After Polly and Alice came to work at the Flamingo, I found myself wanting to see Grace more and more. It was a paradox. Somehow, I knew I was going to have sex with Polly. Indeed, Alice had promised me. It seemed both inevitable and impossible. I might be working with Polly in the concession stand after school, or we might be going with Alice and Pete for supplies in Jacksonville, me and Polly in the backseat while Pete and Alice talked up front, me wishing the backseat were smaller while Polly seemed to be wishing it were larger, me dizzy with anticipation. At those moments when Polly's flesh was most exposed, I was absorbed in thoughts of a world of infinite carnal possibilities. But those moments were seldom prolonged, nor did they happen all that often. Except at night when the Flamingo was open, Polly Jackson usually avoided me. Away from her, I could imagine or remember the sight of her, but it was not the same.

After Alice came to work for us, she took me and Louise into St. Augustine every morning instead of my mother. We had to be at St. Agnes by seven-thirty, and my mother's morning classes were never before 10:00 a.m. (Flagler students were not early risers), so when Alice got a day job in St. Augustine she suggested that she drive me and Louise in while my mother slept late.

Alice was the only Flamingo employee who was ever allowed to have another job. My father had always demanded absolute and undivided allegiance from his people, but Alice was different. She worked at the Booksmith, an old bookstore at the foot of the Bridge of Lions, from eight until four during the week, and then back at the Flamingo for a full shift until midnight or after, and all day on the weekends. Even my father's inflated salary was not enough for her. When asked why she needed so much money, Alice said it was for her college fund.

Until the end of the school year in 1968, Alice drove me and Louise to school and then drove us home when she got off work at the Booksmith. A week after she began her chauffeur duty, Alice added another passenger. When we stopped the first time at the West Funeral Home I began to panic.

"Alice, are you crazy! Daddy is probably watching us right now. And Turner West, too," I said, looking back at the Flamingo, expecting to see my father running down A1A after us, and then at the front door of Turner West's home, expecting one of his sons to come out waving a shotgun.

Louise was unimpressed. "Izzy, calm down. You think we would be doing this if it wasn't okay?" But then she turned to Alice and said, "This is okay, isn't it?" Louise was not quite the actress she is today.

"Everything's kosher," Alice said. "Your mother and I made all the arrangements last week."

"But my father . . . ," I protested.

"Your father and I had a talk after I talked to your mother," Alice said, "and he said it was okay. Have *you* got a problem with this?"

"No, no, nothing," I mumbled.

"So, lighten up," Alice said. "And get out there and hold the door open for Grace."

I stood by the door, wearing my St. Agnes uniform, thinking that Alice had somehow jumped into the adult world of my parents and Turner West and was therefore part of a mystery that I would never understand. Then the tall and dark mahogany doors of the West Funeral Home opened and Grace stepped out into the morning sun.

I use that moment to tell my sons about how I love their mother. I do not really explain anything to them. Can you? Can you explain why you love someone else? You might be able to describe it. But explain? She stood in the doorway, in her white blouse and plaid skirt, and I remembered the first time I had seen her in class years earlier.

Grace walked down the steps toward me, and she never took her eyes off of me. Perhaps that was it. When I looked at her I saw only her, and I realized that I had missed seeing her even though I had seen her the day before in class. When I saw her that morning, I could see how happy she was to see me. I knew then that she *had* to see me to be happy. My sons are skeptical about all this. They are too young. When they are older I will tell them what I told Alice the night I lost my virginity. She wanted to know why I loved Grace.

"She makes me happy, Alice," I had said, exhausted. "And she is the only person I have ever known who makes me calm."

So, until June 1, I saw Grace five days a week. She would have heard stories about the Flamingo from the other St. Agnes students who had worked as temps the night or week before, and I would have to retell the stories, trying to make my father appear less crazy or Polly less of a nymphomaniac (Gary's contribution to the mythology of Flamingo life). As summer approached, I kept trying to figure out ways that I could see Grace as much as I was used to. I could not depend on her father relenting in his refusal to let her anywhere near the Flamingo, nor could I depend on my mother to "make arrangements," or on Alice to, as she said she would, "take care of it."

Tuesday and Thursday were the best days of the week. St. Agnes let out at two instead of three, so Grace and I had two hours to ourselves until Alice got off work at the Booksmith. My mother would give strict instructions on what we could and could not do. Still in uniform, we had to go to her office at Flagler, but only to let her see us, and then we were supposed to go to the Booksmith and wait for Alice. But Alice always told us to go entertain ourselves and be back at four for the ride home.

"You two get in trouble, and I will tell your mother that I had assumed that you were simply next door at the coffee shop," Alice had told us that first week. "I will, of course, be shocked and disappointed that you lied to me." She would laugh. "But I don't really worry too much. You two will never get in trouble."

Louise always went with us to my mother's office, but she never stayed with us after we saw Alice. That was fine with me and Grace. It was not fine with Alice. The first time that Louise did not even bother to go with us to the bookstore after seeing my mother, Alice got off work and searched St. Augustine until she found my wayward sister. For a week after that, Louise had to sit in the Booksmith where Alice could see her. The strange thing was that after a while Louise actually began to like staying with Alice. After Alice punched a Flagler tennis player, for harassing Louise on the Plaza, the Booksmith became a real sanctuary.

Left alone, Grace and I would walk for two hours, sometimes stopping at one of the tourist shops on St. George Street, pricing shells and T-shirts we would never buy, sometimes wandering through the Lightner Museum, another old converted Robber Baron hotel, across from the bookstore, sometimes buying a slice of peanut-butter pie at the Alcazar Restaurant and sharing it. The Alcazar was at the bottom of a drained indoor pool that used to be at the center of the Lightner, a pool surrounded by three floors of gentrified shops and offices that used to be rooms from which a plump capitalist could walk out his door and dive into deep water. We never had profound conversations. We seldom talked about *us*.

When the wind was not blowing too hard, we would walk across the Bridge of Lions and then walk back, stopping in the middle to look at the yachts and giant sailboats in the bay. Once a week, we picked out a different boat and tried to imagine ourselves sailing around the world. But first we had to pick out who we would want to be our crew and fellow passengers. I always started with Gary and Alice; Grace chose her father. I could not imagine my father on the same cruise with me and Grace and the others. Indeed, I did not want him along. But I often thought about my mother and father, me and Louise, just us, getting away from the Flamingo and traveling all over the world, away from Turner West and Judge Lester and Frank the Dog and even Pete Maws. Just the four of us, like it was in the beginning.

In those two months before the summer, the very best times were when Alice and my mother both got off work and took me and Grace and Louise to the old Fort Castillo de San Marcos. The fort had been built by the Spanish in 1672 with blocks of coquina that had been ferried across the bay from Anastasia Island. Sir Francis Drake had attacked it, as had dozens of Indian raiding parties. It was the focal point of St. Augustine, a national park site, where the tourists either began or ended their visits to the Oldest City in America. The grounds around it were immaculate and smooth, and the five of us would take a picnic basket there to spend an afternoon. With the fort blocking the wind coming in from the bay, we would sit in the spring sun and eat and drink and do nothing.

It was at the fort that I had asked my mother why she loved my father. Alice and Louise had gone inside the fort to look at the restored torture and ammunition chambers. Grace was asleep on the blanket beside us.

For a while, as my mother spoke, I did not listen to her. She was not looking at me, or at anything in particular. She had gently lifted Grace's head and put a rolled-up sweater under it for a pillow, talking and doing things at the same time, and I found myself just watching her. Of all the adult walls in my life, my mother was the most solid and impenetrable. That day in 1968 I had the oddest thought. I wished I had truly come out of her body, had been bound to her for those nine months. I thought that if I had been so connected to her then I would have been able to get inside of her now, to understand her, to have my heart beat when hers did, to understand her feelings without her having to tell me. I never felt that way about my father.

With my father, I never felt disconnected. I might have felt, at times, *too* connected. At times, I had to get away from my father.

". . . So long ago," my mother was saying. "We were both much younger, not much older than Alice is now"—but then she laughed—"if Alice was ever young. And he had such dreams about the future. You know, Abraham, your father could have done many things with his life."

When my mother spoke just with me, at times like this, her southern accent was much less noticeable and her voice much softer and slower. Years later, at her grave, my father would tell me about how "breathy" her voice was, especially after they had kissed for the first time. I stood there next to him, helping him up from where he had been kneeling, and I remember how I blushed. My father was a man who never seemed capable of intimacy.

"Like what?" I asked that day at the fort. "What could he have done?"

"Abraham, your father is a brilliant man. He could write wonderful stories. And he could draw. He almost became an architect, and he used to draw pictures of all the houses he was going to build for me, long before he thought about the Flamingo. But he went to graduate school to study books. He never planned on being a teacher. He just liked to read, and he liked to learn new things. With his parents' money, he never had to worry about a job, and he never had to worry about doing things on any schedule."

"But, Mama, he didn't do *anything*," I said.

"You are much too earnest and judgmental, Abraham, just like your father. How can you say he hasn't done anything?"

"Mama, we live in a movie screen! We show dumb movies . . ."

"Hush, sweet boy," she whispered, putting her finger up to my lips. "We live as it was meant to be. Most people in this world would trade places with us."

I wondered if she really believed that. I did not. I looked at her and then heard Alice and Louise behind us up on top of the fort's west wall. They were shouting to get our attention. My mother waved back at them and then motioned to a sleeping Grace. I could see Alice tell Louise to be quiet. When my mother turned back to look at me, I could see over her shoulder to where Louise was raising her middle finger to me. Alice punched her, but then Alice turned back to face me and she did the same thing. Louise punched her. Then they both disappeared back inside the fort.

"Is Daddy the only man you ever loved?" I asked my mother, thinking I knew the answer already.

"Oh, no, for heaven's sake," she said very quickly.

It was the beginning to an answer that I thought I did not want to hear. But I was wrong.

"No, no. I was in love several times before I met your father. My first was in high school. A really charming boy, a senior when I was a sophomore. Russell Tipton Banks the Third. My very first. Then there was Richard Shapiro, but my parents did not approve, for obvious reasons. Then there was Gordon Faulkner, the first boy who was taller than me."

"You loved all those boys?" I asked innocently. "You loved them?"

"I was in love with them, I was sure of that. And there were several boys I liked very much. In fact, when I met your father I was about to become engaged to Alexander Monroe Mitchell. He was going to be *it*, you know what I mean. He's in the Congress now. Always sends me a birthday card, every year."

"Daddy was the last person you ever loved?"

My mother looked directly at me and then leaned back on her elbows, her bare feet pointed toward me.

"Your daddy is the *only* person I've ever loved and been in love with. Ever."

"But you said . . ." I began to argue.

"It was not the same, Abraham, never the same." She looked at Grace and then back at me. "It only happens once."

I thought about Turner West.

"What's on your mind?" my mother asked.

"Do you like Mr. West?"

"I care for him very much."

"Do you love him?"

"Did you listen to me, Abraham? Did you hear me?"

"But Daddy . . ."

"Is wrong," she said sharply. "And he does a disservice to Turner and to himself by thinking otherwise. As do you."

I was in too far to stop. I had to be sure. It was important.

"But Mr. West loves you. Even Grace says that."

"I know that. I know that Turner West thinks he loves me. But he doesn't, really. He loves Grace's mother. And I hope that your father will still love me as much if I should die before him. Turner is a very lonely man, and he is afraid of losing his daughter like he lost his wife. But I am not his lost Grace, and neither is his daughter."

It was enough.

I would tell Alice later that night about this conversation with my mother. We were watching Judge Lester and Pete argue about who should take the film cans to the delivery truck. The Judge was trying to be helpful, but Pete refused to let him inside the booth.

"You should not have asked your mother about those things," Alice said as we sat on the patio. "Some things are private."

I knew she was wrong, but I did not contradict her.

"Do you know what she said right before you and Louise came back?" I said, knowing that she could not, but wanting her to ask.

"Yeah, sure, she said that your father had her permission to make a pass at Polly just as long as he did it in private."

"Alice! That's stupid. Just stupid. How can you say such a dumb thing!"

"Ask a stupid question, Iz, get a stupid answer," she said.

"It wasn't stupid, it was just . . . just . . . ," I stumbled.

"I know, Iz, it was just a figure of speech. I apologize. No reason to be crass. Your mother deserves better."

I did not want to talk to Alice anymore right then. So we just sat there and watched the Judge and Pete bicker. But I had to say something eventually, and Alice was the only one who might help me understand.

"I asked my mother what she had wanted to be when she was a little girl and was thinking about her future. I wanted to know what her plans had been. So I asked her," I finally said.

Alice was silent.

"She said that all she ever wanted to be when she grew up was to be happy. Nothing specific, just to be happy," I said.

"Is she?"

"Very," I said, using the word my mother had used.

Alice just nodded.

Patriotism

Before the Great Fire, the most dramatic thing that happened at the Flamingo in 1968 was when Pete Maws and Alice almost killed a fraternity boy from Flagler. Not by accident: They would have rendered that young man senseless and then dead. He should not have touched my sister.

"You kids ever thought about being in show business?" Judge Lester asked me and Louise as we sat in the backseat of Alice's car on the way home after school. It was the first of May. The Judge was in front with Alice, who was singing along with Bobby Goldsboro on the radio.

" '*See the tree, how big it's grown* . . . ,' " Alice sang, but I'm not sure she was singing with the same emotion that Goldsboro had intended.

"How about it? Do some acting?" the Judge continued, ignoring Alice.

"Judge, we are *already* in show business. And so are you," Louise said, looking out the window as we drove down A1A.

"No, no, I mean some real acting. Be a character, learn some lines, act out a story," he said, starting to twitch just enough to let us know that he had been thinking about this particular idea for a long time and had just worked up enough nerve to make it public. "I've got a promotion idea for your daddy, but it would mean using you kids. I even got a part for big mama here," he tried to joke, tapping Alice on the shoulder.

" '*But friend, it hasn't been that long it wasn't there* . . . ,' " Alice kept singing, looking back at us and then glaring at the Judge.

The Judge was always coming up with promotion ideas for the movies we showed at the Flamingo. When we played a John Wayne movie called *The War Wagon*, the Judge had dressed up like a cowboy and driven a covered wagon rigged up like a tank through downtown Jacksonville. He could not drive a car, so you can imagine how he handled two live horses, both of whom had bowel problems. But he did get his picture in the newspapers, and that is the essence of promotion: free advertising.

" '*Kinda dumb and kinda smart . . . ,*' " Louise began to sing along with Alice in harmony with Bobby Goldsboro.

The Judge was being ignored, and he knew it, but he was also used to it. If anything, the Judge was persistent.

"Your daddy asked me to come up with something for the big one this week," he said, directing his pitch to me alone.

The "big one this week" was another John Wayne picture, but one that had been universally panned by every serious movie reviewer. My father and the Judge, however, had convinced themselves that all *The Green Berets* needed was the right promotion. My father had booked a second feature with *Berets* that he thought was a stroke of genius—*The Sands of Iwo Jima*—but only the Judge saw the genius in my father's choice. *Sands* had probably already been seen by every John Wayne fan in north Florida.

"We get us some uniforms from army surplus, some real-looking guns, maybe advertise that any vet in uniform gets in free, maybe get us a tank to park out front, get some paratroopers to put on a show before we open, have a flamethrower demonstration in the playground . . ." The Judge was speaking faster, almost in full twitch, and I found myself slowly getting interested even though I knew that the Judge was too late.

"So where do Louise and I fit in?" I asked. I should have seen the problem coming by the way the Judge stopped talking, took a deep breath, and did not look at me when he finally answered slowly.

"Well, I thought, you kids being Asian, we could have you dressed up like some Vietcong and have you maybe attack some of us who were dressed up like American soldiers, maybe me and Gary, or maybe we could have a shootout between us and, you know, maybe capture you and . . ."

The Judge meant no harm, I knew that, and I was willing to forgive him, and in its own Barnumesque way the idea made sense. But Alice did not give us time for reflection. Before he could finish, she had swerved off the narrow road and slammed to a stop on the sandy shoulder.

"Get out, you piece of crud," she said, reaching across him and opening his door.

"Look here, Alice, you got no right to tell me to do anything, and I ain't getting nowhere," the Judge said, sitting rigid and looking her right in the eye.

"Get out, Harry, while you can still walk," Alice said very slowly.

I was silent. Only a few seconds earlier we had all been singing or joking, but here we were about to see a test of wills. It was no contest. The Judge crumbled, fortunately for him.

"Look here, Alice, I already talked to Mr. Lee about all this, and he thinks I got some good ideas. Says we might do some of them. Says the picture is a natural for some promotion. Says . . ."

"Did he say you could use his children as prisoners of war? Did he say that, Harry?" she said, and I could see her clenching her right fist.

"Well, no, he didn't say yes, but he didn't say no either, so I'm thinking he was still thinking about everything," the Judge said as he scooted himself backwards toward his door.

I looked at Louise in the backseat with me. She was not actually crying, but I recognized the look on her face, that look of despair like the day Frank had turned on her. Then I looked back at Alice and had a strange reaction. I looked at her and thought only about how pretty she was at that moment. Perhaps it was the angle, behind and off to her right, but I had never seen her look so attractive. She had always been beautiful, but it was an adult beauty that had kept her in a different world from me. But then I blinked, and Alice was an adult once more.

"Have a nice walk, Harry, and keep in touch" were Alice's final words to him that afternoon. In a second, Judge Lester was shrinking on A1A. I looked out the rear window to see him disappear as we drove off.

"Alice, you didn't have to do that," I said from the backseat. "He didn't mean to be—"

"Shut up, Abraham." She cut me off, not looking back. "I'm preparing a speech for your father. You just stay out of the way when we get back. And Louise, you get yourself up front with me. I want some company."

Louise climbed over the front seat. None of us spoke for the rest of the trip home.

Alice did not confront my father as soon as we got back. She waited for my mother to return from St. Augustine, and then right before we opened that night she and my mother demanded that my father justify his existence. I expected him to wither in the face of those two six-foot women, but he was surprisingly firm.

"Both of you relax. And get your stories straight before you start jumping on me," he said, a note of disgust in his voice that was tinged with disappointment.

He was in his pirate costume. I was standing with the three of them just outside the box office. The Judge was lingering near the exit, afraid to get too close because he knew he was the topic of conversation.

"I never said that Louise and Abraham would have to do anything like that," he said, looking at my mother directly. "Have you gotten to dislike me so much that you would think I could actually humiliate my own children? Have you?"

My mother was silent, but Alice was unrepentant.

"I think you are capable of almost anything. I think that you have created a universe with you at the center. I think that you . . ."

My father was getting genuinely angry.

"Alice, who do you think you are! You think . . . you think . . . you think you are part of this family. You think Abe and Louise are your children, or you think they're your brother and sister. You think you know all there is to know about me and my family, but you don't. You never will. Nobody will. Not you. Not"—turning to my mother—"not even Turner West knows enough about me to criticize me."

My mother finally spoke, her voice clear but soft.

"All this is unnecessary. Alice, if Hubert says he had no intention of using the Judge's idea, then we should accept that. Hubert, I am sorry I overreacted. You are an extravagant man, I know that, but I know that the children will be safe with you," she spoke and reached out her hand to touch his arm. "Please forgive me."

With that request, my mother destroyed my father. He began to cry, putting his arms around her, sobbing into her shoulder.

I looked at them, and I can see them now from almost three decades' distance, the enduring mystery of my life. I would never know enough about their life before me and Louise, their life away from us, those walks on the beach, those moments alone together in the Book Room, those whispered or unsaid exchanges about Turner West, those plans they had for an old age together, those plans never achieved because my mother died too soon. I looked at them and could not understand why my father was crying. I could not feel his sense of impending loss. His world, I now understand, was slipping away. As I tell you this now, I am the same age my father was then. It took me that long to understand.

I looked at Alice, trying to make eye contact with her, trying to make her come away with me and leave my parents alone. But she would not look my way. I think I know now what she was feeling, but I might be wrong. Alice wanted to be inside my parents' embrace. But at that moment she had been excluded, pushed out of the circle. Alice wanted to be between my mother and father. I was sure of that, or so I thought.

All over America in 1968 *The Green Berets* played to the disdain of sophisticated movie critics. It was a box office disappointment in most places, but not in the South of Hubert and Edna Lee. On that opening night at the Flamingo, the spell of my parents' embrace was broken by the blare of a Ford pickup's horn. It was at the head of a line of a hundred cars that were impatient to see John Wayne roll back godless Communism and teach the cynical journalist David Jansen that America was doing God's work in the world. Opening night was a sellout. Judge Lester had not had to do a thing to get the public's attention. Vietnam was simply an extension of the untamed American West, and the Vietcong were simply Indians in black pajamas. All week long, and then through a holdover week, every shrimp boat in north Florida rearranged its fishing schedule to be offshore, an armada of nets and rubber boots. With the closing credits, foghorns moaned their patriotic climax.

A half hour into the picture, I knew I should have stayed in the concession stand. Gary knew it too. "Abe, have you been hearing the same thing I'm hearing?"

He had been walking with me checking the single-driver cars. We had already found three, each suddenly with a full carload, usually all male. We had been asking for their ticket stubs, but the response was always "Hey, man, you gotta be kidding. We tossed them as soon as we got in." We would point out that the car tag had been noted at the box office and that the car they were in had driven onto the lot with only the driver buying a ticket. With other movies, the occupants would usually be so embarrassed that they would pay up and buy a ticket from the special roll that I always carried. That first night of *Berets,* the typical response was "That's tough" or "Kiss my backside." And then as Gary and I walked away we could hear someone mutter something about "gooks and fairies."

After the third angry profession of innocence, I looked for my father.

"Abe, let's forget it for tonight," he said. "We'll check them all at the box office starting tomorrow night, before they get on the lot. The Judge and I will handle it. The rest of tonight, you and Gary just keep your eyes peeled for trouble. But you are *not* to do anything. You understand? Just come get me."

Gary was relieved. "Thanks, Mr. Lee. I think you just saved our butts. This is not a Christian audience."

My father and I both laughed at Gary's understatement. Gary could be funny sometimes, more so as he got older.

At intermission, Gary and I stayed near the concession stand. Say what you will about patriotism, those people were big eaters. The intermission trailer usually lasted twenty minutes, not including any separate previews of coming attractions. Dancing cups of Coke, barrels of popcorn, M&Ms jumping into chocolate vats, wieners roasting on an open grill—twenty minutes of sensory overload designed to provoke a conspicuous consumption of sugar, salt, butter, and meat. But the crowd that night, and for two weeks, did not need artificial stimulation.

That first night, Alice did not leave her place at the cash register. I offered her a break during a rare slack period, but she just shook her head. I could tell she was still thinking about that scene before we opened. At intermission, I stood a few feet behind her, scanning the food trays and shirt pockets, looking for any food that might have been conveniently "forgotten," like all those missing ticket stubs. Right at the busiest time, I made the mistake of doing my job the way I had always done it. I saw this young man, wearing a Cardinals baseball hat and a Madras shirt, stuff some Hershey bars inside his shirt and then work his way through the line to the checkout spot. Going past Louise and Polly, he had suggested that we should be selling beer for these hot nights. Louise made one mistake: She agreed with him.

As he reached the cash register, I leaned forward and whispered to Alice about the hidden Hersheys.

"Will that be all?" she asked in her usual voice, staring him right in the eye.

"You bet, honey," he said casually, "unless you're selling something else I didn't see back there in line."

At that moment, a cold chill went through me. I recognized this hulking young man as one of those boys I had earlier asked for a ticket stub.

"Yeah, Duke, I'm selling Hershey bars," Alice said. She was speaking to this young man at the same time she was ringing up sales from the other concession line on a second cash register. The one line was going along quickly; the Cardinals cap's line was stacking up, waiting for him to pay. Everyone was in a hurry to get back to their cars to see John Wayne kill some more Asians.

"Hershey bars, you know," she said calmly, "the kind with nuts."

The young man thought it was the perfect straight line.

"Don't need no nuts, honey, I carry 'em with me."

Before he could finish smiling, Alice had reached across his tray and into his shirt to pull out two melting Hershey bars.

"Then you won't need these, will you . . . honey," she said, tossing them back to me. I remember wishing she had not done that.

The Cardinal was about to say something to her, but as soon as he saw me he just shrugged and paid his bill. He walked past her and muttered to me on the way out, "You'd be smart not to come outside, you chink fag, and you better hope I don't see you somewhere else."

That night, for almost five hours, I heard it all around me. First I was Vietnamese, then I was Japanese. The last night that *Berets* played, after a profitable two weeks, I told my father about all the harassment.

"I should have known all that, have seen all that, have seen what would happen to Louise. Oh, Abraham, maybe Alice is right. I would have pulled that film off the screen that first night and told Warner Brothers to send me a bill, if I had been paying attention," he said. "But I wasn't."

My father found out what happened to Louise that night, but she and Alice did not tell him the whole story, nor did I. So how was he to make the right decision?

With *The Green Berets,* the Flamingo started its usual schedule of repeating the first movie after the second. A customer could come in at intermission and still see both movies if he was willing to stay until past midnight. Usually, however, the field was almost empty after the second show, so we could close the concession stand after a last call, which was given as soon as the first movie began again. Then Gary and I would go around the field turning off the speakers or picking them off the ground and checking for damage. Alice, Polly, and Louise would be cleaning the concession stand, getting it back to surgical purity for the next night. The Judge would stay near the box office and exit gates. My father would be in his Tower office counting money or having his nightly single vodka tonic. After the lot was finally cleared, his ritual was to walk the perimeter of the entire field, locking the gates at the exits and then locking the chains across the box office driveway. Everything surveyed and secured, the

Flamingo was closed. My mother, especially if it was a weeknight, would already be in bed, or she might, if still energized, be reading a book. In 1968, the two of them seldom went to bed at the same time.

That opening Wednesday night in May, north Florida was a steambath. Sweat was everywhere. I had stayed in the concession stand to help them finish cleaning while Gary patrolled the ramps.

I tried to talk to Alice, but she had declared a ten-foot territorial boundary around herself. If your boat wandered in, you could expect to be sunk. Polly, however, was in an unusually liberal mood, especially to me.

"Izzy, you doing anything after we close?" she asked me as I mopped the floor while she held the bucket steady.

I almost gasped. I knew what she was about to say.

"Some homework, I guess," I said, trying to be nonchalant.

She howled, turning Alice and Louise around to look at us.

"You gotta be kidding. Homework! Oh, Iz, you iz priceless. You iz also crazy. You," she said, actually touching my hand, "you have got to relax."

I blushed. It was a mistake, but how could I control it?

"Look at you," Polly said. "You're actually getting darker. But you're still cute."

I was a tanned, blushing Korean, and I was thankful that Polly seemed willing to overlook the blood of my race and the blood of the moment. All night long I had been the object of derisive vision, a manifestation of every white man's burden. The looks had never been subtle, nor the comments kind. Alice told me later that most of those comments had been made by customers who assumed that I did not even speak English. It was the first time in my life that I felt I was on display, a monkey in the imperial zoo.

"Polly, would you like me better if I were white?" I blurted out, shocking even myself. I wondered if she could see my leg trembling.

Louise and Alice were waiting for an answer.

"Absolutely, positively, Iz," Polly answered without hesitating, and my face must have told her how much she had just hurt me.

I think of Polly now, probably married a couple of times, some children, her body betrayed by cellulite and gravity, a drinker but not a drunk, a smoker who probably tries to quit on a regular basis, a watcher of television but not of movies, but still a good mother, a good person. I think that now because I remember how at that moment back at the Flamingo when she had seen my face, and I had seen her own face wince when she saw me, I remember how she rescued me almost at the same time she had cast me aside.

"Yeah, I wish you were as white as Paul Newman, Iz, but I really wish you were taller, older, bigger, and richer. How's that for a wish list? You got a chance to make that list?"

Alice yelled from the cash register, "Give him time, Polly, he'll be as rich as Rockefeller. He can buy you a couple of white guys for Christmas."

Polly laughed and took a deep breath, testing the limits of her sweaty pirate blouse.

"Okay, you can be my sugar daddy when you get older," she said to me. "For tonight, you wanna swim with me and Gary after we close up?"

"I think so," I said without really thinking, but Polly was still being generous.

"Well, you think about it, and we'll *see you* on the beach."

All I did for the next thirty minutes was think about *it*. I forgot the slings and arrows of outrageous fortune, the slurs of Florida rednecks, the towns without pity. I thought about *it*.

Alice was singing that Bobby Goldsboro song again, crooning, " 'And, Honey, I'm being good . . .' "

"Alice, enough! Have some mercy," yelled Polly, snapping me out of that half-hour reverie.

Alice was dancing with Gary at the cash register, half slow and half bop, spinning as she sang about trees and dumb girls in heaven. Then she stopped abruptly.

"Where's your sister?" she asked.

I looked around. Louise was gone. The second showing of *Berets* would be over in fifteen minutes. Gary had come in from the field after turning off the speakers.

"She was talking to some of those guys out on the patio," he said. "I thought you knew she was out there."

Gary went to the patio while Alice and I went out the back door of the concession stand. Polly stayed to watch the inside. Louise had vanished.

Behind the concession stand were five ramps, but there were only three cars in sight.

"She probably went back to the Tower," I said, trying to offer a safe scenario. There was not a breeze stirring. I looked at the screen. John Wayne was in a helicopter blazing away at some huts below. Alice just stared at each of the distant cars, one to the other.

"Alice . . . ," I began to say. I had recognized the car in the farthest corner of the lot. "Alice, that guy who took the Hershey bars. That's his car up there."

"How do you know?" she asked, staring at it.

"It was one of the cars Gary and I checked for single drivers. But it was parked down front before. They've moved it back there. Probably got some beer. You think?"

"Isaac, go get Pete and Gary," she said calmly. "Tell them to meet me at that corner."

"You're not going up there by yourself, are you?" I asked, hesitating, afraid of letting her go up there alone.

"Just a stroll, Isaac, just a casual walk to see how our customers are enjoying the show. You just get Pete and Gary and follow me."

At that instant, we both heard the same scream. Alice went toward the sound; I went for Pete and Gary.

By the time we three got to the corner of the lot, Alice was confronting two young men outside the car. The Madras shirt was one of them. Despite the arrival of reinforcements for Alice, he was not impressed. Pete was short and black; I was short and Korean; Gary was out of breath.

"The cavalry has arrived." He snorted. Then he recognized me. "You looking for a candy bar or just some chopsticks?"

Alice tapped him on the shoulder to get his attention.

"You tell your friends to let that girl out of your car," she said, eye to eye with him.

"In due time," he said. "Due time. She's got to sort of put herself back together before she gets out in public again."

Alice walked to the car door and touched the handle. The Madras' friend put his hand on hers, but he was not expecting how strong Alice was. She threw his hand off and opened the door.

The Madras then stepped between her and the open door.

"Look, Wonder Woman, don't be getting the wrong impression. We're old friends of Louise here, and she accepted our offer of a cold beer on a hot night. Ain't that right, Louise?" he said.

From inside the dark car came a weak "Yes, that's right."

The four young men, two outside and two inside with Louise, were not strangers to Louise. The four were Flagler students, and Louise had once been introduced to them in St. Augustine by her other male friends at Flagler. She had lied about her age, and they had chosen to ignore her St. Agnes uniform. When their friends had told them about swimming in the ocean with Louise and Polly, the four young men had made certain assumptions about Louise. Such assumptions might have been wrong, but they were understandable. The young men were in college, and Louise had probably led them to believe that she was one of those girls who would be the reward in their lives for being young and handsome and wealthy enough to look and sound like they deserved the best that life had to offer. In a few years, Louise would devour such young men and leave their bones and bloody flesh on the side of the road, but on this night she was a month away from being sixteen years old.

"Get out of the car, Louise," Alice said.

My sister emerged from the lair of the young men. She had obviously been crying, and her blouse was ripped. She held on to Alice's hand and stood up next to the door. Alice made her turn completely around, as if checking for damage. Luckily for those boys, we had arrived before things had gotten too far out of hand. Then she made her go over to where Gary was standing.

"You and your friends had better not show up here again. You don't come back here, and I promise not to tell her father," she said to the Madras shirt.

He did not recognize a generous offer.

"Who do you think you are to tell us what to do? You her mother? Her guardian angel? You ain't got the right to keep me out of anywhere me and my friends want to go," he said.

"Gary, take Louise back to the concession stand," Alice said.

His arm around her, Gary escorted Louise away. He and I still smile about that moment. For weeks, all Louise could do was tell her friends at St. Agnes how Gary had saved her. Gary never disputed her perception. He thought being her hero would cause her to fall in love with him. It would not be enough.

With only a few minutes left in the *Green Berets,* I knew Pete had to get back to the booth, but he did not seem to be in a hurry. The young men were also in no hurry to leave.

"You know, we'll be back," the Madras shirt said, his arms folded across his chest as he leaned on the hood of his car. "You can't watch this place all the time. Or we might just see little Louise in town when you are not around. We might—"

"CV-3342," Pete interrupted. He was standing behind the car. None of us understood.

"CV-3342," he repeated. "Your license. This will tell me where you live, or your daddy, since this is probably his car. You bother us again, and we will find *you.*"

The closing credits were about to come on the screen, and there was nobody in the booth to shut down the projector. In a minute or two, the world's largest screen would be glaring white and illuminating the whole field.

"Are you threatening me . . . nigger?" the Madras shirt said, stepping toward Pete while his friend went around the other side. I could see the two in the car start to get out of the backseat. Luckily, it was only a two-door car. Instinctively, I slammed the driver's door shut. Alice stood next to the other door.

There we were: an almost-dwarf Negro, a fifteen-year-old Korean, and Alice the six-foot girl. I remember wishing that my father could see me then. I was absolutely terrified and exhilarated. Something in me hated those young men, but that something paled in comparison to how Pete and Alice seemed to be feeling at that moment. Pete would tell me later: He and Alice were about to be set free. For different reasons, but still set free.

The Madras shirt stood on one side of Pete, his friend on the other. If Alice or I moved, his friends could get out of the car.

"I asked you a question, nigger. Are you threatening me?"

Pete stepped back and pulled out a three-foot crowbar from inside his pants. It was as tall as his belt. Before he spoke, he smashed the right taillight.

"Yes" was all Pete said.

The Madras went berserk.

"You mother coon! You black sonuvawitch!" he shrieked. But he did not notice that his friend was backing off.

Pete smashed the left taillight.

"Stop it! Stop it!" screamed the Madras, but he was paralyzed.

"Denny, Denny, we ought to go now," the Madras' friend had finally said as he edged away. Alice opened the passenger-side door and let him slip inside. "Denny, we better go," the friend said from inside the car.

On the screen, John Wayne had his arms around a young Vietnamese boy, telling him that *he* was the reason that America was in his country.

Denny the Madras took a fateful step toward Pete.

With three centuries of racial history propelling his baseball swing, Pete hit the young man across his stomach with that crowbar. You could hear a lifetime of white air belch out of him as he crumpled to the ground. For a full minute, he crawled on all fours gasping for breath. Then Pete told his friend to get out of the car and help him, but the friend did not move. So Alice lifted the Madras up and sat him on the trunk.

"Got work to do, Alice," Pete said as he handed her the crowbar. "Come see me later, okay?"

Pete ran as fast as he could back to the booth, his short legs surprisingly long-strided. The screen never went white, and within ten minutes the lot was empty except for the Madras' car. Alice had refused to let it leave. She waited until the Madras was coherent again so she could deliver one final message.

"Can you understand me?" she whispered to him, her face up against his, and with the curved head of the crowbar hooked just inside the top of his shirt. With every breath she took, Alice jammed the head of the crowbar into the young man's chest. "You listen to me. You hear me. You will never come here, ever again. And if you see me or Louise or Abraham or *anybody* I know, then you cross the street and act like we're invisible. You understand me?"

The Madras sat on his trunk with his eyes closed, but he kept nodding his head while Alice determined his future.

"You tell your daddy, and your friends tell their daddy, that y'all got jumped in St. Augustine. A gang of Georgia white trash out looking for fun. You were the fun. You ever cause us trouble again, you and your friends will be in jail for rape or attempted rape or something. Your daddy ain't got the money that Louise's daddy does. Your daddy ain't got the connections that Louise's daddy does. You understand me? Her daddy has more friends in the sheriff's department than you got hairs on your crotch. You understand? *DO you understand me?*"

The Madras kept nodding.

As frightened as he was, I knew that he did not really appreciate how much danger he was in. I could see Alice grinding her feet into the gravel as she spoke to him, her one hand pumping the iron bar into his chest, the other holding on to his belt.

"Please, lady, can we go now?" said a voice inside the car.

"One last thing," she said to that voice. Then, in one motion, she yanked the crowbar back, ripping open the shirt, and raised it over her head, holding on with both hands, and, as the Madras youth and his friends thought she had gone completely insane, Alice swung the crowbar down, seemingly straight at his head, but angled to slice right past him and slam into the trunk with a metallic thump that they would hear for the rest of their lives. When the car drove off, the crowbar was still wedged in the trunk.

Me, too. I can still hear that thump.

Death in the Toilet

After the opening night of *Berets,* Alice made my father take a ride with her to Jacksonville.

"I wanted to apologize to him, Abe," she told me the second night of *Berets.* "But I also wanted him to think about booking a different kind of movie instead of all that John Wayne crud. Something for a mellower crowd."

"Did he agree?" I asked her as we were replacing some missing letters from the Cowboy marquee. I knew enough about the booking part of the movie business to understand that in the summer season there was no such thing as a "quick" booking. Everything was usually scheduled months in advance.

"He said he would look for something," she said, handing a giant, red-plastic *A* down to me.

"Did you tell him about Louise?" I asked, wondering if she had talked about anything other than movies or crowd-control problems.

"She asked me to keep it to myself," she said. "I told her we would all keep it to ourselves. No need for your parents to know everything about your lives."

"That's true enough," I said, looking over toward the West Funeral Home, wanting Grace to suddenly appear.

"I also didn't tell him about you and Polly," Alice said as she came down off the ladder. "No need to make him jealous."

"But, Alice, nothing is going on between me and Polly. You know that."

"I know you didn't get to go swimming with her last night. But that was only because she and Louise were going over all the gory details about those Flagler boys. Things calm down, you and Polly will be pollywogging in the ocean."

"Alice, why do you have higher hopes for my love life than I do?"

"Who knows? Maybe I'm just a naturally optimistic person."

I looked her directly in the face.

"You're kidding, right?" I said, noticing that her hair was getting longer and her face was looking more and more like Natalie Wood's.

"You just passed the first test of adulthood, Iz, a subtle appreciation of irony. So, let's see how you interpret this bit of information: Polly has a special present planned for you for your sixteenth birthday."

"Yeah, right," I said, trying not to overinterpret. "And I'm sure she told you all about it," hoping that Polly had, indeed, given Alice all the details.

"Oh, Iz, I know all about it because I gave her the idea. You should be pleased to know that she was not uninterested from the very beginning."

Alice was smirking again.

"Alice, you don't have to tease me all the time, you know. You could—" I said, but she reached out and put her finger on my lips, rubbing it across them slowly.

"Shush, Iz, and cool your jets. I like you, and I like your sister. In fact, if I thought you could keep a secret I would tell you that I like you better than I like your sister. So, if you can keep a secret, I'll tell you that one day. And other things."

I did not speak. Her finger was tracing a line over and then around my mouth. I could not speak. I had never experienced such a sensation, as if all the blood in my body were being pulled toward my face and every nerve ending in my body was connected to my lips.

Alice leaned down and kissed me on the forehead, both of her hands holding my shoulders.

"When you get older, we'll talk," she whispered to me. "I'll tell you all about what Polly wants and how to make her happy."

I tell you all of this now, and I will admit that those were not the exact words. But they are close enough.

My father's penance for *The Green Berets* was a "woman's" picture titled *The Diary of a Mad Housewife,* starring Richard Benjamin, Frank Langella, and a wonderful actress named Carrie
Snodgress, who was a star after this movie but then seemed to disappear. *Diary* was proof that my father's real goal at the Flamingo
was not to make money.

The last week of May 1968, my father and I stood outside the
box office and waited for the lines to form. It was the first of the
seven lowest grossing days in Flamingo history.

"Abraham, would you remind me never to listen to your mother
and her sister Alice ever again about the movie business? Would you
do that for me?" he said, but I could tell he was not unhappy. If anything, he was amused. "Lord almighty, I told them. Women do not
come to the drive-in. Families come to the drive-in. Teenagers come
to the drive-in. Drunk rednecks come to the drive-in. But women do
not come to the drive-in. You know what I mean?"

"So why did you book it?" I asked, feigning ignorance.

My father took the indirect approach.

"Are you going to marry that West girl?" he asked, arching an
eyebrow at me.

"Daddy, I'm only fifteen, and"—I was getting bolder as I got
older—"if you keep making her father mad, I probably won't even
get to sit in the same classroom with her."

"Oh, Abraham, her father and me are irrelevant in the long run.
You'll realize that. If you love her, and only her, and can't see yourself getting old without her, then you'll marry her. Me and Turner
will get lost in the dust as you elope. Turner's problem with me is
not his daughter. But we'll talk about that when you're older."

"Daddy, what has all this got to do with this movie?"

"Love, my son, has got everything to do with everything."

Diary would be one of those weeks when we could all take a
deep breath and slowly exhale. I could feel that the first night. So
could my father, but he must have known it before I did.

"When I told the Universal booker in Atlanta that I wanted this
picture he told me I was crazy," my father said. He was sitting on
the chain that separated the two entrance lanes to the box office. My
mother was a few feet away, threading up the tickets and straight-

ening her cash drawer. Judge Lester was out on A1A, looking for cars. "Said this was a New York or an L.A. picture, not a Florida drive-in picture," he continued. "Said I better run a skeleton crew or have some monster promotion."

"So why did you book it?" I repeated.

Even the Judge couldn't come up with an idea on how to sell this picture. When he heard the title he thought it was another *Psycho*, and his eyes lit up. When I told him the plot, he gave me that glazed look he gets. You know the one.

"So why did you book it?" I persisted.

"Abraham, I already told you why I booked it. Told you a few seconds ago. You got to pay better attention, son, else the big picture is going to slip by you."

My father was calmer than usual. It was seven o'clock in the evening, still daylight, and still very warm, probably over eighty degrees. He was looking at my mother as she worked, and then she looked up and saw him. There was that smile, at first, that I had seen melt my father's heart, but then it faded. She turned away from him and started to clean the box office windows.

"Son, I'm going to have a drink. You want one?" my father said as we walked away from the box office, his arm across my shoulders. I was almost as tall as he, but we were still, both of us, short.

"A vodka toddy for me, Coca-Cola for you. How about it?" he said. "We'll make a toast. Get young Gary, pull Pete out of that booth, call in the Judge. The five of us, lift the grog and make a pirate toast."

I did not know what to say because I did not understand what he meant. He was slowly becoming that other person who was my father, the public showman, the master of hyperbole and gesture, the man who hated Turner West.

My father saw my hesitation.

"Doesn't matter, Abraham. Don't worry about it. But let me ask you a question, man to man, father to son, rich man to heir."

"Is this a serious question?" I asked him.

"Absolutely. A question of grave importance." And then he laughed. "Sorry, son, I really should get serious, I suppose."

"Is it about Mama?" I asked, afraid it was.

"Sort of, since she is the one who asked me to do it."

I waited.

"Turner West wants to put in a twenty-acre cemetery on that scrubby slope behind his building. Do you think he should be allowed to?" my father said, his arms crossed.

"Daddy, why are you asking *me* this question? And where does Mama fit into all this? And you?"

"You know, it makes perfect business sense for him. A classy dignified service and then a solemn burial nearby on land that slopes up and would give you a view of the ocean for eternity. If you were dead, you could see the sun come up every morning. Makes sense to me. And I know that he has been trying to get it done for years. All he has to do is buy the land."

"So why hasn't he done it?"

"Abraham, I own the land. Eventually, you will own the land."

"You own his land?"

"Look, when he started out in his business, he had enough money to get the lot his building is now on. Expansion would come later. But I came along, and I bought every piece of sand for miles around. I even tried to buy him out years ago. No deal. He said he was there first. That was his mistake. So, I own the land behind his building. You said it was *his* land. Well, it never was, and it probably never will be."

"So why are you asking me now?" I said, thinking I had been in another one of those conversations with my father in which he was really only talking to himself.

"Your mother wants me to sell the land to him," he said, shrugging his shoulders. "She says it would make her happy if I would do that."

I knew immediately what he was not saying. Selling that land to Turner West would be a monumental defeat for Hubert Lee. It only took a few seconds, but I deserted my father.

"I think you should sell it," I said. "I think you should leave him alone."

My father rolled his head from side to side, as if he were trying to work some nagging crick out of his neck.

"You're probably right," he finally said as he walked away to unlock the box office chain. "Probably right, you and your mother both. But I can't do it. Not now, probably never."

Diary opened on a Wednesday. We sold less than a hundred tickets. Thursday was even slower. Before we opened on Friday, my father promised Louise and Polly that they could get off work immediately after intermission. My father seemed unconcerned.

"This is good timing, actually," he said to me and Pete that Friday night. "School's not out until next week, and this last week in May is always a bust. Might as well use the time to recharge our batteries. Besides, I think Abe and Gary are happy I booked this one. Right?" He was winking at me.

I knew my father was referring to that scene in the movie where Frank Langella undresses the mad housewife. For almost ten seconds, the world's largest screen is filled with a vision of Carrie Snodgress' bottom. First, just her bottom covered by plain cotton underwear, and then a man's hands slide those panties down and off. But the camera never strays from her bottom. The shrimpers went crazy. Gary and I were not prepared the first time we saw that scene, but for the next six nights we both timed our ramp rounds to arrive at the concession patio and luxuriate in the bounty of female anatomy.

"How can anything be better than that?" Gary would say.

"I've seen better," I would say.

"In your dreams," Gary said the first time.

"No, I've seen Polly," I would say, and Gary would shudder with his own memory of that sight.

"Oh, God, yes. That"—pointing to the screen—"is the world's second-best rear end."

Alice conveyed our sentiments to Polly.

On Friday night, business was slower than expected at the box office, and it was obvious that the few viewers of *Diary* were not big eaters. It was the only Friday in Flamingo history that we did not open both concession lanes.

The few cars that did come to *Diary* were usually filled with groups of middle-aged women, some married couples, and some teenagers who thought it was a horror picture. Scary movies were always great date movies, a chance for teenage girls to cling to teenage boys, but the scariest moment in *Diary* was when Carrie Snodgress kept tapping on her husband's head, asking "Is there anyone in there?" as he ate dinner or watched television. With no screams or blood, *Diary* sent the teenagers to the exit gates long before intermission. The more ingenious teenage boys, however, quickly recognized an opportunity. They would simply move their cars to the back row and use the Flamingo as a motel, substituting their own form of foreplay in the place of a horror movie. Gary and I would act as their security guards, making sure they were not disturbed but also making sure we could see directly into the cars to see that everyone was still breathing. It was all part of our job.

My father was absolutely right about the lack of one particular audience for *Diary*: There were no families, and so we never had to unlock the playground. Except for one adventurous teenage couple whom we caught improvising on the merry-go-round, there was no motion under the Flamingo screen.

A half hour before the end of *Diary* on that Friday night, Alice surprised me and Gary on the patio. He and I had been arguing about whether God was responsible for every tiny detail of life or whether he had simply started the process and let life take its own course, with him, of course, knowing the final outcome. St. Agnes was a progressive Catholic school; Charles Darwin had not been erased from Western Culture.

"You boys still evolving out here?" she said.

Gary and I jumped as if we had been caught smoking by my father.

"Alice, who's watching the cash register?" I quickly asked, trying to shift some guilt back to her.

Alice ignored me.

"You know, you guys ought to write all these deep thoughts down. I especially think that Gary's idea that the female bottom is proof that God exists . . . I think that will seal the case for all those agnostics out there."

"I did not say that!" Gary protested.

"The trouble is, Gary, you haven't seen enough bottoms to make that observation. Take my word for it, a lot of butts out there make the case for Satan. Fat, saggy, hairy, and carbuncled—"

"*Alice!*" Gary and I both sang in unison, trying to preserve at least one of our youthful illusions. To this day, I have been afraid to look up the word *carbuncle* in the dictionary.

"Sorry, I forgot you guys were still just fifteen." And then she turned to walk back into the concession stand.

Left unsupervised, Louise and Polly had begun to throw frozen hamburger patties around like Frisbees. My father had once told me that the market exerted its own form of discipline, so, with no customers, my sister and Polly had become undisciplined. I expected Alice to go back in and restore order, but she was soon tossing those stiff chunks of meat along with the other two girls. Gary and I watched them through the big window in front.

"Why is it that they always seem to be having more fun than you and me?" Gary asked me, his eyes following Polly and Louise as they kept trying to put a frozen pattie inside the other's blouse.

"All part of some cosmic plan, I guess," I said, and Gary thought I was making a joke.

At that moment I saw a woman come in the side door of the concession stand. She was too old to be a hippie, but she was trying to dress like one: beads, scarves, and a zodiac stitched on her skirt. The woman stopped Alice in mid-toss, and I could see the pattie fly past Polly's head as the woman customer started pointing to the back of the building. Alice motioned for me and Gary to come inside.

"This lady says there is a strange smell in the restroom," Alice said.

"Okay," I said slowly, not sure what I was supposed to do about it. "Do you want me to cover the front while you go check it out?"

"No, Iz, I want you and Gary to go check it out," she said.

"Alice, it's the ladies' room," I said, thinking that that self-evident fact would determine who investigated.

"Iz, we have to get ready for intermission. We're still behind on some of the food prep."

"So I saw," I said.

Polly and Louise were suddenly very busy back at the grill and corn popper. Alice just stared at me and Gary.

"Be sweet, Iz, and do me this favor. Okay?" she finally said.

Gary and I looked at each other. Why not, we both seemed to be telling each other by mental telepathy.

We went to the restroom door and knocked loudly on it.

"Anybody in here?" I shouted. No answer. "Coming in!" I said, but I still waited for an answer. Not a sound. I was cautious because I had done this last year and walked in on a woman nursing her baby.

Inside the door, Gary and I wrinkled our noses. There was a distinct smell, some combination of the usual restroom smell and something else. Gary suddenly grabbed my arm.

"Abe, there's somebody in one of the stalls," he said quietly, pulling on me to back out of the room.

That was not too unusual. Sometimes a person in the toilet was too embarrassed to yell back at us when we were checking the restroom.

"Sorry, ma'am," I said politely. "We'll come back later."

We stood outside, away from the door. A couple of minutes passed, but nobody came out. *Diary* would be over shortly, and the toilet traffic would be nonstop for twenty minutes. I had a can of air freshener, forest bouquet, and needed to spray enough to get us through the intermission, but the woman in the toilet would not come out. I stuck my head back inside.

"Lady, we need to do some work in here. Don't mean to rush you, but I thought you might need to know."

My father had always told me that women were not to be disturbed when they were in the bathroom, a rule applied religiously in my relations with my mother and sister in the Tower.

I stooped down, surveying all the floor area, looking for telltale signs of some mess that would explain the smell. It was probably a toilet that had been overused and unflushed. I could see the woman's feet through that space between the floor and the bottom of the stall door. Her feet were pointing in different directions.

"Gary, go get Alice," I whispered to him.

"Send a boy to do a man's job" were her first words to me when she got inside the restroom.

"Alice, I think this woman is sick or something. She won't answer me."

Alice knocked on the stall door.

"Lady, you okay?"

No answer.

"Lady, I'm going to have to open this door if you don't answer me."

No answer. I was beginning to think the worst, so I told Gary to go get my father.

Alice tried to open the stall door, but it was locked from the inside. Then she got down on her hands and knees to look up under the door. There was only about six inches between the bottom of the door and the floor, not enough space to crawl under. I could see her let out a deep breath.

"Iz, go get your father," she said.

"I already sent Gary," I said. Alice was impressed.

"I think she's dead," she said, looking at me with that look she had when she was trying to figure out the answer to some significant question. "Dead as a frigging doornail," she said, but more to herself than to me.

Gary was soon back with my father and with Louise.

"Who's going to run the cash register?" Louise whined. "It's almost intermission time and me and Polly can't run everything by ourselves. We need . . ." And then she stopped, aware that all of us were looking at her like she was an idiot.

"We've got a dead woman in the toilet," Alice said.

Louise considered briefly the possibility that Alice was tricking her, but nobody was smiling.

"Jeez, Jesus God! I'm cooking hamburgers next door to a dead woman! I'm gonna be absolutely fudging puking sick. Daddy, I'm gonna be totally sick!" she moaned, but only Gary thought she was serious. Alice, my father, and I knew when Louise was acting.

We had less than a minute to figure out what to do. My father and Alice had a quick consultation, and they gave the rest of us our orders.

"Gary, you get back on the ramps. Louise, you get back to the kitchen. Abe, you stay around outside the door, just in case somebody gets too curious," my father said, rubbing his hands together.

"Alice will work the intermission, and we'll all meet back here as soon as the second feature starts."

Louise was incredulous.

"We're going to do what? What? We're going to go back to work as if nothing happened? And we're going to leave a dead woman in the toilet while all these other women are peeing around her. Daddy! Are you crazy!" she said, waving her hands. And then you could see a darker thought cross her mind. "Daddy, what if she's not dead? Mary, mother of God, she might still be alive and you could be killing her by not sending for help."

Louise was not acting this time. She was truly appalled.

"Louise, the woman is dead. Trust me, stone-cold dead," Alice said, but there was not a trace of mirth or irony in her voice. If anything, Alice spoke sadly.

Of all the people in the room at that moment, only I seemed to understand how my sister felt. This was not supposed to happen in our world, and only Louise and I understood that what we were doing was not . . . was not right.

"We should call somebody, shouldn't we?" I asked. "Whoever is with her tonight, shouldn't they know? I mean, won't they come looking for her? Daddy, you want us to wait twenty minutes, but her family will find her before then."

"She's alone, Isaac. I talked to her before the show began," Alice said. "She's a widow, said she goes to see all the Richard Benjamin movies. Said she just wanted to get out of her house for a change. She's alone, Isaac, and nobody is going to come look for her."

It was not enough, not enough of a justification for what we were about to do to her.

Even Gary fell in with my father and Alice's conspiracy.

"I checked her car earlier, Abe. The Judge gave me the list of single-driver car tags. She came in by herself. Fact is, we've got about a dozen older women alone tonight. Some sort of record."

I walked Louise back to the concession stand. She could not work, so I let her sit in the storeroom and cry by herself.

I helped Polly in the concession line for the next twenty minutes, not telling her why Louise was crying. Every once in a while I would look at Alice and wonder how she could act so oblivious to the previous scene. But I was slowly being drawn into a tiny world of five people who knew about the dead woman in the toilet. I resisted, but I lost.

Gary had taken my place outside the restroom, but nobody seemed to notice the dead woman. A few women mentioned the smell to him, and he said he would take care of it after intermission.

With the last of the customers out of the concession stand, Alice explained my father's dilemma.

"Your father told me about some state law that says if there is a death on a commercial property then that property has to close down for twenty-four hours for an investigation of all the circumstances. It happened to a hardtop theatre in Jacksonville last year. He is just buying time so he can figure out how to handle all this, that's all."

"Alice, how can you treat her that way? How can you be so . . . so . . . cruel?"

"The woman is dead, Isaac. Nothing we do now will change that."

"That's not the point," I objected.

"So, tell me, what *is* the point? What is the blessed point?"

I was not sure myself. The point was escaping me.

"We don't need to worry about closing down for a night. You know that," I said. "We could close for the whole week and not lose a dime. Money is not the point."

"But what is the point, Isaac? Can you tell me why you are so upset? Can you tell me why we have to rush to tell the world that we have a dead woman in the toilet?"

I could not tell her why, but I kept insisting to myself that there was a reason.

"We should tell my mother," I said suddenly, knowing that her knowledge of this situation would change everything.

"Your mother knows," Alice said.

I had no defense left. No reason to resist the inevitable alliance with my parents and Alice. If my mother knew, I knew, I was no longer a spectator.

After intermission, my parents met me and Alice in the restroom. Gary was posted at the door to direct women into the men's restroom if necessary. Polly was alone in the concession stand.

"I called Turner . . ." my mother began, and I looked immediately at my father, expecting outrage or pain, but he did not seem upset. "As I told your father, Turner had a simple solution."

Now, even Grace's father was part of this conspiracy. There seemed to be no end to the corruption of the adult world.

"If the police are called with this woman on the toilet, she has died on our property. If they are called to investigate a dead woman sitting in her car, then she has died *in her* property."

"She's on the toilet, Mama! She's not in her car," I whispered through gritted teeth, whispered as if the dead woman might hear me.

The three adults did not speak.

"She's not in her car, she's . . ." I started to repeat myself, but then the enormity of their silence told me something I did not want to know.

"She will be when the police find her," Alice said.

I closed my eyes and began to pray, pray that my parents and Alice would be forgiven, and then I thought of Louise alone in the storeroom, crying by herself, and I wanted to be with her.

"Mama, please, this makes no sense," I pleaded with her. "This is a . . . a . . ." I searched for a word. "A desecration."

"My sweet, dear Abraham, please listen to me," my mother said, pulling me to a corner of the restroom where we could sit on two of the vanity cushions in front of the wall-length mirror. She could see that I was about to cry.

"I tell you this now, and you must not think I am trying to be funny or callous, or that I do not understand you. I do not know this woman, her sadness or her joys, but I do know that she does not, as I would not, wish to be remembered by her friends or children as the woman who died on the toilet seat of a drive-in theatre. Do you see that? It is not for your father that I do this, it is for her. This is no desecration."

She held my hands as she spoke, and then, when she finished, she led me back to my father.

I began the process.

"We can't take her out now, not with all those people around," I said, putting part of my life behind me.

"Especially since her car is right in front of the concession stand," Alice added.

"So we have to wait," my mother said.

And then my father became the weakest link.

"But the body, won't it get . . . stiff? We've still got almost four hours until I can clear out the lot."

We looked at him, and even I could anticipate what Alice was about to say.

"She'll be stiff, but she'll be stiff in a sitting position. Makes it easier to slide her back in behind the wheel."

My father, probably without thinking, reached to his left and touched my mother on the arm. She moved closer to him.

My mother then asked Alice the most important question of the night.

"Alice, will you help carry her to her car?"

Alice nodded. Then my mother looked at me, but I shook my head.

"I can't," I said. "I really don't think I can."

"I understand," she said. "But stay with us when the time comes. I am going to take your sister back to the Tower and put her to bed. And talk to her. Perhaps rest myself. Will you do that?"

"Yes, ma'am," I said. How could I say no to my mother?

For the next four hours, Gary and I rehearsed our stories for the police. Pete was our first audience, and then we did it in front of Polly, who thought all this was just another day at the office, so to speak. Pete, however, was not convinced that disturbing the dead was justified under any circumstances.

At half past midnight, my parents, Alice, Pete, Gary, Polly, the Judge, and I assembled for the transfer. As we all expected, the Judge was not much help. When he couldn't find a screwdriver to take the hinges off the stall door, my mother sent him to the exit gate to make sure nobody was sneaking back inside. The Judge seemed to actually believe that someone might want to sneak back in and look at a blank screen.

Polly made it very clear that she was there for the "show," as she described it, but she had no intention of touching the body.

"That's got to be some sort of felony, idn't it?" she said. "Moving a dead body from the scene of the crime?"

"There is no crime, Polly," Gary said.

"Except that moving the body is a crime," Alice pointed out.

When my father built the Flamingo, money was no obstacle. He could have designed it any way he wanted. When he looked at the blueprint for the ladies' restroom, however, his cheap streak interfered with his common sense. He could have gotten stall doors with locks that could have been opened from the outside with a special key, but it was cheaper to just get doors that hooked on the inside. Who would expect someone to die inside? Worse than that, he looked at the original blueprints and decided that there were not enough commodes for the big crowds he expected. Instead of making the whole restroom larger, however, he simply made the individual stalls much smaller. Six narrow stalls were built in the space designed for four stalls. So narrow, in fact, that the toilet paper dispensers had to be put on the back of the door instead of the side walls. More than once, we had heard complaints from very large women about how they had trouble turning around in our toilet stalls. But when we finally got the door off its hinges, we discovered that it was only because the stall was so narrow that this woman was allowed any dignity at all in her death.

She had died and fallen sideways, but the wall was so close that she only tilted a little bit. If you did not know different, you would have thought she had simply gone to sleep on the commode.

Pete removed the door, and the rest of us stood behind him. I remember thinking how muscled his forearms were as he swung the door around and exposed the woman on the toilet. Later that night, as I tried to sleep in my room with Frank the Dog pacing overhead, I tried to imagine how all of us must have appeared in that woman's eyes, those eyes that were still open and staring at us. From her point of view, the door frame would have been like a rectangular picture frame, with Pete in the center and the rest of our heads and shoulders sprouting out from him. A short black man with seven heads.

Seven pairs of moist eyes staring back at her. How did we look to her? For those first few moments, the seven of us did not move, as frozen in life as she was in death. In my bed at night, I wondered if some part of a person stays with them, in their body, even after they die, to watch for that person who will find them. Was it like a coma? Was there something in her that was crying for help? I was only fifteen then. Such questions seemed answerable.

She had been dead for more than five hours. The skin in her face was beginning to sag. She was leaning to her right, and her right shoulder was pressed against the wall. Her left arm was curved across her lap. I asked Gary about it later, and he admitted that he had done what I did at first. We both looked at her stomach, searching for the dark lower triangle, but her legs were close together and her left hand covered most of that personal part, as if a last reflexive thought had been to anticipate this invasion of her privacy. Her open purse was sitting on the floor next to her feet. My mother finally set us all in motion.

"Alice, would you help me for a second," she said, and stepped into the stall. Alice stood behind her, blocking the scene from the rest of us.

My mother was kneeling in front of the dead woman, that was all I could imagine. Then I heard the toilet flush. I could also hear my mother breathing heavily. She was pulling the woman's underwear and slacks back up as Alice leaned over her and lifted the dead woman by the shoulders.

Alice and my mother stepped out. Both of them were sweating. But they had helped this dead woman prepare to die a second time, a death more public and yet without embarrassment.

Polly's disinterested bravado was beginning to wilt, so Gary helped her out of the restroom. For the rest of this ritual, they sat on the patio and watched as we carried the body to the car.

With Gary and Polly gone, Pete then stepped aside and waited for my parents and Alice to finish their unnatural act. He did not speak until the next day.

"You ready?" Alice asked my father, but I could see that he was hesitating.

"Of course. I'm as ready as I'll ever be," he said.

"I'll get her up off the john," Alice said, "and then you can help me get her outside."

My father nodded, and my mother handed me the woman's purse.

Getting her out of the stall was harder than Alice expected. The body was indeed rigid, and so Alice finally had to lift her up and lay her over her shoulder. That was when I noticed how small the woman was. She was like a sleeping child being carted off to bed. Alice grunted, and backed out of the toilet stall.

"I got her," Alice panted. "No need to help now, but I'll need some more muscle when we get to the car."

I led the procession out of the restroom, carrying the woman's purse, followed by my father, then Alice, who was extremely careful not to let the woman hit the walls or door frame as she went through, and my mother came last. Pete stayed in the restroom to clean up.

The woman's new site of death was a 1968 Ford station wagon, dark blue with fake wood siding. It still had the dealer's invoice on the window.

Gary and Polly were holding hands on the patio, watching as my father opened the driver's door and stepped out of the way.

Alice could not get the woman in her car at first. The weight and strain were beginning to show, especially since sliding the woman into the front seat would require that Alice bend her own knees and twist her own body to line the woman up with the driver's seat.

"Alice?" my mother asked.

Alice shook her head quickly.

"No, no, I'm fine," she said, but I could see that she was losing her grip. Without thinking, I raced around to the front passenger door and opened it, slid in across the front seat, and offered my hand to Alice.

"If you can just get her on the edge, I'll pull from this side," I said.

If Alice had hesitated, I would have had time to consider the consequences of what I had just done, but she took a deep breath and swung the woman down into the car, her own knees coming to rest on the ground.

There we were, Alice and me, separated by a corpse, looking into each other's eyes.

"You pull. I'll push," she gasped.

It took less than a second, the last act of violence, and then Alice and I gently removed our hands and closed the doors.

"I'll call the police," my mother said.

Within ten minutes, the Flamingo lot was filled with the flashing red lights of an ambulance and three police cars. Statements were taken, the purse checked for ID and any next-of-kin information, and the woman wrapped in a blue sheet.

If that were all that happened, I could have gone to bed that night and searched for significances as I stared at my ceiling and listened to Frank. But this part of my story, the story of that summer and that Fire, this act requires one last scene.

As I sat with Gary and Polly on the patio, I saw one more vehicle enter our lot. Turner West made his appearance, driven by his eldest son in their blackest limousine. They could have walked, but they rode.

I looked at my father, who looked at me and smiled. My father nodded to me, as if to say, "This is okay, son. This is all part of some great necessity."

My father did not speak, but I understood.

Explanations and Wagers

The day after Alice and I had held a dead body between us, my father and I were driving to Jacksonville to see the cemetery plot he was going to buy for the woman. Her family had immediately accepted his gift that morning when he had called them to offer condolences. Sitting in the front seat with him, I asked why we had had to do what we did. It all seemed so unnecessary.

My father driving was like Judge Lester flying. He was very calm. "You're probably right," he said, steering with his left hand while he tapped his fingertips on the back of the front seat in time with the music from the radio. "It was probably a mistake."

Mistake seemed like the wrong word.

"I just had this idea that I was being tested," he said. "Like if I could get this problem solved, I would prove something to someone. That's not logical to you, Abe, I know that. But, heck, how often do we get a dead woman in the ladies' room? I wasn't really concerned about losing a day's business. I was just a little angry that her being there would force me to close down for a day. Like I had lost a little control over the Flamingo, and I wasn't about to let that happen if I could help it."

We kept driving in silence until he spoke again.

"But it was a mistake," he said, looking for the cemetery entrance.

"Why so?" I asked, seeking some sort of clarification.

"Because I ended up losing control anyway. Your mama called Turner West, and he gave her the idea without really saying we ought to do it. I knew it as soon as he drove through the gate last

216

night. He had solved my problem, not me, and I owe him. I know, even though I won't admit it to him or your mama, I know that I will eventually have to sell him that land behind his place for his cemetery. Sooner or later, he will ask again, and I will have to sell it."

"You don't have to, really, do you?" I asked.

"Yessir, my son, I made a deal. An implied contract, valid in no court but my own, and Turner's. I know it. He knows it. Your mother, especially, she knew it even before I did."

We were having this conversation a month before the Fourth of 1968.

"But it's okay, son," my father said. "The Judge and I already had some plans for the Fourth. I think I can amend those a bit, make some phone calls to Oklahoma, make this Fourth more exciting than last year. Make Turner West pay more than money for that land behind him."

"Daddy, please . . . ," I began.

"Don't worry," he said. "Abe, you worry too much."

Some people think that the only things I photograph are graves, trains, and water, but most of the pictures in my house are of the people I have known. Starting in that summer of 1968, as many pictures of as many people as I could get to pose or pictures of them when they were not looking. I have lots of unposed pictures of Polly, but most of them are not on the walls. They are in my private file cabinets in the darkroom. In that file, I also have an undeveloped twelve-shot roll of Polly naked. She was quite willing as long as they were not too close up. She chose the poses, knowing by then what were her best features.

I had asked her if she was interested in posing like that, expecting a quick rejection, but she surprised me. It was actually Alice's idea to ask Polly, and Alice is the reason I have never developed the film.

"Iz, I'll make a bet with you," she had said that day when I told her I had finally asked Polly to pose. "No shop in this state will develop those pictures for you now. Maybe someday, but not now."

"I know that," I had said, but I did not know that.

"But, don't worry, someday, or somewhere else, you can get them developed. You might even have your own studio. You'll see them eventually. But I'll bet you that you can't wait for a long time before you do."

"How long is a long time?" I asked.

I could see her thinking.

"Until you're as old as your daddy is now. That long."

"I can do that."

"No, you can't," she insisted.

"I could get them developed and not tell you," I said.

"I would win the bet."

"But you wouldn't know. You would never know if you won," I said, pleased that I had bested her in some vague game.

"Nope, Izzy, I wouldn't know. But *you* would. That would be enough for me," she said, checkmating me.

"How do we settle this, when I'm older? How do I prove I can do it?"

Alice handed me a dollar bill.

"We'll go buy the film now. I'll buy. I'll mark the outside of the roll. You take your pictures, and when you're as old as your daddy I'll find you, and you'll give me that roll and I'll get it developed. Be another birthday present for you."

"And if I win?" I asked. "What's the bet?"

"You won't win. You won't be able to resist the temptation," she said, that smirk creeping into her expression.

"But if I do? We have to bet something specific. Something of value."

Alice leaned down and whispered to me, "Anything you want, but you won't really know what you want until then."

That Kodak roll sits in my private file, the initials *AK* almost faded off.

Anticipation, Consummation, Re-creation

Have you ever known any man ever to tell you the truth about how he lost his virginity? A simple rule should be established for all conversations about sex, especially from men about this particular experience: Half of everything said is a lie, and you should be suspicious of the other half.

Everything is anticipation, consummation, and then re-creation.

Two days after my sixteenth birthday, Gary Green and I were at the Duval County Driver's License Bureau. His birthday had been a month earlier, but he had promised that he would wait and go with me so we could get our licenses on the same day. He has been my friend for three decades now.

"Is it true about you and Polly?" he asked me while we waited for our eye exam.

"No comment," I said, knowing that I had crossed a river that he was yet to cross. I was feeling very worldly.

"Well, she's doing a lot of commenting," he said.

I noticed that the hair on his head was already getting thin.

"Well?" he repeated.

"Well, that's bad form on her part," I said, using a phrase that my mother liked to use to describe people who were careless or too casual in their comments. But I was bothered. As pleased as I was about the previous two days, as much as I wanted to tell someone about it—and Gary was the logical choice—I did not want my initiation to be the subject of a public forum.

"Does Grace know?" he asked, exposing the real reason for my modesty.

We were almost at the head of the eye line, and the backwards and upside-down letters were suddenly blurrier than they had been before.

"No, she doesn't, I assume, or I think," I said. "And you won't tell her, will you?"

"Abe, I'm not the one you've got to worry about. And you can probably get Polly to be a bit more discreet, or you can have Alice pound her if she gets too gabby. Not us, Abe, it's your sister you've got to worry about."

"You told Louise!" I gasped, turning heads in the line. My future marriage was ending in divorce before it began.

"Abe," Gary whispered through gritted teeth, "she was the one who told me. Polly told her, she said."

I was at the head of the line, but I stepped out and walked feebly to a bench next to the wall, directly under a giant map of Florida. Key West was a few inches above my head.

Gary gave up his new status as line leader to sit with me.

"Abe, we can fix this. I'm sure. We'll talk to Alice. She'll figure something out. As far as I can tell, your sister knows, and me, and probably Alice, but not your parents or Pete or the Judge. And school's out, so there's no gossip anywhere outside of the Flamingo. We've just got to get to Louise with some leverage, that's all. You got anything to bribe her with? Damage control, that's what we need." Gary began chuckling to himself. "Jeez, I wish I had this problem."

"I'll talk to Alice," I said, knowing that I was compounding interest on a debt I already owed her.

"You're going to tell her about you and Polly?" Gary asked.

"Oh, Gary, she already knows. Why do you think Polly even did it with me!"

He had an absolutely blank look on his face.

"I . . . don't . . . understand," he said very slowly.

"Alice arranged everything. Alice set me up with Polly. Alice promised me weeks ago that Polly was going to do it with me on my birthday. Do you really think that Polly found me irresistible? Polly could have sex with Paul Newman if she wanted to. You think her first choice would be Ho Chi Minh?" As I spoke, I kept looking around to see if anyone was listening.

"Alice . . . arranged . . . for you . . . sex . . . sex . . . with Polly?"

A few years later, Gary and I were in a 70mm theatre watching *2001: A Space Odyssey*. When HAL the Computer was being de-programmed, I leaned over to Gary in the dark and told him that that was how he had sounded when he tried to talk about Alice and Polly and sex.

"Alice . . . arranged for you to have sex . . . with Polly?" It was a statement and a question and a revelation all in one.

"I was a virgin," I said. "Polly probably has this thing about virgins. At least, she did after Alice got through talking to her. We did it after the first intermission, just before midnight in her room in the Tower." I paused to let Gary start breathing again, and then I did something very cruel to him. I was beginning to feel more in control. "It was . . . amazing," I said, purposely letting my voice drop on the last word.

Gary blinked, and then he became my brother.

"You know," he said, "I'm a virgin."

I smiled. He smiled. I laughed. He laughed.

"I'll talk to Alice," I said.

"Would you, please?" he said.

We sat on that bench talking about Polly for half an hour, but I did not tell him anything graphic.

My father had been outside in a brand-new blue Chevy Corvair convertible, his birthday present to me and Louise, and the car we were both to use for the actual driving part of the license test. Louise, however, had refused to take her test the same day as Gary and I did. Tired of waiting, my father finally came looking for us.

"You boys fail the written?" he asked, looking down at us on the bench.

Gary looked at me.

"Oh, gosh, I hope there's no written test for this," he said, and I knew what he meant.

My father stood with his hands on his hips, staring at two hysterical teenage boys.

"Am I missing something here?" he asked.

Another half hour and Gary and I walked out as licensed drivers. An hour after that, I offered Alice a ride in my new Corvair. She put on her granny sunglasses and raced me to the car.

We drove to St. Augustine to pick up her check from the Booksmith. It was one of those Florida postcard days, blue sky and warm breezes. Polly and Louise were the main topics of discussion. I had asked Alice to do something about their talking.

"Still feeling guilty, Izzy?" Alice asked, her hair blowing around her face as I did sixty down A1A.

"No, not guilt," I said, both my hands on the wheel and my eyes straight ahead. "But you know how it is. You know, some things are private."

"And you don't want Grace to know."

"Of course, of course not. Is that so wrong?"

"Not really," Alice said. Then she suddenly swung her body around, put her legs over her door to let them hang outside, and laid her head on my right thigh, taking my right hand off the wheel and putting it on her shoulder. Her head on my leg was not an unpleasant weight.

"I can see up your nose from here," she said.

"Alice!" I protested.

"You know, don't you, Iz, that Grace will be a virgin for you. She will never do it with anybody but you. And she'll assume you feel the same way. And . . . when Polly gets through with you, you'll have to dumb down to act clumsy on your honeymoon."

"So why do you think I want you to keep Polly and Louise quiet, especially Louise, who will blackmail me for the rest of my life?" I said.

"Oh, relax, Iz, I've already talked to them."

Without thinking, I looked straight down into Alice's face.

"Eyes on the road, lover," she said. "I promised your daddy I would make sure you drove safely."

"They'll be quiet?" I asked.

"Tangled webs, Isaac, your life is about to become a bed of tangled webs, and some of those webs will be little white lies."

"Alice . . ."

"They'll be quiet," Alice said. "Polly was easy. You know, I told you before, she actually likes you more than you think she does. And she doesn't want to hurt you."

"And Louise?"

"Ah, your loving sister," Alice said, slowly rolling her head back and forth on my leg, as if she were giving herself a neck massage. "Your sister was a little more . . . difficult. But then I sat her down and recited a string of details I know about her own sex life as well as *other* potentially embarrassing infoe-mation, if you know what I mean."

"Louise's sex life!" I said, sounding more surprised than I should have been. I did not look down, but I imagined how Alice's expression at that moment must have been saying, "Boys . . . so predictable, and so dumb."

"I told her that if she said anything else about you and Polly I was going to tell your mother about her," said Alice.

"Are you going to tell me?" I asked.

"Not a chance, Iz," she said. "That stuff stays in the knitting circle. No boys allowed."

"So she is afraid you'll tell my parents?"

"Iz, I said I would tell *your mother.*"

Alice rolled her head to one side and gently bit my leg.

"Pay attention. Your sister doesn't care, really, if you or your father knows about her. She's not afraid of you boys. In fact, there are only two people in this world she is afraid of. I'll give her credit. She'll take chances that most people wouldn't touch. I admire her for that."

"Two people?" I asked, feeling this part of our conversation about to be closed.

"Your mother . . ."

"And you," I said.

"And . . . Iz . . . I know you're not surprised," she said.

After we picked up her paycheck, Alice took me to a tourist restaurant named The Monk's Vineyard down on St. George Street. I told her about my conversation with Gary.

"This is a big deal with you guys, isn't it, this first time business," she said. "And you and Gary are probably more obsessed than most of the other boys I have ever known."

"Alice, weren't you ever young?" I said, speaking softly because one of the waiters was a senior at St. Agnes.

"Iz, were you?" she shot back, and heads turned.

"I don't understand," I said, and I truly did not.

"Forget it. Just let me ask you this. Gary thinks you lost your virginity to Polly because I set it up, and he wants me to do the same thing for him?"

"Yes." I nodded, as if it were all so logical.

"So, Iz, I'll leave it up to you. I'll do it, and Polly, I'm sure, will do it. As *you* know by now, she isn't a tease or a fake. She actually likes to do it. Gary will lose his virginity to her just like he thinks you did, and you two will be best friends for life, and you'll get old and reminisce about the summer of 1968 and how weird Alice set you up with hot Polly, and boys will be boys and all that crud. In his mind, Polly will be the first for both of you. You will share that experience with her . . . with him. Now, tell me, is *that* what you want?"

"Yes," I said, without a regret.

Alice nodded to herself.

"Tell him it's a done deal."

"Should I wait until you talk to her, just to be sure?" I asked.

Alice cocked her head to one side and stared at me.

"Oh," I said, blushing, "you said it was a done deal."

She softened and then motioned to the waiter for a check.

"So, tell me, did you really tell Gary the truth?" she asked.

"Everything I told him was true," I said.

"Abraham, don't get in a hairsplitting contest with me," she said as she stood up and waited for me. "You may think you're sharp, but I use a razor. Now, tell me, everything you told him may have been true, but you didn't tell him everything, did you?"

"No, not everything," I said, looking down at my plate.

"I knew that, and I know you never will."

Alice stood there, looking at me like I was another problem to be solved, but not a big problem.

"Sorry, Iz," she finally said, "I didn't mean to snap at you. And, besides, whether you know it or not, it wouldn't have been a fair fight."

To Forget God

The day before my birthday had also been the last day of school. There was no air-conditioning at St. Agnes, and I had been sweating all day. Before lunch, Louise had made some snide comment about my having a guilty conscience even *before* I sinned. I asked her what she meant, but she gave me one of those looks that she had adopted from Alice, a look of smirk and sympathy. I kept asking her what she meant until she finally told me to go ask Polly. For the rest of the day, whenever I saw Louise get anywhere near Grace I took a deep breath and practiced my look of incredulity, which I knew would be required if Grace ever asked me about something that Louise may have told her.

The truth is, I avoided Grace that day. I purposefully sat with Gary and some other boys at lunch, and in class I was especially attentive during all the reviews of our final exam results. I was a model student.

I knew what was going to happen the next day. Alice had not been subtle, and Polly seemed, I thought, to be giving me looks that I imagined had been the same looks that Aztec priests gave their virgin sacrifices right before they were laid on the altar.

Louise had been right. I was feeling guilty. It was the last day of school, and I did not know when and how Grace and I would see each other that summer. It might be days, or weeks. I should never have left her alone that last day in school, but I did. I wanted to suspend our relationship, certainly not end it. I wanted to pretend that I had never met her, just for one day. I was damnable, and I knew it.

When the bell rang at three-thirty, a cheer went up in class. Louise and her two best friends immediately peeled off their blouses and skirts to reveal their summer wardrobe underneath, shorts and halter-tops. Sister Mary Francis was not pleased.

I expected my mother to be waiting outside to drive us home, but when we were cleaning out our lockers Louise told Grace and me that we were supposed to go to the Booksmith to wait for Alice. Plans had changed.

"Why didn't you tell me sooner?" I asked Louise.

"I thought Alice told you," she said, shoving her notebooks and uniform into the same bag.

Alice had driven us to school that day. It had been very much a silent trip, with her looking in the rearview mirror back at me and Grace.

As we walked to the Booksmith, Grace did not make me feel any less guilty. Even though Louise was behind us, Grace reached over and held my hand as we walked. Of all the hands I have ever touched, hers are still the softest.

When we got to the front door of the Booksmith, Louise handed me her bag and said, "Tell Alice I'll be back in an hour. I'm going to go buy myself a birthday present."

"But you're supposed to stay with us. That's the rule," I said, knowing that it was a rule seldom enforced.

"Yeah, right," Louise said, and then she walked off.

Alice was alone inside the Booksmith, so I knew she would be busy with stocking or waiting on customers, and she couldn't get too far away from the cash register.

"Hey, it's my two favorite Christians," she said as soon as she saw us. "You got big plans for tomorrow, Iz?" Alice asked as she pulled old magazines off the shelves, innocently fanning her face with the latest issue of *Playboy*. "You and your sister having a big party? You're only sixteen once."

"I don't think so," I said. "You know that we have a new picture opening tomorrow night, and Louise and I have to work. And you know Louise—she doesn't like parties."

"Well, not quite right, Iz. Your sister likes parties. She just doesn't like to share the guest-of-honor spotlight. She told me that when she moves away from home she is going to tell everybody that her birthday is in January," Alice said, motioning to Grace to help her carry magazines.

Grace had not said a word since we entered the Booksmith. That was not too surprising. She was usually quiet when she was around Louise or Alice. Long silences were not unusual, but on this particular day I began to wish that she would at least speak once. I was thinking that she might have been angry with my cold-shouldered behavior all day.

I can tell you all this because I understand it better now, but even back then I was beginning to understand why I was so troubled. It was more than the knowledge that my birthday was probably going to be the day I lost my virginity. I sat in the corner of the Booksmith and thought about the two females at the magazine rack. I was in love with Grace, but Alice was more real to me. I was in love with Grace, but Alice was more interesting to me. I was happy with Grace, calm and happy, but I did not spend time wondering about her, wondering who she really was. I did not think she was hiding anything, nor did I think there was more than one of her.

So, I thought that day in the Booksmith, was I really in love? I had assumed it for the past four years, had even felt it, had talked about it with Alice and my mother, but on the eve of my sixteenth birthday I was looking for a sign of some sort, some moment between Grace and me that would tell me that I was right about us. I knew that *proof* of love was not possible, but on that last day of my fifteenth year I was beginning to lose faith in love. I wanted that faith back. Eventually, the moment came, but I had to wait until my mother's funeral.

An hour later, as Alice was driving Grace and Louise and me back to the Flamingo, and as Grace and I sat in the backseat, I asked myself if I could change the next day. If I knew for sure, and I thought I did, that Polly was coming for me, would I stop her? I looked at Grace's face as she was looking out the window. I looked at Alice and Louise singing in the front seat. I looked in the rearview mirror and saw Alice looking at me. I closed my eyes and pretended to be asleep until we got to the West Funeral Home.

"Will you call me tomorrow?" Grace asked as she got out of the car. "I want to wish you a happy birthday. And I have a present for you."

"I'll come see you," I said. I could sense that Alice and Louise were trying to act like they were not there, as if they were embarrassed. It was behavior I did not expect from them, but I did appreciate it.

"I'll come see you," I repeated, and then I added, "I want to come see you. I really do."

Back at the Flamingo, I kept getting the same question from everyone. "Party tomorrow?" Pete asked, and then the Judge asked, "Big plans for tomorrow?" Even my father seemed curious. "Have you heard anything about a party?"

By the time the box office opened, a party seemed inevitable. When Polly asked me if I had plans for tomorrow, I was beginning to smell a conspiracy.

Business that night was disappointingly slow, but it was not surprising because the whole week had been slow. Gary and I had the lot speakers turned off soon after the intermission, and the few cars that stayed for the second feature, *Two for the Road,* kept their own volume turned down low. Gary and I sat on the patio trying to figure out my father's booking logic.

"You think he just takes the cheapest second feature he can get?" Gary wondered aloud. "Figures that people only care about the main show?"

"Maybe," I said. "But I think that he booked this one because he likes Audrey Hepburn. Did you notice how much time he spent on the patio this last week, most of it during the second show?"

"That's true," Gary said, his feet propped up on the patio chair in front of him. "And she is pretty."

I remembered how many times in the past few years that we had played *Breakfast at Tiffany's* as a second feature. Years later, after my father bought his first television set and then a VCR, he and I would sit and watch a video of *Robin and Marian* over and over. Sean Connery was an old Robin Hood; Hepburn an old Maid Marian. By over and over, I mean more than once a month. My father would cry at the end. He was predictable, just like he had been in 1968, when Alice had Pete play that Bobby Goldsboro song over the big speaker horn on top of the Tower the day after my birthday. My father and I had stood on the lot, and I had seen him get misty-eyed as Goldsboro sang about trees and a dead girl. My mother had gone into the projection booth, jerked the record off the turntable, and instructed Pete and Alice that if *she* ever had to listen to that song again she would personally make life a living Hades for whoever was responsible.

The concession stand closed early the night before my birthday, and Polly disappeared as soon as the cleaning was done. Gary waited at the gate for the film delivery truck so he could carry the new film cans to the booth for Pete to set up. The Judge came by the patio and informed me that he was going to bed early that night. Seems like nobody was inclined to sneak through the exit gates to see this particular movie. By midnight I was alone on the patio.

"Penny for your thoughts."

Alice was behind me, leaning forward and pinching my shoulder as I watched Audrey Hepburn and Albert Finney drive through the French countryside. I did not turn around.

"Alice, do you have to sneak up on me like that?"

"Iz, a herd of elephants could have sneaked up on you just now. A herd of fudging three-legged elephants."

"I was watching the movie," I said. "I *like* this movie."

"Yeah, sure, you and your daddy."

I was silent, but Alice did not go away.

"I have a message for you, Iz, from Polly."

"Alice—" I began, but she interrupted.

"As soon as the field is clear and everybody is tucked in bed, she wants you to meet her down on the beach, where they always go swimming. Bring your swimsuit if you want, but you probably won't need it, if you know what I mean."

It was all beginning.

"A hot night, Iz. A swim in the ocean is what you need. And Polly has a present for you."

"Alice, why are you doing this?" I asked. "Tell me why."

"Five minutes past midnight, Isaac, your birthday has just begun."

There was a half hour left in the movie, and it would take about another half hour for the field to be cleared and the Flamingo to be closed: lights out, gates locked, Lees and employees in bed. I had an hour left until I would meet Polly on the beach. Even if promised eternal life and the adoration of the masses, I could not tell you what I did in that next hour. Those sixty minutes are a void in my memory now, a daze of expectation and transition, the missing last page of a chapter. Perhaps not missing. More accurately, erased.

I found myself walking on the beach at two in the morning. A full moon would have been nice, but the moon was almost totally dark, a tiny sliver. I could not see the horizon, but I could smell the ocean and I could feel the warm breeze. Every sense of my body was working overtime to absorb the outside world.

I could see the two red lights at the top of the Flamingo Tower, and I could see the yellow light on the end of Pete's caboose. I could see tiny white dots far out on the ocean, probably shrimper lights. Those were all I could see.

I was wearing my bathing suit and my Hawaiian shirt. My feet were bare, and I could feel the hard sand. Then I could feel the sand getting moister, the closer I came to the edge of the water.

I walked away from the Flamingo, and then back toward it, back and forth, waiting for Polly to meet me. Just when I thought I had been tricked by Alice, I heard a voice.

"Over here."

I stopped walking and listened.

"Over here," the voice said again.

I did not recognize the voice.

"Over here, Iz."

The voice was Alice's, and I was disappointed.

In the distance, I could see a form move toward me.

"I've been watching you walk up and down the beach," Alice said as she finally stood in front of me. "You seemed lost."

"I didn't see you," I said, but my voice gave me away.

"You weren't looking for me," she said.

"I thought you said Polly was . . ."

Alice stepped closer, less than an arm's length away from me.

"I thought you said Polly was going to meet me," I said, not needing an answer to know that Polly was not anywhere near me at that moment.

Alice's first touch was soft, her hand slowly moving up my arm. She was wearing perfume, something she had never done before as long as I had known her.

I closed my eyes and saw Alice's face as it had looked in the rearview mirror.

"Why, Alice? I don't understand" were my last words for a long time.

"Ssssh, and just listen to me," she said as she bent down and very slowly kissed me. "Just listen to me," she said, kissing me as she talked, her lips warm-wet and magnetic.

Blood was being rearranged in my body, leaving my head and searching for those undiscovered pools of pleasure. I was dizzy, and I was absolutely terrified. I had forgotten Polly, forgotten Grace, forgotten Abraham Isaac Lee. I had forgotten God.

I was on a blanket on a beach, and an ocean was rolling toward me. I was on my back, and Alice was sitting on my legs, pinning me down and moving her hands over my rigid flesh. She still had her dress on.

"Listen to me, Isaac. Listen to me," she was whispering, telling me what was about to happen. "It will be over very quickly for you"—her breathing deeper—"and you will be ashamed and you will think you have done something wrong. But you must not move, you must just lie here and let me move for you. And, much sooner than you could ever imagine, you will be ready again, and we will go very slowly."

Her dress floated around her, and then she moved up over the center of my body and guided me to the center of her body. She descended, and I was inside her.

That is the sensation, that is the mystery revealed. Not the culmination, the loss of control, the climax. Every boy can induce his own release, an easy manipulation of self-love. But as soon as Alice settled herself around me, I crossed into another world.

My body did as she told me it would. I emptied myself in a quick convulsion, almost biting my own lip in an effort to stop.

Alice was leaning forward, her hands squeezing my hands, pushing them into the blanket.

"That was a start," she whispered heavily, "but we're not through yet."

We were motionless for a few minutes, but neither did we separate. I stayed inside her, and then she began to slowly move the center of the universe. A new life was formed. With that, Alice pulled her dress off her shoulders, but not off her body. I reached up and touched her breasts, and she put her hands over mine, not letting me free, and in my palms I could feel the flesh at the tips of her breasts swell and grow rigid. She leaned farther down, and the firm tips of those breasts moved across my chest and then up to find the tip of my tongue and then the circle of my own lips. Taste, touch, and smell swirled around me, and then a whispered hum vibrated down from her throat to the center where we were joined, flowed there and then up my stomach and through my heart to the farthest edge of my memory.

"Don't move," she whispered, anticipating me. "I want to show you something."

I could see nothing.

With the center of her body slowly rising and falling, Alice began to kiss me.

"This is what"—she took a breath—"you will learn from me," she said, her lips tracing mine. "Everything should begin and end with"—another breath—"this."

An hour and a world later, I was still lying on my back on Alice's blanket, looking up at a dark and starry sky. Alice was lying beside me. I was naked. She was fully covered by her dress. I did not know it then, but I was never ever going to see her body.

"You okay?" I asked.

She rolled over onto her side, planted an elbow, and propped her head on her hand.

"That's a strange question," she said.

"I just wondered. If you're okay, you know," I said. "If all this was okay for you."

"I'm fine, Abraham, absolutely fine," she said quietly. "And it was very sweet of you to ask. Nobody else ever has."

We did not speak again for a long time. I think I fell asleep, but I'm not sure about that. I do remember Alice nudging me in the side after a while.

"You need to get back home. The sun will be coming up soon, and you need your rest. Today's the big day. Your parents are giving you a party."

I could see a faint line of purple and orange on the horizon. The tide was coming in.

"You know," I said as I pulled on my bathing suit and buttoned my shirt, "I really believed it when you said Polly was going to do it with me today, that she had a present for me. You're very good at telling lies."

Alice had been walking away from me as I spoke, but she quickly turned around and said, "Iz, I never lie, much, but I wasn't lying about Polly. You *are* going to do it with her today. We have been planning this for a long time. She wants to be your first, so don't disappoint her. Let her believe that, and everybody else, too."

I could not speak, at first.

"You mean I *am* going to have sex with Polly? Today?" I finally said. "But, Alice, aren't we going to . . . do . . . this . . . ," I then began to say, but I knew the answer even before she answered.

"Only once, Isaac, you can only do it the first time . . . once."

"Alice . . ."

"Oh, Iz, relax. You'll live. You'll be fine. I taught you the most important part, and you were a quick learner. But Polly will teach you all the foreign languages, all the Latin and French and anything else you ever dreamed about. You'll bop like bunnies every chance you get, and *you will* see a lot of her body up close and personal. It's okay. Enjoy her body. Lord knows, she does."

"Then this didn't matter to you, all that we did?" I said.

"Is that what you think?"

"I don't know what to think," I almost stuttered.

"I was your first, Iz, but I won't be your last. If you're very, very lucky, Grace will be the last one. The beginning and the end, that's all that matters."

"So this was just the beginning," I said. "And everything in be-tween you and Grace, all that won't matter?"

"Nothing matters, Isaac, nothing at all, eventually not even me."

Before the sun came up, I was back in my room. There was no school, so I could sleep late. As I closed my eyes, I listened for Frank to walk over me. I was very tired.

My Birthday

Part of the pleasure of telling my own story is that I can skip or abbreviate those times that do not fit in with the real story I am telling. Or I can linger on those times that I simply want to relive. My birthday was such a time. You have already heard about how it began, and you might be looking forward to how it ended, how Polly took me back to her Tower room and began my month of sexual orientation. But I will not take you into her room that night, or anywhere else she and I found ourselves alone for the next four weeks. You must use your imagination. If your imagination is as good as Polly's was, well, you will be satisfied.

I slept late on my birthday. It was a tradition with my parents. On our birthdays, Louise and I were allowed to sleep as late as we wished. Even if it was Sunday or a school day. In 1968, I slept until noon.

My dreams that morning were better than usual. Natalie Wood and I were in a theatre, and she was wearing my sister's bathing suit. I was wearing my Flamingo pirate hat. But, like all dreams, nothing made sense. Natalie and I were in the upstairs cry room of an old downtown theatre. A *cry room* is where parents with small children can sit and watch the movie and not disturb other people. The room is soundproof and has a glass wall. But in my dream the cry room has obviously also been used as a smoking room. I could smell stale tobacco as Natalie Wood was taking off her clothes. Then she turned into another woman, another movie star whose name I could not remember, but she had been in a movie I had seen years earlier. In my dream I was not Korean, but I was not Caucasian either. I was like a male version of Louise, and the woman who kept metamorphosing found me irresistible. But just as I began to enjoy myself, the dream melted into darkness, only to begin again with another woman in another theatre with another movie showing on the screen down below us. My father's voice was calling my name, and then I could hear Judge Lester's airplane as it buzzed the theatre.

Almost awake, I dreamed that my mother was in my room with me, looking down at me and then walking around to pick my clothes up off the floor, my clothes from the previous night with Alice, and then she laid out a clean set of clothes on my chest of drawers.

I woke up, and I had the feeling that I was not who I used to be. I was more than a day older than yesterday.

The Tower was quiet. I found some clothes on top of my chest of drawers and put them on. The shirt was new. I looked out my window and saw my parents talking to Pete on the patio. There was not a cloud in the sky, and I knew it was going to be a hot day.

Looking down at my father and mother, I began a habit that I have almost always followed from that moment. I made a mental list of things that I wanted to do that particular day. Eventually, I would begin each day by writing the list in a pocket-size spiral notebook that I would carry with me. These were never major life goals or complicated projects. I would make a note about calling someone or going to a store to get a particular item. As an adult, I would also make a list of things I wanted to photograph that day. The only time I did not keep that list of daily jobs was during the month after my mother died.

Looking at my parents, I made a mental note to ask Alice about the first time she had ever had sex. I also told myself to go see Grace. But the most important item on my list was to get Judge Lester off to myself and find out what my father had planned for the Fourth of 1968. In the long run, I told myself, I was going to have to find a way to stop my father's irrational feud with Turner West. It was odd, the feeling I had there at the window, as if my body had been pumped full of adrenaline and my mind cleared of indecision. I did not know how I was going to shape the future, but I did know that I was going to begin the process.

My parents had noticed me and were waving. Pete did not look up. I waved back, and then I went to the kitchen, where I ate a full box of cereal. I was famished. Hunger satisfied, I started to go to see Grace, but as I came out of the Tower my father met me.

"Don't get too far out of pocket today, Abe. Your mama and I have a party planned for you and Louise, or, who knows, maybe just you, right before we open tonight. And Pete is going to need some help in the booth today. So what's up now with you?"

I did not hesitate.

"I'm going to go see Grace at her place," I said, waiting for his reaction. He seemed unfazed.

"Hmm . . . so I see. Well, you tell her father hello for me," he said, as if I did this every day and he and West were the best of friends. "Why don't you ask her if she would like to come to the party?"

Of course, why not, I thought, and then I corrected myself. There were at least two reasons why I could not invite her: Alice and Polly.

"Good idea," I lied, and then I walked to the West Funeral Home.

Turner West met me at the door. "Hello, Abraham," he said, extending his hand as he always did when he saw me, as if it were the first time we had met. "Grace is not feeling well this morning, so I told her to stay in bed."

I was actually relieved. I would not have to avoid the subject of my birthday.

"She'll be okay, Abraham," West said. "Probably just a bug. She'll be fine tomorrow."

I had nothing to say, but I knew I would start my list the next day with her name on it, and the next.

"Today is your birthday?" West said after an awkward silence.

I nodded.

"Congratulations," he said.

I nodded again.

"I remember my sixteenth birthday," he said.

I looked at him and wondered.

"I have a party planned for Grace's sixteenth," he said, oblivious to my imagination. "I hope you and your sister can come. We will probably go to eat somewhere in St. Augustine. Of course, your parents are invited also."

"You don't mean that," I said quickly, finding my voice again. "You don't want my father to come to Grace's party. And I don't think he really wanted her to come to mine today."

Turner West looked over my shoulder, past the Cowboy marquee and toward the Flamingo Tower. "You may be right, young man," he said. "But I would have done it for her sake. As your father would do for you. Perhaps he is getting as tired as I am. And, yes, I don't really care if your father were to come, but I do hope your mother will. I would like to see her again. It has been too long."

I walked back home thinking about Turner West. He and my father had not had a confrontation for weeks, aside from the sporadic bullet into the Cowboy. But even those shots were becoming more infrequent, and Grace had told me that it was her oldest brother, not her father, who was doing most of the shooting. I sensed that Turner West was winding down, but I was sure that my father was merely resting.

Back at the Flamingo, I looked for Alice, but she and Polly had gone to St. Augustine. School may have been out for me and Louise, but Alice still had to work at the Booksmith. Gary and the Judge had gone to Jacksonville to get supplies. I assumed that Louise was still asleep. My mother and father were in the concession stand. Pete was in his caboose. Frank was in the Tower. Everyone in my world seemed to be accounted for. I was sixteen.

I went to the concession stand and volunteered to help my parents, but they told me to take the day off. It was my birthday.

"Your mother and I can do this," my father said, scraping the grill with a spatula while my mother was up on a ladder wiping off the menu boards. "You and your sister relax."

"Speaking of your sister," my mother said, "would you go tell her to at least get out of bed. She can have a holiday, but I would like her to be conscious for some of it."

"Let her be," my father said. "The kids only have a birthday once a year."

I wondered if this was an argument, but my mother just shrugged and went back to cleaning.

"Hubert, your daughter acts like every day is her birthday," she said, shaking her dust rag directly over the grill that my father had just cleaned.

"Very funny, Edna Marie." He laughed, and I knew they were playing with each other there in the concession stand. It was just like they used to kid around with each other, years earlier. Of course, not having to teach at Flagler during the summer always helped my mother's attitude. I went back to the Tower to knock on Louise's door, but there was no answer. I knocked again. Then I called out her name, but there was still no answer. As I was about to open the door, Louise stopped me. She was behind me, not in her room.

"That's my blessed room, Izzy, and you can stay out!"

"You're up," I said, turning around.

"You always were the smart one," she said, crossing her eyes.

"I mean, I thought you were sleeping late, like you always do on your birthday."

"Oh, is today *my* birthday?" she said.

"Louise, I've decided that nothing you do today is going to make me mad. I'm going to enjoy myself and be happy that it's my birthday."

I noticed that she was beginning to dress like Polly.

"Oh, I've heard about how you plan to enjoy your birthday," she said. "How you get to unwrap your present later tonight."

I was not bothered by the insinuation. Louise obviously did not know about me and Alice.

"Polly wanna cracker?" she said, smacking her lips like she had just finished a cracker herself and was trying to moisten her whole mouth again. "You gonna be her cracker, sweet brother?"

"Louise, at least I am going to get what I want for my birthday. Are you?"

"Izz-zzzy," she said with a hiss, thinking it would irritate me, "I don't want anything."

But I knew that was a lie. The problem was that nobody could figure out exactly what it was that my sister *did* want. Perhaps not even her.

"Are you jealous?" I asked. "Upset because I'm going to have more fun today than you?"

"Nice try, Izzy, but I've *already* had more *fun* in my life than you'll have in all your future."

I could see through my sister at that moment. She was acting. Future movie audiences would only see a character. I would always remember how she had practiced in front of her family.

"And, besides," she said, trying for some vague knockout punch, "it's no big deal. You'll see."

"I'll let you know," I said, not unkindly.

Louise nodded and then looked away. We did not speak for a few seconds.

"Happy birthday, Iz," she finally said, smiling.

"Happy birthday, Louise," I said.

I wanted to hug my sister, and I was sure she wanted to hug me. But we did not physically cross the space between us. That was okay. We both knew.

"You'll be at the party, won't you," I asked.

"I guess." She sighed. "Can't let you have all the fun."

My parents had arranged for the party to be in the Tower dining room. Louise and I, being the guests of honor, sat at the ends of the long table. I was in my father's seat; Louise in my mother's place. Everyone was there except Pete.

Louise was flanked by Polly and Alice. Gary and the Judge were next to me. My parents sat across from each other at the middle of the table. The party began at four in the afternoon. By the time the box office opened at seven, everyone except me and my mother was drunk.

The table was full of presents and food, but as soon as my father began proposing toasts to his children we all forgot about the food.

"To my children," he began, standing, lifting his champagne glass and pointing it to each end of the table. "A long and happy life."

That wish seemed safe enough.

Toast finished, he gulped down the full glass. Judge Lester did the same, as did Alice and Polly. Always in the past, as part of a ritual invented by my parents, Louise and I were given a glass of champagne on our birthday. It was a gesture toward our eventual adulthood. Always in the past, Louise and I would take a sip but never finish the full glass. It was an unspoken assumption by us that our parents had never intended for us to really drink the champagne. Besides, I never liked the taste.

On our sixteenth birthday, as my father drained his glass, Louise looked right at me and then downed hers. Only my mother and I noticed, but my mother did not stop her. I did not see that directly beside me Gary was beginning a long life of drinking too much. My birthday was also the official day of his coming to live with us for the entire summer. He was away from his parents for the first time.

With that first toast, a full bottle of champagne was consumed. Then the Judge stood up.

"To the prettiest children in north Florida"—but then, seeing both my parents glare at him—"I mean, in the continental United States. May your life be full of success and happiness."

I looked at my father, who was looking directly at my mother. They smiled at each other, and I remembered how they were always happy on their children's birthday. The Judge lifted his glass, only to discover it was empty, but he did not hesitate. He tilted it back as if it were full, but my father did not let him escape.

"Harry, your glass is empty!"

"Yessir, I know that," the Judge said sheepishly.

My father had reached behind him to an ice chest that was sitting on the floor. A new bottle of champagne emerged, and he went around the room filling glasses, pausing by my mother to lean down and whisper something in her ear, something that made her smile momentarily, a smile that I could see was quickly stifled, as if she thought my father was the funniest man in the world but she was not going to let him entertain her too easily.

"Harry! Another toast!" my father said, sitting back down, but with a third bottle next to him ready to be opened.

The Judge tried again: "To Abraham and Louise. The future king and queen of the Flamingo."

My father applauded as the others drank their second glass, then he downed his. In five minutes, six people had emptied two bottles of very expensive champagne. Looking at Louise, I realized that Gary had been the only alcohol virgin at the table.

"Gary!" my father directed.

My then and future best friend stood up and raised his newly refilled glass.

"To the smartest person in the Catholic world"—nodding at me—"and to his sister"—nodding at Louise—"the most beautiful."

Louise and I blushed, but everyone else laughed and clapped. Polly and Alice were even tapping their forks on their plates. My mother was looking at me, smiling, that look of pride and love that I saw on her face whenever the subject of discussion was her children.

Polly stood up, and I held my breath. I also tried very hard not to make eye contact with Alice, but I knew she was watching me.

"To Louise, on her journey to the big screen." And then, looking at me: "To Izzy, on his journey to the . . . to the priesthood."

Polly had unwittingly turned the key in the lock of a door that I did not know I had been standing in front of. As she spoke about my sister, I started to see the future. You must suspend your disbelief here. I do not mean I imagined the future. I *saw* the future. I saw my sister as an actress. The others might have thought that Polly was using a cliché, but I saw my sister in focus for the first time in my life. All the clues had been there. How she had always watched the movies not as a fan but as a student. How she always memorized lines from her favorite scenes. How she had, in some ways, been more like my father than I was, more theatrical, more able to shift personalities in a split second. As Polly spoke, I saw Louise then as she is at this very moment, as you now hear this story, a woman in her forties, an actress who has been in almost thirty movies. A woman whose look and voice change with each role, whose own character is still a secret. I saw Gary as a balding professor, my father as an old and frail man, Polly as a pudgy mother with a pack-a-day cigarette habit. I peered through that door and looked for Alice and my mother, but before I could see them it shut quietly.

Alice had gotten up to make her toast.

"To Louise Janine, the sister I never had . . . ," she began, and we could all hear Louise whisper "You mean the daughter" under her breath. Without missing a beat, Alice dipped her fingers in her water glass and, without looking at her, flicked water in Louise's face. "May she be as successful in life as she is at strip poker."

From some secret shared experience, Polly and Louise both laughed uproariously at Alice's reference. Before Alice could continue, Louise interrupted her.

"Be sure to invite me to your wedding, Alice. I'll have a toast for you."

"You'll be my maid of honor, but can you wait that long?"

"Sure, but would you please do it before I go through menopause?"

"Louise . . . ," my mother said, but not too harshly.

The Judge, Gary, and I were all blushing. My father was pouring another round for everyone.

"And to Abraham Isaac," Alice continued, "may his life"—she turned to face me—"may your life be filled with wonder and grace."

I was still holding my first glass of champagne, and it seemed that I was the only male at the table who understood the veiled reference to Grace. Polly and Louise both snickered until frozen by a look from my mother.

"To the true son and daughter of Hubert and Edna," Alice said as she tipped her full glass and emptied it with one gulp.

Everyone looked at my mother. It was her turn. My father was standing across from her, a glass in one hand, another full bottle in his other hand, as she rose from her chair.

"To my babies, my *true*"—she nodded to Alice and then to me and Louise—"my true children. I wish you what I have found"—she looked directly at my father—"one person to truly love."

My father sagged, his hands dropping to his side, the champagne almost spilling from his glass. The party might have been over at that moment, but, of all people, the Judge rescued us.

"Right on!" He belched, the first tipsy signs of champagne beginning to slur his speech. "Hear! Hear!"

Alice looked at me, and I knew what to do. I quickly stood up.

"To all of us," I said, raising a warm glass. "To my sister and my parents. To my friends. To the future."

I was the center of attention, and my parents were happy again.

"Let's cut the cake," Alice said, and the party continued.

Three hours later, after a conspicuous consumption of cake and fried chicken, after eight bottles of champagne, after three hours of jokes and gossip and bad imitations of all the white-trash customers we had ever had, after Louise pouting and then laughing, after Polly letting slip that she was going to wait to give me my birthday present and Alice nearly choking on a chicken bone when she said that, after Gary telling Louise that he wanted to marry her, after the Judge telling everyone that he really really really loved them, after my father standing on his chair and reciting verses from Dante, after Alice telling us about the faculty at St. Agnes and thus making my father immensely satisfied at the frailty of human flesh, after me noticing that my mother and father were touching each other's feet under the table, after me wondering who was the first person Alice had had sex with, after that brief moment when everyone was singing but my mother and me and she came to sit beside me and asked how Grace was feeling and I told her I did not know, after me watching Louise and Alice whisper back and forth and then laugh, after me thinking about how in a few hours I was going to see and touch Polly and continue the sensation of the early morning of my birthday, after I realized that sex was like a drug that was offered free the first time but that you then spent your life seeking to recapture those moments of euphoria over and over, after three hours of studying my parents' faces and seeing lines I had never seen before, after seeing Alice stand behind my mother and rub her shoulders and my mother reaching back to pat Alice's hand, after seeing the Judge try a hundred times to make a spoon stick to his nose, after seeing a dozen furtive glances toward me from Polly and then one long stare as Louise whispered to her, after my parents had given Louise and me each a pair of keys to the new car that was to be ours as soon as we passed our driver's test, after the Judge gave me a model airplane kit that was meant for a third-grader, after Gary gave Louise a charm bracelet and me a billfold, after Polly gave Louise a cigarette lighter that my father politely ignored, after Alice gave Louise a new diary with a Houdini-proof lock, and, finally, after Alice gave me my first camera, after all that, it was time to open the box office.

Fortunately for the Flamingo cash flow, my mother was sober at the ticket booth. In the concession stand, Alice handled the cash register as if the champagne had been water. My father was especially impressed with her ability to match him glass for glass and not totter at all as she walked.

Thus, the customers that night were processed quickly when it came to extracting their money, but getting them served in the concession stand was a major problem. Louise and Polly did not get to the stand soon enough to prep all the food, so the first few customers saw a comedy of dropped beef patties, burned popcorn, undercooked hot dogs, and Coca-Cola that sometimes tasted like Dr Pepper. Polly and Louise were having a gay time entertaining themselves, and they were drunk enough to ignore Alice as she yelled at them. Instead of their pirate hats, they had put large cardboard popcorn buckets on their heads.

I offered to help in the concession stand, but the Two Stooges yelled "Get out of the frigging kitchen" at me as loudly as they could while brandishing ladles and forks. The customers just stood there and watched them. They had heard rumors about the Flamingo.

Of all of us, Gary was in the worst shape. His initiation into the world of bubbled wine forced him to sit on the patio most of the night, close enough to the men's room for any emergency trips. Alice, for fun, would sometimes take a meatball sandwich out to him and ask if he was hungry.

"Just remember, Gary dear," she would say to him, "it's not the Ides of March you've got to worry about. It's the grapes of wrath!"

If we had been busy that night, the Flamingo might have been in real trouble, but there were only about fifty cars on the lot. A bad opening night for the summer, but a price my father was willing to pay in order to maintain another one of his traditions. As part of our birthday celebration, Louise and I were allowed, months in advance, to pick the movies to be shown the week of our birthday.

In 1968 I had picked *Lawrence of Arabia.* I had never seen it, and it had never played a Florida drive-in, so my father thought it might be a fair box office draw, especially on the biggest screen in the world. Louise had picked *Rosemary's Baby.* My father was not pleased with the combination, but a deal was a deal.

Lawrence was given top billing, and Alice pointed out to me before it started that I might have done myself a disservice by choosing a three-hour movie about camels and deserts.

"Three hours, Izzy, means that the first intermission won't be over until after midnight."

I had been taking pictures with my new camera.

"And?" I asked.

"And that means Polly won't be free until after your birthday is over. Not much to get sentimental about if you lose your virginity on the day *after* your birthday."

I took her picture.

"I thought about that already," I said as I looked at her through the focus of the camera she had given me. "Pete can put an intermission strip in at the end of the fifth reel. Be about ten-thirty. A twenty-minute break, and Polly will be free to roam."

We went out to the patio, where I took another picture of her.

"Getting awfully cocky, aren't you?" Alice said.

"Hadn't thought about it like that, Alice. It just seemed like the thing to do."

"Yeah, the thing to do," she repeated.

"Smile, Alice." I pointed the camera at her again. "And answer me one question," I said.

"You always have one question, Izzy. Were you born with one question?"

"Not with this one," I said. "Who was the first person you ever . . . you ever had . . . you ever made love with?"

"Other than you?"

"Alice!"

"Give me your camera, Iz," she said. "I want you to have a picture of you on your birthday taken by me. Save it, so every time you look at it, you remember who took it."

"You think I could forget you?"

"Not really, but why take chances, I say."

"Who was your first, Alice?"

She took my picture. "An older man, a long time ago, somebody I trusted. He said he would not hurt me. How's that, Iz: tragic and mysterious enough for you? And, really, why ask?"

"I made a list. That question was on it."

"I'm on a list?"

"Not like that, Alice, you know that."

If ever given a second chance, if born to live again, I would not ask Alice that, nor would I tell her it was a question on a list. It was the most ungracious moment of my life.

"I know, Iz, I know. No offense taken." She shrugged and handed me back my camera. "So, tell me, what else is on your list?"

"I want to ask the Judge about my father's plans for the Fourth of July."

"Why not ask your father?"

I realized that I did not have a good answer for that question. It had simply not occurred to me to ask him.

"I don't think he would tell me the truth," I finally said, and that seemed like a reasonable answer.

"Probably not," she said, relieving me. "But, heck, who does?"

I wanted to change the subject.

"Is Polly still planning to see me later?"

"Oh, absolutely, Iz, and you have to act surprised. She is going to ask you before intermission. Maybe slip you a note. Nothing specific, but enough to get you to where she wants to go."

I felt like I was glowing.

"Go see the Judge, Iz, and then come back here to help at intermission. Louise and I can close the place down. We have an agreement."

Just as Peter O'Toole was being interrogated by the Turks, I found the Judge asleep on a swing in the playground. When I touched him, he sprang up and began apologizing, "Jesus Lord, I'm sorry, Mr. Lee. Must have dozed off. Sorry sorry sorry." But then he realized it was me and relaxed. "Oh, young Abraham, thank goodness it's you."

"You have to tell me, Judge," were my first words to him, "exactly what my father has planned for the Fourth."

Did he see a different me? I don't know, but I did know then that the Judge seemed afraid of me, as though if he did not tell me what I wanted to know, then I would tell my parents about his being asleep in the playground. But there was no reason for him to be afraid of my parents. They had forgiven him much worse.

"Can't do that," he said, shaking his head.

"Why not?"

"It's a surprise. He told me to keep it a surprise."

"Judge, I don't think my mother likes surprises, especially after last year."

"No, no, Abraham"—he seemed to flutter—"this is not a bad surprise. This is safe, your daddy guaranteed me. He's got a triple-money-back guarantee from the fireworks company. They promised a foolproof Fourth. You and your mama will see. It's safe."

"Tell me, Judge," I said again, reaching out to steady his shaking shoulders.

"I'll tell you, but you have got to act like you don't know. Is that a deal?" he finally said, standing up to stretch his arms and to try to pour some sobriety into himself.

"A deal," I said, and I was not lying. I was going to keep it to myself, but I was also going to make sure nothing bad happened on the Fourth.

"Sooner Fireworks has a new product. A sky banner. Like those banners I fly around to advertise the shows. But this one is a long banner that lights up. Message of your choice. Lasts about thirty seconds, like those big exploding ground displays at the end of the show. You know?"

The Judge was getting excited as he described the effect, clenching his fists and boxing some unseen opponent. "You have to see it the way your father described it," he said. *Happy Fourth 1968!* That's what it will say. Just as the regular fireworks finish, I'll be flying overhead and the big finale will be that banner exploding behind me and then floating down with letters blazing and pinwheels popping at the corners."

"Floating down?" I asked, starting to see the obvious flaw. "You are going to let it free-fall down?"

"That's the beauty, Abe. All the sparklers are timed to last just long enough that it gets about a hundred feet from the ground. Of course, depending on how high up you drop it and how the wind's blowing. But they all fizzle out at the last second and then there's this giant boom. This pants-wetting boom. The crowd will love it."

The Judge was body-punching his phantom foe when I left him.

Three hours later, Louise and I were sitting alone on the patio watching the birth of Mia Farrow's devil-child.

"I could play this part," she said.

"The son of Satan?" I said, trying to be funny.

"No, Iz, the woman who had sex with the Devil."

"I was joking," I said.

"I wasn't," she said, but then she reached over and patted me on my arm, letting her hand stay there all through the ending credits.

"How long have you wanted to be an actress?" I asked her just before Pete turned on the Tower lights.

"A long time, a very long time, Izzy."

"Will you still come see us if you're a big star?"

"I'll fly you to Hollywood, some chartered studio jet, with a starlet just for you, my favorite brother," she said, still squeezing my arm.

"No, Louise, I don't want to go to Hollywood. I want you to come back here."

We watched the few remaining cars drive slowly out the exit. We could hear Pete closing down the projection booth, film cans clattering, and then the steady nightly sweep of his broom. The screen was dark. On top of the Tower, two red lights were blinking. The booth door closed, and we could hear Pete's feet walk across the gravel toward his caboose. "Good night, children," he said to us as we sat under a moonless sky. "Night, Pete," we both said at the same time. I wondered if Louise remembered that our birthday was also the day Pete showed up at the Flamingo.

"You tired?" Louise asked me as soon as we saw the lights in Pete's caboose go off. I thought we were alone.

"I think I am," I said. "At least, I think I should be, but I'm not really. Does that make sense?"

"So, how was it?" she asked, but not in her usual sarcastic tone. Her voice was softly concerned.

"How was what?" I asked, and for the briefest of moments I genuinely did not know what she meant. But that innocence did not last.

"Polly," she said. "How was she? How . . . was . . . *it?*"

I told my sister the truth, and she seemed happy for me. "It was very good."

"Will you tell me all about it sometime?" she asked.

"Will you tell me about your first?" I asked her.

"You'll be the third person to know." She laughed. "Right after me and whoever the lucky guy is."

Even at sixteen, my sister was beginning to be a wonderful actress.

My First Twelve
Pictures

What follows is a description of the first twelve pictures of my career, taken between 6:30 p.m., June 4, 1968, and 2:00 a.m., June 5, 1968, with critical commentary.

1. Gary, Louise, Polly, and Alice as a group. Gary in the middle, grinning. Polly, Gary, and Louise in sharp focus. Alice, who moved at the moment I pressed the button, face blurred. Gary is holding a champagne bottle.

2. Looking down at the West Funeral Home from the Tower. The hearse and three black limousines clearly visible. One of the West sons washing one of the limousines. If you look closely, you will notice that the front bumpers of all four vehicles are lined up to be exactly even with each other. I tried to frame the picture to exclude the Cowboy marquee, but was not successful. Louise had gone with me and Pete to see Frank, and then I went to the top of the Tower by myself.

3. Gary sitting on the patio. His eyes are closed. Head back.

4. Louise and Polly in the concession stand, popcorn buckets on their heads, both of them making an obscene gesture toward the camera. I remember that there were customers watching us. Not well framed. I wish I could have had them under the menu board

nearby. The top line copy was PACK YOUR TRAYS
WITH OUR TREATS.

5. Pete's caboose. It completely fills the frame. You can
see spots of the original red paint where the sea-blue
is peeling. I made an extra copy of this as soon as it
was developed. Had it enlarged and gave it to Pete.
My first picture gift. He still tells me how much he
appreciated me doing that for him. I often take pictures now and make prints for people. Sometimes
the people do not even know they have been pho-
tographed. They just get an anonymous eight-by-
ten in the mail. Nothing incriminating, sometimes
just a picture of them or their house, or perhaps a
close-up of their hands or face or their children. I always make sure the picture is of publishable quality,
artistic, a picture that magazines would pay to have.
I imagine my pictures framed on the walls of people
who have never even met me.

6. My mother and father standing together outside the
box office. The best picture ever taken of them in
their lives. They said it, but I knew it as soon as I
took it. It was the first picture that I knew was going
to come out as my eye had seen it. Their hair—
perhaps it was how the sun was setting in front of
them—was blond and red again. I had that sensation for the first time, the feeling that the camera
lens and my eye were the same. I saw them as they
looked before I was born, as they must have looked
to each other that first time in Chapel Hill in the
Dante seminar. When I showed them the picture,
even my mother was moved, almost to cry, but she
stopped herself.

7. Alice at the cash register, from behind. She hated
this picture and tore it up when I showed it to her.
I made a reprint, but did not tell her. She was right.
It was a bad picture. Taken without thought or
composition.

8. Alice at the cash register, looking over her shoulder toward me at the concession-stand door. A good picture. Her face like that of a model or actress, but her hair a bit frazzled. Still, that look is there, that measuring look she often had when you were the object of her interest.

9. The picture Alice took of me. The only picture of me on my birthday by myself. I am leaning on the front rail of the patio, the screen behind me. I am wearing my Hawaiian shirt, but not my pirate hat or eye-patch. I am looking right at her, not at the camera. My mother especially liked this picture. My black hair is wet and combed straight back.

10. Polly.

11. Polly's bed. Just the bed. My second flash picture. Pillows on the floor.

12. Me and Louise on the patio. A flash picture. Louise's favorite picture of me and her together. Mine, too. Both of us in our Hawaiian shirts. Her gorgeous, as usual. Hard to take a bad picture of Louise. Neither of us looks sixteen. Much older. But you can tell we are brother and sister. It is the only picture I have in which we look genetically bonded. I look less Korean; she looks more. The flash illuminates just our faces. Everything else is black. Alice took the picture. She had come to the patio after the show was over. Said that she was going to walk us home. Make sure we were safe. Last shot on the roll, she told us not to move. We waited until she was ready. Could not see her, but she could see us. We waited, the flash blinded us for a few seconds, and then we all walked back to the Tower.

Free Will and Fate

Sixteen, and a licensed driver, I had three weeks to figure out how to alter the future. I was also getting a Darwinian education from Polly about natural selection and survival of the fittest. In that school, I was two weeks ahead of Gary Green.

More important than my tutoring from Polly was my desire to control the Fourth of 1968. If I could do that, I knew it was going to be a good summer. To control the Fourth, I knew I had to get more information out of Judge Lester. His allegiance to my father, weakened by alcohol on my birthday, had soon risen again to the level of patriotism. The Judge loved my father, but he was becoming suspicious of Hubert Lee's son. Whenever I approached him with a direct question about the Fourth, he would mumble and change the subject, or tell me to go ask my father. But I knew he would not tell my father that I was asking; he still did not remember exactly what he had told me on my birthday.

For the week after my birthday, my father had booked a movie combination that made almost everyone at the Flamingo happy. A Steve McQueen double feature: *The Thomas Crown Affair* and *Bullitt*. Gary and I spent the week watching *Bullitt* and imagining ourselves racing my Corvair down A1A as we chased some Florida gangsters. But *Bullitt,* the older movie, was the bottom half of the bill. Most of the customers were there to see *Thomas Crown.*

I did not tell Gary, but I eventually came to like *Crown* better than *Bullitt*. Part of my appreciation for *Crown* was that I saw how it affected everyone else, especially the women in the crowd. In fact, it was one of the few movies that my mother actually arranged to watch herself. She and Alice traded jobs opening night, and then I was put at the concession cash register as soon as the first feature started. I could see my mother and father sitting on the patio watching the movie together. They had never done that before.

At certain points in the movie, every night, Louise and Polly would take turns going out to the patio to watch particular scenes. On the second night, when Alice asked me to relieve her at the register so *she* could watch it, I knew I had to see the whole thing.

On Friday night, Gary and I finally got to see *Crown* from beginning to end straight through. Crown was not a tough-guy loner turtleneck sweater detective like Bullitt. He was a three-piece-suit banker: sophisticated, handsome, and lonesome. If the phrase "cool" meant anything, it meant Thomas Crown. Gary wanted to be Bullitt; I wanted to be Thomas Crown.

I also wanted Grace to see *Crown* with me. As soon as that late show was over, I told Alice how I had wished Grace was there to see it with me. "So ask her," Alice had said.

"Sure, it's that easy," I said, a little impatient. "You think her father is going to let her waltz down here to watch a movie with me this late at night?"

Alice and Louise and Polly had been watching the end of *Crown* that Friday, but they had had to close the concession stand, so they had missed the first thirty minutes. It was 1:30 a.m. Saturday before they could get to the patio, and, at first, they sat by themselves away from Gary and me. Eventually, he and I moved to sit behind them.

"You think her father is going to keep her away from you?" Alice said. "Or are you afraid that she just might say no for herself?"

Soon enough, everyone else on the patio had gathered around to offer me advice.

"Call her tomorrow," Gary said. "All she can do is say drop dead."

"Why do you want her to watch *this* movie with you, Iz," my sister asked, but I think she already knew. "You gonna be Steve McQueen for a night?"

"I bet I know why," Polly said, nudging Louise with her elbow. "He's going to ask her to play chess with him. I bet you're a good chess player, aren't you, Izzy?"

Somewhere in your past, you have probably seen *The Thomas Crown Affair*. If you did, you will remember the scene where McQueen and Faye Dunaway play chess in front of his fireplace, and how the camera starts to move slowly around them as it becomes obvious that they are attracted to each other, and how their faces come closer together as the fire gets brighter behind them, and then the camera is swirling faster around them as they begin to kiss, and the kiss does not stop until the fire and the faces seem to be the same and the scene blurs out of focus and then fades to black.

"How about it, Iz, you a good chess player?" Alice smirked and then stood with Louise and Polly. "Does your Knight always get the Queen?"

" 'Wild nights, wild nights! Might I but moor tonight in thee, wild nights would be our luxury,' " Louise recited, her hands folded across her chest.

Polly looked at Louise like my sister was from another planet, but Alice knew the source.

"How about this, Iz," she said, pointing her hand at me like a pistol. " 'My life had stood a loaded gun . . .' "

"Stop it! Both of you," I said. "I simply said I wanted to ask Grace to see this movie with me and you guys . . ."

Gary caught up with us at that moment.

"Hey, that's Emily Dickinson. We did her a month ago in school. But all I remember is that one about her waiting for death or something, and that funeral in her brain."

"Who is this Emily girl?" Polly asked, turning to Gary. "And who did her? Did you do her?" Then she turned back to me, almost looking angry. "Did *you* do her?"

I looked at Polly, and I was embarrassed for her even though she herself was not embarrassed.

It was all too much for Alice.

"Oh, for Christ's sake, Polly, have you ever read a book in your god-blessed life! Emily Dickinson is a dead walleyed poet. Not Abe, and nobody else, *did* her!"

At that moment, I liked Polly better than anybody else on the patio. She and I had had sex every day for the previous nine days. It may have been carnal, it may have been clinical, and her reasons might not have been sentimental or emotional, but she was not a bad person. She did not deserve to be the object of ridicule. Polly, however, did not need my sympathy.

"Oh," she said. "Well, then, that's okay. Dead girl poets don't count."

All of us looked at her, and we all, I knew, liked Polly very much at that moment. Alice put her arm on Polly's shoulder and leaned down to kiss her on the top of her head, whispering just loud enough for the rest of us to hear, "Don't worry, you were the first."

Gary, standing behind me, jabbed me in the back. Louise, on the other side of Alice and Polly, rolled her eyes.

Polly then surprised all of us.

"Iz, why don't you ask your mother to talk to Grace's father about letting her come to the movie? You ask Grace, your mother will take care of the old man."

Only Alice and I could really appreciate how much generosity there was in Polly's suggestion, and I thought I could read Alice's mind at that moment, looking at me with her arm around Polly, looking at me as if to say that she had been right about her choice for my official initiation. Alice, I could tell, was very proud of Polly.

"Polly's right about your mother, Iz," she said. "But let me talk to her myself, and your father. Cover all the bases so there are no surprises."

"I'll talk to Daddy, too," Louise added.

"Is it settled?" Polly asked, rubbing her stomach under her shirt. "We'll work out all the details for your date. You just be a perfect gentleman."

"And you can have the patio to yourself," Gary said. "None of us will get near you. A deal?" he said, looking at everyone else.

Everyone nodded, even Alice.

"So, if that's settled, does anybody want to go swimming with me?" Polly asked, unbuttoning the top two buttons of her shirt. "And, Alice, you don't bring your flashlight."

"Don't worry," Alice said. "You kids go fishing. I'm going to bed."

I remember that night, how I hoped that I could keep every one of those people around me for the rest of my life. I trusted all of them, even my sister, and I wished I knew how to repay them. It was a long time ago.

The next night, actually Sunday morning, Grace and I had the patio to ourselves. I had walked down to the West Funeral Home to get her, and I walked her back when *Crown* was over, after three in the morning. She did not see Alice or Polly, or, at least, she did not acknowledge their presence behind us in the concession stand. Gary brought us some popcorn and Cokes, said hello, and then disappeared. Grace and I sat in the first row, our feet sometimes propped up on the rail in front of us. Before Steve McQueen and Faye Dunaway played chess, I had already put my arm across the back of her seat. Chess Kiss consummated, Grace rested her head on my arm.

I discovered something about myself that night. If I truly cared about someone, I wanted them to share everything with me. Well, almost everything. But if I liked a movie, or a book, or a song, or the look of a building, I would try to re-create that experience for them. Buy the book or music, take them to the building. Sitting with Grace that night, I wanted her to have seen all the movies I had seen. So, VCRs and videotapes have become an essential part of my life. Especially with my sons, I will have them sit with me at night and watch old movies that played at the Flamingo in the past.

The older boys are now at that unattractive age when all children try to break away from their parents, but Dexter is different. Dexter will sit with me and watch anything, anytime. Sometimes, I will find him watching a tape that he and I have already seen. He especially likes the old science-fiction movies from the fifties. Last night, he and I watched *The Incredible Shrinking Man.* I was touched. He is as scared of spiders as I am. Tonight we are going to watch *Them,* the movie that marks my earliest film memory. Giant radioactive ants roam the sewers in a big city and eventually kill James Arness. I had nightmares for weeks.

. . .

I remember *The Thomas Crown Affair* for more than just my patio date with Grace. *Crown* also had a scene that was the wedge I needed to pry more information out of Judge Lester.

It was near the end of the run, Monday night. The Judge was in the playground watching the scene in which Crown flies his glider. It was an odd angle from which to watch any movie, right there almost directly under the screen.

I was walking the ramps when I saw the Judge sitting on a bench near the playground gate. I expected him to be surprised to see me, but he did not move when I sat down beside him. Over us, Steve McQueen was gliding solo, looping and soaring as the sound track played "The Windmills of Your Mind."

"I always wanted to do that," the Judge said, his own head slowly swaying from side to side.

"But you do that three or four times a week, Judge," I said, looking up with him to see how the sunlight refracted off the glider's canopy.

"No, no, not be a pilot. Be a glider," he said.

I turned to look at the Judge, his face brightly lit by the light reflected off the screen. I could see then the man that my mother, Louise, Grace, and even Alice had described to me, the man who was perfectly calm in the air.

"Flying is wonderful, Abraham, but I have always wondered how it would be to fly without the noise or the vibration of the engine, to see how long I could stay up, how far I could go. Know what I mean?"

I just looked at him.

"You see, young Abraham, flying my Piper is something that I can do really good." He laughed to himself but kept looking at the screen. "I know you and your mother don't think I can do anything good, but I can."

"My mother tells me that you are a very good pilot," I protested.

"She does?" he asked. "She really does?"

"Absolutely," I said.

"That's good," he said softly. "I'm glad to hear that. Real glad.

I wasn't sure how she felt. She always seemed to like it. Told me she wanted me to fly her at night sometime, over the ocean and this place here. See the lights on the road and on the boats offshore. But she never told me she thought I was okay."

"You're okay, Judge," I said.

The gliding scene does not last too long in *Crown,* just enough to get the "Windmill" song sung. When it was over, the Judge did not move. His guard was down.

"Are you still flying that exploding banner on the Fourth?" I asked him, trying to appear only mildly interested.

"Oh, sure. Fact is, Abraham, your daddy ordered two of them. I've already practiced with one, just to make sure the timing is okay."

"You've already done it once? Why didn't we see it?"

"Did it yesterday afternoon. Flew way offshore so nobody could see it. See, the tricky part is making sure the whole thing is unfurled before you hit the switch."

"Switch?"

"Sure, you can't light this thing like you do ordinary fireworks. It's hooked up to an electric wire that ignites a fuse that sets the whole thing off. Lot safer that way. No matches or flares needed. I just sit in the cockpit and pull this special switch. Ten seconds later it's HAPPY FOURTH."

"Did *everything* work the way it was supposed to?" I asked.

"You mean did it fizz out when it was supposed to on the way down? Right on cue." He beamed. "Every letter at the same exact second. If you're under it, you might think it's coming down on top of you, blazing *H*s, but it goes dark in plenty of time."

I then knew my father's plans. He would know that Turner West and his sons would be out on their roof with hoses, prepared for the worst, and they would see this burning banner coming down out of the sky toward them, and they would think that my father had gone completely mad and was trying to burn them to the ground. My father would be back at the Flamingo, perhaps on top of the Tower watching the banner descend, knowing that it would extinguish itself at the last second but also knowing that Turner West would be petrified. It was to be a joke. My father would laugh as he told the story for years afterwards, how West's heart must have almost burst up until the last split second, how impotent West must have felt. But I also thought that I knew that my father's plans would not go as he intended. The banner would fall, but the timing would be off, or the wind too weak or too strong, and the banner would fall to the roof, and garden hoses would not save the home of Turner West and his family.

The fire would not be intentional, but it was inevitable.

A few minutes later, the Judge had returned completely to earth. The effect of the glider scene had worn off. He sighed and then said he had to get back to work at the box office.

The Judge had told me more than he knew. More important than just helping me imagine how the Fourth would happen, he had implicitly told me that the fireworks were already somewhere nearby. I had to locate them, and then I had to figure out a way to make sure the banner did not work. I had fourteen days.

For the week after the Steve McQueen double feature, my father had booked a Sidney Poitier double feature: *In the Heat of the Night* and *The Defiant Ones*. Pete was very pleased. Business was surprisingly good, especially since the mayor of St. Augustine at that time was a Kleagle in the Klan and had once bragged about having shut down the only "colored" movie house in town after it was used for an organizational meeting of the SCLC. A health problem, he had said, too many roaches. Jacksonville had been a little bit more sophisticated in its response to the civil rights movement. I know this now because I have gone back and read all the old newspapers from that time. Back in 1968, Pete was my only racial barometer.

My world was very insulated, I'll admit that. I sometimes think now that I was, indeed, possibly very aware then of all the strife outside of the Flamingo, and that I have simply forgotten much of it. But I also know that I do not forget anything from my past. If it happened, I remember it. The war and the marches, the dogs and hoses, they were pictures in *Life* magazine. But they did not happen to me.

In 1968, I was two years way from the draft. It might as well have been centuries. Gary once mentioned the draft to my father. We had been unloading an early film truck. Gary had only been joking, but my father turned and pointed his finger at him, telling him, "My son will never go over there. Nor will you." Gary did not talk about the army ever again.

After the opening night of the Poitier twin bill, after nobody called in a bomb threat or even let slip a slur about dark skins when they saw me or Louise, after I saw some of the younger white kids walking around the concession stand at intermission imitating Poitier's line "They call me Mr. Tibbs," after I saw lots of black and white customers standing in line together piling the food on their trays and actually helping each other reach for the hard-to-get popcorn boxes at the back of the warmers, after I saw black and white kids playing in the playground together, after I saw Pete smile for the first time in a long time, after all that, my father and I let out our tightly held breath.

Alice told me to not get too optimistic.

"You see any of the white teenagers mixing with the Negro teenagers?" she pointed out the second night. "And, if that so happens to happen in the next few days, you watch to see all these cracker faces if some Negro boy and white girl walk in this concession stand holding hands. Watch Polly, especially her face."

"Alice, why do you *always* see a half-empty glass?" I tried to joke with her, using one of my mother's favorite metaphors. "Why not half-full?"

We were locking up the concession stand after the last intermission on opening night. Polly and Louise and Gary had gone to the beach to go swimming, along with two St. Agnes temps. Alice was sorting the receipts for the night. My father always appreciated how obsessive she was about tightly bundling the cash with all the bills facing the same way and all the coins rolled.

"Iz, you've got to remember," she said as she smoothed out a crumpled ten-dollar bill, "this drive-in ain't America."

Money safely bagged, she added, "Heck, this drive-in isn't even a drive-in. Know what I mean, jelly bean?"

"Alice, I have no idea what you mean, jelly bean yourself."

"Oh, sure you do. You just don't know it yet," she said, tossing me the bag of money. "Let's go see the Wizard in the Tower, and then you can go swimming."

"Are you going with us?"

"Do I ever?"

"No, not yet."

"So, stop asking, Iz. The answer is always going to be the same," she said.

After I walked with Alice to deliver the receipts to my father, I went back to the projection booth to see Pete. He was sitting on a lawn chair outside the booth door, watching the end of *The Defiant Ones*. Just inside the door a big fan on the floor sucked warm outside air into the even hotter booth. I wanted to ask Pete about the Fourth.

"Are you in charge of the fireworks again this year?"

Pete kept his eyes on the screen. Sidney Poitier and Tony Curtis were about to be lynched by a crowd of angry whites, but Pete was smiling.

"I saw this movie ten years ago," he said, fanning himself with one of those folding hand fans that had some advertisement on it. "Had to sit in the balcony, but I knew that Poitier boy was going to be a star someday. I've seen all his movies."

"Pete, I can't imagine you having time to see any movies. I thought you were on the railroad all the time."

"Abraham, why do you think I stopped here eight years ago?"

"Your truck was broken down," I said, but I knew that my explanation was not the real reason. It was too literal.

"That's right. Falling apart under me. Wheels flat on the trailer and a transmission that had seen better days. But I would have stopped anyway. Or some theatre. Truth is, I always wanted to work in a movie theatre. Some sorta luck or fate just put me here."

At that moment I wished I had my camera with me. I was seeing a picture. Pete still has that lawn chair, the seat and back restrung a dozen times, but the same aluminum frame. That night in late June of 1968, I saw Pete in the future in that chair on the back of his caboose, saw him in the future, saw him in 1968 as I saw him just yesterday.

"Did my father say anything to you about something different for the Fourth?" I asked him.

"Just that he was going to be more careful this year," Pete said. "Keep the shrimpers disarmed, keep you and Harry off the Tower. But nothing special."

"Nothing about an exploding banner?"

"No, Abraham, all I know is that young Gary is supposed to work the booth while I work with those Oklahoma people out on the barge. Do you know something different?"

"I think my father is planning a special display that he thinks will . . . will irritate Turner West," I said, but I did not tell him that I thought my father's plan would be disastrous.

Pete shook his head and sighed. "Yes, your daddy would do something like that. He can be a small man sometimes."

"I think he is going to have the Judge drop a banner over the funeral home," I said.

"Well, if there is a way to do it wrong, Harry will find it. He is very predictable."

Pete understood my dilemma, I could tell, and I knew I could trust him.

"You should talk to your daddy," he said.

"Pete, my father will not listen to anyone when it comes to Turner West, you know that."

Pete nodded, and then said, "It is strange, how he feels about that man. And your mama, she does not deserve her grief about knowing Mr. West, all that tension all these years. Strange man, your daddy, afraid of losing things that can't be lost. Your mama, she can't be lost."

"So you understand, Pete? I can't talk to my father, but I do have to stop him. I have to stop him from hurting all the people around him. If he does this thing on the Fourth, something bad is going to happen. I know that. So I have to stop him."

Pete was silent.

"When do the fireworks get here?" I asked him.

"They're here already, Abraham. In the Tower. Been here a week or so. I helped Harry and your daddy unload them when you and the others were in St. Augustine. I checked them all in, checked them against the invoice sheet. But there's no banner there. Just more of the same as last year."

"You checked everything?"

"There is no banner, Abraham. I swear to you."

"The Judge said there were two of them," I said, desperate for some clue.

"They're not in the Tower. Never were," Pete said.

"There's one left, Pete. It must be somewhere."

Pete stood up to go inside the booth to make the reel change-over. Every twenty minutes, for every show, he had to stand between the old projectors and wait for the cue marks on the corner of the screen: one cue to tell him that there were five seconds left and that he had to start the other machine and then the second cue to tell him to flip the switch on one Simplex and open the shutter gate on the other. In eight years, he had never missed a changeover. Perfect hand-eye coordination.

Seeing the first cue, he told me where to look.

"It's probably already in his plane in St. Augus"—changeover—"tine. Look there."

A week later, my mother asked me to drive her to St. Augustine so she could get some things from her Flagler office. It was the first time ever she was to be my passenger. I was tempted to tell her all about the banner, but I did not want any more friction between my parents.

I looked at my mother that afternoon in the Book Room and wondered about her and Turner West. If I had known all about my own future, I would have known that my mother, and my father, every parent, had a secret life from which their children were excluded. It was necessary, I suppose, for their sanity, for mine now. Back then, I also realized that my mother did not know everything about me. Surely not. Polly? Alice? How would my mother know about them? Why should she? Why should I have to know all about her and Turner West?

My mother was sitting on the black leather couch, a stack of books on the end table next to the couch and a stack of magazines on the couch itself. She read every day. Books for her courses, mostly, academic journals, and some weekly magazines. When Louise and I were very young, we would sit on that couch with my mother between us. She would read to us every night, usually with my father sitting in his big chair across from the couch. Nursery rhymes and fairy tales and Bible stories. When we were very very young, we would hear Bible stories that had been simplified for children. By the time we were six or seven, she would read directly from the giant Bible that had been read to her when she was a child. King James, from her Baptist upbringing. Louise and I would also take turns reading as my mother moved her forefinger along under the lines. Old Testament names would always trip up Louise, and she would giggle, try again, fail, giggle, and try again. My mother would feign exasperation, but my father would laugh along with Louise. Then he would begin to make up a limerick using the name but always heading toward some conclusion that involved a bodily function. My mother would stop him, but we all knew how it would have ended. Then we were put to bed, my mother tracing the sign of the cross on my forehead and kissing me, my father patting my chest.

Ten years ago, Louise and I drank too much at one of her parties, and I reminded her about all those nights when our mother read to us. I thought she was almost going to get sentimental, but she stopped herself when she saw that another actress was trying to overhear our conversation. It was the last "Hollywood" party she ever invited me to. In fact, the more famous she became as an actress, the less she went out in public. In her most recent movie, however, there is a scene in which she plays a mother reading a Nancy Drew mystery to her daughter. When I asked her about it, knowing how she had loved Nancy Drew, Louise shrugged at first. But then she smiled. "That was for you," she said.

Looking at my mother that night in 1968, I slowly realized that I had to do more than just find the Judge's plane and the banner. I had to start making choices about other things as well. I asked my mother if I could invite Grace to go with us.

The next day, my mother sat in the back, and Grace sat up front with me. We had the top down on the Corvair, so Grace and my mother had scarves tied around their heads. My hair looked like my finger was attached to the battery. The radio was playing "Sgt. Pepper's Lonely Hearts Club Band" and then some forgettable songs, and then a Mason Williams instrumental called "Classical Gas," which, if you are driving, makes you speed up. I looked in the rearview mirror to see if my mother noticed, but she was looking out toward the ocean as it appeared between sand dunes. I thought I was flying a jet. Just as I went past the speed limit, my mother said my name and I let up on the accelerator. I thought I was in trouble, but she pointed out that she could not hear the radio if I went too fast. And, besides that, she said, she wanted to hear the song that was on at that particular moment, the theme from *Thomas Crown*. I slowed down and let the other cars pass me, but my mother and Grace were happy.

After we dropped my mother off at the front entrance of Flagler, Grace and I walked over to the plaza across the street. We sat on a bench next to one of those Spanish cannons left over from the eighteenth century.

"I need your advice," I said to Grace there in the plaza.

"Is it about my father and your mother?" she asked.

"Not directly. But it might affect them. I want you—"

"Isaac, I want to ask you a question before you go any further," she interrupted. She had moved to the far end of the bench so she could turn and face me more directly, but there was still that noticeable gap.

"Do you know what I think about when I'm at home?" she asked.

I thought I did, but I was wrong.

"I think about us," she said, looking over at the Booksmith.

Why was I surprised to hear that?

"About us? You mean you and me and our parents?"

"No, just us. You and me. I look at a clock and wonder what you are doing at that exact moment. I look out my window at night and see the front side of the Flamingo Tower, all that pink neon. I wonder what you are doing, especially late at night when I can't go to sleep."

I started to say something, but she waved her hand to stop me. "No, no, let me finish. I think about us. About when you kiss me, especially the last few times when it was so different, so nicely different. I get scared. I don't think you can imagine how happy I was that you asked me to come with you today. I think silly things. Like how our children would look if you were the father and I was the mother. Isn't that silly? I mean, we're only kids ourselves. But I think about how beautiful our children would be. I think about living with you all the time, away from all our parents, away from this place. Do you know what I really want to tell you, Abraham?"

I shook my head, seeing Dexter almost a quarter century in the future. I looked intensely at Grace on the bench, trying to see her more clearly in that future. I could not make her come into focus, but I knew she would eventually. I would see it all before it happened.

"I want to tell you that I love you," she said. "I hope you love me, too."

I had never told her. In four years, even though it was obvious to me and everyone around me, I had never told her.

I need to tell you something now, as you hear this—my only chance, probably—and you have to ignore how ponderous, how patronizing I must sound. If you feel it, and you know it, then you must say it. You must never let that other person wonder if you love them. I should have told Grace sooner. I should have been the first. There is only one first time.

"I love you, Grace," I said, truly and deeply.

She smiled, almost grinning, and then she said, "I knew you did, I mean, I know you do. I just wanted to hear you say it."

We both took a deep breath at the same time, and we both laughed at each other at the same time.

"Something else, Abraham," she said, moving across the bench closer to me. "I think I know more about you than you do about me. I have a life that you need to know about. I think if you were to tell someone about me they might not see who I really am. Does that make sense? I want you to come see me more at my house. I asked my father, and he said it was all right. Will you do that?"

"I would like that," I said.

"He talks about moving away from here, up to Jacksonville. So I have been thinking about how hard it might be to see you, especially if I have to go to another school."

I was only mildly surprised by the possibility that Turner West would be moving. As quiet as it had been for the past few weeks, I knew he was tired of my father. But if I could alter the Fourth of 1968, I thought to myself, sitting there with Grace, then perhaps our parents would reach some sort of adult understanding, like adults were supposed to do. If my father's banner did not fall on the Fourth, I thought, Grace might be able to stay just down the road from me. If it did fall, there was no hope.

Grace and I sat there, and I knew what I needed to do to change the future. But I needed Alice's help.

A Trip
to the Airport

I would do the right thing. I would not ask my mother or my sister or Grace about the Judge's airplane. I had decided to ask Alice. It was to be our second partnership, something less public than putting a dead woman back into her car.

"You said you were going to ask me to help you do something," she said. We were in my Corvair cruising down A1A, Alice driving, and I was switching radio stations every time a commercial came on or whenever Bobby Goldsboro began singing.

"I want you to tell me where the Judge keeps his airplane. You've been with him on flights, so I thought you might have been with him when he parked his plane, or whatever it is you do with a plane when it is not flying."

"Abe, you don't need me for that. You must know he keeps it at the airport out on Highway One," she said, not looking at me directly.

"The airport, yes, but *where* at the airport? It's not outside. I've looked. And there are a dozen hangars, most of them locked up. I need to know exactly where and how to get in. Can you help me?"

"Why do you need to know all this?"

"I just do, Alice, I just do. Can you trust me until after the Fourth of July fireworks? I will tell you everything then."

I wanted her help in finding the plane, but I did not want her to be actually involved in whatever I had to do to stop the banner drop.

"You want me to trust you? But you don't want me to know why you need to find that plane? That right?"

I nodded.

"Does anybody else know about this plan of yours? Now or ever? Is it really truly between just us?"

I nodded again, and almost at the same moment Alice hit the brakes and we did a screeching U-turn on that narrow blacktop highway, scraping shrubs and scattering gravel along the side.

Fifteen minutes later, I was standing in front of the Judge's red Piper Cub. Alice was sitting outside in my Corvair, prepared to hit the horn if she thought someone was going to catch me. I imagined I was Sean Connery playing James Bond.

Once I was inside that hangar, the Piper was easy to spot among the half dozen other planes. Closer to it, I could clearly see the banner attachment. A makeshift metal chute had been strapped to the bottom rear part of the fuselage. Even when I think about it now, I can still remember how obvious it was, how obvious what I had to do was. Inside the Piper cabin, I looked for the wire that the Judge had described. At first, I was confused because there were two wires that had been newly rigged to the control panel. I traced them both down along the floor and back to where they went through the rear cabin wall. I realized that one wire was to release the banner and the other was to ignite it. I cut both of them, taking a full inch out of each one where they passed under a floor mat.

Unless he was looking for trouble, he could not see that the wires had been tampered with. Flying alone at night, the Judge would pull the release switch and wait for the jerk as the banner flew out to its full length and then became a drag on the plane. But there would be no banner released. He would not be able to fly the plane *and* search for the problem, so he would have to return without dropping the banner. My father would be upset. The thousands of customers who had been promised something different this year would be disappointed.

And I would tell my father what I had done.

Walking back to the Corvair, I must have been smiling. Alice was sitting on the hood. She gave me that look of hers, that look that nobody could ever directly face.

"You find what you were looking for?"

I nodded.

"You do what you need to do?"

"I think so," I said.

"Everything okay?"

"Alice, I'll tell you everything after the Fourth. But for now I'd like to keep this a secret between us. Is that still all right?"

"Will I be surprised?"

"Are you ever?"

"Not too often," she said, shaking her hair away from her face and sliding off the hood down to the ground. "In fact, never. No surprises, no disappointments."

"So, does that make you happy?" I said, raising my eyes to meet hers.

"Nope, Iz, it just makes me feel safer."

I was about to say something else, but she interrupted me.

"Whatever . . . You sure about this?" she said.

I took a deep breath and looked right into her eyes. Neither one of us blinked. "Absolutely," I said.

She stuck her right hand out to me, as if we were about to shake hands. "Okay then, Clyde, done is done. Let's go rob some banks."

Six Pictures Taken 7/4/68, Before the Box Office Opened

1. Grace on the beach at sunrise. We had sneaked out of our houses while it was still dark. Our parents were still asleep. Grace is midway between the line of the tide's edge and the back of the Flamingo seawall. Strong wind. She is framed by the concrete and saltwater lines. The water line goes to the top of the picture. The Flamingo seawall stops about halfway up. Her face is darker on the right side as she faces south.

2. Polly and Alice in the Booksmith in St. Augustine. Alice had written BOOK on a large sheet of paper, with an arrow from the K to the edge of the paper. She was holding the paper next to a real book, the arrow pointing to it. Polly is scratching her head, acting dumb. The picture was Polly's idea.

3. Alice and Louise singing a duet on the plaza across from the Booksmith. Louise is sitting on top of one of the old Spanish cannons, her legs wrapped around the barrel. I thought the pose was too obvious, and a bit vulgar, but Alice insisted, saying, "Sometimes a cannon is just a cannon."

4. My father and me, side by side next to my Corvair. Alice took this picture. My father and I are the same height. I am wearing the usual Hawaiian shirt, but I

had just that day convinced him to let all of us forgo the eye patches and pirate hats as a uniform requirement, just for this Fourth. Everyone was very grateful to me. My father had been very easy. "All you had to do was ask," he had said. One of my father's favorite pictures. Except for some gray hair, I look exactly the same today.

5. Grace and her father in the parking lot of the West Funeral Home. I had worked very hard for this shot. Turner West was at first uncomfortable with posing. So I faked some shots, twitching my finger and making clicking sounds with my tongue three or four quick times in a row, my face hidden by the camera. When he couldn't maintain his pose any longer, he involuntarily relaxed and that is when I really snapped the picture. He is looking down at Grace. Her head is leaning into his chest, and her right arm is around the front of his stomach. In the background is the hill where West had wanted to build his cemetery.

6. Alice and Louise and Grace. An odd shot. The only picture I have of them all together. Alice and Louise had been walking down A1A to come get me for the opening of the box office. I had been gone for over an hour. They had walked past Grace's house and she had come out to see them. My sister was actually being nice to Grace, inviting her to watch the fireworks from the patio. Grace had declined, as Louise knew she would, but it was a sincere offer by my sister. They are standing under the Cowboy, Alice on the end. In this particular picture, you can see the edge of the West Funeral Home, the legs of the Cowboy, the neon Flamingo on the Tower in the background. A1A is full of cars. Grace and Louise are talking. Alice is looking at me, holding a blazing sparkler high over her head, bright sparks against that dark sky, a thin bracelet around her wrist. It

would have been a better picture if I had gotten closer and focused on them, but I wanted to get in as much as I saw at that moment. Grace went back inside, and then Alice and Louise and I walked back to the Flamingo to play our parts in my father's annual Fourth.

Consequences

The Fourth had begun with my father's own version of psychological warfare. With my mother and most of the rest of us in St. Augustine that afternoon, my father had had Pete turn on the Tower speaker horn and play Handel's fireworks music as loud as possible. And then again, and again, for all the time we were gone, relentlessly and needlessly reminding West of the previous Fourth. West, of course, had scheduled no services for either the third or the fourth of July. He was too busy getting ready to defend his home and business.

When we had gotten back to the Flamingo from St. Augustine, I could feel the air getting thick with another storm like we had had the year before. It was cloudy and very humid. The wind was blowing strong in from the east. All day long, I had expected the rain to come, but by the time we opened that night the wind had calmed down, and the only signs of meteorological trouble were the clouds and an occasional rumble of thunder, but no lightning.

My father had spent extra money advertising this particular Fourth, even though we had always had a sold-out lot. This time, however, he made it very clear in the ads when the show was actually going to start. First feature to start at 9:00 sharp, running time one hour and thirty-seven minutes; a twenty-minute intermission; the Handel overture for three minutes; and then, as the music continues to play, precisely at 11:00, the Fourth of July, 1968. A twenty-minute extravaganza, bigger than last year, and then, as advertised, a finale that had never before been seen in the continental United States.

"You ready? Abe!" my father had shouted to me as Alice and Louise and I ran past him to our places on the lot. I waved at him.

The Judge was unlocking the chain across the box office entrance. By the time the first car was on the lot, we were all in place. I remember the Judge giving me a thumbs-up sign as I raced by him. My mother waved at me from inside the box office.

"About time!" Polly yelled at us as we got to the concession stand. "I thought y'all were going to leave me with all these virgins." She pointed to the four St. Agnes temps that my father had hired for this Fourth night: Amy Smith, Connie Farley, Gretchen Smiley, and Cindy Mitchell.

"Gretchen is the only virgin in this building," Louise shouted as she put on a full-length apron. "Probably the only virgin in St. Augustine."

"Louise!!" Gretchen squealed, and we all laughed as she blushed.

"Louise, you just keep the food coming," Alice said, putting the money in the cash register. "Both lines open from the start."

"Are you really a virgin?" Polly asked Gretchen, handing her a tray of french fry baskets. "I thought you had—"

"Polly!" Alice interrupted with a slam of the cash drawer. "Leave the virgin alone and concentrate on your fudging grill."

"Alice!" Gretchen shouted.

"Gretchen!" we all shouted back in unison. Gretchen was always the first temp my father hired when he needed extra help. She was a serious worker, and too pretty to stay unblemished for long, especially surrounded by my sister and her friends. Gretchen's chastity was always pointed out to her, but she liked the attention, and we liked her.

"Skinny-dipping party tonight after the last show!" Polly yelled right before the first customer came in the door. "Gretchen is"—just then Gary came in looking for me, and Polly did not miss her new opportunity—"going to be Gary's surfboard. How about it, Gar-ree, you going to paddle out on Gretchen tonight?"

"Uh?" was Gary's first response.

You must have had this experience some time in your life. Pent-up expectation finally being let out. You have worked for a long time on a project, it was finally coming to a conclusion, and everything was working out as you had planned. Everyone else seemed to be fitting into some role you had assigned them. Dammed-up adrenaline made everything go faster and easier. It was like the air was totally pure oxygen, and you were pumped full of carbohydrates and your sugar level was in some red-level zone. That was what those first two hours were like that night at the Flamingo. My father's crew and all the temps were in perfect sync. The lot was full in a half hour, and the concession lines did not stop. I was in and out of the concession stand in between my rounds along the speaker posts and down to the playground. Gary and I would cross paths, exchange a status report, and then we were off again on our rounds.

In the concession stand, I would see if they needed any special replenishments from the Tower, and we would all joke and work at the same time. Polly was getting nastier and nastier the more Coke she drank, but also funnier. Louise was trading insults with Alice, and doing better than usual. I heard Gretchen call Cindy Mitchell a "hippie whore" and Connie Farley a "Polly wannabe." Connie said she would not want to be Polly even if the only other choice was to be dead. In unison, Polly and Alice told Connie they could arrange that. A pregnant woman threw up in the restroom, and Amy Smith, being the youngest, was ordered into the toilet by Louise. Gary came to get me to help him break up a fight in the playground between two nine-year-olds who turned out to be brothers. Alice sent me to the box office for more quarters, and I disappointed my mother by telling her I could not stay to talk because Alice needed the quarters as soon as possible. I promised her we would take a walk on the beach the next day. My father did his pre-show routine flawlessly and then came into the concession stand waving his sword and grabbing for Polly, who, I noticed, did not seem bothered by his lingering arm and wandering hand. And I remembered certain other times, but I did not care because I was too pumped up about the whole night.

I know, I know, I am probably making all this sound too easy. That night, those two hours. I remember most of it. That's all. I remember thinking even then that I wished I had kept my camera with me, but, then again, I was too busy to really look for pictures. Some pictures from those two hours would have been helpful in telling this story, but I was too excited. Actually, the only picture I wish I had taken that night would have been one of my mother looking at me as I raced back to Alice with those quarters. I was walking away from her, backwards, almost running, waving at her with a roll of quarters in each hand. She smiled at me like she did at my father when they were happy.

An hour into the first feature, with everything flowing smoothly, I began to smell salt in the air. A storm was coming, but I did not care. Rain or not, there would be no banner dropped. I was only worried that if the rain came too soon then the regular fireworks display might be ruined, but that would not be the end of the world.

If you have been listening carefully for the past few hours, you will have begun to hear the faint, small steps of the approaching future. An hour into the first feature on the night of the Fourth of 1968, I heard them for myself.

I went back to the box office to talk to my mother, but she was gone.

Alice was in the box office, talking to my father, who was standing next to the window.

"Where's Mama?" I asked, thinking that she might have had to go to the restroom, and Alice was just there to relieve her.

"She drove Harry to the airport," my father said.

Alice looked at me as if she thought I should have known about my mother's plans.

"Drove the Judge to the airport?" I asked.

"You remember, Harry doesn't drive himself anywhere," my father said. "He had to get to the airport, and your mother insisted that she be the one to take him. I had made other arrangements, but she insisted. You know your mother. She insists, we do it her way."

"Why did the Judge have to go to the airport?" I asked, confusing myself because at that moment I could not think of any reason for him to be there.

Alice and my father looked at me like I was seven years old and they had just picked me up off the ground after I fell off my bike. I was hearing doors, some opening, some closing, muffled but somewhere near me.

"Isaac," my father said to me in a patient voice, "you *know* why he had to go to the airport. I know you know."

"Your mother asked the Judge to take her flying tonight," Alice said.

My father and I stared at her.

"You didn't tell me that," my father finally said.

"She asked me to not tell you. I promised to keep her secret," Alice said, looking at me.

Back in the projection booth, Pete, about to go out to the fireworks barge with the Sooner pyrotechs, was giving Gary some last-minute instructions about changeovers and weak frames in the print of the intermission trailer. Louise was doing Alice's job at the concession-stand cash register. Polly was telling the temps to get ready for the intermission rush.

"Did you know about this, too?" my father asked me, his voice rising. "Am I the only one in the dark around here?"

"No, Daddy, I didn't . . . I didn't know."

I can tell you all this now, and I can tell Dexter sometime in the future, but I have known all the parts ever since that moment when my father asked me if he was the only one in the dark. All the choices made, the acts of will, the merging decisions.

"She told me she was going to drive him, not fly with him. But I should have known, ever since we argued about the banner, I should have seen her getting in the way. I suppose she's right, but it would have been harmless. There was no need for her to interfere tonight," my father said, shaking his head. "No need for all this."

How did she know about the banner? I asked myself. But then it became obvious to me that her knowing about it was a good thing. The Judge might have done something stupid all by himself once he found out that he couldn't drop the banner.

"I told her not to worry," my father said. "Said that Harry and I had practiced all this. Harry told me that he had found some trouble with the banner but that he had fixed it. Everything was fine. I told your mother not to worry. She worries too much, I told her that."

The Judge had found something wrong. What did that mean? Did it really make any difference? My father was right. My mother would not let him drop the banner.

I looked at Alice, who was looking right at me.

"Did the Judge tell you what was wrong with the banner?" I asked my father.

"Nope, just that it was a simple problem, and he would have it fixed by tonight. Isaac, are you okay?"

I was not okay, but I could not tell him. Or Alice. I just walked away.

"Isaac, are you okay?" my father repeated.

I went to the kitchen in the Tower and called the airport. Surely, I thought, someone could call the Judge on his radio and I could talk to my mother. Surely, there was a way I could tell her about the wires. There was no answer at the airport's main number. It was late. It was a small airport. Surely, there was time.

The next thing I heard was Handel's music. Three minutes. I went running to find my father. He was on the patio, his face turned up to watch the exploding sky. I was breathless. The crowd was entranced. Horns blaring, collective gasps of pleasure. The box office was closed. Alice was standing on the seawall at the edge of the lot. I could see her clearly. Nobody was in the concession stand. Polly and Louise were laughing, one on either side of my father. There were so many fireworks going off that it seemed like they were a string of firecrackers all lit at once. Starry bursts of reds and blues and golds and thundering claps of exploding gunpowder. Circles and lines of disintegrating light.

I talked to my mother. I told her about my future, about Grace and the boys and Dexter, about college and my first trip back to Korea, about all that I was beginning to see as I waited there that night looking at my father.

I was the only one there, I knew, who could hear, between the bursts, the drone of the Judge's Piper gliding toward the Flamingo. Then I saw what my mother must have seen at that moment as she flew toward her home that night. From miles away, she would have seen the lights and how gorgeous it all was, and she would have held her breath as the Judge dropped down to only a few hundred feet off the ground and then she would be carried across the Flamingo lot and she would look down to see all of us waving at her. The Judge would dip his wings as he flew directly over the patio, and my mother would see her husband and her children on the ground at the edge of the Atlantic, and then she would look back toward us as she flew farther out, and we would all be getting smaller, and then we would disappear.

"There they are!" my father shouted as soon as he heard the Piper engine.

I did not look.

My mother flew past us, but I did not look up. I could hear the engine as it came so close over us that it temporarily drowned out the sound of the fireworks, and then it faded as the Judge pointed his plane out to where he could turn around and head back.

I just looked at my father. He did not know what was about to happen, but I did. The plane was coming back, and I knew that my mother had not stopped the Judge from dropping my father's banner. She had simply told him to drop it offshore but close enough for everyone to see. It would seem like an eminently fair compromise. But the Judge would have misconnected the wires that I had cut. There would be no moment for either of them to think about anything. He would simply pull the switch to free the banner, but the crossed wire would ignite the banner instead. It would be very quick.

I looked at my father as the sound of the engine got closer. Then I watched him die.

There was an explosion and then complete silence, and my world had been reduced to my father's face as he saw, as his eyes reflected, my mother falling into the ocean.

On Eagle's Wings

Sometime in the future I will have to talk to Dexter about all those storybook initiations that are waiting for him, especially sex and death. I will tell him that the difference between sex and death is the difference between sight and sound.

When I first touched Alice on the beach all of my senses were overloaded, all except sight. I was in the dark. I could see nothing. But I could feel, hear, smell, and taste. All of those senses were panting, as if I were pumped full of some magic drug that told my body to absorb everything in excess, everything except light.

As I looked at my father's face late on the Fourth of 1968, as the Judge's plane exploded over the ocean, over the barge that Pete was on, as I stood there on the patio and felt the sound wave of that explosion coming toward me from behind, pushing the salt air out of its way, all my senses shut down, all except sight. I was deaf. Touch and taste and smell were gone, too, but I noticed their loss only after they returned at my mother's funeral.

I looked at my father's face and saw everything in razor-like focus. The explosion had torn apart the letters of the banner, and they flew in a dozen directions, single fiery letters spinning like pinwheels away from my mother, and then, as the Judge had promised, they vanished.

I was frozen, as was my father. We could not move. I looked at Louise. She was screaming at him, tearing at his shirt, screaming at him to do something. In my mind, I could hear her, but the sound did not come from the outside. I was reading her lips, seeing the words almost like print. She turned to me and screamed again, but I knew I had to stay with my father. She ran toward the water.

The fireworks display was over, and I realized that the crowd thought that the Judge's plane was part of the show. They had gotten their money's worth, and my father had been truthful in his advertising. Headlights were flashing on four hundred cars, off and on, bright and dim, and I knew that their horns were honking, those sound waves bouncing off a blank screen and heading out to sea. The crowd was happy, but the next half hour was very ugly. Expecting a second feature, they soon began honking in annoyance, not exultation. North Floridians came looking for the manager, shaking their fleshy knuckles in my face, jabbing their stubby fingers in my father's chest, demanding a refund, cursing a theatre that no longer existed.

With Pete on the barge offshore, and my father and me sitting on the patio, Gary Green assumed command of a sinking ship. He had seen the explosion, knew what had happened, and knew the show was over. He immediately turned on the large floodlights at the four corners of the concession stand, and then he turned on one of the Simplexes, projecting a white light on the world's largest movie screen. The field was illuminated like a cloudless noon day.

He called the police, but with so many of them already on duty around the Flamingo to deal with the expected traffic jams, they were already swarming the lot trying to steer the crowd out the exits. But since A1A was also packed with other spectators of the Fourth, there was no way to get the Flamingo lot cleared quickly.

Gary got on the PA system, trying to calmly inform the crowd that due to technical difficulties there would be no second feature. Seeing the mounting hostility, he soon came up with an idea that probably saved the Flamingo from total destruction. He told the crowd that they would get a three-for-one ticket refund if they would just come by the box office tomorrow. He told me all this later, weeks after my mother's funeral, told me how he was afraid he might be doing the wrong thing, making decisions like that on the spur of the moment. But my father told him he had done the right thing. My father was very proud of Gary, as was I. When Gary went to Notre Dame with me, my father paid for it.

Polly had rushed into the concession stand at the same time that Louise ran to find my mother. The other temps were hysterical, but Polly yelled at them to remain absolutely calm.

Why were Polly and Gary so prepared, I have always wondered. Gary and I talk about that night every so often, and he still doesn't have a good explanation for why he did what he did. We both still shake our heads in wonder at how Polly knew to start giving away all the concessions free. Anyone else would have hesitated, but Polly not only started giving everything away free, she loaded up trays and went out on the patio to seek out customers, forcing them to take some popcorn or a slice of pizza, interrupting their verbal assaults on me and my father, telling the twitching swarm of customers that everything was on the house, or something like that. Looking at Polly that night, I remembered what Alice had told me about her. Don't underestimate Blondie, she had said.

Gretchen, Amy, Connie, and Cindy were in the concession stand, crying and cooking. If Polly had not gone in after the lot was cleared and literally grabbed their hands, they would probably have been cooking through the next morning.

I was in the center of a silent movie. For that half hour I sat there and watched a thousand people stumble over each other in their frenzy to get free food, or to get out, or simply to vent some vague and personal wrath that had been provoked by their being told about the absence of a second feature in their lives that night. I saw Gary step between my father and a man wearing a cowboy hat and boots, saw Gary grab the man's hand as it flew toward my father, saw Gary shove the man's hand back into the man's shoulder. Gary was very strong when he was young.

I saw Polly offer a bald man a free Coke, but he knocked it out of her hand. I saw the words come out of her mouth as she shrugged and told him that she could replace the drink but he couldn't replace his hair. She was funny. The top of the bald man's head turned red, and Polly offered him another drink. Gary was standing behind the bald man. I looked at Polly and Gary, and I wished they would fall in love with each other and get married. They would have been good together. But I could see the future. It was not going to happen. She had been his first, but he would never find his last.

I sat there knowing that Louise would never forgive me or my father. How could we just sit there? My father was paralyzed from shock and grief. I don't think Louise had ever understood, and still does not, how much my father loved my mother. He did not move that night because he was no longer alive. I did not move because I knew there was nothing to do at that moment. She and Alice had roles to play. I did not.

By midnight, the lot was clear, and I could see the wake of the crowd. Over a hundred speaker posts had been knocked down. Dozens of decapitated speakers lay on the ground, their wires ragged where they had been torn from the posts. The playground fence had been battered by careening cars. One of the plate-glass windows of the concession stand had been shattered. The concession stand itself was a shambles, food and boxes all over the floor. The doors on the restroom stalls had been knocked off their hinges, the mirrors broken. One sink had been pulled out of the wall and water was gushing out of the pipes.

Polly had the four temps off in one corner of the patio, holding Gretchen's hand and speaking low to the others. Gary was talking to three deputies. The only cars on the field were police cruisers, red lights flashing. The screen was still white.

I was standing behind my father as he still sat, my hands on his shoulders. I was talking to him, telling him what was about to happen. In my ears, the sound of my voice was like hearing a tape recording. You've had this happen to you. You hear yourself on tape, but you do not recognize yourself. But, still, it is you. A disembodied voice, but yours. I leaned down, putting my voice right behind his ear, whispering to him to look out toward the water. My mother was coming back.

If you were there, you would have heard a chugging motor as it pushed the fireworks barge toward shore. The tide was out as far it was to go that night, and there was almost no wind. The barge was huge and flat. At each corner was a pole light, each pole taller than Pete Maws, who was standing in the center of the front edge of the barge. Pete was directing some phantom crew, those unseen Oklahoma pyrotechs who were at the back of the barge, directing them to keep the barge plowing straight ahead, like one of those giant sea turtles that must plod themselves onto the sand to burrow a nest for their eggs. The barge came straight toward us, almost grunting as it heaved itself onto the beach. Planted on the shore, Pete raised his right hand, motioning to his crew to turn off the motor. Standing in the center of the empty barge were Alice and Louise, each soaking wet. My mother lay between them, covered.

Pete jumped down off the front of the barge. Louise and Alice carried my mother over to the edge and handed her down to him. He was much smaller than my mother, but he seemed to have no trouble carrying her, one arm under her knees, one arm under her shoulders. By the time he reached his caboose, Alice had raced ahead of him to be there to open the door for him. Pete took my mother inside.

Louise came back to the patio, but she did not sit with me or my father. Alice came to the patio with two quilts that Pete had given her from his caboose. We were all waiting for Turner West.

West did not arrive as soon as I had expected. Grace would tell me later that he had waited until he had been able to call his two oldest sons, who were in Georgia and South Carolina. With them notified and on their way back home, he had sat with Grace in his office, telling her stories about her own mother. He did not talk about my mother, but Grace understood. Turner West had to go back to the past to avoid thinking about the present.

At three in the morning, West's youngest son drove him to the Flamingo to pick up my mother. The hearse floated through the exit and parked next to Pete's caboose. My father was standing at the foot of the steps to the caboose, waiting for West to appear.

Face-to-face, the two men shook hands, and then they walked off to one side of the caboose for a private conversation. Their feud, so often a farce, had ended. They would never forgive each other, but they each had ceased to care about the other.

The two men made arrangements. West had wanted the land behind his building for a cemetery. My father wanted my mother to be buried on that hill. A deal was made. Land was transferred. The oral contract was binding. My father assumed that West would prepare my mother's body. West said that *he* could not, but he had called in all his sons. They would handle the body.

West pointed out that the land behind his building was not ready to be a cemetery yet. My father told him that he would make those arrangements. Every landscaping company in Jacksonville and St. Augustine would be called, and all would be hired at once. Round-the-clock shifts, my father promised, would create a cemetery in seventy-two hours. Permits and zoning? West asked. My father shook his head: No problem. Coffin? West asked. Your choice, my father said. Services? The ceremony itself? Each man looked at the other, then they came back to the steps of the caboose to see me.

Services? The ceremony itself? My voice told them that Grace and I would make those arrangements.

The door of Pete's caboose opened.

Do you remember early in my story, when I told you that only one other person had ever been inside Pete's caboose? This was that moment. Turner West ascended the caboose steps, carrying a large dark-blue blanket with gold trim, and walked inside. He was there for a long time. After a while, Pete stepped out and stood on the back platform of his caboose, leaving West alone with my mother. I remembered my eighth birthday, when Pete had first stepped out on that platform, looking down on the Lee family.

When West came back out again, I was afraid that he might stumble. He looked pale and shaken, but he held together. He motioned for Pete to help him, and the two men took a canvas stretcher inside and then came out again, carrying my mother, now covered in the gold-trimmed blue blanket, carried her exactly parallel to the earth, even as they descended the caboose steps, carried her out of the caboose down to the hearse, which then carried her to the home of Turner West.

At noon the next day, Turner West and Grace, my father and I, sat in West's main parlor. Just the four of us. Louise stayed in the Tower, burning bridges between herself and her father. The two men sat at opposite sides of the large room, each in an oversized Queen Anne chair. Grace sat across the room from me on a Victorian couch. I rested on an amply padded footstool. At the other end of the building, the six sons of Turner West were standing around my mother, preparing to bring her back from death to sleep.

For five hours, none of us spoke. My father and West did not move. Grace would sometimes leave the room to go check on her brothers, coming back to smile at me but shake her head. I looked hard at West and my father, to see if they could hear each other. They must have been talking to themselves, and then to each other. The room was silent, but I knew they were speaking.

I looked at the walls and saw pictures on them that I had not taken yet. You can go there now and see my first ocean pictures. In 1968, one wall in West's parlor was covered with a few standard prints of famous paintings, mostly French Impressionists, and another wall had a few enlarged photographs of famous American landscapes. It was not a good mix, and I was surprised that West had not seen the obvious clash before then.

At five o'clock, Grace's oldest brother came into the parlor and whispered something to his father. Turner West stood up and we all followed him, my father last.

As I walked down the hallway to a viewing room, I began to feel weak. I was almost nauseated. I knew my father was feeling the same. I was afraid to see her. It would be proof.

Grace went in the room first, and then my father. I stood away from the coffin, purposefully making sure that Grace or my father would block my view. Instead, I waited for my father's reaction. I waited for him to turn to me, waited to see his face.

His back to me, my father stood there several minutes. He put his hands on the edge of the open casket, leaning forward for support. I saw him reach inside the casket, then I saw him reach inside his coat pocket and take something out and put it in the casket. Later, I asked him what he had put in with Mother, but he told me it was a "personal something" between the two of them.

I heard him sob, softly, and I heard him take a deep breath. I closed my eyes. When I opened them again, my father was looking at me, and I knew everything was okay. He held out his hand toward me. I walked over to stand beside him and see my mother.

She was in her wedding dress. I had seen the old photos. Her blond hair was flowing around her face. That was one thing different from her wedding, when her hair had been tightly pinned up. The only other difference was that she also had on long white gloves that went past her elbows, and the dress sleeves came down over the edge of the gloves. The only skin I could see was her face and neck.

Her gloved hands were folded across her stomach. Everything below her waist was hidden by the lower half of the coffin lid.

I wanted to talk to her, but I told myself that she was sleeping and not to be disturbed.

I looked at my mother, and then over to Grace, and then to the door where Turner West stood with his head down. How could my father have ever hated these people, I wondered. My mother had been destroyed, but the sons of Turner West had brought her back. I looked at West. If he had taught his sons how to do this, how to be both artists and welders, alchemists who took death and made it . . . made it, I don't know, not life, but not death either, how could my father envy or resent this man? How often had he and his sons been able to do the same thing for a thousand other families?

Grace walked over to get her father, the most reluctant of us to see my mother. My father and I stepped aside while Turner West looked down at the work of his sons.

West clutched the edge of the casket and stared at my mother. He began to weep, stifling some emotion that was working itself out of him. Then he began to sob more uncontrollably than even my father had. His knees buckled, and he slumped down beside the casket, his hands still on the open edge. Without thinking, I knelt down beside him just as Grace did, and the two of us helped him up. I thought I heard him, through clenched lips, whisper some damnation of a god in which I knew he did not believe.

Years later, Grace told me I was wrong. Her father, she said, was actually thanking God for his sons' art. I must remember, she told me, that of all the people in that room at that moment, only *he* had seen my mother as she was *before* his sons had transformed her, as she had been in Pete's caboose.

But I heard God damned, I was to insist. "You did not hear that from my father," she told me. "You heard it from yourself."

Except for sight, I was senseless until I heard Grace sing at my mother's funeral service.

My father had been right to let Grace and me handle those arrangements. I like to think that at that moment outside Pete's caboose, when he and Turner West looked at each other, I like to think that my father saw himself absolutely clearly, that he recognized that if he allowed himself to handle the arrangements then my mother's funeral would have been too gaudy and exorbitant, too much of a drama to show his loss, as if layers of procession and music and flowers and speeches were public proof of *his* love for her. I like to think that.

I had asked him about music, and he had said that he wanted to hire the Jacksonville Symphony Orchestra. I did not ask him about anything else.

The service was to be Catholic, with a pall over my mother's expensive casket. The Bishop would preside. He had known my mother for years. Services would be in the St. Augustine Cathedral, where Turner West had first seen my mother and where my father had never set foot.

For music, Grace honored the request of the Cathedral choir that it be allowed to sing. My mother had sometimes sung with them in the past, but she had not been a regular member. I contacted the Jacksonville Symphony and hired two musicians: a violinist and a pianist. The choir sang a few of my mother's favorite hymns. The Jacksonville musicians took the theme music from my mother's favorite movies and blended them into a long medley that transformed all of them into something more solemn, more significant. I told them which songs to use.

I sat with my father in the front row. Every so often, I would glance at him and try to hear what he was thinking. When he was not looking at the casket, he was letting his eyes travel around the Cathedral, trying to absorb all those images that my mother must have seen in all the years she had been going there.

I looked at him and then around, and I had an odd thought. The inside of the Cathedral, I told myself, was like the inside of one of those Fourth of July fireworks. Sitting there, I felt like I was inside a silent explosion of holiday color. Gold and blue and red and silver were everywhere, brighter than I had ever seen them, erupting colors that had been frozen so that you could study where all the lines went and how the colors interconnected. If it were possible to take a precise picture while inside one of the Oklahoma starbursts, I would see the inside of the Cathedral.

Then it occurred to me that I would see even more in that starburst if I could enter it. Surely, I thought, beyond light and color, such an explosion in the sky would be composed of all these other images there around me in the Cathedral. With a special film and a special camera, I could photograph what must surely exist within that burst. It had to have been there every July above the Flamingo, right before our eyes.

I saw the inside of the Fourth: the Stations of the Cross, the Annunciation, the Martyrdom of Saints, Birth, Crucifixion, Resurrection, the bleeding wound and crown of thorns, the dying face of Christ as he called out to his father. I saw all that, sitting there next to my father, saw everything my mother must have seen at her very last moment.

Louise sat on my right, staring straight ahead. She had refused to sit by my father, as she had refused to go with us that first night to the funeral home as our mother was being restored by the West sons. Louise went to see her the next day, alone, and two more times, but always alone.

Alice, Gary, Polly, and Pete sat behind us. Turner West and his family sat in the front row across the aisle from us. Behind us, the Cathedral was full.

I did not hear the choir sing nor my musicians play, but I could feel voices and notes inside me. There was a lull in the service. No one moved. No one spoke. Then Grace stepped up next to the casket, followed by Alice and Louise. They had not told me about this part. Tallest of the Trinity, Alice stood in the middle.

I felt the piano begin playing my mother's favorite hymn.

Alice and Louise and Grace began to sing "On Eagle's Wings." The piano was barely audible, but it was clear. Of the three girls, Alice's voice was the least smooth, but their combination obliterated any individual weakness. It was almost as if they were singing a cappella. My father, who had often heard my mother sing this song at the Flamingo, began to tremble.

With the end of the first verse, Alice and Louise fell silent. The piano also stopped, and then, as the single violin began to vibrate, Grace sang the refrain solo.

With Grace's voice, I began to hear again, to inhabit all of my body, not just my eyes. And I began to hurt. Like frozen hands plunged into warm water, the extremities of my existence came to life again, but only after a thawing pain that I cannot describe to you, a pain that told me that I was not up in the casket with my mother, not in that plane with her, and worst of all, that I was never going to be back on the beach with her, never again going to see her smile at me like she smiled at my father.

For the first time since the Fourth, I began to cry. Hearing me, my father took a deep breath, put his own pain to one side, and put his arm around me.

Hearing Grace sing, I began to see everything that was going to happen to us in the future. I saw the death of her father, the eventual death of mine, our marriage in the Cathedral, our sons, whom she had already tried to imagine, my picture-gallery house kept to myself. I saw her growing older with me; I saw her nursing Dexter with that look on her face that must have mirrored mine as we both saw him as a miracle; I saw a hundred sad and happy scenes.

I knew all of those scenes led back to that day when Alice and I went to the hangar to find the Judge's plane, that week before the Fourth, when she sat outside as I cut two wires, when she looked at me as I came out of the hangar, and I knew she would always keep my secret.

As my father promised, the Turner Cemetery was completed in three days, but my mother was not buried as soon as it was finished. In addition to the cemetery, he had also commissioned stonecutters to build a small mausoleum of Georgia granite, so small that only two caskets could be placed in it. My father did not want my mother under the ground, nor himself.

Because the granite had to to be sculpted as well as cut, the mausoleum would take more than three days, so my mother had to wait almost ten days inside the Turner Funeral Home until she could be laid to rest. My father went to see her every day. I wondered if he was still jealous of Turner West, especially since West had even this temporary possession of my mother.

When the walls and other parts of the mausoleum arrived, my father and Turner West co-supervised its placement. Almost two weeks after the Fourth, I stood with the two men early in the morning at the spot that they each agreed was the ideal location, at the crest of the hill, on a gentle slope.

The sun was just coming up, but there was a shadow over the future site of my mother's grave, a shadow that my father was finally coming to see.

The Tower was blocking the sunrise.

"It's in the way, Daddy," I said.

Turner West looked at my father.

"Daddy, it's in the way," I repeated.

My father was staring at the only home I had ever known. He looked at West and me, then back toward the Tower.

"It's been there a long time," West said.

"It's got to go," my father said; then, looking only at me, "so your mother can see."

"Mr. Lee . . ." Turner West began to speak, but then he just looked down at the ground and began shaking his head, not knowing how to finish his thought.

"I'm going to burn it down, burn it down to the ground," my father said, letting out a deep breath. "Down to nothing."

The Great Fire

It was to be my father's last grand gesture.

I sat with him and Pete on the patio. The screen had been blank since the Fourth, but Pete had already done all the repairs necessary to reopen. The posts had been replanted, the speakers reattached. Except for being at the funeral, Pete had worked every waking hour to patch the cracked egg that was the Flamingo.

"Do you understand what I want?" my father asked a few hours after he, West, and I had been at the cemetery.

"Yessir" was all Pete said at first.

I wondered if he resented that all his labor had been wasted.

"Do you disagree?" my father asked.

"No, sir," Pete said.

"You know that you can stay here as long as you like. I'll still need someone to watch the grounds."

"I appreciate that," Pete said.

"Turner West will probably ask you to do some odd jobs for him."

Pete grimaced, but then he noticed my reaction.

"Nothing against Mr. West," he said. "I just don't want to work there."

"Not in his business, Pete," my father quickly said. "Just some small maintenance jobs around the building, the parking lot, some landscaping on the grounds behind him, you know. And I would appreciate you looking after Edna on those days I might not get there. Would you do that for me?"

"Yessir, I'll do that for you," Pete said. "Didn't mean to be so sharp a second ago, just misunderstood."

The two men did not speak for a few minutes, nor did I. The three of us were reluctant to get up to begin the end of the day.

Late that afternoon, my father gave Polly a hundred-dollar bill and told her to take Louise to St. Augustine.

"You girls go to a movie, buy some things, spend every penny of this, and don't come back until you do," he told her.

"You sure you don't need some help around here?" Polly asked, insinuating some knowledge that she should not have possessed.

"No, we're covered," my father said, unable to look her in the face.

Polly looked at my father, then she stepped closer and put her arms around him, hugging him tightly.

"How long do you think you'll need?" she asked him as she let go. "Midnight?"

"Not that long, but close. Just give us about six hours."

Polly nodded, folding the hundred-dollar bill, and then she looked at me. "Will I see you again?"

"I'll be here when you get back, don't worry," I said.

She shook her head. "No, I mean when this is all over."

"Oh, Polly, we'll see each other," I said, but we both knew that we were not talking about the same thing.

As soon as Louise and Polly drove off in the Corvair, my father and Alice began the dismemberment of the Flamingo. Calls were made. Plans confirmed. Trucks arrived. Men in coverall uniforms began hauling out the insides of the Tower. Alice and I were in charge of telling them what to load in the trucks and what to leave. My father had given me a list of particular things that he wanted: the furniture and the pictures. The books were not on his list.

I told the men that everything in Louise's room was to be saved. Gary was there to take out the few things that he had accumulated in his apartment. He asked if he could have the Judge's new color television, and my father agreed. I had asked Polly earlier in the day if, by any chance, there happened to be a fire in her room, and she was not there, what would she want me to save.

"But, Iz, none of it belongs to me, except my clothes," she had said.

"But if you could pick anything to save . . . ," I had said.

"I *would* like to have that bed," she had said, and I was touched that she was almost blushing. Polly never blushed.

I did not have to make a decision about Alice's room. She had a suitcase packed as soon as I told her what was going to happen.

"Always travel light," she told me as we watched the truckers haul furniture out of the Tower, "so you can make a quick exit."

Gary was going back to his parents. Polly was going to move into a St. Augustine apartment that my father was renting for her. Pete was going to stay in his caboose. Louise and I were moving to a house my father had bought in St. Augustine, an old Spanish three-story right next to St. Agnes. A real-estate agent had described it to him over the phone.

As chairs and beds piled up in front of the box office, waiting to be loaded on the Bekins van, a long flatbed truck with a crane pulled up next to the Cowboy marquee. Within an hour, the Cowboy's head was severed, its arms and legs disconnected, its body and appendages loaded and hauled to a warehouse in Jacksonville where it rested until my father sold it for scrap.

From the top of the Tower, as I stood there for the last time, I could see Turner West standing at his door, Grace beside him, watching the Cowboy disappear. Alice was with me.

"Where will you go from here?" I asked her.

"I think I'll go north. I know some people in Chicago," she said. "Florida is a great place to vacation, but I don't think I could live here."

"But, Alice, you grew up here."

"But I sure as heck am not gonna die here," she said, punching my shoulder.

From the top of the Tower, I could see the spot where Turner West and my father and I had stood that morning back in 1960. I could also see my mother's mausoleum.

"So you're the reason for all this," Alice said, interrupting my view of the new West cemetery.

I hesitated, trying to interpret that line.

"Reason for what?" I asked, walking over to the east side of the Tower, the side facing the Atlantic. Somewhere out there was the un-recovered Judge.

"The fire," she said, walking behind me and talking to my back. "Your father said you wanted to burn it all down."

"Alice, I just agreed with him. It was his idea. Were we wrong?"

"No, Iz, you guys aren't wrong."

"And . . . reason . . . I am not the reason for all this. There is no reason for this fire. For anything. No reason that we found my mother's body so quick but have never seen a trace of the Judge."

"No, probably not," she said. "No reason for nothing. Still, reason or not, your father was right. This place has got to go. Just like me."

"You don't have to, you know. You could stay."

I meant every word.

"Sorry, Iz, you and I are headed in different directions."

"My father could—"

"Your father gave me five thousand dollars," she said, "and his blessing. I like your old man, ever since that first interview with me and Polly when he asked us if we had ever wanted to be in the movies."

"Five thousand! Why did he give you five thousand dollars?"

"Beats the fudge out of me. I only asked for a thousand."

"Alice, why did you even ask for . . . ," I began to say, but then I gave up. There was really only one more important question. "Will I see you again?"

We had walked back to the entrance to the ladder to go back down and get ready for the Great Fire. Alice went over the edge first, lowering herself down until only her old and lovely face was showing. Then she said, with that irritating smirk, "Every blessed day for the rest of your life."

At nine o'clock that night, Pete and my father went through the apartments at the base of the Tower and began pouring gasoline in every room. The five-gallon can from the projection booth was gone by the time they finished the Judge's room, but they had hauled in extra fuel. "A job worth doing," my father had said grimly, "is worth doing right."

Pete had suggested they do it at night. There would be less traffic along A1A, and by the time most people had heard about the fire, Pete said, it would be over. He said this way we could cut down on the number of sightseers who were sure to come. None of their business, he said. Do it while they're asleep.

My father had called the Duval and St. Johns County sheriffs. They told him it was illegal, officially, but that they would have some cars nearby in case they were needed. They said there might even be some fire trucks out on training exercises that night, and that if they saw a fire, they might want to investigate, just to make sure it did not spread. My father told them he would be grateful for their consideration.

By ten o'clock, everything was ready, and Polly and Louise were still in St. Augustine.

"You ready, Abe?" my father asked. "I'd like to get this started before your sister gets back."

"Yes, Daddy, I'm ready."

"Everything is out that you want to save?" he asked.

"Everything," I said.

My father and Pete then walked into the Tower.

Down the road, Turner West was on his roof with three of his sons. He knew what was coming, and he knew that if something as big as the Tower burned, the heat would scorch everything within a half mile. He and some of his sons were already soaking the shingles on their roof with water. They would stay there as long as the Tower burned. He had his other sons in the parking lot with hoses to keep the limos and hearses watered down. His cemetery had a built-in underground sprinkler system that was being tested for the first time. The new sodded grass was covered by dozens of misty water fountains that seemed to pulse out of the ground.

Gary and Alice and I parked my father's old Buick about a hundred yards down A1A South, set up some lawn chairs, and waited.

Pete and my father were very methodical. With most of the rooms on the ground level soaked in gasoline, they had to allow themselves enough time and space to get out quickly as soon as the match was dropped. Pete had also made arrangements to protect his caboose. Two lawn sprinklers on top of his roof were twirling even before he went into the Tower. Two window fans were pulling air from the inside of his home, anticipating how hot it was soon to be.

It was a good night to burn the Tower. There was very little wind, and what there was was blowing more northerly than westerly, so the smoke would probably drift out over the ocean before it got to Jacksonville.

I noticed how quiet it was, and how dark. So did Alice.

"Too much like a frigging funeral," she said in disgust, and then she got up and began walking toward the Tower.

"Alice!!" Gary and I yelled at the same time.

"Keep up or drop out. You boys make up your mind," she said over her shoulder.

Gary and I went after Alice, getting our instructions from her as we all ran to the Tower. Just as my father started to light a carton of coffee cups in the storeroom, Gary had found the switch to the Flamingo neon marquee. The giant pink bird began to bob up and down, lifting its leg and dipping its neck, for the last time. The glow lit up the night. Just as Pete threw some flaming rags in the corner of the cup room, Alice and I found her favorite Mick Jagger album. On our way out of the projection booth, we flipped on the switch to the RCA speaker horn on top of the Tower and were already halfway back to A1A before the first song began. "At least for the first twenty minutes," Alice said as we ran out of the projection booth, "we can dance *and* burn."

But we did not dance when we got back to our lawn chairs. We just sat there with my father and watched the Flamingo smoke and the Tower burn while we listened to Johnny Mathis sing.

"Johnny Mathis!!!" Alice had screamed as soon as she heard his voice, but it had been too late to turn back. The Tower had already begun to burn. I had grabbed her hand and held tight, pulling her toward me with all my strength, shouting at her that we did not have time to go back. Alice swore that she would search out and destroy whoever had put the Mathis record inside a Rolling Stones album cover.

Alice was not happy, but my father, sitting on the hood of his 1952 Buick, calmly told us all to be quiet. "I like Johnny Mathis. So did Edna. This will be okay."

Alice looked at Gary and me, shrugged, and then said, "I knew that."

As smoke poured out of the creases in the Tower, Johnny Mathis sang about chances and tides. Pete had gone back to his caboose to keep it watered down and to make sure no burning fragments fell on it. Gary, Alice, my father, and I sat on or around the Buick, watching the flames, waiting for Louise to come back from St. Augustine.

The cup room burned slowly. There was lots of paper in it, but all that paper was packed tight. It was not until a flame finally reached an open gallon jug of gasoline that Pete had left on the floor that the Tower fire really began. After the small explosion, the flames spread quickly to the next room, which was soaked in gasoline. The chain reaction was quick and increasingly dramatic.

Within ten minutes after Pete and my father had left the Tower, the ground level was blazing from end to end, and the fire began weaving itself toward the voice of Johnny Mathis. Of course, long before the flames got to the top, the speaker wires had been incinerated lower down. So, eventually, before Louise came back, the only sound most people heard was that of the world's largest screen tower combusting and disintegrating.

Two pumper trucks from the St. Augustine Fire Department had arrived, but they had driven up slowly and without their lights flashing, as if they were coming back from a fire, not going to one. A handsome fireman named Fred Tymeson, his name printed in large letters on the front of his uniform, had a private conference with my father. I could see the two men speak slowly, and then Fred patted my father gently on his back, as if to console him.

At eleven o'clock, the Flamingo neon began to explode, showering the road with red-hot glass shards, some flying across A1A and landing in the palm trees on the west side. A few of the palms began burning, but Fred and his men quickly put them out.

My father had assumed that he could control his fire, but when Fred came to suggest that we move farther away from the Tower, I began to sense his anxiety. Fred had asked him about any other combustible materials in the Tower: paints, cleaning fluids, pesticides, anything explosive.

"All those things," my father had admitted.

Fred was like a doctor giving a patient some very bad news.

"We should get some more men out here. I've already made that call, but all of you need to get farther away. There's a big difference between that thing"—pointing to the Tower—"*burning* down and it *falling* down."

I thought about Pete. His caboose was closer to the Tower than we were. Just then a palm tree a hundred feet away suddenly burst into flames, spontaneously, without having been touched by anything from the Tower except its heat. Fred made a quick motion to his men, and the palm was extinguished. "We're going to need some more water," I heard him say to himself.

"Pete's caboose?" I said.

"Nothing we can do about that," my father said. "Pete is there. He'll be safe. Worse comes to worse, he can get into the ocean."

"Look!" Alice yelled.

The asphalt in front of the box office was bubbling.

When I describe this to Dexter, I make a simple observation. You must remember, he is very young. I tell him that the Flamingo was the world's largest screen tower. So, I say to him as I tell this story as he goes to bed, he has to imagine the world's greatest fire. Flames a thousand feet into the air, heat visibly pulsating out in every direction. Burning palm trees, explosions shaking the foundations. Pete on the roof of his caboose holding a hose over his own head to keep himself soaked and protected. Plastic utensils in his kitchen melting into flatness. The unprotected concession stand catching fire, plate-glass windows shattering, wooden seats on the patio popping their slats, the projection booth dissolving. Directly at the base of the Tower, the playground disappearing as the Great Fire began to inhale all the air in the world to feed itself, sucking air toward it, creating elemental winds rushing past all the playground equipment, winds turning the childless carousel in horizontal circles, spinning the childless Ferris wheel in vertical circles, lifting the childless swings in ever-widening arcs.

If I tell this story right, Dexter can see the white screen leaking smoke and then the flames escaping from between the seams of those screen panels, flames that at first form red outlines around the panels, and then the panels, like melting film, turning black in the middle, and then those black dots becoming bubbling black rings, and the flaming panels beginning to fall onto the flaming play-ground.

Pete sees all that, I tell Dexter, and then Pete feels the water pouring over his head turn warmer and warmer as the Tower heat seeps into the earth itself.

Dexter loves this story, but he never seems to make the connection between the Great Fire I describe and the Flamingo world I have described to him at other times, never seems to realize that the Great Fire cancels out the Flamingo. He still thinks that I will take him there someday.

I do not tell Dexter about the real sound of the Great Fire, just as I have told no one else. Not even Grace now, or Alice then. But I heard it. The only other person to hear it was Louise.

By the time Polly and Louise got back from St. Augustine, the rest of us had moved to watch the fire from in front of the West Funeral Home. Polly and Louise would have gotten back sooner, but the police had blocked off A1A two miles back in both directions. The two girls had left the Corvair at the roadblock and walked, then run, to the fire. My father had been preparing himself for her return, but Louise went for me first.

"Where is he?" she screamed at me, grabbing my shirt and pulling me close to her.

My father reached for his daughter, but she pushed him away, yanking at my shirt and beginning to cry. "Where is he?" she screamed again, my shirt tearing, her fingernails clawing into my skin. "I heard him. I heard him. Where is he?"

"Louise . . ." I spoke as softly as I could, grabbing her hands and forcing them down. "He is dead."

My father and the others looked at me.

"I left Frank in the Tower," I told them. Of all the people there, gaping at me, only Alice understood. I think she did.

Louise hit me in the face as hard as she could.

Louise had heard Frank just as I had, but she had been miles away in our Corvair driving back. I was closer. I heard him first. I heard him sniff the smoke coming up through his floor above my bedroom.

I heard him pacing back and forth. Heard him growling at first, and then scratching at the floor, feeling the heat under him. Heard him begin to whimper, then growl again, and then begin to howl until he began to gag on the smoke that was flooding his dimly lit room.

As I had stood with my father and the others watching the Tower burn, I began to hear what Frank heard. The rushing wind inside the Tower, the groaning California redwoods and Texas oaks, the steel beams clanging as they fell against each other. And then I saw Frank in the center of his flaming room, his fangs bared and his black eyes wide and shining, his paws jerking up and down as he tried to levitate himself off the floor that was beginning to fall out from under him. I heard his curse, that last second before he fell into the past.

I had not lied to my father when he asked me if I had gotten everything out of the Tower that I wanted to save. I was not surprised that he did not mention Frank at that moment. He was a distracted man. Pete must have remembered Frank, but he said nothing to me. It was to be my choice. Louise, and I knew this when I made the decision, Louise would never understand. Nor would she forget, or forgive. My father had killed her mother. I had murdered Frank.

Of course, when I tell Dexter this story, Frank does not die. Louise rushes back to find us helpless in the face of disaster, so she rushes into the Tower looking for Frank. She has always been braver than me. But she, too, is trapped. That is when handsome Fred the Fireman goes into a burning building to save her and her puppy. Fred is a hero.

A good story, with a happy ending, and partly true. Louise did start to limp toward the Tower, but Fred Tymeson was right there in front of her. He *was* a handsome man, and he did stop her, picking her up and carrying her back like a child, holding her in his arms until she stopped crying. Louise still talks about him.

Pete and my father had underestimated the tenacity of the Tower. The Great Fire lasted all night and then well into the next night. The Jacksonville Fire Chief had said it was like watching a lumber factory burn. The crowds that Pete thought we could avoid finally had enough time to see the Tower burn, even if they had to walk two miles to get close. The morning after the fire began, dozens of boats were floating offshore watching the famous Flamingo consume itself. That night, there were close to a hundred boats offshore.

When I told Pete about hearing Frank howl in the fire, he assured me that I was probably hearing some of the shrimp boat foghorns that he heard as he stood on his roof. I told him he was probably right.

Two days after it began, the Great Fire was over. Within a week, my father's money had provided the bulldozers and trucks to raze and remove the debris and ashes. The speaker posts were pulled out of the ground, the seawall leveled. Pete's caboose was restored with new paint and windows. Someone who had never seen the Flamingo would not believe it had ever existed.

My father moved me and Louise to St. Augustine, the oldest city in America. Polly got a job at a bar called Scarlett O'Hara's. Pete stayed at the beach.

Alice disappeared for a week after the Great Fire, but I knew she would be back to say goodbye. She called Gary and Polly, telling them to take care of each other, but I knew there was no future for them together. She also went to see Grace and her father, before she sought out my father. When Louise told me that Alice had seen Pete, and then her, at Pete's caboose, I began to think that she was avoiding me.

"Oh, Isaac," Alice assured me when we did finally meet, "I was just saving the best for last."

She was sitting on a bench on the plaza across from the Booksmith. It was a humid, windless day in Florida, and I was standing in front of her.

"Stare much?" she said, looking over the top of her sunglasses at me. She was right, I was staring.

"I just want to remember your face," I said, instantly anticipating her response.

She laughed. "Oh, Iz, that is so absolutely wonderfully romantic, and just borderline sappy sentimental. But I'm glad you think that way. You'll always be the sweetest boy I ever knew."

I was sorry to see her go, but I couldn't think of a way to stop her. Finally, I asked, "Why do you do that, Alice?"

She did not speak for a moment, and then her voice changed.

"Do what?" she asked, looking hard at me.

"Throw that wall up around you," I said. "Get close to people but not let them get close to you. I was serious. I want to remember you because you and I . . . we did something together . . . you and me . . . that changed everything."

"Iz, that night was special, but don't get stuck in time and—"

"I wasn't talking about *that* night. I was talking about me and you at the airport," I interrupted.

She took off her sunglasses and looked away from me. Then she turned back to me and spoke very slowly and precisely.

"For the record, I was just your getaway driver."

"But you knew," I began to protest. "You were there. You knew."

Alice nodded. "I figured it out soon enough, even before she left that night with the Judge." She paused, watching me start to tremble.

"Alice . . . Alice, I am guilty. And we—"

"Stop this, Isaac! Stop it immediately!"

"But I am responsible—"

"Responsible for being a part of something that I thought *you* would understand, you more than Louise or your father. A part, Isaac, a part, just like the rest of us. A part! In *my* cynical world, we are all just bit players in some fudging cosmic joke. But my world is not yours, Isaac."

"Alice, why are you so bitter?" I asked.

"Forget me! I'm not raising you. And I am not bitter!"

I could see that she was chewing on the inside of her mouth, her jaw tensing and relaxing. I changed the subject away from her.

"Alice, what is it that I should understand, that you're so sure I should understand, because, right now, I don't understand anything."

"Sit down, Isaac."

Alice and I changed places. Then she knelt in front of me, resting her hands on my knees.

"You're so full of grief and anger and guilt that you can't see that you have something I wish I had."

I just shook my head.

"The first thing that will come to you after I'm gone, Isaac, is that, sooner or later, you'll remember that moment in that building over there"—she pointed to the Cathedral—"that moment at your mother's funeral when you were looking up at the ceiling. I saw how you looked. I was watching you. I looked up but all I saw was a ceiling. You were seeing something else."

"Alice, I thought I saw what my mother saw when she died."

She looked at the Cathedral again and then back at me.

"And that is what you will eventually understand."

"Understand?"

"Isaac, you are your mother's son."

She stopped talking, as if she expected me to say something, but I was silent.

"You have her faith. Her world is your world. You and Grace are there together. Your father, your sister, Grace's father, they are all in a different world. In your world, your God forgives you, your mother forgives you, and you will eventually forgive yourself. And you will find comfort. In time, everything will be fine."

"Where are you, Alice? Which world?" I asked.

She put her sunglasses back on and covered her eyes completely.

"I'm a tourist," she said, "and my bus leaves in a half hour. You, lucky boy, get to carry my bag."

We walked to the station, three blocks away from the plaza.

"Are you going to see us again?" I asked, even though I knew the answer.

"Iz, I'm getting on that bus and not looking back. No offense, partner, but I got other hearts to break."

There was the beginning of a breeze, and her summer dress swirled just a little as we stood at the station. I handed her bag to her, and she leaned over to kiss me on my sweaty forehead. Then, for the last time, looking over the top of her sunglasses, she gave me that smirky, quizzical look.

As she walked to the bus, I called to her, "Be careful, Alice, and you take care of yourself."

She stopped, and I thought for a second that she was going to turn around and speak, but she didn't. She just hesitated, and then she raised her right hand back over her shoulder and waved at me.

Then she was gone.

Abraham's Voice

After I tell Dexter about the handsome fireman Fred saving Louise, I tell him to go to sleep. He will usually tell me not to be sad, that the Flamingo is still there. Then Grace will come in and kiss him good night. We both sit there and watch him as he breathes deeper and deeper, clutching a brown stuffed bear that he has had since he came home from the hospital. It is a necessary ritual.

Right now, I am waiting for Dexter to wake up, so we can take a walk on the beach to see Pete. I am sitting by his bed. He has been sick more and more. Allergies are a problem, and sometimes he gets so weak from fighting the effects of the allergies that he gets sick with something else. Doctors have not been much help. But I don't worry. He will grow up and be healthy.

Much of my life now follows a regular cycle. I take care of my children. I spend several hours a day taking, or thinking about taking, pictures. I go to my private picture gallery at least once a week, usually more. I see my father every day. I spend money without thinking. Within my routine, there is some flexibility, and nothing is rigid as to when I must do it.

Only one habit is absolute. I go to Mass every Sunday. Louise laughs at this, but I do not mind.

Pete still lives in his caboose. We see him often, especially in the summer when we all live at our beach house near him. In that season, in the early darkness, my father and I and Dexter will get Pete to go for a walk with us. We did it yesterday. And, as we always do, standing there on the sand, three old men and a boy, we waited for the rise of the morning sun.

A NOTE ON THE TYPE

The text of this book was set in Sabon, a typeface designed by Jan Tschichold (1902–1974), the well-known German typographer. Based loosely on the original designs by Claude Garamond (c. 1480–1561), Sabon is unique in that it was explicitly designed for hot-metal composition on both the Monotype and Linotype machines, as well as for film setting. Designed in 1966 in Frankfurt, Sabon was named for the famous Lyons punch cutter Jacques Sabon, who is thought to have brought some of Garamond's matrices to Frankfurt.

Composed by North Market Street Graphics,
Lancaster, Pennsylvania
Printed and bound by R. R. Donnelley & Sons,
Harrisonburg, Virginia
Designed by Virginia Tan